WITCH DUST

BY THE SAME AUTHOR

Relatively Strange
Even Stranger

"What a brilliant unique book. I couldn't put it down" - *Off-the-Shelf Book Reviews*

***

"Beautifully written, this book will grab readers on a visceral level. Stella is both heroine, victim and villain, and one of the most compelling characters I have encountered in some time." - *For the Love of Books*

***

"… keeps you both on your toes and at the edge of your seat throughout each chapter. A must-read." - *Elisheva Sokolic. Under Cover*

***

"I spent the first few chapters of this brilliant novel wondering if it really was a crime book, since it seemed to be a very funny description of Stella's mad relatives – then I got swept up in the story, and after I'd finished I couldn't quite see what else it could be. Imagine a John Wyndham character strayed into a McDermid, Kate Brannigan novel, that might give you an idea of this quirky book. If you want to try something a bit different, I'd really recommend this." - *Promoting Crime Fiction*

***

"A Stephen King-like Dark Tale of Strange Occurrences" - *Breakaway Reviewers*

WITCH DUST

MARILYN MESSIK

Matador
9 Priory Business Park,
Wistow Road, Kibworth Beauchamp,
Leicestershire. LE8 0RX
Tel: 0116 279 2299
Email: books@troubador.co.uk
Web: www.troubador.co.uk/matador
Twitter: @matadorbooks

ISBN 9781788033725

British Library Cataloguing in Publication Data.
A catalogue record for this book is available from the British Library.

Printed and bound in the UK by TJ International, Padstow, Cornwall

Matador is an imprint of Troubador Publishing Ltd

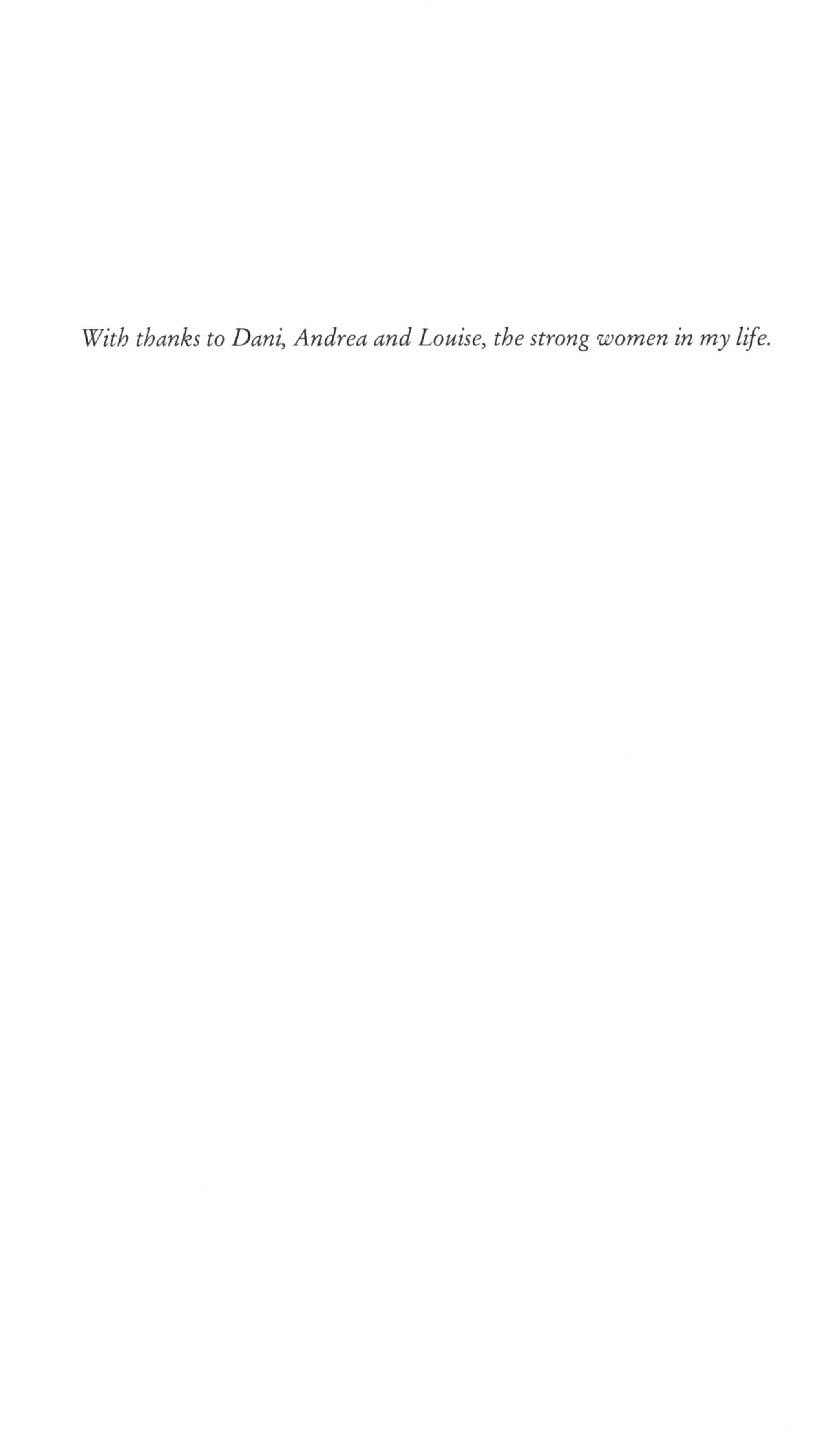

With thanks to Dani, Andrea and Louise, the strong women in my life.

About the author

Marilyn was a regular feature and fiction writer for national magazines when her children were small. She set up her first business, selling toys, books and party goods, from home, before opening first one shop then another. When she sold both shops she moved into the world of travel, focusing on Bed and Breakfasts and Country Inns in New England, USA. Her advisory, planning and booking service flourished and she concurrently launched a publishing company, producing an annual, full-colour accommodation guide.

In 2007 she set up a copywriting consultancy, to help businesses shape their messages to optimum effect. She's the author of the Little Black Business Book series and the novels Relatively Strange and Even Stranger. She's been married to her very patient husband for more years than he deserves and they have two children, five grandchildren and, somewhat to their surprise, several grand-dogs.

CHAPTER ONE

My Mother had a lumpily-packed, Louis Vuitton carpet bag clamped under one arm, a stout black cat struggling under the other and a brown envelope gripped damply between her front teeth. She appeared, without warning, in the middle of my living room. I really hated it when she did that.

"I've just killed your Father." She said.

Martin, emerging from the kitchen with two mugs of coffee and a box of chocolates was, not unreasonably, startled to see her. He jumped violently and a jet of hot liquid scalded his wrist, before splashing dark brown across the cream sofa. The chocolates went flying. The cat, with a yowl, jerked free and hit the ground running, whilst my Mother sank soulfully into an armchair and Martin started sneezing – he had allergies.

"What the… ?" He was baffled and incensed in equal measure. I sighed, picked up a couple of stray chocolates which had landed in my lap, and prepared to extricate myself and the Mother-from-hell from yet another situation you couldn't dream up if you tried. I'd spent a lot of my thirty years doing that.

CHAPTER TWO

You'd probably recognize my Mother if you saw her, my Father too – Adam Adamovitch and the lovely Ophelia. You might have been to one of their stage shows, more likely you'll have seen them on television – they did a Christmas Special for years; or perhaps you caught them, not that long ago on Graham Norton. Most people have simply got used to seeing them gazing adoringly at each other in innumerable red-carpet press shots – a premiere here, a society bash there or simply champagning it on the slopes of Gstaad.

Adam and Ophie, or as the media love to label them, Mr and Mrs Magic. Purveyors of illusion; delusion; sparkling eyes; flashing teeth; little-left-to-the-imagination costumes and death defying stunts. Sword; flame; guillotine; water-tank; all thrillingly enhanced with their trade-mark sizzling chemistry although naturally, that's not an aspect on which a daughter likes to dwell. Not a shred of doubt though, a fair old amount of high voltage smouldering took place, both onstage and off. His tall, olive-skinned good looks charmingly offset by her petite, curved blonde ones had, over the years, put the extra into some extraordinary performances, resulting in consistent bookings, a vertical career path and egos the size of the national debt.

Me? Well no, you wouldn't recognize me, why should you? Mind you, I believe I did do a turn or two, way back when I was small. I vaguely remember, toddler-sized, being hauled out of a hat rabbit-fashion then befrilled and becurled, tottering across the stage arms outstretched, to be scooped up by one and tossed, uncomplaining to the other. The audience loved it, clapped their hands sore, rocking with excitement that Adam and the lovely Ophelia – looking no more than a child herself – had sealed their union with a predictably gorgeous baby. But of course, a baby's one thing, a sulky six year old quite another. And unsurprisingly, as time passed and stomachs had to be held in ever more tightly, buttocks clenched ever more constantly and make-up applied with an increasingly lavish hand, a spottily awkward teenager was the last thing they wanted in the public eye.

No, don't get me wrong, I'm not grumbling, I certainly wasn't neglected, it's just some people aren't natural parent material, and whilst there was never any shortage of loving hugs and expensive gifts there was, it has to be said, a corresponding and disconcerting degree of absent mindedness. As a child I was accustomed to being regularly, if inadvertently, left behind at numerous hotels, stations or airports. The Stage Manager would assume I was with the PR people, the PR people would be convinced I'd gone on with Props and my parents generally omitted to give it much thought one way or another.

Whilst never thrilled by this evidence of my importance on the scale of things, I was fairly philosophical and would wait patiently, never fearing abandonment. I knew, sooner or later, someone would come rushing back in a panic to get me, and such incidents were invariably followed by Ma and Pa descending briefly into darling-we're-such-terrible-people-you-must-hate-us-what-can-we-possibly-do-to-make-it-up-to-you mode. This was generally the most tiresome part, because I then had to spend time and effort reassuring them they were the best parents anyone could ask for – which we all knew wasn't remotely true – but it drew a line under the whole thing, until the next time.

On the whole, I suppose my relationship with my parents wasn't so very different from the norm, although birthday parties, for which they usually insisted on providing the entertainment, were pretty excruciating. There can't be many of us who spend our formative years hissing at our Mother, 'For God's sake, *put some proper clothes on!*' But like most children, I did want to shine in their eyes and whilst fully anticipating, was invariably disappointed when they were unable to make school plays, sports days and prize-givings. Mind you, their rare attendance could be considered a mixed blessing. They once arrived at a Nativity play I was in – complete with film crew and sound team to record the performance. That's not a comfortable memory. When it came to the finale Pa, channeling Spielberg, insisted on four re-takes. The whole thing turned so stressful that the English teacher came over all unnecessary, Herod got into a fight with the donkey and the Virgin Mary threw up over two of the three Wise Men. As I said, a mixed blessing.

CHAPTER THREE

As soon as I was old enough to suss the lie of the land, I daily thanked my lucky stars for Murray Silverstone, who pitched up in loyal loco parentis for every single one of my plays, hockey matches or parents' evenings throughout my school years. In fact, Murray it was who laboured long into the night, tongue tip protruding pinkly between concentration-pursed lips, as he sewed name tags into my uniforms; Murray who cajoled me to dentist and doctor with promises it wouldn't hurt and reasonable explanation if it did. And it was always Murray to whom I ran howling with scraped knee, cut hand or wounded pride.

Murray had been with my parents from almost the instant their career took off. He never gave much away about his background, refused to talk about his own childhood and, as far as I can recall, didn't ever take holidays. He certainly always seemed to be around. He ruled our lives with an iron fist in an iron glove – dresser; props supervisor; travel arranger; rock in a crisis; port in a storm. He was the only person totally unintimidated by my Father's roaring rages and patently unimpressed by my Mother's histrionics.

His lack of height, never diminished his authority, although you had to get up early to catch Murray without his built-up shoes, for which he regularly paid a small fortune to a clever cobbler, off Bond Street. Vertical challenges notwithstanding, it was a brave theatre manager who'd risk making last-minute changes to one of Murray's meticulously drawn up schedules, and a mere murmur of 'I'll just mention that to Murray, shall I?' was usually more than enough to bring stroppily creative tv directors swiftly to heel.

Over the years, his bright red hair softened to a silky dollop of pure cream, topping cherubic features that had only become ruddier with age. If the increasing purple veining of his nose belied his ferocious tee-totality, his rounded, cheerful chappie exterior was even more of a let-down. Despite the fact I adored him unconditionally, even I had to admit, pessimism was his middle name, misery his mantra and hypochondria his hobby. 'How are you Murray?' was a question wisest not to ask – not unless you had an awful lot of time on your hands.

Murray's relationship with my parents was often stormy – well, stormy on their part, millpond unruffled on his.

"You've done *what*?" My Father would bellow at the top of his impressively mellifluous voice, which never needed benefit of microphone to resonate right to the back of an auditorium.

"Given 'im 'is cards."

"He was one of the best bloody stage-hands we've ever had – get him back. There you go again Murray, making decisions without checking with me first. Who the hell pays your flaming wages, just tell me that?"

"He's kept a notebook hasn't he? Every single bloody trick."

"Good God! Are you... ?"

"Sure? Yup. Burned it."

"Has he... ?"

"Yup, Daily Mail."

"Dear Lord, can you...?"

"Sorted."

"Right. Well... um... good man Murray."

Fallings out with my Mother were usually over costume decisions – hers, and costume revisions, his.

"*Murray*, what the blazes is this grotty piece of rubbish Betty's just handed me? I specifically told her I wanted it tight and sequined like the last one. See to it."

"You need it draped."

"I most *certainly* do not. When will you learn, *I* and not *you* decide what I will and won't wear."

"Last scene. You're up on that podium sideways and you're back-lit."

"And your point... ?"

"Stomach's sticking right out in the tight costume."

"How *dare* you, you odious little man!"

"Okey doke. Have Betty make up the tight one then, shall I?"

"Indeed you will and in future, kindly have the courtesy not to countermand my instructions and keep your insulting opinions to yourself."

"Right you are."

"No. Hang on a minute. I'm not giving Betty extra work and an excuse to walk around like a wet weekend in Warrington. I'll wear the wretched thing as it is. But in future, I'll thank you not to stick your nose in where it's not wanted. Understand?"

"Understood."

As I grew to appreciate, the relationship between the three had very clearly defined boundaries which seemed to satisfy all parties, but anyone else, even me, overstepping the mark, was a step too far. I learned this early, I was probably about seven or eight then. Murray had forbidden me to do something, can't even recall what it was now, but it was certainly world-shatteringly important at the time and I turned and hissed at him through clenched teeth, borrowing, with no compunction whatsoever, my Father's tone.

"Horrible little man," I yelled, "Your trouble is you don't know your place." Whereupon my knees buckled, as my Mother delivered a totally unexpected whack to my rear end.

"Don't you *ever*," she said, "*Ever*, let me hear you speak to Murray or indeed anybody else in that way again. Do I make myself *absolutely* clear? Apologise, immediately!"

"Sorry Murray." I muttered ungraciously.

"Properly, please!" She snapped.

"Really sorry spoke like that to you Murray, won't happen again." I mumbled. He nodded and we both looked at my Mother, who appeared somewhat in shock at having sounded for once like a proper parent. Apparently not quite knowing where to go from there, she swiftly reverted to type and drifted off, hand to head, in search of a headache pill. Naturally, that didn't put an end to my struggle against authority, Murray-shaped as it usually was, but I knew thereafter, there were lines not to be crossed.

CHAPTER FOUR

My parents' passionately volatile relationship was founded on mutual, albeit not uncritical adoration. They also shared the conviction that God had placed them on this earth to bring a little light into people's lives, and it was therefore people's reciprocal responsibility to bring quite a lot into theirs.

In my Father's case, this innate certainty was relieved with frequent flashes of unexpectedly self-deprecating humour, overlaid with an almost child-like delight in the good things of life. This ensured he was able, most of the time, to effortlessly charm the birds off the trees – and I'm not just talking the feathered kind. He was a sucker for a well-turned leg, whoever's hip it was hung from and if it was fishnet-clad and chorus-girl long, so much the better. Luckily, he was generally rather too lazy to follow through on flirtations, relying on the eagle eyes of my Mother and Murray to see off any opposition before it got too serious. Murray probably made more women disappear offstage, than my Father ever did on.

Adam was so inordinately and fiercely proud of the way in which, from humble fumblings with bunches of spring-open artificial flowers and strings of coloured scarves, he'd surged to the very pinnacle of his profession that I don't believe he ever really stopped to think how it all came about. Neither, oddly enough, for a long while did I. After all, when you're brought up watching your Father saw your Mother in half most nights, it's not always easy to know what's what, and whilst I was aware from an early age, things weren't always quite as they seemed, it was a good few years before I put a far firmer finger on it.

***

They met in the early '70's, she was just eighteen and he was twenty-four. It was, they never tired of telling people, grand passion at first sight. Adopted, she'd had a rotten upbringing, knowing nothing about her natural family and, I gathered, with no urge as she reached adulthood to investigate who or where they might be. Her early years, as she recounted them, sounded like something out of Dickens with the sob factor turned up. Childless when they took her in, her adoptive parents then went on to have two, unexpected offspring of their own and, according to my Mother, there was clear distinction indeed between little orphan Ophie and their own kids. She'd run away from home when she was seventeen and had no contact since.

She'd made her way to London with her few possessions in a pathetic bundle – Dick Whittington minus the cat – and secured a job in Liberty on Regent Street. She started as a junior in Millinery, but within a very short while, had worked her way up to saleswoman status.

She was exceptionally successful, scoring the highest sales in her department, probably because customers fell in love with hats modelled disingenuously above her lovely face and blonde curls convinced, usually erroneously that they too could look as good. She was stepping out, at that time, with Peter Pollard in Gentlemen's Underwear, an earnestly adenoidal young man with a larger pay packet than hers and a touching willingness to spend it. The story was, they'd gone out for supper one evening and then on to a small night-club where, as fate would have it, my Father was performing.

He asked for a volunteer from the audience, spotted Ophelia and their glances locked across the crowded room. In an instant, he'd crossed the distance like a thing possessed, swept her close and led her transfixed, back to the small stage. He produced a bunch of flowers, several coins and a couple of doves from about her person and the rest, as they say, is history. Poor old Peter Pollard and the others in the audience might just as well not have been there, in fact probably heartily wished they weren't – trust me, I've spent enough time sitting on the sidelines, watching my parents exchange heavy-lidded looks, to know just how superfluous to requirements you can feel.

Departing retail with relief and no regrets my Mother, like a dolphin making it back to water, plunged headlong and happily into show business. Their successful stage partnership was born and so, scandalously, within nine months was I.

When they eventually found the time between bookings, they officially tied the knot at Chelsea Register Office, she in a white crochet mini dress and full-length hooded fur cape, he in a Regency suit, sporting a flourishing Zapata moustache and flowered cravat. The photo album shows, even at that point, they'd managed to accrue a fair old smattering of celebrity friends and there, rubbing elbows with Mick and Bianca, was a younger, slimmer Murray with extravagant flares, sideburns to die for and me, sound asleep in his arms.

CHAPTER FIVE

From things Murray's said or rather left unsaid, over the years, I gather the Match Made in Heaven came in the nick of time for Adam Adamovitch (previously Sydney Blomblot, but what kind of a stage name would that have been?) who, up until then, hadn't exactly been hitting the heights. Doing the rounds of some of the less salubrious pubs and clubs, he'd had his share of raucous heckling from punters keener on socialising than on sleight of hand, and usually too far gone to recall, or indeed care, which card they'd picked. He was in desperate need of a gimmick and when my Mother turned up, hey presto she was it, and then some! From that moment on, they never looked back.

There's no doubt, they made a stunning couple, and the camera loved them so much it practically followed them around with its tongue hanging out, begging for more. The fact that they were married, legitimised for all ages of audience, the amusing, often slightly risqué double-entendres that became one of their trademarks without, as my Mother always stressed, the tone being lowered in any way.

And to give them their due, they never rested on their laurels, never stood still, constantly re-inventing the act, creating ever more complicated feats of apparently life-threatening scenarios that had the audience on the edge of its seat, fingernails gnawed to the knuckle. As they moved further and deeper into the realms of illusion, their reputation grew proportionately. What Adam Adamovitch and the lovely Ophelia did today – levitating higher, vanishing faster, staying underwater longer – was studied long and hard by peers and aspirants alike, with the goal of doing it better tomorrow. My Father was fond of quoting 'All the world's a stage.' and indeed to them, it always was, they were both consummate performers through and through.

Of course, all I ever wanted was to live a life more average. Growing up as I did, with people extracting coins from ears, rabbits from hats or levitating in the living room, I absolutely adored being invited to friends' houses, where normality was the name of the game and parents never seemed to feel the urge to ham it up over the egg sandwiches.

Having people back to me wasn't half as much fun. I knew full well that if Adam and Ophelia weren't in evidence at our large Maidenhead home with its lawns sloping gently down to the river, my friends would be deeply disappointed and I'd feel I'd fallen short. However, I also knew how much worse it could be when they *were* there. I lost count of the number of times I was abandoned without a backward glance, in favour of entertainment of a more magical kind. I certainly couldn't keep track of the number of occasions I stormed out in a huff to go and watch television on my own, without anyone so much as noticing I'd left the room. Whilst accepting from an early age, my parents were never going to be feet-on-the-ground folk, I did feel they could occasionally make an effort to at least hover within landing distance of sensible and remember which of us were supposed to be the grown-ups.

It should have been no surprise I suppose, that they wouldn't tolerate being called Mum and Dad, said it made them sound middle aged and worse – suburban. I was always told to use their names, but that didn't feel right to me, so most of the time we compromised uneasily on Ma and Pa. They in turn had lumbered me with Serenissima, and try dealing with that when you start school with missing teeth and a resulting lisp. The name was bad enough, the icing on the cake being them explaining to all and sundry it was chosen because I was conceived in Venice – just a little more, I felt, than anyone really needed to know. As soon as I was old enough, I made a unilateral decision and insisted on the far more prosaic Sandra. I'm not proud to admit the name thing turned into an ongoing war of attrition, me Mum and Dadding them to annoy and they Serenissima-ing me back because they knew how mad it drove me.

***

Because I toured for a portion of every year with my parents, both in this country and abroad, there were long periods when I was tutored on the road. I grew adept at finding small corners in which to study, whilst heated planning sessions, language to make a sailor blush and rejected props flew over my head. Unlike the succession of put-upon and faintly bewildered tutors, stringently interviewed and employed by Murray to oversee my education, I never had any problems concentrating. I was used to being surrounded by sawing and hammering as sets were created, erected and dismantled, and I loved the security and familiarity of my Mother's Chanel No. 5, overlaid by the cigarettes and sweat of stage hands and dancers.

Spending a lot of time as I did, observing from the wings, I was aware early of all sorts of things. I knew for example that my Father, much as I adored him, was in truth not half as clever as he and everyone else thought he was. With the sure instinct of a child and the critical eye of one brought up in the business I also knew, but hoped he didn't, that on his own he wasn't actually very good. On the other hand, the lovely Ophelia, for all her blonde dizziness and addiction to her own image – neither of my parents ever passed a mirror they didn't like – was as sharp as a tack in spotting new opportunities and innovative in her exploitation of every one of them.

There was, I was aware, much more to my Mother, histrionics and all, than immediately met the eye and although I can clearly remember to the day when suspicion was finally confirmed, realisation had been sneaking up and clearing its throat to get my attention for quite some time.

There's always been for me, a definitive and clearly delineated difference between real magic which was what my parents performed on stage and all the other stuff that went on. Real magic, once you knew how it was done and had spent hours watching carpenters and mechanics sweat to get it right, was all the more seamlessly brilliant for the effort that went into it. What I labeled *Funny Business,* was another and far smellier kettle of fish altogether.

CHAPTER SIX

Our Christmases were always way-over-the-top affairs; designer decorated tree, famous-name guests and an event planner person meticulously organising everything from the first canapé to the final cracker. I should also add that for us this happened not once, but twice a year. Once in July, to be photographed for one or other of the glossies, when we all sat around sweating like pigs, dressed in suitably themed Xmas jumpers and then all over again, on the proper date. Both these occasions, naturally included a perfect chef-cooked turkey, which my prettily flushed, aproned and triumphant Mother would bear in from the kitchen to a huge round of applause – as if she'd actually had anything remotely to do with it. Oh yes indeed, so much of the time we lived in a kind of cloud cuckoo land.

One particular year, I suppose I must have been about eleven, it was our December Christmas and my Mother opened an intricately wrapped and beribboned box, cautiously as instructed. With shrieks of delight, accompanied by even louder shrieks from the encircling guests – showbiz folk are never restful to be with – she extracted a somewhat confused, jet-black, Persian kitten, weighed down by an elaborate diamond encrusted collar, almost as big and certainly twice as heavy as she was.

"Something precious for my precious." Intoned my Father, for whom a humble 'Hope you like it.' would never have sufficed. Murray, always looking for and finding the bright side, muttered,

"Scratch the furniture to blooming shreds that will, and don't expect me to clear up when it craps on the carpet." My Mother though was immediately totally enchanted, well aware just how perfectly the black sleekness of the kitten would contrast in photographs against her own flawless peaches and cream, and an instant, mutual adoration society was formed.

Stuck, not unlike myself, with a ridiculous pedigree name, which in her case was swiftly shortened to the more useable Ink, kitten almost didn't make it to cat, when one day she happened to spot several sparrows landing a little way away and leapt, like a mad thing, out the open front door and down the drive. Unfortunately, she was hurtling down the drive at the same time as Fred the Grocer, in his battle-scarred white van, was hurtling up.

Accustomed as I was to my Mother's hysterics over most things, the scream which rent the air on this occasion, was truly panic stricken and I dashed to where she stood, just in time to see the ball of black fur streak in front of the van, with fatal impact inevitable. Brakes squealed, the kitten shot vertically upwards and the van ploughed to a swerving, gravel-spraying stop beneath her rather than the other way around. I thought for one dreadful moment that she'd been hit and hurled upwards. But strangely, for a beat or two, she simply hovered in mid-air, looking more surprised than alarmed, before sinking slowly back down to the ground and making a dash for the safety of my Mother's outstretched arms. Fred exited the van shakily, removing his tweed cap and scratching a sparsely haired head.

"Bloody 'ellfire and damnation." He said, "See that, did you? Never seen a blinking cat do that before and that's for sure." My Mother, chiding and cooing simultaneously, had already turned back inside, so it fell to me to take an agitatedly muttering Fred, along with the fruit and veg, through to the kitchen. But he wasn't wrong, I'd never seen a cat do that before either.

***

A few months after that, there was the knife thing. For a year or so, knife-throwing had featured as part of the act. My Mother, smiling valiantly, buckled to a revolving wheel, legs and arms spread-angled would be sent whirling, while my Father – blindfolded to boot – would rapidly hurl a succession of lethally sharp knives at her. When the wheel was halted, she'd be carefully unstrapped, lifted down and escorted triumphantly away by a couple of the dancers, leaving her perfect body shape, perfectly outlined by the still quivering blades. I'd watched them rehearse and perform this to the point of boredom, and it was only by chance, that one day I happened to glance up from where I was slumped over two seats in the empty auditorium reading, while I waited for them to finish. I saw a hurtling knife suddenly pause, shiver impossibly in mid-air then fractionally alter angle, before continuing headlong to embed itself safely, centimeters from my Mother's elegantly blushered cheek.

I knew I wasn't mistaken, but nobody else seemed to have noticed anything out of the ordinary. I nodded quietly to myself, wandered off to find out from Murray what time we were going to eat, and simply added what I'd seen to an oddities file which perhaps, until that point, I hadn't realized I was compiling.

CHAPTER SEVEN

It probably wasn't until a good couple of years after that particular incident – I must have been coming up for thirteen then – that accumulated concerns coalesced into uncomfortable confirmation. Whilst I'd always known Ophelia was out of the ordinary, it transpired she was rather farther out than I could ever have imagined.

Murray had, as he did fairly frequently, hit the roof,

"Are you out of your teeny tiny mind?" He'd shrieked, when my Father announced his plans to introduce a lion into the act. "…And where, may I bloody ask, are you planning to keep the frigging thing?" My Father, who usually exploded immediately Murray did, maintained for a brief while, before he lost it, a saint-like demeanor. He explained that the strict rules and regulations governing the appearance of performance animals meant there'd be a fully qualified trainer on hand at all times. Additionally, the necessary authorities had to be completely happy with the conditions under which the animal was to be kept, as well as entirely confident about safety and security.

Murray remained as unmollified as I'd ever seen him, and there followed a great deal of shouting and gesticulating from both parties. My Father finally told Murray where about his person he could stick his old-woman worries, while Murray suggested to my Father that he might like to find similar accommodation for the lion, its bleeding trainer and its sodding cage.

Despite all the drama and hoo-ha, my Father got his own way. The lion duly joined us on tour and from his mournful expression, viewed the whole enterprise in much the same dubious light as Murray. His trainer, Johnjoe was a tall, skinnily anaemic young man, who appeared to have outgrown himself height-wise and always looked in imminent danger of suddenly folding over in the middle. He was a bit short on conversational skills and thrown into frequent blushing incoherence, by the brevity of the costumes worn by Ma and the other girls. But he was a sweet chap, always found time to answer my numerous big cat questions and, when he wasn't busy mucking out, was always happy to muck in.

Languid, as we nicknamed him, although no doubt a fine specimen of lionhood, was not a stage natural and unlike my parents, didn't perk up and perform at the first whiff of the greasepaint or roar of the crowd. His natural inclination seemed to be to lie down and sleep a lot. This was so far from what was required, that all sorts of desperate measures had to be resorted to, including dubbing. Poor old Johnjoe was dispatched to London Zoo, armed with a tape-recorder and strict instructions not to return without some blood curdling sound-effects. These were duly played over the theatre's sound system when the cage was rolled onstage. Sadly, Languid never really got used to that, invariably jumping out of his skin and dropping into a defensive crouch, convinced he was under attack by another lion. My Father was livid,

"He's nowhere near wild enough." He yelled at a hastily convened crisis conference, "We want pacing and roaring."

"We want, doesn't always get." Muttered Murray, living dangerously as always and smug in the knowledge he'd vetoed the idea from the start. Johnjoe scratched his head and averted his eyes from a group of dancers in the skimpiest of leotards, energetically rehearsing on the other side of the stage.

"P'raps I could give him his supper a fair old bit earlier, so's he's hungry again by time he comes on?"

"Well, why didn't you damn well say so before?" Snapped my Father. "And for God's sake can't you spray him with something, he stinks to high heaven."

Johnjoe was as good as his word, and it was a very different lion who rolled up for the next performance – languid no longer. What the audience was supposed to see, was the animal inside the cage doing his law of the jungle-untamed stuff, while my Mother entered an adjacent, square cabinet which was then elaborately padlocked left right and centre. Whilst this was going on, from two apertures in the cabinet, a slim white arm and an elegant foot would be extended and wiggled, to show she was all present and correct. With a number of dramatic flashes, explosions, drum rolls and gymnastic efforts from the support dancers, a voluminous, silver star-studded black cloth was lowered over both cage and cabinet and whipped back in almost the same instant.

Revealed then, would be my Mother and Languid transposed. She pirouetting prettily in the cage, he ostensibly trapped in the cabinet as evidenced by a lion tail, lashing from where her arm had been, together with a lot of lion-type rocking, rolling and roaring. No sooner had the audience begun to gasp and clap, the black cloth would again descend and re-ascend. And lo and behold there they were – Languid livid in the cage and Ophelia liberated, completely unruffled from the cabinet. With all the effects in place it was enormously impressive, even to those like me, who'd watched it numerous times and knew exactly how it was done.

There was naturally, some pretty nifty footwork required by all involved, not least Languid and Johnjoe. But a hungry lion isn't always a co-operative lion and one night at the London Palladium, things went spectacularly wrong. Ophelia disappeared from the cabinet and duly pitched up in the cage, only to discover Languid, still in residence and mighty unimpressed to find he'd acquired a room-mate.

The audience's gasp of horror was echoed by that of the cast, who knew the routine and were aware this wasn't it. Languid raised his massive maned head, opened wide his jaws and finally gave throat to just the sort of roar for which my Father had been begging. From my position in the wings I watched Adam, his face rigid with fear beneath the thick stage makeup, as a peeved and peckish Languid decided to find out whether Ophelia was as deliciously edible as she looked. The huge animal, horrifyingly close to the slim woman in the cage with him, crouched, snarled, sprang and vanished in mid leap into thin air.

The audience was still surging to its feet applauding wildly, when the black cloth was swiftly lowered and raised again and yes, there was Languid, back in his cage – large as life and twice as confused. And there, safely back in the cabinet, was my Mother. Murray and I had clutched hands. When we stickily untangled, we had matching rows of nail indentations and as I turned to him I saw reflected my own relief, as well as something else I couldn't quite identify.

"*What happened*?" I hissed.

"Blinking trap-door mechanism jammed, didn't it?"

"But..."

"No harm done, they got it sorted."

"But..."

"Have to get it checked." And he headed off swiftly, picking his expert way over props and cast as he went. Turning back, I saw my parents taking their bow. They milked the applause extravagantly as normal and ran off, glowing, to the approbation of the rest of the team, who weren't exactly sure quite what they'd seen either, but had leapt to the only conclusion possible. Wiley old Adam had pulled a fast one. And there indeed was wiley old Adam, preening, winking, laughing and talking about keeping everyone on their toes. But I'd seen the shock and fear on his face. Something didn't smell right and it wasn't just Languid.

CHAPTER EIGHT

My Mother was also working the crowd, kissing, being kissed, laughing and accepting congratulations for a great show. As she moved towards her dressing room, I was right behind her. I waited quietly in the corner while Betty, her dresser, belying her impressive girth, flashed round the room like a highly motivated whirling dervish. She swiftly helped my Mother out of her costume and then her fishnet tights, tutting at a rip and gathering up assorted rollers, Leichner sticks and discarded tissues along the way. She was grumbling and muttering the whole time about damn fools, working with wild animals.

"Mark my words," she said, "One day something'll go proper pear-shaped and then where'll we all be laughing? T'other side of our faces, that's blooming well where!"

Conjuring order from chaos, and having helped Ophie into her after-show, blue velour dressing gown, ensured she had everything she needed to clean off her make-up and still holding forth at length, Betty bustled out bearing costume for laundering and tights for darning. Before she left, she'd boiled the kettle for the customary cup of Earl Grey which now gently steamed on the dressing table. I had an uncomfortable, unidentifiable feeling in the pit of my stomach. The sort of discomfort you get when you're at the dentist's and he's umming and aaahing and the next news you're expecting to hear is sure to involve needles and a hypocritical 'This won't hurt a bit'.

"Ma?" I said.

"Ophelia." She tutted.

"Ophelia then."

"Mmm?"

"What happened?"

"When?"

"For goodness sake, just now, out there."

"Oh that. Just a new bit your Father and I..."

"No."

"What d'you mean, no?"

"Adam knew nothing about it – I was watching. He was as shocked as anyone."

"Rubbish. You know he loves nothing better than playing to the gallery."

"Where did Languid go then?"

"Languid?" She was sipping tea, eyes closed, savouring the fragrant warmth.

"Yes, Languid, you remember – bloody great lion?"

"Don't swear darling." She hovered elegant, crimson-nailed fingers over the biscuits Betty had put out for her, opting for the chocolate one. "Languid disappeared, isn't that the whole point of the trick? Now run along sweets, I've got a head coming on."

"Ma, he's taken out through a trap door." I could hear my voice rising, "I know as well as you how it works, but tonight he didn't go out the trapdoor – he just *disappeared*, I *saw* him."

"Clever, n'est pas Serenissima?"

"*Sandra.*" I hissed, and with the anger came unexpectedly hot, scalding tears. I must have been far more frightened than I'd realized, out there in the wings, preparing to watch something dreadful happen to her. She swung around on her chair, saw my distress was genuine and held out her arms. Kneeling awkwardly on the floor I buried my head against her stomach although, even in that instant, I felt her tauten instinctively, lest it seem too squashy. I wasn't short of affection, we always hugged and kissed a lot, but they were generally fast, showbizzy efforts, finished almost as soon as they started, with maximum 'mwah, mwahing' and not too much body contact. This longer embrace felt strangely unfamiliar, but I knew it was a pivotal moment. I could leave well alone – or not.

"I want to know how you did it." I said

"Told you." She pulled away from me, turning back to the mirror and slapping on some Nivea. "Now I need to get dressed, your Father'll be in any minute, we're eating with the Caines and the Connerys and he'll rush me, you know he will and I so hate that."

"You didn't."

"Didn't what?"

"Tell me."

"Oh, for God's sake, just leave it alone, can't you?" Ophie's patience, not plentiful at the best of times, was rubbing rapidly thin. "It's no big thing, just something I did."

"Did? What do you mean *did*?"

"Sometimes I just... " she waved a dismissive hand, "Oh I don't know, make things happen if I need to."

"Happen?"

"Don't echo."

"What things? How?"

"Things... oh I don't know, stop badgering me." She snapped.

"Show me." I demanded.

"No."

"I want to see." I said. She grimaced in anger, muttered something under her breath and with no warning whatsoever disappeared, right in front of my eyes.

I'd sat back on my heels on the floor after our hug, so she was only a foot or so away, I could still smell her perfume all around me. I felt a little light-headed and a lot frightened. I leaned forward and waved my hand feebly above the dressing table chair, nothing. This was oh so definitely not magic as I knew it, this was irrefutably something else entirely.

"Ma?"

"What?" She was suddenly back. We stared at each other, shocked and defensive respectively.

"How... ?"

"For God's sake, stop making such a song and dance about it." She turned the chair decisively back to face the mirror and dolloped more cold cream calmly. For a few seconds, I couldn't think of what I wanted to say next, then,

"Does Adam know about... this?"

"Naturally." She tissued, turning her face from side to side, ensuring she didn't miss any greasy patches, at the same time not meeting my anxious eyes in the light-bulb rimmed mirror. "Your Father and I don't have any secrets." But I knew when she was lying, I'd seen it often enough.

"He doesn't, does he?" My indignation grew. "How can he possibly not know something like... " I paused and shrugged at the enormity of it, "...this?"

She crumpled the used, now pinkly stained tissue, threw it into the bin at her feet and turned towards me. I rarely saw her, nobody did, without artfully applied make-up, stage or otherwise and her face looked strangely undressed; younger, yet far less vulnerable than I'd have expected. I began to wish I hadn't embarked on this fact-finding mission.

"Some things we just don't talk about much, your Father and I." She said.

"Well what does he *think* happened today?" I persisted, she shrugged a shoulder,

"Sometimes Adam has more than enough on his plate, sometimes it's my job to just get things sorted." I digested this, turning it over in my mind for flaws and finding plenty.

"But how can he not want to know what happened?"

"Told him it was something I organised – a surprise – he was thrilled."

"A *surprise*? That's ridiculous." I yelped. Her face hardened, so did her tone.

"Ridiculous? And why would that be? He's happy, the audience loved it. We'll get great reviews, a longer booking next year. Not ridiculous at all – it's our living, don't knock it." I couldn't fault her argument, but was dimly aware of moral implications palely loitering. Trying, but failing to grasp them fully, I reverted to the original issue.

"How can you do 'things'?"

"Just can. Honestly Serenissima, I'm very surprised at you, you've been brought up with all sorts of illusion, this's only more of the same." She was sponging on creamy foundation now, her lovely face untroubled. She made it all seem so completely normal. Indeed, and oddly enough, the thing that seemed to be bothering me most was the change in the way I viewed my Father. Confirmation though it was of what I'd suspected, I felt my world shift a little on its axis.

"Does Murray know?"

"Murray?" She sniffed, "Murray knows what Murray chooses to know. Enough questions now. Off you trot poppet, give me a bit of peace before I have to go out and send Betty in with some pills for my head."

***

When we're young, we're pretty adaptive, aren't we? You're probably thinking 'How on earth…?' – as indeed am I, reading this over, but despite having been shown something that would have rocked most people back on their heels, my biggest concern at the time, was the reassessment of my parents' relationship. I do remember though, as soon as opportunity arose, broaching the subject with the surest source of knowledge on all manner of troublesome issues.

"Murray?" I said casually, sitting myself down next to him one day. "Have you noticed anything kind of odd, about Ophelia?" Murray snorted, turning the richly embroidered costume he was darning – we'd gone heavily medieval in the swords-through-the-casket illusion.

"Ophelia, odd? Is the Pope Catholic? Course she's odd. Blimey what do those ruddy dancers do in these outfits to fray 'em like this?"

"No, I mean *really* odd?" He bit the cotton off and stowed needle and thread in the mending kit he carried around with him. It was a bit like the Tardis that kit, just a small square box, but whatever anybody needed was always there and usually in a choice of colours. He turned and looked at me over the little half-moon glasses he'd acquired for close work, much to the amusement of the rest of the crew. With the ruddy complexion and creamy hair, they made him look even more like he'd mislaid a pointed hat and fishing rod.

"Listen to me, Sandy love," he said, "Not everyone in this world's the same as everybody else, it'd be boring as all-get-out if they were."

"And?"

"And nothing."

"That's it?"

"That's it."

"But." I persevered, "She's really, *really* different isn't she?"

"She leans towards the unusual, give you that."

"Murray, if she leaned any farther, she'd fall flat on her face." I said. He gave his short, rarely heard, bark of a laugh,

"I'm saying nothing. Least said soonest mended."

"But," I abandoned oblique for outright. "She does… you know… things."

"Ask her about it."

"Have, but…"

"Well ask her again. Nothing to do with me."

"But Adam, what about Adam? If she's not telling him the truth about things, It's just not right is it? In fact it's downright wrong."

"Now listen here young lady, listen hard and listen good. Your Ma and Pa love each other in their own way, what they do or don't do, see or don't choose to see, is their business, not yours, and certainly none of mine."

"You mean, you think he does know, but she doesn't know he knows?"

"Bloody 'ell, Sandy – you're giving me 'eadache not to mention earache. Drop it now."

"But..."

"And fetch me a couple of aspirin – throat's dead scratchy too." He shook his head gloomily, "My luck, it'll spread to my chest, I'll not shake it off all winter."

So, there it was. And there it stayed. Not exactly out in the open but perhaps not quite so much in the shadows as previously. Was I really any the wiser? No. Was I curious? Yes. Should I have asked a hell of a lot more questions? Certainly. Did I actually want to know the answers? Probably not. After all, growing up, you adjust to a heck of a lot, don't you? And you see the things you want to see and you turn your back firmly on those you don't. Perhaps I just turned my back more firmly than most.

CHAPTER NINE

"You haven't really killed him, have you?" I asked now, with some apprehension. My Mother absentmindedly selected an errant chocolate from amongst those strewn over the coffee table and popped it thoughtfully in her mouth.

"I suppose if I had, the police would have been round by now to tell you, wouldn't they? He must have a cast iron head, goodness knows I hit him hard enough – you know that bronze horse… ?" I sat up straighter and stared at her appalled.

"Good God, Ma, that thing from the fireplace? What were you thinking?" Accustomed as I was to my parents hurling things at each other in the midst of one of their ferocious rows, this sounded a blunt instrument too far. I reached for the phone,

"I'm calling an ambulance."

"No, no, no." She flapped a hand, "Murray's there, it can't be that bad or we'd have heard. You can ring him later and check if you want. Anyway, what about my poor ankle, it's agony." She'd cracked it sharply on the wrought iron leg of the coffee table when she arrived and now she raised, for my inspection, an elegant if rapidly swelling extremity.

"Serves you right." I was unsympathetic. Materialising unexpectedly was, of all Ophelia's unsettling proclivities, the one I disliked the most.

If you're thinking, at this point, that I wasn't half as agitated as you might expect, I should probably point out that my Mother leaving my Father was not an infrequent occurrence, their relationship being nothing if not explosive. Over recent years, as he hit his fifties and had been caught, ever more frequently leching in the direction of the girls in the company, hysterical showdowns had become even more regular. One or other of my parents was always storming off in high dudgeon, swearing they never wanted to see the other ever again and not to bother arguing, because teams of flaming wild horses wouldn't be able to drag them back!

These partings were invariably acrimonious and accompanied by bellowing (Adam), hysteria (Ophelia) and frantic phone calls to their patient, albeit put-upon solicitor for urgent divorce settlement discussions. Luckily the spats, although always heavy on the glassware, usually only lasted a few hours. I think the longest had been when my Father yelled he was getting on a plane and didn't care where it took him, as long as it was far away from her. Unfortunately, just after he flew out of Heathrow, the airport closed down, due to fog. He couldn't get back for four days and was forced to cool his heels and bad humour elsewhere. Of course, whilst the arguments and dramatic walk-outs were unsettling, the inevitable making up periods were even more so, and not the sort of thing you really wanted to be around for.

I rose from my chair to extract a pack of peas from the freezer for the ankle and some milk from the fridge for Ink, who'd spread herself expansively on the sofa – she'd lived through almost as many of these dramas as I had, and tended to take them in her elegant stride. Martin not surprisingly, had departed a while back, almost certainly I thought glumly, for good.

"You just didn't hear the doorbell," I'd said, he'd looked baffled as well he might, it's hardly a huge appartment.

"What're you talking about?" He'd hissed, "One minute she wasn't there, then she was! I was only in the kitchen, it was like she just appeared out of thin effing air and why didn't you tell me she was coming round?"

"I didn't know." I'd said honestly, ignoring the first part of his comment which was too close for comfort. "Honestly Mum," I'd said, turning to her, "I do wish you'd call first." She must have been upset, she didn't even rise to the Mum bait, but nevertheless made a stab at flirtatious.

"Martin, my dear, I am so very sorry. Of course I should have phoned first, I've completely ruined your evening and now you probably think I'm the most dreadful woman ever." She paused for protest, but got no argument from Martin, who'd cordially disliked her from the moment I'd introduced them a couple of months back – rather a plus in my eyes – my Mother didn't meet many people who weren't instantly susceptible to her charms. Mind you, she hadn't taken to him much either.

"Since you ask, I thought he was exceptionally boring." She'd commented to me after I'd succumbed to his repeated requests, taken him to a show and then brought him backstage.

"I didn't ask." I said. "And he's not boring, just normal."

"Same difference darling. You can do so much better."

"He's not an exam." I'd snapped. I was rather taken with Martin, who seemed to me to be the epitome of stability.

"What did you say he did?" She'd asked.

"Chartered accountant."

"Ah, well, there you are then."

CHAPTER TEN

"So, what exactly is it Pa's done this time?" I asked reluctantly, because I wasn't sure I wanted to know.

"Betrayed me. Utterly betrayed me. See for yourself." She was gingerly applying peas to the swollen ankle and nodded towards the brown envelope she'd brought with her, now lying a little soggily amidst the chocolates on the coffee table. I hesitated, I so didn't want to see photographs.

"For God's sake." She said. "It's only his credit card statements." I leaned forward and extracted the sheets. My Father was never the sanest of shoppers and there was the usual horrendous total at the bottom. I raised my eyebrows.

"So?"

"Look a little closer," she spat, "Hotels, restaurants, jewellers. None of them *with* me or *for* me."

"Ah..."

"And I caught them this evening."

"Caught them?" I enquired weakly. I thought back wistfully to just a short while ago, when my biggest worry had been the cliffhanger at the end of Coronation Street.

"In the dressing room, in flagrante!" She started to cry. Ink woke up, ascertained it was only Ophelia, hysterical as usual, and went back to sleep.

"Who?" I asked.

"Sasha Barrington, you know the new dancer. The little slut!"

"Goodness, but she's..."

"...Young enough to be his daughter. Yes, well, no fool like an old fool." I'd been going to say she was such a quiet little thing but true, she could only be about twenty-three, a good seven years younger than me. I was starting to get a bad feeling. This wasn't the first time by a long chalk that Adam's eye had wandered, but it wasn't usually allowed to linger long enough for any harm to be done.

"D'you know what she had the gall to say to me?" I shook my head.

"She said," and my Mother adopted, with cruel accuracy, the high, slightly breathy lisp of young Sasha, 'Ophelia, I hope thith doethn't mean we can't be frienth.' "*Frienths* hah! I'll give her frienths!" She paused, choked with rage and recollection before continuing, "Then she said – listen to this – 'You're probably finding everything, the act and all, just a bit much for you now, maybe it's time to take things a bit easier?'" I winced, I didn't give much for young Sasha's chances of reaching twenty four.

"What'd he say?" I asked cautiously.

"Huh, he was too bloody busy trying to pretend he hadn't had his hand up her jumper, said it was all a big misunderstanding, begged me to stay, said the act wouldn't work without me." Her eyes iced over. "Too right, it wouldn't. He'd never have amounted to anything if it hadn't been for me. I love the so and so, you know I do, but I won't be made to look a fool. And right now, my heart feels as if it's broken in two." She clapped a hand firmly to one turquoise-cashmered breast and looked thoughtful, "I feel I need to get back to my roots." She said. I looked at her in astonishment. I hadn't the remotest idea what she was talking about, the only roots I could think of were the ones she had done every six weeks in Knightsbridge.

"I need," she said, "To re-connect. With myself, with my past, with my family." I was now completely baffled,

"Me and Pa?"

"Darling, must you always be so self-centered? I do have other family you know."

"No, you don't."

Normally she was the only woman I knew who could cry and still look radiant, tonight though she was pale and drawn, her hair lacking its usual sheen. Her skin was dull and there were delicate mauve shadow stains below each eye. I realized, with faint shock, she hadn't even lipsticked before she left, things must be serious. I felt an entirely unexpected stirring of sympathy. I reached out to touch her arm and said gently,

"Ma, they were dreadful, horrible to you. You ran away. You don't really want to have anything to do with them now, do you?"

"No, no," she said impatiently. "Not them. I just made them up." My hand fell away from her arm,

"I'm *sorry*?" I said.

"Well my sweet, be honest, you were always on and on at me weren't you? Questions, questions, questions all the time – so I simply made up the odd interesting story or two – you know, just to keep you quiet." She smiled absently and re-adjusted the peas.

I got up abruptly and walked into the kitchen. On past occasions, when I've wanted to put both hands firmly round my Mother's elegantly slim white throat and squeeze the living daylights out of her, leaving the room has proved an effective avoidance strategy. For no good reason, I put the kettle back on to boil and watched it absently while it worked itself up to a pitch of excitement and then switched off. Then I went back into the lounge again.

"Ophelia," I said, calm as you like, "Can I just get this straight please. Are you telling me your adoption, the ill-treatment, the running away – it's all a complete pack of lies?"

"Not exactly a pack of lies sweetie, why must you always exaggerate everything so?"

"If you made it up." I pointed out evenly, "It isn't true is it? Hence, it's a load of lies."

"Well if you're going to nit-pick." She said.

"*Did* you run away from home?"

"Yes."

"Because they ill-treated you?"

"Not exactly."

"What does 'not exactly' mean? Were you even adopted?"

"No."

"Wait a minute." With an effort, I kept my tone measured. "Wait one bloody minute. Are you telling me that you – we – actually have family? Relatives? People related to us?"

"Don't swear and yes."

"But you brought me up," my voice was rising despite my best efforts, "Believing we didn't have a soul in the world. No-one. Not one single, solitary family member. Nobody on your side, nobody on Pa's."

"Goodness, you do make it all sound so dreadfully dramatic." She sighed in a heavily put-upon manner and I bit my tongue so hard it hurt, because when it came to dramatic, I'd learned from the best. "It's true for your Father, he doesn't have any siblings and lost both parents before he was twenty." She added sanctimoniously, "But you know all about that. I've told you time and time again."

"Well you told me time and time again about your childhood too," I protested, "But talk about changing your story. How the hell could you lie so well, for so long about something so important?" Another thought occurred. "Does Pa know, does Murray, is it just me who's had the wool pulled?" She waved that airily dismissive hand,

"Goodness me, I really don't know. Anyway, it hasn't been talked about for ages now, has it? I suppose I'd just sort of forgotten what I'd said, so I never really put you straight." There was an awful lot I wanted to say, so much in fact that I really didn't know where to begin, so I didn't, I might not have known where to stop.

"Never mind," continued Ophelia blithely, "Look on the bright side, it's actually rather a nice surprise for you, finding out about this now isn't it? Will you drive me down there tomorrow?"

"Drive you? Where?"

"Near Stratford-on-Avon." She said, "I'll give you the address." I took a deep breath, held it for a few seconds, then let it out very slowly to see if that might help – it didn't.

"No." I said.

"No?"

"No. Firstly, I'm working. And secondly you can't drop a bombshell like you've just done, and expect me to simply take it in my stride. I need to get my head round it, then I need to decide if I can ever, ever again, for the rest of my life, believe a single word that comes out of that mouth of yours. And," I was in full flow now. "What on earth is it you're planning? You can't just descend on them out of the blue. How do you know they're still there?" I paused as yet another unwelcome thought struck home, "Please, please don't tell me you've been in touch with them all this time?" I realised my voice had now heightened to what might, uncharitably, be called shrill. Ophelia had the grace to look slightly sheepish,

"Just on and off, now and then, you know, nothing regular and of course they're still there." She got back into her stride quickly. "Surely you can take one little day off to do me this teensie weensie little favour? You know Serenissima, all my life I've made sacrifice after sacrifice for you, and when was the last time I asked you to do *anything* for me?" Even accustomed as I was to Ophelia's view of her own world, she still had the ability to amaze me. Taking tense silence for some sort of consent, she now pressed a trembling thumb and forefinger to her brow,

"Thank you darling, I knew you wouldn't let me down. Now, I'm quite beyond exhausted, with a thumping head coming on. Two of those little pink pills from my bag, quick as you can and I could probably manage a very weak cup of tea. Is it too much to hope you've anything other than Typhoo? Did you put my case in the bedroom? You'll be all right on the sofa, won't you? And pack a few things for tomorrow, we may well decide to stay over."

CHAPTER ELEVEN

Call me an idiot, but experience has taught me, however awkwardly inconvenient, aggravating and downright wrong it is to do what Ophelia wants, it's infinitely less exhausting than sticking to your guns and not doing it. Which is why, still furious and entirely against my better judgment, 11.00 o'clock the following morning saw us beetling down the M40, Stratford-on-Avon bound.

Sal, my business partner had been less than thrilled when I called to tell her.

"Oh, dear Lord." She moaned, "Please tell me this is a joke, Sandy. If we don't get those proofs for Potter & Kleins, finished and signed off today, we won't get them to print on time and I'll slit my wrists." I clenched my jaw – sometimes it felt I'd simply swapped one drama queen for another. I moved automatically into soothing, God knows, I'd had enough practise.

"I know, but not to worry, all in hand, I'll have my laptop with me. Send me the pdfs as soon as they're ready, I'll proof them and get them back to P&K, they won't even know I'm not in the office. If they sign off on them right away, we'll be fine." The phone emitted a drawn-out, hard-done-by sigh.

Sally Leigh had proved somewhat of a disappointment to me. Lusciously built, with long red hair tendrilling around an even-featured face of pale serenity – she looked like one of those patient angels Botticelli slipped in when there was a space to fill and he'd used up his cherub quota. We'd met when I was with an events company, and had worked comfortably together on a few projects over a couple of years. When she'd suggested I think about joining her in her small design business, I'd thought it might be even further away from my hysterically theatrical upbringing than my current job. Unfortunately, deeply fond though I was of her, and successful as our growing business proved, beneath that serenely unruffled exterior it turned out, she possessed an outlook that made Murray look perkier than Pollyanna on Prozac. Still, I suppose the benefit of working with a glass-half-full type is it makes you, of necessity, consistently and determinedly more positive.

Before we left home, I'd also rung Martin to let him know I might be away for a few days. He greeted the news with supreme indifference.

"Let's hope... " he said, on learning of my unexpected family reunion, although it didn't sound as if it mattered much to him, one way or another, "...that they're not all as fruit-loopy as your Mother." I ignored that and said I'd call him when I got home. He said he was pretty much tied up for the next few weeks, but yes, of course, we'd do dinner sometime. I said goodbye and mentally consigned him to the tried and failed drawer – in a fit of pique, filing him under E for exceptionally boring.

Naturally, the very first of the series of calls I'd made that morning had been to Murray, to let him know Ophelia was with me and to check how Adam was.

"Like a bear with a sore head – literally." He reported glumly, "Had to cancel that Day in the Life piece they were doing on him, you know, for the Sunday Times. Mind you, not that we could have gone ahead without her here anyway, they wanted the two of them."

"What's he said?"

"Says it's for the best. Says this is the end of the road. What about her?"

"Same." I reported. Murray sniffed noisily,

"I don't know Sandy love, this time things don't look so good."

"You don't mean that."

"I do. That Sasha's a sly little minx, who'd 've thought she had it in her. She's already told the others she's doing the show with him next week.

"She hasn't!" I was genuinely shocked, "He'd never go on without Ophelia."

"Tackled him on it. Says he will."

"Oh God, Murray, what're we going to do?"

"Search me. Not much we can right now. Look, sit tight, I'll work on him today."

"Right, and just so you know, I'm taking her to Stratford-on-Avon."

"Gordon Bennett girl, are you nuts? D'you really think this is the right time for a day-trip."

"She says she's got family there. Murray, she's only been fibbing her head off all these years, all those stories about her childhood – completely made up, can you believe it." I paused, but had to ask, "You didn't know, did you?"

"No, course not." He was as indignant as he was incredulous. "You sure you got it right? You must've have got it wrong." I shook my head, which was silly because he couldn't see me,

"Driving her down today, soon as she's ready."

"Blimcy." It was a long time since I'd heard Murray nonplussed.

In the confusion of her dramatic defection, Ophelia had grabbed Ink, but not Ink's basket. Luckily, there was a vet down the road and I went to purchase a ridiculously expensive cardboard effort, for which they presumably thought they were entitled to charge £15, because of the *Pet à Porter* printed in fancy letters on the side. Unfortunately, Ink took the view that this was a distinct and insupportable downgrade from her usual mode of transportation – a luxurious wickerwork contraption, furnished with made-to-measure cushion and with a large Perspex window.

Whilst there wasn't much to choose between Ink and my Mother on bloody-mindedness, when it came to speed, the cat had the edge. I spent twenty sweaty and increasingly frustrating minutes, haring round the flat, trying to grab the wretched feline and bundle her into the box, against which she'd taken, with a vengeance. When my Mother wandered in, freshly talcumed and gently glowing from a hot bath and suggested I needed to be a bit firmer, I lost what little temper I had left.

"She's your bloody cat, you do it."

"Don't swear, sweets." And she turned her eye on the cat. "Ink. Box." Whereupon Ink, who'd been attempting to haul her portly self up the curtain, an exercise threatening to rip the rail away from the wall, suddenly shot through the air. She hovered bulkily over the box for a second or so, before descending rapidly inside with a resounding thump and a small mew.

"Well, don't just stand there Serenissima. Shut it." Said my Mother.

CHAPTER TWELVE

I don't remember too many details about our drive down to Stratford-on-bloody-Avon that day. I think I was pretty much on auto, focusing on the many and varied things I wanted to say to the wretched woman sitting next to me. I was also distracted at an early stage by Ink, who utilised a paw to punch a large and defiant hole in the cardboard box, squirming out of it, bit by painful bit. It took her about twenty minutes to finally emerge triumphant, like a rather hefty butterfly from an ill-fitting chrysalis. She spent the rest of the journey sitting complacently on the back seat, her expression clearly indicating that if she had fingers, she'd be putting two of them up at me and my box.

I wanted to tell my Mother exactly, and in some detail, what I thought of the dreadful deceit she'd perpetuated through the years. And when I'd finished expressing myself on that, there were a ton and a half of questions to which I wanted immediate and comprehensive answers. Unfortunately, everything was left to swish frustratingly back and forth inside my head because once the Ink incident had resolved itself, Ophelia put her seat into recline and went to sleep. She's always had a world-class ability to nap neatly – never a drooping jaw or unladylike dribble – whenever, wherever and for however long she wants and once she's gone, she's gone. She hadn't even bothered to ask whether I'd spoken to Murray to find out how my Father was – or wasn't. For all she knew, or apparently cared, he could be lying on a slab somewhere with a label on his toe and she could be a fugitive from justice.

I honestly didn't know what to think about these hitherto unsuspected relatives on whom we were to imminently descend and indeed, I was still pretty sceptical. The whole enterprise had more than a whiff of the wild goose about it. I wouldn't have put it past her to have made everything up on the spur of the moment, purely for dramatic effect. I was half prepared to drive for a couple of hours only to end up with her wiping away a wistful tear and stating sadly, the old folk must have moved on.

I wasn't even entirely sure what I was hoping for. I was feeling an acutely painful sense of dislocation. All my life, throughout all the hysterical ups, downs, shenanigans and odd goings on, I'd borne in mind the terrible childhood she herself had endured, and felt allowances needed to be made. But last night, she'd casually trampled over all of that. I now had no idea at all of where or who she'd come from, why or when she'd left and whether she'd all the while been in clandestine contact. There were a hundred and one questions I could have asked had she been in answering mode.

***

We made good time, it being mid-week with lighter traffic. If I hadn't been so preoccupied, I'd have certainly enjoyed the drive more and once off the motorway, roads were scenically lined with trees decked out and dressed up gloriously in burnt orange, not yet completely decimated by spoil-sport winds. My little Fiat, which had seen better days, but of which I was very fond, for once behaved impeccably with none of the bumps and starts to which it was prone. All in all, it was an uneventful journey – until I mowed down a little old lady.

Ophelia had woken grudgingly when I nudged her for directions.

"That's if you remember?" I said.

"I'm not half-witted, of course I remember." She sat up indignantly and unhesitatingly issued instructions, which had us negotiating some disconcertingly narrow lanes and passing through several sinisterly named villages, until I was fast on the way to losing both my bearings and my patience. Finally she said, with enough relief to confirm she'd been as doubtful as me,

"Look, there. Turn right down there, then sharp left at the bottom. I glanced over to see whether she felt as apprehensive about this whole crazy business as I did. My eyes were only off the road for an instant. When I looked back, there was a figure smack dab in front of me, hands outstretched as if to ward off the lethally approaching vehicle. I threw all my weight on the brake. Ophelia and I jerked painfully forward against seatbelts and I felt a ghastly, solid thump as we hit the woman, echoed by another blow as Ink catapulted off her seat, smacked into the back of mine and bounced off onto the floor.

I could feel adrenaline in the frozen tingling of scalp and fingers, and for a second or two couldn't unclasp my grip, as if by force of hold on the steering wheel I could pull the car back from whatever terrible damage it had done. I staggered out on jellied legs, dreading what bloody sight might meet my eyes.

Struggling to sit up in the middle of the road, was a woman, head haloed by fine, curly silver hair. My first impression was late fifties, but as she looked up, I adjusted that to a fair bit older. Relief surged, she wasn't dead thank God, not even unconscious. She was cradling her left arm in her right, shoulders shaking. I looked a little closer and made another revision, not sobbing, laughing. Laughing?

Blood that had departed my head, in the general rush to keep my heart going, started to trickle back to work and I felt slightly dizzy. I mustered moisture in a fright-parched mouth, and moved forward even though my legs were urging me to lie down, but two of us on the tarmac wasn't going to do anyone any good.

"I'm *so* sorry," I croaked, "I just didn't see you. You came out of nowhere, are you all right?" Replaying in my mind was the sheer solidity of the sound as we hit her, she had to be hurt in some way. I knelt down beside her in the road. I was a bit hazy about what to do next, aren't you supposed not to move someone, internal injuries and all that. An ambulance, that's what we needed, an ambulance.

"Look, you mustn't move." I put an arm round thin shoulders to support her and looked back for Ophelia who, unbelievably, was still sitting in the car,

"Ophelia." I shrieked, "Ambulance – call an ambulance, mobile's in my bag."

"No, no, no dear, goodness me, don't need an ambulance, nasty noisy things. I'm fine... not hurt, other than pride that is and bit of a sore arm." The injured party giggled, she seemed to be a jolly old soul. "So silly... my fault entirely... don't know what I was thinking... completely misjudged the distance. Could you um... " she gestured vaguely with her head and I wondered, should I be putting her in the recovery position, or did that only apply if someone was unconscious?

"I'm fine, really." She reiterated, "I assure you. Just assist me to stand and perhaps you wouldn't mind... a lift home? Just the weeniest bit shaky." She giggled again breathlessly, I wished she'd stop doing that – injury, indignation and shock I was geared for, giggling was unexpected.

"Do you think you can stand?" I put both arms around her and we rose a little unsteadily, hanging on to each other. She was short, reaching only to my shoulder and so finely boned it was like holding a child. Close up, she was certainly considerably older than my first impression, although her skin was softly unlined. Under an open, moleskin-brown, padded jacket she was wearing a pair of now-dusty black trousers and a soft pink jumper which, I absently noted, she had on not only inside out but also back to front. She smelt mustily of lavender and I sniffed again, hoping for something alcoholic, that might account for a lot and would make me feel less guilty.

"Rostropovich." She said suddenly.

"Pardon?"

"Rostropovich." She repeated, casting round anxiously and my heart started to thud again. It was odd that the frail bundle of bones in my grasp had been hit with such a resounding wallop and yet was still in one piece – but if there'd been two of them. Maybe he was under the car. I crouched down again, forgetting in the stress of the moment I was still holding her, and she obligingly scrunched down with me.

"What are you looking for?" She asked, as we both craned to see into the shadows under the car.

"Rostropovich."

"Well he won't be under there, dear." She said reasonably.

"But maybe I hit him."

"No, no, he was definitely behind me."

"Well where is he then?" We straightened up and were now both looking round vaguely, perhaps it was catching, perhaps any minute now, I'd start chuckling too.

"Probably my own fault," she said. "I'm afraid I didn't have him on the lead and he's a bit highly strung. Must have had a fright, but not to worry, he'll find his way home."

"Oh, a dog?" I said. She smiled absently and swayed a little and I hastily grabbed her again, the sooner we moved on the better. Ophelia, wretched,

wretched woman that she was, hadn't budged off her bottom and was just sitting there, gazing absently out at the scenery as if it was still passing. Opening the back door, I unceremoniously shoved an already aggrieved Ink out of the way and folded our new passenger inside. I got her seat belted, patted her encouragingly on the uninjured arm and slid into place behind the wheel, turning back to look at her,

"Can you direct me?"

"Well, let me see... a minute... goodness, never quite sure, must get my bearings."

"Next right, follow the road down to the end then take a sharp left." said my Mother firmly.

"You always had a good sense of direction." Said the little old lady.

"Hello Mother." Said Ophelia.

CHAPTER THIRTEEN

"*Well*," I said, and if a touch of bitterness crept in, who could blame me. "Well, well, well. Isn't this nice? Hello Grandma, and thank you very much Ophelia!" After all, I thought, what's one shock more or less, when you've just nearly killed someone? That the person in question turns out to be a Grandmother you've only just discovered you have, is just the flipping sugar-pink icing on the cake. It wasn't just the surprise, it was Ophelia's way of handling things – with maximum theatricality and minimum consideration for anyone else's feelings.

In truth, the woman did have an uncomfortably familiar look about her. Matter of fact, I thought grimly, eyeing her in the mirror, she looked much as Ophelia might, were you to add a couple of decades and subtract hairdresser, health farm and Estée Lauder.

I waited a beat or two to see if any more revelations or indeed relations were forthcoming, but neither passenger seemed inclined to add anything. As I carefully pulled away – running over the missing Rostropovich, at this point, would just about finish me off – I wondered what I might have expected. Probably not a falling on each other's bosom and weeping kind of a reunion. On the other hand, a 'Well, so how've you been?' wouldn't have gone amiss. But next to me, my Mother had her compact out and was powdering her already impeccably powdered nose, whilst the newest addition to the family was busy muttering to Ink in the back. At least I think it was Ink to whom she was muttering, to date she had more of the Loopy Lou about her than I'd have preferred.

Still shaky and driving slowly and carefully, I followed Ophelia's instructions, stopping before the sharp left turn she'd indicated, because it obviously wasn't the right place. An ornately lettered sign told me it was *The Home Hill Country House Hotel and Spa.*

"Well I never." Observed Ophelia with interest.

"You mean this is it?" I said.

"Indeed it is dear," a whiff of lavender and a chuckle from the back seat confirmed the last ten minutes hadn't been a bad dream. I turned in between the couple of open, somewhat rusty, wrought iron gates trailing former glories and a fair amount of ivy, and we bumped and jerked down a not very wide, winding drive bordered and darkened by canopied trees, sunlight breaking through only with persistence and intermittently. I devoutly hoped there wasn't going to be anybody bombing down the other way. The drive was in a dreadful condition and our progress was punctuated unnecessarily at every lurch, by irritated little tuts from Ophelia. I was about to point out testily that I wasn't doing it just to annoy her, when the drive widened into a circular gravelled area, fronting a large rambling building whose slightly neglected appearance, couldn't conceal an original pleasing symmetry of design. In the centre of the gravel in a grassed circle, a moss-greened mermaid was perched on a plinth clasping, without enthusiasm, an urn from which a trickle of water splashed desultorily into a small pond. Wide, slightly chipped stone steps led up to open black, gold-knobbed, double doors flanked by two large terracotta pots whose contents looked in need of urgent floral first aid.

A couple of vehicles were already parked to the left of the fountain, so I drew up alongside them and got out. The place seemed pretty deserted. I turned to extract my back-seat passenger, helping her out before quickly shutting the door in the face of an indignant Ink who, I hoped was just curious and not answering an urgent call of nature. She'd just have to wait. Ophelia was already standing on the other side of the car, gazing at the house with an unreadable expression.

"Come along then, no point standing out here, we'll go in the back way, shall we?" The sight of home, if indeed that's what it was, seemed to have galvanised the new-found grandparent and before I could protest, she'd grasped my hand in a surprisingly firm grip and, pulling me briskly with her, was trotting towards the side of the building. Ophelia, despite raising her eyes to heaven as she caught my glance, had grabbed her handbag and butter-soft leather jacket from the car and was following at a more sedate pace, no doubt counting the cost of gravel scrapes to her elegant heels.

Rounding the side of the building, we ran full tilt into a woman surging the other way. An imposing figure with a slightly grubby white medical-style coat, buttoned and straining over an impressive bosom. She had fine cut features and a face made paler by a slash of deep red lipstick and kohl-rimmed eyes. Jet black hair, hauled high on her head was held with two tortoiseshell combs.

"Mimi, there you are." She snapped. "Take this... no, on second thoughts you'll only drop it. You hold it." She thrust what she'd been carrying at me and I automatically put out my hands to take it. It turned out to be a baby in a grubby pink dress. The infant and I contemplated each other in mutual astonishment.

"Can you cook ducks?" Said the woman. I stared at her, was she being affectionate or specific?

"Well, I... "

"Come on, haven't got all day." She placed an authoritative hand on my waist and whirling round, propelled me briskly back in the direction from which she'd come. I hastily readjusted the babe in my arms to avoid it plummeting to the ground.

"Look," I said crossly, "I think you're mistaking me for someone else."

"Why?"

"Well, I only just arrived. With my Mother."

"Ophelia?"

"Yes." I looked helplessly over my shoulder to where Ophie was following us, picking her way gingerly along the flag-stoned path which ran around the back of the building. Typically, she appeared more concerned about her Jimmy Choo's than anything else that might be going on.

"Well, unless she's changed a hell of a lot," said the white-coated one briskly, "She wouldn't know her arse from her elbow in the kitchen, always next to useless when it came to anything practical, so, can you tackle duck?"

"Well, I... "

"For goodness sake girl, yes or no. Don't faff. We've five booked for dinner and Gladys is having one of her turns."

"Just hang on a minute." I stopped dead against the propelling hand. Mimi who'd been trotting too close behind and couldn't stop in time, barged into us both. Ophelia tutted, Mimi giggled and the baby, who I'd almost forgotten I was holding, gave a small yelp and rammed a fist into its mouth. "Who exactly are you?" I demanded.

"Bella."

"Cousin." Muttered Ophelia sourly in my ear, catching us up. "Always was a bossy so and so."

The hand was in place on my back again and whilst I was still largely unenlightened, it was impossible to resist such onward pressure. We surged briskly onwards then swiftly through an open back door, arriving in a large, square, chilly and distinctly un-gleaming kitchen. Initially I thought it was empty, then realized with a fright that made my heart hammer, there was a thin, dark-clad woman sitting cross-legged on the floor in the far corner of the room. She had her eyes tightly closed and was, disconcertingly, rocking back and forth and crooning softly in a high sing-song. She didn't seem to hear us, certainly didn't acknowledge us in any way, and as if that wasn't weird enough, none of the three women with me spared her so much as a glance.

A massive brick-built walk-in fireplace took up a major part of the wall opposite the back door. It was bordered on one side by a carved and weathered, high-backed wood settle, on the other by a glass fronted dresser, holding a large assortment of mismatched china. The adjacent wall hosted an elderly fridge chugging loudly, alongside a more modern chest freezer, dishwasher and a capacious white porcelain sink. To the left of the door we'd come in by loomed a gas cooker that, from the look of it, hadn't seen a Brillo pad anytime in the recent past and centre stage was a four-square, not particularly well-scrubbed, pine table on which a heap of ingredients were piled higgledy-piggledy – potatoes; vegetables; three still cling-filmed ducks; herbs spices and one solitary saucepan.

CHAPTER FOURTEEN

"Please tell me," said Bella, indicating the table, "That you can do something with this little lot. I'd have a go myself but I've got a soak and wrap at 3.00, a colonic irrigation at 4.00 and a Miracle Rejuve at 5.00, Elizabeth says she's bitten off far more than she can chew already and Devorah's as much use as a sick headache."

"Nice welcome." Ophelia, having ostentatiously dusted a kitchen chair with her handkerchief had seated herself at a little distance from the table, fastidiously turned away from the ducks.

"What were you expecting?" Enquired Bella politely, "A brass band?"

"Now, now girls," interrupted Mimi, "No bickering, I hate bickering. It's not that we're not pleased to see you Ophelia dear, you know that. Things are just a little… tense right now."

"Nothing new there then." Said my Mother.

"Oh, please don't say that dear. It's all just a bit awkward… "

"For God's sake," Bella snapped "Call a spade a spade, can't you Mimi. What she's trying to say Ophelia is that we don't all have your financial resources."

"Is that what all this hotel stuff is about?" Ophelia asked with interest.

"Hush, oh shush," Mimi fluttered agitated hands at the two women facing off across the kitchen table. "You know Etty doesn't countenance money-talk, if she hears you, there'll be trouble. Now… here's an idea, why don't I take charge of dinner?"

"No!" Ophelia and Bella spoke as one, then looked at each other and laughed and in the softening of both faces, despite the different colouring, I saw resemblance and shared history. Bella turned back to me,

"Serenissima?"

"Sandra." I corrected automatically.

"Don't blame you – Sandra then. Can you possibly help out? Wouldn't ask if we weren't up the creek without a paddle." She looked at me hopefully. I glanced at Ophelia, who gave an up-to-you shrug.

"I'll have a go." I said reluctantly, "I think I owe Mimi that much. Look, you're sure you're not hurt, injured in any way, should I run you to the nearest hospital to check?" Mimi shook her head firmly,

"Right as rain dear, never better."

"Fine." Bella appeared monumentally incurious about whatever might or might not have befallen Mimi. Clearly this blithe unconcern was a family trait shared with Ophelia. She clapped her hands together decisively. "That's all settled then. Thanks a million."

"No, wait a minute," I said, things were moving too fast altogether – there were so many explanations I wanted, I honestly didn't know which end to start. "What about her?" I indicated the woman in the corner "Is she drunk?"

"Gladys? Good God, no." Exclaimed Bella indignantly. "Certainly not, never touches a drop, not to worry, she's fine, it's just Sitting Bull, Ophelia can fill you in." I'd no idea what she was talking about, but there was another, more pressing concern, which was wriggling in my arms and starting to feel somewhat damp around the nether regions.

"What about the baby?" I held her out.

"Damn, I'd forgotten." Bella began to look fraught again. "Mimi, can I trust you to take her upstairs? She's fed, she just needs changing and then she'll go down for a good few hours." Mimi nodded and took the child from me. She placed the now fussing baby against one shoulder, supported the lolling head with a firm hand, and vanished. I think I might have staggered a little then. I know I must have looked pretty awful, because Ophelia rose and pushed a chair towards me and Ophelia didn't put herself out unless a situation really screamed for it. I felt the rim of the seat against the back of my knees, not a moment too soon and sat down abruptly. I hadn't anticipated *that*. It simply had not once crossed my mind.

"What on earth's the matter?" Bella looked anxious, less I thought for me, than for dinner.

"Search me." Said Ophelia. I looked up at her and she smiled vaguely, "Better now darling?" I was torn, as so often in the past, between a desire to scream until I was hoarse and the urge to spend a productive few minutes, banging her head against the nearest floorboard.

"Your family." I said levelly.

"Mm hmm?"

"They're like you?"

"Well, people did used to say I had a look of Mother, but I could honestly never see it myself."

"I don't mean *that*," I hissed, "And well you know it. They're *like* you, aren't they?"

"Well, technically darling, I suppose I'm like *them* but… "

"For God's sake Ophelia, why didn't you tell me?"

"You didn't ask."

I slapped my fist down hard in frustration on the nearest thing, which happened to be the kitchen table, the ducks jumped, as did Ophelia. I could hear my voice shrilling upwards, along no doubt with my blood pressure.

"Well *excuse me*, but don't you think such a snippet might have been worth sharing, after all we've just been sitting in the bloody car together for two hours."

"May I ask what this unseemly racket is all about?" The voice was mild, nevertheless it was a tone that brooked little if no opposition. It carried across the room and sliced through the rising tension like a knife, if only to replace it with tension of a different kind.

A diminutively upright figure was silhouetted in a doorway at the far end of the room. For a moment it was difficult to define feature or age, but authority emanated from every autocratically restrained inch of her. I was aware of Ophelia and Bella beside me, straightening imperceptibly.

She advanced into the room and although she moved easily, as her face came clearly into the light, I saw she must be well into her eighties, despite a tautly unjowled jaw. Her skin was finely cross-hatched, and thinning silvered hair stretched starkly back from high cheeked, hawk-nosed features and folded into a chignon, low on her long neck. Although she carried a carved, bird-head topped, walking stick, she leaned on it hardly at all and I'd been in show-business long enough to know an effects prop when I saw one. A brown tweed, mid-calf skirt swung as she moved, above elegantly pointed, heeled shoes strapped over the instep. A crisp white shirt contrasted with the softness of a black pashmina, draped evenly over her shoulders. She glanced briefly at the swaying figure in the corner,

"Sitting Bull?"

"'Fraid so," said Bella. The woman turned a startlingly piercing green gaze back to us, inclining her head slightly.

"Ophelia." She said, "Presumably there's trouble in paradise, or we wouldn't have the pleasure of a visit."

"I thought it was about time." Ophelia, aiming for defiant, reached only defensive.

"Hmm, after how long is it, I quite forget? Your girl, I assume?" I stood, stepped forward a little and extended my hand. I may have had a series of shocks, the implications of which I hadn't even yet begun to consider, but damned if I was going to be intimidated by some little old battle-axe, especially if I was being co-opted as emergency chef. She ignored the hand, staring intently at me with those unsettling eyes. I sensed she used silence as a powerful tool.

"I'm Sandra." I said.

"Well, you've not got your Mother's looks and I hope you haven't been blessed with your Father's brains." She responded. Charming. I threw a sideways glance towards Ophelia, normally she responded to any slur on my Father with fury, unless she'd been the one to make it, but she was busy not catching my eye.

"And you would be?" I kept my tone neutral, I'd mixed with egos all my life, this one was no different.

"Etty Goodkind. Your Great Grandmother. Now, I came to get tea organised, can you see to it for me? Tea and biscuits for two in the library and sooner, rather than later would be appreciated." Another one not into heavily emotional re-unions. And why was it everyone instantly assumed I was here to help with the catering arrangements?

"Good Lord," said Bella suddenly, looking at her watch. "That the time? Must fly." I looked round apprehensively, the way things were going it wouldn't have surprised me if that had been exactly what she did, but thankfully, she was just bustling out the back door.

"Tea? In your own time." Etty, also moving briskly out of the kitchen, rapped her cane twice on the stone-tiled floor to get my attention, although succeeded only in getting up my nose.

"I'm sorry, but no." I said firmly, "I may have been coerced into doing dinner, but I'm not the new maid. You want tea? Get someone else to make it." There was a brief silence, broken only by the mutterings of the rocking woman in the far corner. I met the chill green gaze of my newly acquired Great Grandmother evenly. The woman was obviously a bully, habitually getting her own way, but if there was one thing I was used to, it was dealing with selfish prima donnas. For a few beats we took each other's measure then,

"Sandra," she said, "My most sincere apologies. I really shouldn't be asking favours of you so early on in our acquaintance, but circumstances have forced upon us some staff shortages. It would help me immeasurably, if you could see your way clear to helping me out, just this once." She paused. "If only for appearances sake in front of my guest." Well, she'd got me sussed – guilt and good manners, my two weak spots. I didn't say anything, but she took it as read. "I am in your debt." She inclined her head graciously and left the room. As I placed a somewhat battered kettle on the hob to boil I had to admit, her tactics threw my Mother's into the novice class, I couldn't help but be impressed by that.

CHAPTER FIFTEEN

Needless to say, Ophelia had taken advantage of my temporary distraction to make herself scarce. I ground my teeth, a habit I've been trying without success to break for years. I'd been livid with her time without number, but on a scale of one to ten, right now I was fast speeding towards twenty. Frustration was doubled, because she hadn't even had the grace to hang around and receive the mouthful she so richly deserved. Of course, when I eventually did get hold of her I knew full well, there'd be small chance of conveying just how angrily hurt I felt about all the things she had and hadn't told me – guilt lingered as long on my Mother, as water on a duck's back.

Talking of which, I eyed the pallid, cling-filmed items awaiting me glumly on the table and then glanced around the dimly lit kitchen to see if there were any cookery books on view. Committed as I now seemed to be, not only to tea and biscuits in the next few minutes, but also to this evening's dinner, the coming hours were going to be fully occupied. Once beyond those few hours though, there was no doubt in my mind.

Perhaps I should have been intrigued and excited, itching to find out all I could about the new nearest and dearest but frankly, I'd had it up to here with eccentricities of all kinds. I'd grown up with Ophelia's, but had long since come to terms with and incorporated them into everyday life. I'd dealt with them the only way I knew how, by simply not thinking about them.

Head in the sand? You might say. Turning a blind eye? You bet. But it had worked for me to date, and as far as I was concerned if something was working, why change it. One thing I knew for sure, I didn't have the space, time or inclination for anything else in the way of 'goings-on' and if there was anything painfully evident, in the brief time I'd spent in the bosom of this new-found family, 'goings-on' looked as if they might be thicker on the ground than daisies in May. It was crystal clear to me, the sooner I turned the car round and made good speed back up that motorway, the very much happier and more relieved I was going to be.

***

Kettle boiled, tea-pot unearthed and warmed and vaguely matching cups and saucers acquired from the dresser, I looked around for a tray. It wasn't that I was unduly intimidated by the old lady with the chill green gaze, but tea and biscuits isn't a hugely complicated production and I didn't intend to be judged by Ophelia's levels of incompetence. I suddenly became aware, all had gone silent in the room, the woman in the corner had stopped chanting and was regarding me warily with deep-set, button bright, dark eyes.

"Hello." She said cautiously, "Do I know you?"

"I'm Ophelia's daughter, she's… "

"I know who she is."

"Right, well, I'm looking for a tray, where do you keep them?"

"Why?"

"I'm taking tea upstairs."

"You'd better use this then." She beckoned me over. I advanced cautiously, she seemed to be fairly rational, but I was taking no chances.

"Give me a hand up?" She was struggling to rise, hindered by limbs stiffened in their cross-legged position. She wasn't a young woman and cadaverously thin with graying hair tied up and back, pink-ribboned in a girlish ponytail. She thrust out an arm for assistance and I took a bird-thin, work-reddened, cold hand in mine. If she was normally in charge of the kitchen, no wonder they had problems, she didn't look as if she'd have the strength to crack an egg, let alone give it a good beating.

"There." She moved clumsily away, stretching her back and bending to rub her knees. "There." She repeated, inclining her head impatiently. On the floor was a large silver tray. She'd been sitting on it. "Silver," she explained. "Solid. Excellent conductor." I nodded as if I understood and bent to pick it up.

"Thanks." I said.

"Pleasure. Now just make sure I have it back when you've finished, we've others, but this is the best." She smiled absently and moved across to one of the kitchen chairs. She sat, leaned across the table and gently poked one of the ducks with an exploratory finger.

"Oh my," she said, and a solitary tear ambled slowly across one cheek. "I did try you know." She heaved a deep sigh. "I tried ever so hard, I knew tonight was important." I carried the heavy tray across to the table and handed her a tissue from my bag which I'd hung over the back of a chair.

"D'you mean the meal?" I said. "Look, don't worry, it's certainly nothing to cry over. I'll give you a hand, we'll get it sorted, only thing is I'm not sure of timings, do you have any cookery books?"

"Cookery books?" She shook her head vehemently, "Well of course I don't. *They* wouldn't let me, would they? Don't you see, they'd take huge offence. But I've let the family down haven't I? Let them down dreadfully. But it's just that he's so strong. Can you understand that?" She shot out an urgent hand and grasped my arm before I had a chance to whip it out of reach. "Ah, but you're strong too, aren't you? Very strong indeed I can see. Did you know you have a powerful aura?" She looked up at me hopefully, "Perhaps together we can relegate him. Not," she added, lowering her voice cautiously and looking briefly over her shoulder, "That I don't appreciate what he does for me, but quite frankly he's a dreadful cook, and the ingredients my dear, well naturally, there's no chance of me getting half the things he asks for." Releasing my arm, she put both of hers on the table, rested her head on them and started to cry in earnest. I ineffectually patted one heaving scrawny shoulder.

"Look… Gladys, is it?" Choked assent. "Well, Gladys, not to worry, I'm sure we can sort it out between us, I may not be Delia Smith… " She raised a tear-blotched face hopefully,

"Oh my dear, but I might," she said, "I might well be her by the time you come back. I'll try, I'll really try, I promise."

"That's the spirit." I said encouragingly. Poor old bat was obviously so far round the bend it wasn't worth chasing her. I fished another tissue out of my bag, pushed it into her unresisting hand to supplement the first sodden one, filled the teapot and bearing the full tray, headed out of the kitchen. I was halfway down an uncarpeted corridor, illuminated by light filtering through the glassed upper halves of the double doors at either end, before I realised, I'd absolutely no idea at where I was going.

CHAPTER SIXTEEN

Old Etty Grand-manners had said the library, and I briefly debated backtracking to quiz Gladys but didn't think she'd be much help, she hadn't looked as if she could find her way out of a paper bag with a map and a torch. Naturally enough, Ophelia hadn't reappeared either, why would she if there was a chance she might be able to do something remotely useful? I pursed my lips and utilised my bottom to push open one of the two heavy double swing doors in front of me.

I followed the now carpeted hallway and found myself heading towards what must be the main entrance to the house which was set up as a reception area. A couple of worn green leather, gold-studded, upright chairs stiffly flanked an inlaid wood coffee table bearing some suitably country style magazines and an art deco bronze of a woman, leaning back against the pull of two leashed and straining dogs.

Opposite, on a wide and high, dark wood, ornately carved reception desk was a thick register with a pen in a stand, a phone, a small wooden postcard holder and one of those circular bells you only ever see in hotels. I stifled a strong urge to go and bang it with the flat of my hand and keep banging, until someone sensible came along,

Backing the desk was a half-open door onto a small office – empty. The adjacent wall held a board with a range of keys on numbered large wooden fobs. Parquet flooring in the reception area was softened with judiciously spaced rugs and whilst the black, gold-knobbed front doors standing open to the drive where we'd first drawn up, were letting in some welcome light, there was also a steady stream of dried, fallen leaves borne in on a chill wind that wasn't going to do much for the heating bills. An imposing, elaborate, wrought-iron balustraded staircase swooped upward from the middle of the hall to a galleried first floor.

I surveyed the range of doors on either side of the hallway, any one of which could be the library and opted for the nearest, because it was ajar. I edged it open with my foot, the wretched tray was feeling heavier by the minute, and found myself at one end of a substantial living room. It was furnished with an eclectic mix of darkly mottled, over-stuffed leather sofas, the sort you either immediately stick to or find yourself sliding right off of.

The sofas, together with some hectically flowered and cushioned armchairs, had been arranged in groupings round a selection of glass-topped coffee tables. Lurking uneasily over each seating area was an old fashioned, heavily fringed, pink-shaded standard lamp and above a large, blue delft tiled, empty fireplace, a wide mantelpiece was crowded with assorted sizes of slightly tarnished, silver framed photographs. It was a pleasantly proportioned room, but the high arched French doors leading out to the gardens, were firmly shut and from the musty smell, hadn't been opened for quite some time.

I backed out to try another door although reaching it, realized I didn't have a hand free to turn the handle. Placing the tray carefully on the floor, I found this one opened into a dining room, with the same pleasingly square dimensions and high arched windows. The room held about a dozen clothed, un-laid tables. To my vast relief, there was at least someone here I could ask for help. A tall, well-built woman in a black dress was bent over, industriously assembling cutlery from the drawers of a dresser at the end of the room.

"Hello?" I waited for her to turn. She ignored me. I tried again, slightly louder, still nothing. This was silly and I had tea going cold outside. Crossing the carpeted room, I reached up and touched her shoulder. She jumped and swung swiftly round, hand to chest, wide-eyed and open-mouthed with such undisguised fright that I jumped too. Late fifties, she had a disconcertingly doll-like face with large long-lashed brown eyes, snub nose, rosebud mouth, hectic dab of rouge on each appled cheek and sleek, dark wings of short, straight hair hanging neatly below her ears from a rigidly controlled centre-parting,

"Good God in Heaven above," she yelped, looking down on me, she must have been nearly six foot tall. "What kind of a game you playing, sneaking up on a body like that, you'll have me stone dead on the floor you will."

"I'm so sorry, I did call out, you didn't hear."

"Course I heard." She snapped, "Was concentrating is all. Anyway, what time do you call this and what's that you've got on?" Disconcerted, I glanced down at my jeans and sneakers.

"White shirt, black skirt or trousers, didn't they tell you?" She said sharply. "Might do you a piece of good, m'girl if you listened a bit more yourself, 'stead of creeping around frightening folk out their wits. Here..." She thrust a key into my hand. "Cupboard next the larder, find something to fit, then get yourself back here and get these tables done, we've only five in tonight, but we need to set the others too, make it look busier. What're you gawping at now? Get skates on." I swallowed any comment, I really didn't have the strength for what were obviously going to be complicated explanations as to who I was or wasn't, but I did still have the ruddy tea tray to deliver. She'd turned back to the dresser and didn't hear me ask again. I had to touch her shoulder to make her look at me.

"Well, *what is it now*?" She tossed her head indignantly, making the hair wings swing back then forward again.

"The library?" I asked.

"Third on the left, what you want that for anyhow?"

"Tea." I indicated the tray sitting on the threshold.

"Who's asked you for that then?"

"Etty."

"*Miss* Etty – mind your manners if you please. Well best get on with it hadn't you."

Third door on the left; tea-laden, ton-weighing tray; another ornate door handle; still no hands. Enough was enough, patience was running on empty and this wasn't the Savoy, so I gave the door a couple of hefty kicks. There was a pause in the murmur of voices coming from the room and I was about to re-plant foot on wood, when it opened and a tall, skinny chap with a pair of glasses perched where his hair should be, arched an eyebrow at my drawn back leg.

"Murder to kick down, aren't they?" He said. "A lot of people just opt for using the handle." Great, a wise guy, just what I needed right now.

"Hands full." I said shortly, nodding downwards.

"Well there's a relief, sounded like we were being raided." He stood aside to let me enter.

The room revealed, was indeed the library. Darkly draped maroon curtains obscured much of what was left of the fading November light and an unenthusiastic fire was stuttering nervously in the grate, trying and failing to raise the temperature. Similarly sized and proportioned to the other rooms I'd seen, three of the four walls were book-lined, producing that unique smell, the heady amalgam of leather, ink, binding glue and age-foxed paper. There was a magnificent, ornate gilt, heavy-on-the-cherubs mirror which presided over the fireplace, a black, full-sized grand piano in one corner of the room and a harp in another. And seated rigidly on a small sofa, at right angles to the feeble fire was Etty, her expression chillier than the tea I was bringing. She waved an aristocratic hand.

"Milk and sugar for Mr Heywood, black no sugar for me. Thank you."

"Right, I'll be Mother then shall I?" I muttered, taking a certain amount of grim satisfaction in seeing the tea emerge in that turgid, non-steaming way that bodes no good at all and, as I placed a plate of custard creams on the bow-legged coffee table in front of the sofa, spotted with pleasure the almost imperceptible grimace of her guest as he took a sip. Etty herself was drinking her tea with every evidence of enjoyment, but I caught her chill eye momentarily and any small smugness evaporated. I certainly didn't like the woman and her high-handed ways, especially as she'd so obviously tarred me with the same brush of uselessness as my Mother, but there was something about her – an implacability that demanded grudging respect. She inclined her head in thanks and dismissal and restraining myself from bobbing a satirical curtsey, I shut the library door quietly behind me.

Making my way kitchen-ward, tea duties discharged, a guilty thought suddenly assailed me – poor old Ink was still shut in the car. It was, of course, just possible Ophelia might have already retrieved her, but as I hadn't observed any airborne pink pigs, I deemed that unlikely, and hastened out the front door to make amends. Serve me right if she'd made a mess. Ink however had behaved like a perfect lady and, other than a reproachful glare as she jumped heavily out on to the gravel, didn't seem to be bearing any grudges, although she didn't hang about, but made with alacrity for a convenient flowerbed.

While I waited, I strolled up and down a little, crossing my arms across my chest as the evening chill closed in. Close up, the down-at-mouth mermaid still looked as miserable as the trickle her urn was producing, and the water had a dankly unpleasant smell to it. It was very peaceful though, not even the remotest grumble of traffic – lovely spot, delightful building, shame it had been allowed to run down in the way it had.

I noticed there was a slightly more modern, single-storey annexe, set back a little and stretching to the right of the main house. It too looked in need of a bit of re-pointing and painting and in one of the lighted windows, I could see a white coated figure moving around busily – no mistaking the shape of bossy Bella. What was it she'd said – a mud soak and some kind of irrigation? I shivered in the spiteful little wind that was ruffling Ink's magnificent plumed tail as she came trotting over in answer to my call, although I put her cooperation down to hunger, rather than either obedience or affection. She answered to only one mistress and it wasn't me, but I started inside, confident that in expectation of a bowl-full of something tasty, she'd follow. I was startled when she suddenly hissed, an unexpectedly loud and hostile sound. The only other time I'd heard her do that was when Adam accidentally caught her tail in a door. I turned to see what had alarmed her. It was a wolf.

CHAPTER SEVENTEEN

I blinked hard and looked again. Yes indeedy, I was no David Attenborough, but there could be no mistaking the coarse silver-gray fur, high ridged back, easy lope and golden eyes, black pupils slitted in the fading sunlight. It was a bloody big, real-life wolf and it was heading, in a business-like way, out of a thicket of trees to the side of the circular driveway, moving fluidly and disconcertingly swiftly across the gravel towards us.

"It's a wolf." I muttered out loud, as if pronouncement might make sense of the situation – it didn't. At my feet, Ink didn't seem to be in much doubt either, every inch of fur was standing at right angles to her body. Good try, but my guess was, it might take more than a very fat cat to put the wind up a wolf.

Bending I swiftly scooped her, still hissing, into my arms, backing hurriedly through the open front doors and trying to push them closed behind me. But they were both fastened firmly back against the wall and, fingers made clumsy by mounting panic, I couldn't find the catch to free even one of them. Concluding it might not be in my long-term interest to hang around, I turned and headed down the hall at speed, hearing with mounting horror, the unmistakable click and patter of claw and pad on parquet, as the animal entered the front door and started briskly down the hall after me.

In my initial panic, I was dashing for the stairs until it flashed through my mind, that as a deterrent for a determined predator, that might not work, why wouldn't he just take them in his stride? No, what was required was definitely something in the barrier category. I needed to head for the double swing doors at the far end of the hall. They'd take me back to the kitchen, where there must be a phone, although I wasn't clear at that point whether I'd be screaming hysterically for police, RSPCA or just for the hell of it.

It was pure bad timing that Etty and guest should choose just the moment I was speeding towards them, to emerge from the library. To avoid a head-on collision, I tried to stop. Unfortunately, the rug I happened to be hurrying across, didn't. It slid smoothly along the polished parquet at a rate that had a certain inexorability about it. Etty's guest reacted instantly and commendably calmly, looping an arm around her waist and whipping her back out of my path.

"*Wolf*!" I shrieked as Ink and I glided past, "...don't worry, phoning for help." After all, I'd have hated anyone to think I wasn't in control of the situation. And then, probably because I wasn't paying the attention I should have been, the rug and I took a slight swerve and reached the stairs. This time the rug stopped and I didn't. My foot, toe-crushingly hit the bottom step and I measured my length with a thwump that knocked Ink out of my arms and air out of my lungs.

For a short while, I lost touch with priorities and could only contemplate with interest, the densely patterned but faded royal blue carpet under my nose, at the same time as trying not to inhale more dust than was healthy. Then reality rushed back and I gasped, choked on a chunk of blue fluff and flopped clumsily over on my back in full expectation of hot foetid breath on my face and rabid fangs at my throat.

"I assume," said Etty, "No one's told you about Rostropovich?" Looking up, I met the amused eye of Mr milk and sugar Heywood.

"Rostropovich?" I echoed weakly.

"...is quite harmless." Etty said. "I'm sorry if he frightened you. Mimi's supposed to keep him well out of everyone's way." I sat up cautiously. A headache with big potential was starting to make its presence felt, just above my right eye and the bits of me that had hit the stairs were aching.

"Are you hurt? You went down with quite a thump." Heywood was straight-faced but only, I felt, with an effort.

"Fine." I lied firmly, the way you do when you've made too much of a prat of yourself to do anything else. Rostrobloodypovich meanwhile had planted himself right next to me, far too close for comfort, tongue lolling in an eager way, head to one side. I stood up cautiously. I'm usually quite good with animals, God knows I had history with a lion, but that was under more controlled circumstances and this creature, close up, looked no less wild and wolfish than from a distance, apart from which you just don't expect wolves in Stratford-on-Avon. A disturbing sort of rattle was issuing from his throat and as I moved, so did he, pushing forward to rub his huge head against my reluctant leg. I backed up a couple of steps,

"Sit." Snapped Etty and I very nearly, despite myself, did. "You see," she turned to me. "He's totally tame and very well-trained. He's not even pure-bred, he looks more wolf than he really is."

"Why's he making that noise?" I asked, she sniffed,

"He thinks he's purring. Your Uncle bought him home when he was just a cub, goodness only knows why, and he was adopted by one of our cats who'd just had a litter and gone into maternal overdrive. Stupid animal's grown up under the impression he's a cat." She turned to the Heywood man,

"I really must apologise for all this ridiculous furore, what must you think of us? May I introduce my Great-Granddaughter, Serenissima who's kindly helping out for a few days." I was still digesting the mention of another relative, an Uncle no less and had absently put out a polite hand when the 'few days' hit me. I glared at her, where on earth had she got that from? I'd committed to cooking some flipping ducks, that was all. Once I had them done and dusted, I was heading out of this mad house faster than a bat out of hell.

"Should I fetch your cat for you?" Heywood had retrieved my hand from where I'd left it hanging in mid-air, shaken it and given it back. Ink had settled further up the stairs and was washing her nether regions enthusiastically. I eyed them both with equal disfavour she, recovered totally from her earlier fright, he with glasses still perched idiotically on his head.

"Thank you, no. She'll come when I call. Ink," I patted the side of my leg encouragingly. Ink paused, looked at me thoughtfully for a beat or two then went back to what she was doing.

"Ink," I snapped, "Come along now."

"I don't think she wants to." He observed helpfully.

"Well, of course she doesn't want to, poor sweet baby, she's scared half to death. I can't believe you let that wild animal roam around like this." From the first floor landing my Mother, changed now into flowing black trousers and beaded kaftan, came swooping gracefully down. She bent, gathered a stoical Ink to her bosom and bestowed on Heywood one of her, I'm-distressed-but-going-to-be-very-brave-about-it smiles. "I don't believe we've met?" She said.

"Actually we have, but it was years ago. How are you Ophelia? Shouldn't think you'd remember me, last time I saw you I was about six. Mark, Mark Heywood. Simon Heywood's son, I used to come here sometimes with my Father. You were always very sweet to me, gave me an ice-lolly once." He grinned, "Favours like that, you don't forget in a hurry." I could see she didn't have the vaguest recollection but she flashed another smile, this time going the full hundred and fifty watts.

"Why of course I remember, fantastic to see you again. That's what's so lovely about coming home, seeing all the old faces." He returned her smile pleasantly, although I was gratified to note, not as drop-dead, star-struck as many I'd seen. He turned politely to Etty.

"I didn't know Ophelia was going to be visiting."

"Neither," said Etty, each word an icicle with the end snapped off. "Did I. She sprang it on us. Delightful surprise." Any sub-text was winging its acid way above his head as he stooped to retrieve his bag, set down hastily when collision needed to be averted.

"I'll be off then Mrs Goodkind. Pleasure to meet you Serenissima." I bared my teeth in what he could choose to take as a smile. It wasn't that I had anything against him personally, but you're never at ease with someone who's just seen what an idiot you can make of yourself. "Delighted to see you again Ophelia." My Mother bent her head graciously, I suppose one thing you could say about her was that she rarely thought anyone not worthy of the full Ophelia charm. Etty and guest headed, talking quietly, to the front door and I turned to glare at Ophelia, I had more than a bone to pick with her – in fact with a cupboard full of skeletons, it was difficult to know exactly where to start.

"Naughty boy, I couldn't think where you'd got to?" Mimi had suddenly appeared beside the wolf. I wanted to think she'd walked along the corridor from the kitchen, but feared that wasn't the case at all. I swiftly stopped thinking about it and noted that nobody had yet pointed out, she still had her jumper on every which way but right.

"Come along now, or we'll both be in the dog-house." Grabbing a collar, nearly obscured in thick neck fur, she tugged it decisively. The animal rose amiably enough to its feet, pushing against her affectionately and she staggered. Next to her tiny frame it looked even more massive and its powerful jaws could have crushed any part of her without undue effort. Pure bred or crossed with something else, it still looked like a wolf to me. I moved a step further up.

"Oh my!" Mimi paused suddenly, her gaze sweeping over Ophelia and me, still on the stairs and Etty returning down the hall, silver bird-headed cane striking the floor with each decisive step, "Isn't this just too wonderful? Look at us. Four generations of Goodkind women. What an occasion eh? What an occasion." If she expected a round of hurrahs she was disappointed, perhaps we each had our own thoughts on the matter. Certainly, given the crazy events of the last few hours, I was thinking I might be wending my way home sooner rather than later and screw the ducks – after all, what did I owe these people? I'd grown up believing I had no family and having now met them, couldn't help feeling I was better off that way.

"Serenissima."

"Sandra." I corrected Etty automatically. She ignored me and continued, "I suppose after your little encounter with Rostropovich you won't be feeling up to dealing with dinner, I know your Mother always used to get very stressed by any little… upsets." I instantly drew myself up.

"I am not my Mother."

"No, but… "

"I've said I'll do dinner and do it I will." She nodded briefly and turned away, not before I'd caught a green-granite glimmer of satisfaction. I could have kicked myself. Gracious, but she was good. She was very, very good.

"Just one minute." I said, my tone as cool as hers and as peremptory, she paused without turning.

"Yes?"

"I'd like to make something clear."

"I'm listening."

"Once I've sorted this meal for you, I'll be leaving, going back to London." Ophelia opened her mouth to say something, but I raised a hand – I can do imperious too, "Ophelia, if you're coming with me, please be ready to leave within the next hour or so."

"I didn't somehow think you'd be the enquiring type." Etty murmured, but I wasn't as green as I was cabbage looking. I wasn't going to rise to that, I wasn't going to let her paint me again into whichever corner she chose.

"Well you were spot on then weren't you?" I agreed, and with a brisk inclination of my head to include all three of them, and a cautious but dignified circuit round the wolf, I headed back below stairs.

CHAPTER EIGHTEEN

Friend Gladys had disappeared, but the ducks hadn't budged. I surveyed the gloomy kitchen. Daylight was fading and the light switch, sticky with something that smelt like Marmite, produced only feeble illumination from a hanging centre fixture which, given the room's general state of cleanliness, was probably no bad thing. I was damned though if I was going to deal with the ducks under cover of darkness. I rummaged around and came up with half a dozen candles which I banked together on a tin lid, filched from an almost finished box of Sainsbury's Continental Choice, and they instantly imparted a kinder glow to the room. Whatever minimal warmth they provided was also more than welcome, whilst the main parts of the house were chilly, once you got back to the staff areas, it was perishing. I debated going to get an extra jumper from the car, but decided even that had too much of an air of permanence about it.

It took me a while to ferret out everything I needed, basics were secreted in the oddest places and I found a vegetable knife with its blade worryingly embedded in the side of the dresser. Maybe they'd never heard of knife-blocks, still it did cause me to glance nervously over my shoulder, I wished I knew exactly where Gladys had gone.

It came as no surprise to discover the pilot light in the old-fashioned oven had gone out and that contortions, for which the human body wasn't really designed, were required to get it re-lit. Gradually however, order began to emerge. Potatoes peeled, parboiled, oiled and seasoned stood ready, as did three plump birds, pricked, salted and ready for action on iron trivets in two roasting tins. The oven, at first reluctant to play ball, was now warming up and hiking up the temperature in the room a welcome few degrees, for which I was grateful. In my explorations, I'd come across a nearly full bottle of white wine and on the principle of it may not help, but couldn't do any harm, I'd splashed it liberally into the roasting tins. As an afterthought, I'd also poured myself a reviving glass. If ever anyone needed an alcoholic boost, it was probably me more than the ducks.

Bella bustled back in – for a woman who bustled so much she seemed to get very little done – and cast an approving eye over my efforts, patting my shoulder in passing.

"Good girl, knew you could do it. Table's reserved for eight thirty, what about starters and dessert?" I reached for the wine glass and tersely pointed out, no-one had mentioned starters and dessert. Bella smiled encouragingly,

"You'll think of something, can't stop, middle of a treatment." I stared resentfully after her, what did they think I was, bloody meals on wheels? What a bunch of liberty-takers, although of course, life with Ophelia had given me a great grounding in people taking unashamed advantage. I was muttering crossly and at length to myself as I thrust the various dishes into the now hot oven and left them to their fate, then realised I was sounding rather more Gladys-like than was comfortable, so I shut up and reached for my handbag and mobile to give Murray a call. I owed him an update, not to mention I could do with talking to someone with a better grip on reality than anyone I'd had contact with all day. I could visualise him, standing in the hall at the house, absently polishing the toe of one already immaculate shoe against the back of the other leg. He was, as ever, not happy.

"Bleeding fun and games here." He said.

"Oh?"

"Brought Sasha down to stay, hasn't he? Mrs M's in a right old strop." Mrs McTeer was our long-suffering lady-what-did, although in truth, she never actually did that much. She was nevertheless a much-loved part of home life and, having put up with Ophelia for years, was normally fairly imperturbable. Sasha must have worked hard to upset her so quickly.

"What's Adam playing at?" I said. "Should I talk to him?"

"Out." Murray was succinct, "Walking by the river, then booked for a romantic dinner at Albertini's." I sighed, Albertini's was my parents' favourite restaurant, venue for all special occasions and celebrations through the years. "Ophelia," said Murray, "Needs to pull her finger out sharpish and get her backside back here, before it's all too late."

"I'll try and tackle her again, make her see some sense."

"Where are you anyway?"

"With her family." I said. Murray whistled through his teeth,

"She wasn't 'aving you on then? Who'd have thought, all these years?

Can't get my mind round it, wonder why she pulled the wool over our eyes like that?"

"I don't."

"Don't what?"

"Wonder why. They're… "

"What?"

"Like her." There was silence at the other end of the phone. "Murray, you still there?"

"Course I'm still here. You mean… ?"

"Yeah."

"Blimey. Blimey O'bleeding Riley!" He whistled through his teeth again, a sound so familiar it made me feel even more homesick.

"Look," I said, "I've got to go and finish dinner."

"Eh?"

"Long story, they've got this hotel and the woman who does the cooking's had a funny turn. Tell you properly when I get back."

"Tonight?"

"You bet, sooner I'm out of here the better I'll feel."

"With Ophelia?"

"Hope so, um… Murray, listen I've got to go now." I ended the call abruptly and put my mobile slowly on the table, heart pounding hard again. Outside the kitchen window, darkness had descended and something terrifying was looking in. A chalk-white apparition with distended eyes was mouthing something at me. I would have run, but my feet seemed to be stuck firmly to the floor, not sure whether with old food or fear. The disembodied horror bobbed up and down a bit, then a pale hand materialized and rapped knuckles sharply three times on the glass of the kitchen window. At the same instant, another hand fastened hard on my shoulder. I leapt round, screaming long and loud. The girl whose hand was on my shoulder started back and screamed too.

"Why you screaming?" She shrieked.

"Look at the window, the window." I shrieked back, pointing. She looked, saw what I'd seen and screamed again. And then the back door began to creak open and we backed away, clutching each other. Whatever it was that was out there, was starting to come in from the cold.

CHAPTER NINETEEN

"Hello there," it said. The girl, who'd been digging her nails into my hands as deeply as I was digging mine into hers, suddenly let out her breath in a rush, chuckling shakily.

"Oh frigging hell," she said, "It's all right, we're OK, it's just one of Bella's women."

"Bella's women?" I squeaked, still hanging on to her for dear life.

"Yeah," she said, trying to extract her hand from mine. "Some of the treatments have like, really odd side effects, she really shouldn't leave them on their own."

The ghastly apparition, on closer inspection, turned out to be middle-aged, paper mob-capped and wearing a thin, blue, floral-patterned gown, fastened precariously at the back with nothing much else on other than paper knickers, a pair of fluffy blue slippers and the rigid white face mask that, up close and personal, looked more painful than petrifying.

"Came out for a glass of water." She announced, "But," she giggled and raised a hand to her head, "Actually feel a teeny, tiny bit out of it... " She had it in mind, I think, to reach a kitchen chair and sit down, but her legs started to fold ahead of time. The girl and I, two minds, single thought, each grabbed an arm just as Bella re-appeared, tutting,

"Mrs Bertram, my dear, thank goodness, couldn't think where you'd vanished to, only took my eye off you for a second. Now, didn't I say to just lie still and relax, you'll catch your death running around like that." Mrs Bertram, strung between us like a substantial bit of washing on the line, bobbed her head up and down merrily in agreement and Bella reached forward, putting one arm firmly round a blue floral waist "Sorry," she said to us. "Give you a bit of a turn did she? I'm trying out something new – not got the balance quite right yet. Never mind, she'll be tickled pink with the results." She hauled her limp charge out the back door with no little effort, and I shut my eyes for a brief moment, I felt I needed a break. When I re-opened them, the girl was staring hard at me.

"You'll be Serenissima then." She said

"And you'll be?" I asked tersely. She grinned,

"Guess."

"Sorry," I snapped "Do I look like a woman in the mood to play games?" She was young, early twenties, lustrous dark brown almost black hair, long and curling to her shoulders, capacious bosom emphasized by a small waist and a tight white, low-necked jumper with a considerable amount of cleavage on display, what Murray would call approvingly, a womanly woman. She jutted a petulant lip.

"Oh all right then. Devorah. Bella's my mum and you've already met my daughter, Simona." I started to shake my head then realized who she meant,

"The baby?"

"That's the one."

"So, you're my... ? "

"Second cousin or is it once removed? Not sure, anyway, welcome to the clan, nice to finally meet you."

"You knew about me?"

"Well, more about your Ma really, seen her and your Dad on tv. You look like him." She added judiciously, and clearly didn't mean it as a compliment.

"So I've been told."

"Well, fire away then." She settled herself comfortably at the kitchen table, pulling forward another chair on which to rest one shapely, tightly jeaned leg, casually appropriating my wine glass and re-filling it to the top.

"Fire away?"

"You must have a ton and a half of questions." She said, "Must be like, dead exciting, meeting us after all this time. Long-lost family and all that stuff." This cousin, second, once removed or whatever, was starting to get on my already frayed nerves. Excited couldn't be further from what I was feeling right now and whilst there were any number of questions I could think of, I had a suspicion I might not like any of the answers. Quite apart from which, I still had to sort out starters and desserts for this ridiculous dinner challenge I'd been conned into.

I eyed Devorah with disfavour, she looked perfectly, if not more than able-bodied to me, I couldn't see why she wasn't the one doing what needed to be done in the kitchen in the first place. I reached out and took back my glass of wine. She smiled, amiably enough, glancing over to one of the kitchen cupboards whose door swung instantly open. A wine glass left the shelf, bobbed gently across the room, turned itself the right way up and came to rest on the table. She poured, picked it up, sipped and wrinkled her nose slightly, she wasn't wrong, it wasn't the best I'd ever tasted either. I felt rather sick. She looked up and caught my expression,

"What?" She said. I jerked my head at the glass. "Yeah, I know," she said. "Awful, isn't it? Etty always insists on the cheapest she can get."

"Not the wine." I said.

"What then?"

"All that... business with the glass."

"Oh. Sorry, I thought, family and all that. Don't you... ?

"Certainly not."

"But Ophelia...?"

"Doesn't do anything like that."

"Well she could if she wanted to couldn't she? And you are her daughter aren't you?" She said. And there it was, metaphorically slap bang on the table, the issue I'd been determinedly not thinking about ever since Mimi's first little vanishing trick. I swigged back too large a swallow of the sharp wine, and Devorah reached over to thump me companionably on the back as I choked. After a couple of moments, my throat re-opened for business and I sprang up to do a trawl through the fridge. A repository that big had to conceal something I could use to top and tail this ruddy meal, and any kind of activity seemed preferable to either talking or thinking too hard about anything other than the menu.

CHAPTER TWENTY

Devorah watched my activities with interest, sipping wine and chewing on a piece of gum extracted, not without a struggle, from the pocket of jeans so tight they must have been sprayed on.

"This is not," I pointed out testily, "A spectator sport, please feel free to join in and help at any time. In fact, just as a matter of interest, why aren't you cooking in the first place?" She laughed out loud,

"Don't do cooking. Not my thing." She said. I tutted and turned back to the fridge, from whose murky depths I'd unearthed a large airtight container, the contents of which looked, smelt and tasted like vegetable soup. Working on the Occam's razor principle, I took a chance and decanted it all into a saucepan which I placed on the hob for when it was needed. A further forage produced a beautifully decorated and glazed apple flan and some double cream that was slightly on the turn, but could get away with it under the banner of crème fraiche. I wasn't too clear what the set up for tonight's booking was, but if they were looking for a varied menu choice they'd picked the wrong place.

Flan plated, cream jugged, ducks and potatoes now happily co-habiting and sending out mouth-watering aromas. My work here was nearly done. I could move on and the quicker the better. I simply had to gather up my Mother and draw a line under this whole, highly un-thrilling episode. In future, should Ophelia feel the urge to visit the green, green grass of home, she could damn well catch the train and do it on her own. As if summoned by the thought, Ophelia walked into the kitchen,

"There you are." She said to me and to Devorah. "Hello sweetie, no mistaking who you are, you're the image of Bella at your age. Mmmm," she sniffed appreciatively, "Smells good, what time's dinner?" I shrugged, I'd been running myself ragged, catering for the paying guests, what was on the family menu wasn't really my concern, they'd have to fend for themselves. After all, they'd got along without me before they met me, they could get along without me now. Traitorously, my own stomach suddenly produced a small grumble. We'd stopped for coffee and a sandwich at a service station on our way down that morning, but a whole lot had happened since then. I was, I realised, ravenous.

"Come on." I said to Ophelia, "We'll find a nice restaurant on the way home."

"Home?" She said sharply, "We're not going home yet."

"Yes we are."

"We can't leave. Not now we know what's going on."

"Going on?"

"All this," she waved a hand, "All this crazy hotel stuff, you can see they don't have the first idea what they're doing."

"Not our problem."

"I might think differently."

"Oh, come on! After how many years is it? Suddenly you're all family-minded, pull the other one why don't you? Look, I've spoken to Murray; I didn't want to tell you, but Adam's taken Sasha down to the house. You need to get back there pronto and sort everything out with him." Her mouth tightened,

"What your Father chooses to do is his own affair – or should I say affairs. Anyway, he'll be out of that house soon enough, it's in my name."

"But… "

"I don't want to talk about it now Serenissima, I've already told Etty you'd be happy to stay and help out for a bit."

"You've done *what*?"

"It's obvious, all they need is a bit of organising and you're so good at that."

"A bit of organising! Are you stark staring bonkers?" I didn't know whether to tear my hair out at the roots in frustration or just laugh till I dropped. "Ma, for Pete's sake, take a look around you, this place is falling so far apart at the seams, it'd take a fortune to put things right. There's a delusional lunatic running the kitchen, and a bloody great wolf running everywhere else. There's one loopy old lady who keeps appearing and disappearing and another loopy old lady who's enough to scare the bejesus out of any guest mad enough to book in. Oh, and let's not forget Alice bloody blue-gown out in the annexe, being driven demented by whatever beauty treatment your crazy cousin's giving her right this very minute."

"Well, there you are darling," said Ophelia, "See. I knew it, you've instantly put your finger on all the little problems, you've always been so good at that. You could tell them how to put things right. It's the sort of thing you do all the time for clients, isn't it?" I started to do some calming breathing, then decided calm probably wasn't what was called for right now.

"*Why*, in the name of all that's holy, would I want to help any of them do anything?" I snarled.

"Because it's family." She said firmly. I clenched my teeth again, I was so livid I could have knocked her into next week and beyond.

"How have you got the nerve?" I hissed, "How *dare* you say that? You spring these, these... people on me, out of the blue, after lying to me all my life and you expect me to feel something for them. Well I'm sorry, I don't and I don't believe for one single solitary minute you do either, so drop the prodigal daughter routine, it really doesn't suit you."

We stood, as we'd stood so often before, toe to toe, glaring and I could see her swift calculation. Should she match my anger, pull parental authority or head straight for the sympathy vote. The latter won by a nose and immediately her blue eyes sparkled, filled and overflowed – if she'd chosen a different branch of the business, she'd have had Oscars coming out her ears. But I'd been here too many times before. I reached behind her and decisively lifted my bag from the chair.

"Don't waste the waterworks Ophelia. I'm off. You can't thrust a bunch of ready-made relatives under my nose and expect love and loyalty. In real life – something you don't have too firm a grip on – things simply don't work that way."

"She's not wrong you know Ophie, I always said you were mad, not telling her the truth." I looked past her. A slim, blond haired man, mid-forties, was leaning casually against the wall by the back door, one elegantly suede-shod foot crossed casually over the other. I'd no idea how long he'd been there. I eyed him coldly and he smiled at me and nodded briefly to Devorah, who grinned at him as he advanced into the room, setting down on the floor a comfortably worn, brown leather briefcase. Draped round his shoulders was a long, camel, cashmere coat which swung gracefully in the way only expensive coats can do. Beneath it he was wearing a perfectly cut, charcoal three-piece suit. He looked immaculate and completely out of place in the shabbiness of the ill-lit kitchen.

CHAPTER TWENTY-ONE

Ophelia swung on her heel to face him. He held out his arms. After a moment's hesitation, she moved into them. He hugged her hard, picking her up easily and whirling her round in a gesture that would have screamed staginess from anyone else. He set her down gently, holding her out at arm's length, examining her face closely, fingers along her jaw, thumb tilting up her chin.

"Not bad," he said, in that beautifully modulated light voice, leisurely and smooth as milk chocolate, "Odd laughter line here and there, but on the whole, my darling girl, looking pretty good for your age." She gave a small snort of disgust and moved her head away from his hand. "You do look tired though," he continued, "And," he touched her hair briefly, "This colour, far too harsh for you now I think, several shades lighter really couldn't hurt. Aren't you going to introduce me to my lovely niece?" He dropped his arms from her and moved towards me. I was in no mood for either a hug or a hair colour analysis and stuck out a hand, he took in the thought behind the gesture, grinned again and shook the hand gently.

"Roland." He said, inclining his head.

"Sandra."

"A very great pleasure indeed to meet you Sandra," It was strange seeing my Mother's face in his, the resemblance was uncanny. "You're absolutely right, you know."

"Right?" I repeated.

"It'd take a great deal more than one young woman could do – however determined, clever or organised – to put this place right. Not only does it need more money than any sane investor would dream of pouring in, but it needs to be run as a business, not a rest-home for relations who can't be bothered to find anywhere else to live." He winked at the seated Devorah, who raised two unabashed fingers at him. "And," he picked up my glass of wine by the stem, turning it reflectively so it sparkled attractively in front of the flickering bank of candles, before tossing back what was left and grimacing wryly at the taste, "As you've already so accurately assessed, money and disrepair are only a part of the problem. Even if by some miracle, all that's wrong could be put right, it's never been marketed in any way whatsoever – could be the most wonderful place in the world, but if nobody knows about it…" he shrugged philosophically, "Which brings us full circle, doesn't it. Marketing equals money we don't have. I'm absolutely sure Ophelia's faith in your abilities is justified my dear, but," and he looked me up and down and patted my shoulder in kindly fashion, "I'm afraid getting this place back on its feet would take rather more than you'd be able to bring to the party."

"You're wrong you know." I said. He'd taken off his coat and draped it over his arm, I didn't blame him, I wouldn't have put something that good on one of the kitchen chairs either. He raised an interrogative eyebrow,

"Don't think so, sweetheart."

"You probably wouldn't get investment," I conceded, "Someone'd have to be mad to do that, but if you're stuck with a disadvantage, you simply have to turn it round, convert it and make it work for you, not against you." He smiled politely again.

"Sweet idea, but, if you'll forgive me, a little naïve and a tad too Pollyanna." He chuckled, "Methinks you've been to one too many marketing seminars." He bent to pick up his case.

"Don't patronise me." I snapped. If I'd had any doubts he was my Mother's brother, they'd high-tailed it out of there without argument, he had exactly her knack of winding me up. He straightened and turned back towards me, holding out a beautifully manicured placatory hand.

"Sandra, my complete and abject apologies. The last thing I would ever do is patronise. I've also done my share of motivational workshops, even led a good few in my time, and whilst the reasoning's sound and the delivery inspirational, in truth what you pick up, can very rarely be put to practical use." I shook my head briskly,

"You're wrong and that's such a blinkered view. You just have to make a virtue out of necessity, take what you've got here, all the shabbiness, the shortcomings and the eccentricities and turn them into selling points." He chuckled,

"Indeed? And why on earth would people… ?"

"Because everyone loves a gimmick, an angle."

"An angle?"

"Well of course," I was impatient with his slowness, "Can't you see? You simply have to capitalise on what you've got and what you've got is a pretty weird set up. You take that, enlarge on it and make it – I don't know... wait, yes I do. A haunted hotel. All you'd need would be enough special effects to scare the pants off a few people. And God knows," I said wryly, glaring at Ophelia and Devorah, "You've certainly got the means to do that. You wouldn't need to add anything, you'd simply be working with what you've already got." He nodded slowly, frowning slightly.

"What about getting publicity?" He asked.

"Trust me, you lay on enough *weird* and you'll have journalists biting your hand off – people love nothing better than being scared to death, and this sort of thing writes its own headlines."

"Hang on a minute though," he said, "We wouldn't have the faintest idea of the first thing to do."

"Well, I have. It's what I used to do for a living." I said.

"But a project like this, it's way, way too ambitious." He said, shaking his head dubiously.

"I've handled bigger."

"But, forgive me, didn't I hear you say you were leaving right away? Mind you," he paused, struck with a sudden thought, "I suppose if Ophelia could see things getting sorted out here, she'd be able to move on and focus with an easier mind on what I understand is going on at home. Sandra, my dear, I'm totally overwhelmed you feel you could take this on for us – how could we ever repay you? I am most unusually, lost for words." He moved swiftly forward and enveloped me, unresisting, in an expensively after-shaved hug. He wasn't the only one totally overwhelmed. I was aware I'd just been very professionally had – again. Crossly I jerked away and met his amused blue gaze.

"I didn't say I'd do it, did I? I'm only putting forward some suggestions." There was a silence as all three of them looked at me. I mentally weighed up the options. Getting Ophelia back home if she'd made up her mind not to be budged or committing myself to getting things moving in this crazy set-up. I really wasn't sure I was up to the effort required for either, it felt like a rock and a hard place situation

"Bloody hell!" I muttered ungraciously. "All *right* then, but two, three days tops, just long enough to get the ball rolling, after that the rest of you are on your own, like it or lump it."

"Understood." He said warmly. "Look let me just pop upstairs for a wash, get out of these work things and then we can have a confab." He'd just bent again to the briefcase, when the door of a full-length cupboard at the end of the room burst open and Mimi, a mop and several dusters fell out.

"Oh," she muttered, "Not the broom cupboard again. Hello Roland, you're home early, good day at the office dear?" She patted disarranged fine silver hair and kicked a couple of dusters away from under her feet. I retrieved my glass from the table where Raymond had left it and poured myself some more wine.

CHAPTER TWENTY-TWO

I can't say I slept very well on that first night at the old homestead. This was because I was suffering from information overload, Gladys's cooking and was sharing a room, not only with my Mother – something I don't think we'd done even when I was a baby – but also with Ink.

To the many and varied revelations of a trying day, I was able to add the fact that Ophelia snored surprisingly lustily and Ink was given to getting up every hour on the hour, stretching, purring and settling down again with the maximum of fuss. I also now knew that Gladys produced scrambled eggs of a consistency that promised to remain welded to my stomach lining, at least for the foreseeable future.

I was relieved that the dinner guests last night, three women and two men, had arrived; been treated to my culinary offerings; hadn't complained and departed, seemingly quite happy with what they'd had. All in all, I felt that there was a breach into which I had successfully stepped, at the same time proving to all and sundry that whilst Ophelia might be the weakest of reeds on the practical front, I was not.

Preparing for bed last night, was the first time my Mother and I had spent alone together since we'd arrived, but if I was expecting explanation, justification or apology, I was in for a long wait. Lying stiffly in the bed across from hers, I was exhausted, exasperated and disturbed in equal measure – there she was, sleeping the sleep of the just, while today's events were relentlessly playing themselves over and over like tape loops in my aching head. And if in an evening spent trying to clarify the situation, more questions than answers had reared their ugly heads, well, that seemed about par for the course.

***

Roland, good as his word, last night had returned to the kitchen in under ten minutes, suit discarded in favour of a well-worn pair of soft green cords and matching polo shirt. He was obviously one of those annoying people who wear clothes well and would probably have brought a sense of chic to a bin bag. He helped himself to a fresh glass of wine and rested one elegant hip against a kitchen top. In his absence, Devorah had dusted down a disorientated Mimi, still chuckling and chiding herself. I'd noted absently, that Ophelia, who normally automatically assumed centre-stage of any room she was in, had remained quietly on the side lines. Maybe this sudden exposure to family life and all its funny little ways had subdued her as nothing else ever did – an odd change of status, but down here in la la land, nothing was quite as you'd expect. In fact, I had serious doubts about inside-out-jumpered, daffy Mimi. Amidst all that dizzy old biddy, what-a-fool-I-am stuff there was, every now and then, a fleeting sharpness of glance that led me to believe she wasn't half as addled as it suited her to make out.

"Right." I'd said, taking charge of what seemed to be an ad hoc meeting and looking at my watch. "It's coming up for 7.00, so we've got to be quick, why don't we start with how you've managed to get even five people booking for dinner tonight – I mean," I waved a disparaging, if honest hand, "Look at the state of this place." Devorah reached past Mimi and pulled open a kitchen table drawer. Like all such drawers, it was crammed with those irritating bits and pieces that go in happily in the first place then shift about as soon as the drawer's closed, so it can't be re-opened. After a couple of tugs though, this one succumbed to brute force and a few seconds rummaging through the usual detritus of saved string and old receipts, produced a crumpled page of newsprint.

"Good reviews," she said triumphantly, "Look." Smoothing the paper against the surface of the table, I saw the by-line was Jonathan Harper, 'Restaurant Rover' and sure enough, the food he'd sampled at Home Hill, had him rhapsodising in that self-conscious style food writers often feel obliged to adopt.

"But this is great," I looked up, "Who did the cooking when he came?"

"Don't know." Said Devorah.

"What d'you mean? How can you not know, was it Gladys?"

"That's the problem, you see."

"No, I don't see." I looked from Devorah to Roland who sighed gently,

"You've met Gladys?" He said. I nodded,

"Briefly, she was sitting on a tea tray I needed."

"Ah," said Roland, "Then you'll know she has her idiosyncrasies. Been with us for years and we're all very fond, trouble is she's not always... consistent."

"Consistent?" I queried,

"She can only perform under the influence."

"You mean drink?"

"No, Delia Smith."

"Sorry." I shook my head, which was a mistake as a headache which had been hovering in the background biding its time, inched forward gleefully. "You've lost me."

"Delia Smith, Gordon Ramsay, Jamie Oliver, Nigella Lawson. She says she tunes into them and they cook through her."

"Cook through her?" I was aware I sounded like little Miss Echo, but he wasn't making much sense.

"What can I tell you? Gladys cooks in a trance." He shrugged, "I mean really, in a trance. Calls it automatic cooking, says they tell her exactly what to do. What to order in, how to prepare it, how to cook it. And, to be honest, she has produced some truly astonishing things." I looked round for Ophelia, to share an eyes-raised-to-heaven look, but in the last couple of minutes she'd apparently drifted out of the kitchen. I sighed, true to form or what? I turned back to Raymond.

"Don't people have to be dead?" I enquired, keeping a determined straight face, "Before they can come through, I mean?" Roland shrugged again,

"Apparently not."

"And Chief Whateverhisnameis?"

"Sitting Bull. Yes. Well I believe *he* is in fact an ex-chief as it were, lived some 400 years ago, according to our Glad. It's actually him and a few others that cause all the problems. They sort of get in the way – like static interference she says, when you're trying to tune a radio."

"And that's not good?" I asked. Roland shook his head firmly,

"Disastrous apparently. To be honest, it was never really an issue when it was just us she was cooking for, we simply got used to the rough with the smooth, but since all this hotel, spa thing – well, it does lead to a certain unpredictability."

"OK," I said neutrally. "Well, why not simply hire someone else to do the cooking?" Roland and Devorah exchanged a shocked look,

"Etty wouldn't do that to Gladys." Said Devorah.

"Couldn't afford it anyway," added Roland, "Certainly couldn't afford anyone to match her on a good day." I nodded, there was a certain skewed logic to that. I decided we'd probably covered as much on the subject of Gladys as I was ready for at the moment, and moved swiftly on.

"Right," I said. "If I'm to offer any constructive suggestions to try and get things moving, I need to get a few more things straight in my own mind." Roland nodded earnestly and came to take a place at the table with Mimi and Devorah. I'd planted myself at the head and could hear how bossy I sounded, but didn't care much one way or the other, I wasn't here to build bonds.

"Hang on a moment," I said. "Just have to check… " All three turned to look expectantly at the oven door, as if it was going to obligingly open to show them what was going on inside. With a qualm, I realized that might be exactly what one of them had in mind and I nipped over sharpish, to do things the normal way. Whilst we'd been talking, the ducks had finished themselves off nicely and looked ready for action, although it was still only 7.20. I turned everything right down and another thought occurred.

"Who's going to actually serve this little lot?" I asked.

"Don't worry, my sweet," said Roland, "Not you, you've been brilliant getting it to this stage, I'm sure Elizabeth can take it from here."

"Elizabeth? Bit hard of hearing?" I said, Devorah nodded,

"Deaf as a post, bless her heart, but won't have it, insists we're all just mumbling to take the mickey." I wasn't reassured. From my disconcerting conversation earlier with Elizabeth, she appeared convinced I'd been drafted in from somewhere to help on the waitressing front. Still, one problem at a time. I spotted a notebook and pencil in the still open kitchen table drawer and pulled them out, opening it officiously to a blank page. If I'm going to do a job, I like to do it properly.

"So, I presume this was previously just the family home," I asked. All three nodded, "And I'm assuming this hotel thing was started, to generate some income?" They nodded again,

"You don't work here though Roland?"

"No, I'm a barrister." He said, "Chambers in London." I raised my eyebrows,

"Lucrative?"

"I wish, tough at the moment. Really tough."

"You?" I looked at Devorah,

"No, I can't work," she said happily, "I've like got the baby." She seemed to be a bit of a lost cause and one without a conscience at that.

"Well," I said repressively, "I'm sure we can find you some constructive contribution to make." She started to interrupt, but I was in full bossy mode.

"Now, when did you start this hotel thing?"

"Just after last Christmas?" Roland raised an inquiring eyebrow at Devorah, she nodded in confirmation.

"So, it's been going about ten months? How many bedrooms?"

"Fifteen in total," supplied Roland, "Seven for family. The rest for letting."

"Right. And staff? One chef – on and off. And Elizabeth, who is… .?"

"Well officially she's the housekeeper, although she turns her hand to most things – real trouper, been with the family for years, carries this place. Married to Alfred."

"Alfred?"

"Alfred Heylow, gardener, plumber, decorator; we need it, he does it, wonderful chap, retired languages teacher."

"Really? Ah now, that's a selling point for foreign visitors."

"No."

"No?"

"Well only if they're ancient Greeks."

"Right." Silly me, why would I have imagined anyone round here could offer much in the way of practical help. "Who else?"

"That's it really, we get agency staff in on a temp basis when we need them – for waiting in the dining room if we have several tables booked, that sort of thing."

"Blimey," I said. "How does a place this size run, with so little help?"

"Not well. Although," added Roland cheerfully, "Looking on the bright side, as we've never had too many guests, it's never really been too much of a problem."

"It is," I pointed out tetchily, "If you're trying to earn a living."

CHAPTER TWENTY-THREE

We'd been interrupted at that point in the discussion by the entrance of Elizabeth, who had to be disabused, at full volume, of the notion I'd been sent by the agency and that she'd caught me sitting down and socialising on the job. She was even more unimpressed when informed who I actually was. Ophelia's stock here didn't seem to be that high.

"Huh," she grunted and, "Well that's all fine and dandy, still means I'm on my own again tonight as usual. Bloody stupid hotel lark. Well, it's no use you lot sitting there on your backsides, take yourselves off out of it, go on, off you go. You," she trumpeted, I turned. "As there's no one coming in for serving help, you'll have to do, I'll call you back if I need you." I nodded reluctantly, there seemed little point in arguing.

On our way out of the kitchen, we bumped into a subdued Gladys, making her way back in.

"Bad turn today Glad?" Enquired Roland solicitously.

"Terrible sweetheart, terrible! Nigella does a lovely duck, so I was aiming for her, but... " she dropped her voice, looking anxiously over her shoulder, causing us all to automatically scan the hallway behind her too. "...you-know-who came through instead," she continued. "And once he's here, he doesn't half hang around. Anyway, I'll bring you all some scrambled eggs on toast shall I, in the living room, it's warmer in there and," she nodded at me, "You can get something down, before Elizabeth wants you.

We adjourned to the room I'd seen before and Devorah busied herself with the curtains, whilst Roland put a match to the ready-laid fire. The artificial light was softer and kinder than sunlight, lending the room a minimal shabby cosiness. Roland and Devorah seated themselves on a sofa facing me and Mimi planted herself deep into one of the sagging flowered armchairs that appeared to have had most of the stuffing knocked out of them.

"We shouldn't forget Bella's health and beauty stuff." Said Devorah, carrying on from where we'd left off. "Now that's starting to get known again, it's bringing in some income, and with word spreading we sometimes get two or three women coming in together and staying overnight, you know, making a party of it."

"What exactly does she do?" My earlier alarming experience with Bella's work-in-progress, hadn't gone into my boots.

"Well, it's not the same as when we were in London." Said Devorah hastily. I held out my hand in a stop gesture,

"Haven't you always lived here?"

"Goodness, no." Said Devorah, "We've moved around a lot, although in the last few years we stayed longer in fewer places, because Bella said it wasn't good for Henry, all that chopping and changing of schools.

"Henry?"

"My brother, haven't you met him yet?" I shook my head warily. "Well, he's glued to his screen most of the time, but he comes out regularly for meals and school and things. We lived in London for about three years or so," she continued, "It was like great. Business was doing really well. Bella rented a couple of rooms in a clinic, just off the King's Road, posh receptionist and all, and we had a smashing big flat not five minutes walk away. Anyway, the stuff was going so well, she paid a designer to put together some packaging and took on a PR woman – worst mistake she ever made, we were doing well enough with just personal recommendations. Told her it was getting too big and there'd be trouble." I held up a restraining hand again, I was starting to feel like a traffic policeman.

"Hang on a minute, what was it she was doing exactly?"

"Cosmetics and creams, natch," said Devorah, "Well actually, like what they call cosmeceuticals – you know the sort of thing, make-up that does you good. Bloody brilliant most of it was too. Anyway, we started to get all sorts of publicity." As she was speaking, an uncomfortable connection was worming its way into my consciousness.

"What were they called?" I asked with apprehension.

"*Bella Donna Treatments*, maybe you heard of them?" I sat forward in the chair, good God, of course I'd heard of them, everyone had heard of them, I could even picture the distinctive black and gold packaging.

"*Bella Donna?*" I said. "*For Women Who Like A Walk On The Wild Side.*"

"Yeah, great line wasn't it?"

"So she's… ?"

"Bella Belinfante." Confirmed Devorah with a touch of defiance.

"My word," I said weakly, less than thrilled. "She was all over the papers, and tv – didn't that guy from Watchdog try and get an interview and someone threw him and his cameraman down the stairs?"

"Yeah, well that was all like a bit unfortunate." Devorah conceded. Unfortunate? That's hardly how I'd put it, although it had of course made for riveting television and some great newspaper headlines.

"But didn't those cosmetics do dreadful things to people's faces?" I asked. More and more of the story was coming back to me, "Weren't the police involved?" Devorah sat up straighter and transferred the ever-present gum from one cheek to the other, battle-light in her eyes – I wondered whether it was her or the formidable Bella who'd done the down-the-stairs throwing.

"Honestly Sandra," she said. "You know very well you simply can't believe all you read in the press. Truth was, they worked like, amazingly." She paused. "It was only when they wore off, that people made a ridiculous amount of fuss and bother. For heaven's sake, they were only face-creams, if they were after permanent, they should have gone for surgery or just waited for a bleeding miracle."

"Nobody's grateful for anything these days." Mimi contributed unexpectedly, Roland patted her hand.

"Not wrong there, Mother."

"Well, anyhoo," Devorah continued, "Bella'd been approached by this like, ginormous cosmetics company and a deal was all drawn up for them to buy her out – it would have meant a shitload of money, we wouldn't have had to worry any more – ever. But with all the rotten publicity, the deal fell flat on its face, dead in the water. And what with all the scare-mongering and stupid fuss in the papers, there was no way she could carry on at the clinic and we weren't sure what to do for the best. London suddenly wasn't very comfortable any more." She paused for a moment, her flushed face reflecting the extent of the upset and disappointment. "And of course," she continued, as though it were somewhat of an afterthought, "I was pregnant by then, so we came here." Roland gave her an affectionate mock shove with his shoulder,

"To re-group, as it were, right?" He said. I was intrigued, it was the nearest thing to normal family interaction I'd seen. But I well remembered the whole Bella Donna scandal. It had been a lean time news-wise, so the media fell on the story with unashamed alacrity and there were numerous before and after shots of women who'd purchased the ludicrously expensive face treatments.

It seemed, contrary to their life-changing claims, the miraculous results were remarkably short-term, one of the main complaints being that the further down the jar you got, the less effective the contents. That though wasn't the main issue, the big problem was the rashes that set in after a few weeks of using the stuff. The Daily Mail, becoming ever more hysterical by the day, had roped in lots of disgruntled Bella Donna users, who all recounted a remarkably similar story. Whilst they'd seen fantastic results initially, from there on in it was a slippery slope and many of them, the paper shrieked, swore they looked far worse when they'd finished using the product than when they'd begun – and with a whole range of angry red blotches to boot!

I remember Ophelia and I discussing it one morning, over the breakfast table, when I was there for the weekend. There'd been numerous pictures of Bella, dashing in or out of somewhere, with her hand raised and offering 'no comment'. There was no way Ophelia wouldn't have recognized her, but she'd said not a word, not a single solitary syllable. I wrenched my attention back with an effort and a grimace.

"I hate to ask." I said, "But these creams Bella was producing, were they um . . ?" I paused, not quite sure how to put the question, not even sure I wanted to hear the answer, but Devorah caught my drift, surprised I think that I'd even asked.

"Duh!" She said, "Natch." I didn't think there was anything natural about it at all, but that was beside the point, and I wasn't sure I wanted to know further details. Call me an ostrich, but hiding my head in the sand and not thinking where, why and how, when it came to my Mother's oddities, had worked well enough for me in the past, although I was realising it might not work quite so well in the here and now.

"So, these treatments she's doing next door.... ?" I enquired cautiously, Devorah nodded again, baffled I think that I needed to ask. I sighed, noted Health and Beauty in my notebook with a question mark on income or indeed outcome and continued, "Is there any other money coming in at all." The three of them exchanged a look.

"What?" I demanded.

"Well, Etty always has a small cash stash." Murmured Roland, "Well, not so much *has,* more *makes.*"

"Right."

"Only in very small amounts of course," he added reassuringly, "So It doesn't make a huge difference, I mean we can never use it for anything big, too many rules and regulations on money laundering. You simply can't move cash any more, so we only use it for small everyday expenses."

"Isn't that forgery?" I'd unconsciously lowered my tone to a horrified hiss. Roland looked affronted.

"Certainly not. It's just she..."

"No." Up shot that traffic police hand again. "Don't tell me any more, I don't want to know. Think I've got the overall picture. I'll put together some strategies and ideas for you – for you to implement, but as I said, once I've done that, that's it. I'll get you started, but then you're entirely on your own."

CHAPTER TWENTY-FOUR

"Morning Murray."

"Sandy, you all right? Thought you was coming back last night."

"Change of plan, we stayed over and, um… we're probably now staying on for a couple of days more."

"Why the hell you doing that?" He was indignant.

"Said I'd help them out. Everything's a bit of a mess here."

"Well, what they expect you to do about it?"

"Help them get organised."

"What, with the hotel thing?"

"Sort of."

"Blimey, what d'you know about hotels?"

"Stayed in enough of them." I said. Murray snorted,

"And that qualifies you to do what exactly, ring for room service? Aren't you flipping listening to me Sandy girl, I told you, Ophelia needs to get her backside back here, more than sharpish."

"Murray, I know, I do know. I'm as worried as you, but when has anybody ever been able to make the wretched woman do anything she doesn't want to until she's ready to do it? Truth is, quicker I get things ironed out here, quicker I can get her home. Is Sasha still there?"

"Still here? Course she's bloody-well still here, got her feet right and proper under the table, hasn't she? Right now she's busy re-arranging the furniture, says the way it is, is bad Fang Shooey or some such."

"You're joking."

"You hear me laughing?"

"Ophelia'll go mad."

"Sandy, I gotta tell you, it looks pretty serious with this girl and Adam, he's like a dog with two tails, haven't seen him like this for years and Ophelia's the one walked out, isn't she? I don't know, maybe they really have got to the end of the road."

"But they adore each other. You know they do." I was disconcerted to hear a catch in my voice and realized just how miserable all this was making me. They may not have been the best parents in the world, but they were mine, and the solidity of the marriage and the continuity of the stage act, formed a security backdrop to everything I knew.

"Now, look," he said, "Don't go getting your knickers in a twist, maybe it is just a flash in the pan. All the same, you know Adam's a real soft touch and that Sasha's no fool, for all she's so young. She's a bloody quick mover with an eye on the main chance and right now, that's Adam. Best thing we can do is get your Ma and Pa talking again and quick."

"I'll do my best." I promised.

"OK. And Sandy,"

"What?"

"Be careful."

"Meaning?"

"They sound like a right rum lot down there – stick your nose in too far and you might not like what you smell."

"Murray, listen, about Ophelia's 'funny stuff', the others here..."

"Gotta go now pet." He interrupted. "Talk later, eh?"

"Oh, OK." He'd already hung up on me, not like him. All that was known territory, seemed suddenly much farther away than the few miles which in reality separated us. It was my own stupid fault of course, all these years I'd deliberately not seen or heard things because I simply didn't want to and now my three-monkey policy – hands tightly over eyes, ears and mouth was coming back to bite me in the bottom. Probably served me right.

Murray's concern was as warming as his warning was chilling, but he needn't have worried. I'd categorically made up my mind, I was going to poke my nose in only as far as was strictly necessary. That way I could get this lot kick-started and hopefully inject a bit of common sense into the whole operation. In the long reaches of that first night, interrupted by the combined efforts of Ophelia and Ink, I'd had more than enough time to think, and I had the basis of what I felt was a well-shaped and workable plan.

***

Although I'd risen early on what was to be my first full day, Gladys was in the kitchen before me, unautomated, so far as I could tell. She gave me an anxious little smile and a bob of the pony-tail in greeting and hustled to get me some coffee, although I refused on grounds of self-preservation, her offer of a cooked breakfast. I opted instead for a couple of slices of toast, for which she produced butter and a dusty china pot of jam which looked as if it had been hanging about, aimless and uncovered for some while. I scraped off and jettisoned the top layer as a precaution when her back was turned.

Gladys was not a restful person to be around, she had an unnerving habit of sliding her eyes away and downwards whenever I looked directly at her, provoking me, oddly enough to do the same, so conversation was conducted geisha girl fashion.

This morning she was attired in baggy gray track suit bottoms and a long, shapeless black and white striped jumper, which loitered uneasily round her knees as she walked. She'd topped this snazzy ensemble with a flowered overall, and was wearing once-white sneakers which protested squeakily with every step. As a fashion statement, it didn't say much, as professional chef's garb, even less.

It was a bright, crisp morning, but she had the light on because the sun was fighting an uphill battle to get even a ray or two through the grubby glass of the back door and adjacent window. There was a lingering odour of roast duck which was warring with the newer one of coffee and burnt toast. Gladys didn't sit still for a moment, although none of her activities looked to be on the constructive side, maybe I was making her as nervous as she was making me. Something would really have to be done about the state of the kitchen, not to mention the state of Gladys, I couldn't even begin to imagine the effect both would have on a health and safety inspector. You didn't have to be au fait with the latest catering rules and regulations to know we might be working with more than the odd infringement.

"Gladys," I said cautiously, "You know I've agreed to see if I can help get things moving for you all?" She nodded,

"Yes, heard you last night."

"Well, I think it might be a good idea to start in here, what do you think?"

"Here?"

"Well, there's a bit of ship-shaping called for, isn't there?" I said tactfully. She looked around in vague astonishment,

"Well, I s'pose I could wash up the breakfast things."

"Oh for goodness sake," I said, throwing diplomacy out the window – sometimes I worried that there was more of Ophelia in me than I imagined. "Look at it woman, the room needs scrubbing out and disinfecting from top to bottom." Her face fell and I thought for a moment she was going to break down and start crying again. Still, needs must and time was short.

"Gladys," I persisted firmly. "Didn't you have to get a license in the first place, to run this as a hotel I mean?"

"Course we did, a man came round to look at everything. Here for hours he was."

"And he was happy?"

"Happy as Larry; said it was one of the best equipped kitchens he'd ever inspected." She looked up, caught my baffled expression, gave what could have been a wink or maybe was just a twitch, and looked quickly down again, "Etty was here with him all the time," she added. "He said he only wished all the kitchens he saw were up to this standard, we were a shining example of what could and should be done."

"Right." I said grimly, "Got it." I'd resolved to do all this on a need to know basis and whatever kind of jiggery pokery Etty had pulled, came under the heading of superfluous to my requirements. I lurched back to practicalities like a drowning man to land.

"This staff agency you use, do they supply cleaners?"

"Suppose so, Elizabeth organises all that, but," she looked apprehensive, "It'd be awfully expensive wouldn't it?"

"Ophelia's treat." I said firmly, hoping that in her rapid exodus my Mother had remembered cheque-book and credit cards. "Speak to Elizabeth, get her to organise a couple of people," I'd been absent-mindedly pushing my thumb nail along the table surface and glancing down, I saw it now bore a solid chunk of gunk, I wiped it hurriedly on my jeans. "Actually, let's make that three or four people, and say we want a really thorough, deep-clean job. Now, why are you looking so worried?" Gladys drew air in sharply between her teeth,

"Etty won't like it, especially not if Ophelia pays." She warned.

"You leave Etty to me." I said. She was unconvinced, but took herself off in search of Elizabeth, untying the overall and slipping it over her head as she went. She passed Ophelia in the doorway with a murmured greeting, and we could hear her muttering anxiously to herself, as she padded and squeaked along the uncarpeted corridor.

CHAPTER TWENTY-FIVE

"Good morning my darling girl. Did you sleep well?" My Mother surveyed the kitchen warily as one would do foreign territory – which in a way it was, the only time she spent in our own starkly modern, stainless steel and mercilessly shiny-surfaced area, was when she was being photographed for a magazine spread.

"Not particularly. You snored and Ink snuffled."

"I do not snore, never have done never will," she said indignantly. "You must've been dreaming. I suppose the only coffee is instant?" She looked pained and as I made no comment, gingerly made herself a cup, wrinkling her nose fastidiously and joining me at the table.

"I've just been speaking to Murray." I said. She shook her head sharply,

"No, not interested, thank you very much. Don't want to know. A camel can only handle so many straws before it breaks its back and gets the hump and for me," she said, mashing metaphors to suit, "Sasha was just the icing on the cake." She tasted her coffee, adding a little more milk from the jug on the table and tutting as she noticed a chip out of the china.

She was as always, fully made up, albeit her lighter daytime look and she'd swept her hair back to the nape of her neck, tied with a thin black velvet ribbon. She had on a pair of black, fine wool trousers and a mint green shirt, although how her clothes always emerged from her case as crisply laundered as they'd gone in, was a mystery to me. I noted absently her swiftly critical glance at my own unruly brown locks, which had suffered mightily from a night of tossing and turning and were, right now, without benefit of a good brush, let alone a wash and blow dry. I could, if I worked at it, get my hair to hang straight as my Mother preferred, but laziness tended to get the better of me and I usually let it do its own thing. The hair issue was an ongoing one between us and therefore could be continued without benefit of words – one critical glance and my ignoring it – conveyed in mother/daughter shorthand, all that needed to be said.

"OK." I murmured, "Your funeral. Can't force you to listen, but I think you'd be mad to throw away all those years, just like that. And that's not all, what about the act?" She ignored me, and as I knew she could continue with the silent treatment indefinitely, I gave up and changed the subject.

"I need you to make a phone call for me this morning." I said.

"I've already told you, I am not phoning your Father, nor Murray for that matter."

"Not them. I want you to get in touch with the journalist who did this restaurant review." I leaned across and opened the packed kitchen drawer, pulling out the printed piece. She smoothed it out to read, holding it awkwardly at arms-length and squinting – she needed reading glasses, but hell would freeze over before she'd admit it.

"Listen," I said, "You need to tell him that you followed his recommendation to this hotel. You had dinner and stayed overnight – and you and your husband were never so terrified in your entire lives. Actually, make it that you came with a couple of friends and you all had a horrible experience. You have to say you think it's absolutely disgusting he should write a review on somewhere like this, without giving people fair warning."

"Fair warning?"

"Well, the wretched place is haunted, isn't it? All four of you 'saw things' you couldn't explain. You consider yourself lucky to have got out in one piece – in fact," I warmed to my theme and leaned forward in my chair, "You were so scared, you packed up in the middle of the night so you could leave at first light, you couldn't get away fast enough. And you've been on tranquillisers ever since. Can you do all that?" Ophelia smirked, she'd lost the tearstained, strained look with which she'd arrived at my flat and for that, I was relieved. I was used to her being difficult, it was vulnerable I couldn't cope with.

"Darling, need you ask? I'll give him the full works. I see exactly where you're coming from, great idea. And then… ?"

"We'll hit him from a couple of other angles too," I said, "I'll do an email as well, from someone else – he can't help but smell a story."

"Or a rat?"

"Not if we play our cards right."

"Clever girl." She grinned at me. I treasured those rare genuine grins of hers – from the heart – not posed, best-profile-to-camera and not the polite, slightly absent effort when her mind was a million miles away. I tapped the newsprint,

"This's the guy."

"Phone number?"

"He writes for the local paper, Google it, my laptop's in our room. He'll be there, or they'll be able to get hold of him." I stood up, brushing the back of my jeans which seemed to have acquired a coating of God-knows-what from the kitchen chair.

"What are you going to do now?" She asked with interest.

"A quick tour of the place, get my bearings, decide exactly what we can lay on for Mr Restaurant Rover, and Ma,"

"Hmm?"

"I might have to ask you, and maybe one or two of the others to... perform a little." She glanced up disingenuously,

"Perform?"

"You know darn well what I mean, though I'm hoping we won't even need it."

"You always were peculiar about it." She said, I glared at her,

"What do you expect? And don't think for one moment I've forgotten or forgiven you for the unspeakable way you've behaved. I still can't get my head around how you bare-faced lied to me."

"Interrupting, am I?" Bella, in a cleaner white outfit than yesterday's, strode across the kitchen, kettle-bound. Now I'd pinpointed where I'd seen her before, I could also see the change wrought in her appearance by the hair style. All previous pictures had been with her hair down, darkly framing her face. Upswept as it now was, it gave her features a completely different slant.

"Ah," she said, noting my scrutiny with amusement, "I suspect Devorah's given you the low-down."

"What I don't understand," I said, "Is why anyone would still risk coming to you?"

"Well," she considered the question. "I'm working under a different name, so most of them don't even know it's me they're coming to. But even if they did, vanity's everything my sweet – the results I produce are rather startling, even if I say so myself. I'm working on making them longer lasting though, and getting rid of those annoying little allergic reactions. Not too long-lasting of course, otherwise they won't be back for more. I'm working on a whole new line now – completely different image this time, sophisticated's out, natural's in – *Grandma Etty's Cottage Preparations*. What d'you think?"

"Etty must be turning cartwheels with excitement." Observed Ophelia dryly.

"Oddly enough she was fine about it, you know she never ever reacts quite the way you think she's going to – anyway, it's all really low-key; home-spun but classy, earthy colours and brand new slogan." She paused expectantly, it seemed only polite to look interested.

"*Beauty As It Used To Be.*" She pronounced, with a flourish. "Like it? I rather feel it captures the zeitgeist. Now, tell me what plots you're hatching." She helped herself liberally to Muesli from a nearby cupboard, seating herself opposite Ophelia, flooding the bowl with milk and munching with gusto. My Mother drew back slightly, breakfasts weren't really her thing and she blanched at a brioche, let alone a hearty fibre-full bowl.

"Ophelia can fill you in." I said briskly, "I've things to do. Oh, and Ma, nearly forgot," I paused on my way out, "I told Gladys to get some agency cleaners in and you'd cover that, thought you wouldn't mind. Did you bring your cheque book and cards?" She smiled,

"Not just mine, darling. And if I can slip a little expensive aggravation into a certain someone's life, then my day will have not passed in vain."

CHAPTER TWENTY-SIX

I couldn't find Elizabeth, or indeed anyone else in the downstairs rooms, but when she'd taken us up last night to our bedroom – it was the only one made up, which was why we'd had to share – the door hadn't been locked anyway. Maybe they were all unlocked and I could simply have a look around on my own. I'd start from the top and work my way down, by which time Elizabeth would probably have turned up.

Ascending from the first-floor landing was a further, smaller winding staircase, bannistered by a thick and fraying red cord attached to the wall at intervals by peeling gold fixtures which didn't seem to be nearly as firmly attached as they should be, I hated to think what would happen if you lost your balance and made a grab. It led up to what looked like three further bedrooms one at the end and two on either side of a surprisingly wide corridor, I assumed this area had been converted from the original attics.

The first room, to the right was unlocked, unoccupied and unheated, although it was quite a reasonable size and well-lit by a window that climbed up one entire wall and continued into the dormered roof to become a skylight. Spitting on my sleeve and cleaning a spyhole in the dust of the window pane, I could see the view from here was stupendous, uninterrupted as far as the eye could see by any other buildings and overlooking reasonably well kept gardens, presumably the responsibility of the erudite Alfred. The gardens extended to either side, backing the whole width of the house and sloping down to a small ornamental lake where a large weeping willow was doing some graceful, drooping stuff, partially obscuring a weathered wooden bench beneath it. The view alone would sell this room and make for some great shots for a hotel brochure. I mentally pulled myself up, my involvement here was strictly short-term.

The second door I tried was the one at the end of the corridor. This wasn't locked or unoccupied. It was a smaller room than the previous one and full to the gunnels with electronic gadgetry. Pieces of equipment were stacked haphazardly, one on top of the other, most in some stage of dismantlement or re-assembly and all trailing a myriad of wires heading off in every direction with an agenda of their own. There was a narrow if hazardous path through the mess, presumably to allow access for the boy seated at the far end of the room in front of a flickering screen, next to a single, unmade bed. A bit of fresh air wouldn't have done the atmosphere any harm at all, but I couldn't immediately spot a window, presumably it was currently obscured.

"I'm so sorry," I said, "I didn't realize you were here, otherwise I wouldn't have barged in."

"S'okay," he swung round on the chair, a solemn-looking fourteen or so, with skin just heading into spotty and voice cracking. There was a wire, taped with Elastoplast to his right temple, from where it snaked into the back of one of the computers. He eyed me up and down, "Nice bod!" He remarked with a leer he'd clearly been practising in the mirror, but hadn't nearly perfected yet.

"Don't be ridiculous." I said sharply.

"Sorry." He was immediately chastened.

"Henry, right?" I said.

"Yup and you're Whatshername's daughter."

"Ophelia. What's that?" I indicated the wire and he raised a hand to ensure the Elastoplast was holding.

"Evolution of the mouse." He said. I looked blank and he tugged gently at the wire, "The disc at the end of this, see – once I've prototyped it, it'll do away completely with the mouse as we know it." His voice was running up and down the scale, full of enthusiasm and then, as if ashamed of that, he had another go at the leer.

"You." I said grimly, "Have been having way too much screen-time. How's it work?" A thought struck me and he must have read my expression because he sneered,

"Nah, none of that stoopid mumbo jumbo family stuff – this is pure science, utilising brain waves. Going to sell it and make millions."

"Good for you, that'll come in handy. Does it actually work?"

"Course – dead simple, only problem is trying to teach thickos how to use it – I'm working on an instruction manual right now."

"Will people want to sit at their computer with a wire stuck on their head?" I asked. He groaned,

"Duh! There won't be wire when I've finished it, just a tiny thin disc, so big," he spaced thumb and forefinger to show me. "Self-adhesive, disposable, people'll buy packs, use 'em once, throw 'em away, built-in obsolescence, neat huh?"

"I'm impressed." I said honestly.

"So you should be. And Sweetpea, feel free to come up and check all of my wires, any damn time you want." I told him sharply to mind his manners and shut the door briskly, continuing my exploration with a glance at my watch, just gone 10.00, I was already behind on my self-imposed agenda of practical action, I needed to get a move on. I tried the third door, the one opposite the unoccupied room but this one was locked. I was heading back downstairs, when it abruptly opened behind me and a woman clutching a pink quilted dressing gown closed to her neck, peered out.

"Have you brought breakfast?" She demanded, "I did ask for it to be brought early this morning." I gaped at her for a second or two, I could have sworn Elizabeth said last night and Gladys confirmed this morning, there weren't any guests staying at the moment. But such was the management style round here, perhaps this was just someone they'd forgotten. And one thing we, I hastily amended that to they, couldn't afford to do, was antagonise a paying customer.

"I'm terribly sorry, it must have been overlooked, can I get it for you now?" I asked. She tutted impatiently,

"I'm not impressed with the service here you know, not impressed at all." Birdlike, she put her head on one side and blinked at me expectantly. "Well?"

"Sorry?"

"On what do you plan to take my order?" I whipped out pad and pencil, which I'd stowed in the back pocket of my jeans, "I'd like half a grapefruit, segmented of course, pith and pips removed properly mind." She said. "One portion of cornflakes, milk in a jug please, not in the bowl – it came up like that the other day and was soggy, soggy, soggy. Two slices of wholemeal bread toasted – but only very lightly and I think I might manage a bit of jam today," she tossed a long gray plait over her shoulder and patted what looked like a concave stomach, beneath the faded dressing gown. "One has to be so careful if one isn't to slip into a portly middle age." I glanced up surreptitiously, a portly middle age wasn't something I would have thought she needed to worry about, she'd be lucky if she saw sixty again. "And a pot of tea for two." She added. "And please don't forget both cups this time."

"For two?" I queried.

"I believe that's what I said, didn't I?" She said sharply and loudly, maybe she was used to talking to Elizabeth.

"Right, I'll just run down and get all that for you. I'm so sorry you've had to wait, Madam." I wasn't quite sure about the madam, but it seemed the right sort of room servicey thing to add and I headed down the stairs at speed to a now deserted kitchen although, I crossly noted, Bella's empty bowl still sat on the table, alongside Ophelia's cup.

"What'd their last bloody servant die of?" I muttered to myself, "Probably food poisoning." I came back quick as a flash – honestly, I could keep myself amused for hours. I really would though have to insist that everyone pulled their weight, otherwise this enterprise was going nowhere, except further to the dogs. I thrust the offending crockery into the sink and got busy with the breakfast order.

CHAPTER TWENTY-SEVEN

Finding everything I needed took a little time, although I felt I was coming to grips with Gladys's unorthodox storage methods. For reasons best not delved into, she kept cutlery in a cupboard, saucers and plates in a drawer and eventually, after a frustrating search, I stumbled across a couple of slightly shriveled grapefruit, hanging around with a gang of apples in a string bag and sharing a hook with a wall calendar that was still showing August. Segmenting, I discovered was not my forte, and as no psychic assistance was forthcoming from Delia and co, the results of my labours looked decidedly ragged. To cap it all, the only tray I could find was still the big silver effort, which seemed to have put on weight overnight. I was all too keenly aware of the passage of time – if I didn't get my skates on, I'd be dashing up with an early lunch rather than a late breakfast. I'd just have to bank heavily on the fact that my upstairs friend had opted to stay here for character rather than class.

I staggered up one flight, pausing to catch my breath and rest the tray on the landing. The only bright side of this whole episode, I could currently see, was that I'd almost certainly lose some unwanted pounds through a combination of stress and weight-lifting. By the time I'd hauled my load up to the third floor, I swear I could feel my arms working their way out of their sockets and I was pretty certain, if I put the tray down to knock on the door, picking up again might not be an option. There was a strong temptation to simply bang my head against it, I restrained myself and sang out,

"Breakfast."

"Enter." She said. Sod it, I thought.

"I'm sorry, you'll have to open the door for me," I said, "No hands free." There was a lengthy pause, during which I could feel my sinews straining, then the door swung open and I surged in, desperate to find a surface on which to put the ruddy thing down. It was only because I had no strength left in leg or lung that I didn't immediately turn tail and flee, screaming. The room was choc-a-bloc, full of people.

I'm not much given to hysterics, that's always been Ophelia's area of expertise and even as a child, I was aware I couldn't compete, but at this point I was seriously contemplating trying. In my defense, I was tired and it had been, to put it mildly, somewhat of an eventful couple of days, so it took me a good few moments of noisy hyperventilating before I realized what I was surrounded by – they were models, sculptures. And they were good, incredibly good. Standing, sitting, lying, each one totally individual and bursting with petrified life. Full size figures; truncated torsos; faces, numerous differently featured faces – some masks, others full heads – and, reaching from shelves ranged up and down the walls, dozens and dozens of artfully created arms and hands of every shape and size, filling every available space, beseeching, forbidding, beckoning – all with the same incredible quality of movement.

She'd cleared a small space on a table and on it I plonked the tray. As initial shock diminished, I could see the room was double the size of the other two I'd been in on this floor. Longer and with two of the skylight arrangements, allowing sunshine to flood in unimpeded. In the far corner, under the dormer roof and guarded on either side by more silent white figures, was a neatly made bed. Call me Sherlock, but the room didn't feel like that of a woman who'd just popped in for a weekend leisure break.

"Who the hell *are* you?" I demanded.

"Felicia. Who the hell are you?"

"Sandra. Ophelia's daughter."

"Ophelia, gracious, haven't seen her for a while, you don't look much like her, do you? Is she here too?"

"Downstairs."

"Really? Well, tell her I'll try and get down to see her later." She'd moved back to the door, holding it open and clearly waiting for me to leave. "Thank you for breakfast."

"I thought you were a guest." I said resentfully,

"I know." She said, and shut the door firmly behind me.

CHAPTER TWENTY-EIGHT

Halfway back down the stairs, I expelled a shaky laugh. I hadn't even been a complete twenty-four hours in this wretched place, but most of that time had been spent scared witless or ready to commit aggravated homicide with the nearest weapon to hand. I know they say you can choose your friends, but not your relations – even so, I felt fate had dealt me a poor hand. On the plus side though, when it came to putting haunted hotel plans into action, I reckoned I'd have more than enough special effects to do the business and then some. Pulling myself together, I decided to take a swift look at the rooms on the first floor, just to check whether there were any more, up-till-now, unmet family members lurking.

The room Ophelia and I had occupied last night was now, in the daylight, a little musty and dusty, but nothing a bit of fresh air and a judicious application of polish wouldn't banish. It had a large window overlooking the garden and each of the two beds had its own material-draped bedside table and pink over-fringed lamp. That the bedspreads bore evidence of long use and clashed more than slightly with curtains boasting a bilious orange motif, wasn't the end of the world. The room was also big enough to take a neat, two-seater sofa and low table, set in front of a fireplace. Above the mantelpiece hung an oval gilt, mercifully cherub-less mirror and placed at various intervals on the walls, were a couple of landscapes and a still life – an assortment of vegetables on a table with a very dead pheasant hanging folornly over the edge. There was though more importantly, an en-suite bathroom and if, as Ophelia had remarked disparagingly last night it was hardly big enough to swing a cat, it was to be hoped most people coming for a few days R and R, wouldn't want to. I made a note on my pad to organise the purchase of some good bath sheets. The towel I'd used, after standing for a long time under the feeble shower earlier that morning, was less effective than if I'd drip dried, and I'm a firm believer that the shortcomings of any bathroom can always be ameliorated by a thick and thirsty, body-swamping sheet.

There were twelve rooms in total on this level, ranged along two corridors which ran from either side of the galleried balcony. Additional doors at the farthest end of each corridor turned out to be sizeable cupboards, unevenly stacked with linen and towels.

I reflected that this whole property, together with its extensive grounds, must be worth a fair old bit, I'd have to find out if they were already mortgaged to the hilt, or whether that could be a way of them getting some money in hand to fix things – I presumed Roland would be the best person to ask, and made a note to tackle him.

The six doors to my left were all unlocked and obviously destined for guest use. A couple of them even had four poster beds – great selling point, we could charge more for those and, best of all, they too had their own bathrooms – cramped, true, and certainly nothing to write home about, but there nevertheless, which always beats having to tramp self-consciously down a corridor, complete with towel and toilet bag. I reckoned if luxury was the market we were aiming for, we'd miss by a mile, but we could probably scrape by reasonably well on full-of-character, with good food – Gladys and friends permitting!

Continuing along the right-hand side of the stairs I opened another door onto Devorah, nursing baby Simona. I apologised, but she cheerfully waved me in. Her room, as I might have imagined, was chaotic with clothes strewn everywhere and a distinct odour which, as I moved over to the window to look at the view, I put down to the discarded nappy on the floor. Simona, happily latched on, showed no inclination to let go but followed me with her eyes as I moved around, little jaws working firmly, matching her mother's mastication of the ever-present chewing gum.

"Well?" Devorah said.

"Well what?"

"Are we standing by for hordes of guests yet?"

"Give me a chance – look do you mind if we talk while you're er..." I indicated Simona who managed the admirable feat of grinning at me, without for one second stopping what she was doing.

"Fire away, she'll be on for ages."

"I met Henry." I said.

"He needs some slapping down."

"I noticed. And then I met Felicia."

"Ah!"

"Thought she was a guest." I said wryly, "I took breakfast up." Devorah pealed with laughter, shaking Simona up and down as she did.

"Way to go, Felicia."

"Who is she anyway?"

"Mimi's sister, Etty's other daughter. There were three of them originally, Mimi, Felicia and my Grandmother, Phoebe, who was the youngest."

"And where's Phoebe now?" I asked apprehensively.

"Dead – years ago." Said Devorah cheerfully. "When Bella was like just a baby, though Etty's always clammed up whenever I've asked about her. Bella was too young to know anything and Mimi's always so damn vague. But I know Phoebe wasn't married when she had Bella – big no-no then of course, shit-storm all round. Far as I can gather, Mimi brought Bella up, alongside Ophelia and Roland – God help them all, surprising they turned out so normal." I snorted, I had my own views on that.

"Obviously, Etty's always been around to oversee." She added. I had my views on that as well, maternal wasn't the first word that sprang to mind whenever I thought of Etty.

"And Mimi's husband?" I couldn't help but be curious – my Grandfather, after all. Devorah turned her mouth down.

"Roger?" She shook her head dismissively. "Not good news. Real charmer at first glance apparently, looked very much like Roland does now, but with one of those funny thin moustaches, you know, looks like it's been put on with eyeliner – I've seen photos – bit film-starrish I s'pose he was. Good looker, smooth talker, full of big ideas and money-making schemes, but Etty took against him from the start. Didn't want Mimi to have anything to do with him. Mimi wouldn't have it, besotted I gather. Anyway, there were ructions and in the end they eloped, got married, came back when she was pregnant with Ophelia. Don't know all the ins and outs, although I think Etty was as far from thrilled as it's possible to get, but because she didn't trust him, thought they'd be better under her eye than not, so she let them move in." She shivered theatrically, "Must have been frigging frosty around here for a while."

"And what happened?" I asked.

"He was a thoroughly snide piece of work apparently, up to all sorts and not always on the right side of the law either. Spiteful too; once they were married and he had his feet under the table, the charm went out the window. He was supposed to be in some kind of property business I think, but I don't know that anybody ever saw him do a day's work. Course, this is all only what I've picked up over the years, but he didn't treat Mimi well.

"What, violent?"

"Don't think it was ever anything physical, more like, you know, emotional stuff, there's a special name for that, isn't there?"

"Abusive?"

"No... well yes... but Etty called it something else, talking to Bella once, didn't realise I was just outside the room, listening to the whole conversation – gaslighting, she said, that's what he was doing. It stuck in my head because it sounded so odd. It was all like, showing her up, putting her down, making her think she'd forgotten things, unpleasant, nasty stuff. She was pregnant and not having an easy time and even when the baby – Ophelia – arrived, she found it difficult to cope, maybe a bit of post-natal depression, no surprise under the circs. Anyway, he had her convinced she was a sandwich short of a picnic."

"And isn't she?" I asked, from what I'd seen, it certainly looked that way. Devorah frowned at me sharply.

"She may be now, but I don't think she was then and you shouldn't be so flipping quick to judge. I know she plays the daft old bint, but there's more to her than meets the eye. She was beautiful you know, Ophelia looks like her, I've seen pictures – that's what pulled him in, in the first place I suppose."

"So, what happened?" I leaned forward.

"Well, I think Mimi kept trying to make a go of it, don't think she could bear to let Etty see how right she'd been, and they went on to have Roland, but things got worse and worse. He and Etty were always daggers drawn, then one day he upped and offed."

"Upped and offed?" I repeated.

"Yup, disappeared. Like, never," she said with satisfaction, "Seen again."

"What happened to him?"

"No-one knows." She grimaced and winked, "Or if they do, no-one's saying." I stared at her, horrified but wondering and she laughed.

"Oh don't worry, it was all like above board, reported to the police and everything and a big hunt went on, but he just never turned up. Turned out he owed an unhealthy amount of money to the sort of people you really shouldn't owe money to. The general thinking seemed to be, when no-one could find hide nor hair, he'd gone one step too far, once too often and..." She drew her finger swiftly across her throat. "For God's sake though, don't try asking Etty or Mimi about him. Mimi'll have hysterics and Etty'll clam up." She removed Simona, who let go reluctantly, but only after a struggle, and started patting her on the back. "Anyway, why you so interested, it was all way before our time." The baby let out an enormous belch and looked startled but pleased, and Devorah planted a congratulatory kiss on the top of her head. "Clever girl." She said and put her on to the other breast, before turning back to me. "If you want, there are some brilliant old photo albums down in the library, they go back years, some of the photos are like – whatdoyoucall'em, funny-coloured things."

"Sepia?"

"Yeah, I'll show you sometime if you want."

"Thanks, but I don't plan to be around too long, as you know. Although," a thought occurred, "I wonder if I could take out some of the photos, get them framed and hung – nothing like a bit of sepia for atmosphere – the Americans love that sort of thing. And if Etty won't talk to me about family history, I can find out more from Felicia."

"Shouldn't think so."

"Why?"

"You'll be lucky if you ever see her again."

"No, she's coming down later. Said she'd be down to see Ophelia." Devorah laughed, jiggling breast and baby all over again.

"Felicia doesn't come downstairs."

"What? Never?"

"S'right. Some kind of a disappointment with a man – don't know exact details, as I said, everyone's always so damn secretive around here, you'd think they all worked for bloody MI5. Anyway, she took to her room – and I mean, like in a big way. Hasn't stepped outside the door in twenty years." My mouth dropped open as I digested this.

"You're kidding me. Bathroom?"

"Up there, leads off her room."

"Eating?"

"She's got a little gas ring I think and a sink. Elizabeth buys whatever stuff she needs, leaves it outside the door – Felicia usually won't open up while anybody's around, nobody's been in her room for years, that's why I couldn't believe you'd seen her."

"Well, she let me take her breakfast in."

"No! You're kidding me. You actually went *in*? What the hell does she do in there? I hear her thumping around at all hours."

"She sculpts."

"*Scalps*?"

"Sculpts! People, figures, brilliant stuff actually, gave me the most terrible shock." I paused, terrible shock didn't even begin to describe how my mind tried to rationalise what my eyes thought they were seeing. "But," I said, "She must need clay and stuff in the first place, tools all that sort of thing."

"Elizabeth again I s'pose, or Alfred. Here, could you?" I looked up to see Simona, finally asleep, head lolling and a trickle of milk on her chin, sailing gently across the room towards me – I automatically put out my arms and she landed solidly in them, Devorah was buttoning her shirt.

"Bloody hell, I wish you wouldn't do that." I said crossly.

"Sorry, forgot."

"Not with other people, I hope?"

"Course not, Etty's dead strict about that. But you're family." I grimaced, no denying that unedifying fact. I transferred the sleeping, surprisingly heavy and delightfully warm armful to my shoulder. I'd never had much to do with babies, but this one seemed amenable enough and happy to be pass the parcel. I absently rubbed her back as being the sort of thing I'd seen people do and she rewarded me with another fulsome belch.

"Well done," said Devorah, to both of us. "You can dump her now." She nodded towards the cot in a corner of the room with a helicopter and teddy mobile, gently turning in the breeze from the window. I carefully laid the sleeping baby down and covered her with the blanket. When I turned, I saw Devorah had flopped on to the bed in similar boneless fashion. Catching my expression, she was defensive,

"Night feeds, I'm shattered."

"Two more quick questions – where do Elizabeth and Gladys sleep?"

"Gladys has a room at the back of the annexe – you know, where Bella has her studio. Elizabeth and Alfred have a cottage in the grounds, other side of the pond, well Etty calls it the lake but it's really not that big. You can't see the cottage from here, hidden by trees."

"And the lake belongs to the house?"

"S'right." She already had her eyes closed.

"Listen, I want all of us to meet up, in the library this evening, about 5.00 – Devorah, d'you hear me?" She grunted, which I took to be assent and I shut the door gently behind me, heading downstairs just as Ophelia emerged from the kitchen corridor, looking like the cat that'd swiped the cream.

CHAPTER TWENTY-NINE

"There you are my pet." Ophelia said, "Journalist mission done and dusted."

"You spoke to him?"

"As instructed."

"What did you say?"

"Everything you told me."

"How 'scared' were you?"

"Sweetheart, I was Academy-Award-winning scared! And halfway through the conversation I had to ask him to just hang on while I ran and got a glass of water, because talking brought it back so vividly and I'd come over all dizzy."

"Well done, that woman." We smiled at each other, a rare moment of accord.

"What next?" She said. I looked at her in astonishment, usually one task a morning was all Ophelia liked to undertake before sloping off for an Earl Grey and a nap – not that different from Devorah, now I came to think about it. Still I wasn't in a position to look any gift horses in the mouth.

"I'm going to email the paper now." I said. "You go and check Gladys and Elizabeth have got the kitchen cleaners in, before we poison anyone and make sure they're doing a really thorough job." She made a face, "Ma, I'm not asking you to put rubber gloves on and dig in – just see that they do. Also I want everyone together for a meeting at 5.00 this evening. It's no good me organising all this if the family won't co-operate, they're the ones who are going to have to carry on with what I'm getting started. What's the matter?" She was frowning,

"They're not big on get-togethers."

"Tough. I'm relying on you to round everybody up."

"Actually, darling, I think I've one of my heads coming on, I'll just… "

"No," I interrupted sharply, "No, you won't. You will not slope off as usual and leave everything to me. You got us into this crazy situation, the least, the very least you can do is pull your weight to get us out." She opened her mouth, but I was just getting into my stride, "If, Ma, you decide you want to leave at any time, that's just fine with me, say the word and we're out of this like a shot. It isn't *my* guilty conscience that's keeping us here – these people may be your family, they're not mine. As far as I'm concerned, they're just a bunch of nutty strangers. We stay, we go, your choice." I paused for breath and she tutted.

"I honestly do not know, Serenissima where you get such a mouth – and that hard streak, not from me that's for sure."

"Is that so? Well let me tell you... " we were interrupted by a series of agitated pings from the bell on the reception desk in the hall. I stepped out from the shadow of the staircase to take a look. There was a young woman with her back to me, shifting from one sturdily-shod foot to the other. Outside the front door, I could see a small car drawn up – honestly, they really shouldn't leave that door open all the time when the reception desk was unattended. I looked down at myself, I was hardly a picture of sartorial efficiency, but someone would have to go, I put out a hand to grab Ophelia who was, as always, dressed impeccably and could easily play receptionist. Needless to say, the instant I'd turned my back, she'd seized the opportunity to slope off, leaving me with no choices. Bloody woman.

"Morning," I said brightly, making the best of things and moving forward. The woman jumped and swung round to face me. She was younger than I'd thought with a black knitted hat pulled down over a mass of curly, hectically red hair, the freckles that go with it and a nose either reddened by the wind or a streaming cold. She had a black leather coat over her arm, a document case under it and a chunky jumper tucked into the waist of her trousers, which was doing her no favours in the tummy region.

"Oops, you made me jump." She said, "Sorry about the bell, I never know whether these things are really meant to be rung, but there didn't seem to be anybody around?" She had one of those speech patterns that make a question of every statement, voice rising plaintively at the end of each sentence seeking, doubting or inviting comprehension. It was one of my business partner Sally's most annoying habits and I hated it that after a while in her company, I'd find myself doing it too.

"No, I'm terribly sorry, there should have been someone on duty." I indicated my jeans apologetically, "Bit of a housekeeping blitz." I moved into place behind the desk, on which sat the large, closed registration book and was about to haul it open in an officious manner until it occurred to me, it might reveal an appalling blankness of page, so was probably best kept closed.

"Do you, um, have a reservation?" I asked.

"No. No, actually I don't."

"Ah." I sucked some air in through my teeth, to indicate this wasn't good news. She looked swiftly over her shoulder, reminding me of Gladys, although she needn't have worried, the hall was hardly thronging with cocked ears, nevertheless she leaned forward and lowered her voice.

"Look," she confided, "I'm actually in a bit of a pickle." Great, I thought, just what I needed, someone else in a pickle. I waited politely for her to go on.

"I really, really don't know whether you'll be able to help me out?"

"Well, you'll have to give me a clue."

"Yes, sorry, sorry, silly billy me, I'm in that much of a tizz – you see we were all set up for Westerly Manor. But there's been a bit of an issue."

"An issue?" my questioning tone echoed hers, despite my best efforts.

"God yes. See their chef's only gone and run off with the owner's wife, the Dalmation and all of last week's takings." I sealed my lips and looked suitably shocked, though if she thought Westerly Manor had issues, she should get a load of ours. "Anyway," she continued, "Oliver Owen – the owner, you probably know him don't you, he's in the most dreadful state – she was last year's overall Crufts winner, the dog I mean, not the wife." She paused for breath, "Thing is, all the prelim work's been done, but he says he simply can't go ahead now and of course he's right, we can't film him, he's either cursing or crying and that doesn't look good, does it? So I've been driving round and round all morning and someone finally sent me here." She paused again, taking in the surroundings and looking suddenly doubtful, "This is a hotel isn't it? I mean you are a going concern?" I lied swiftly and without compunction.

"Absolutely."

"And you haven't been in business all that long?"

"Well... "

"God! Sorry, sorry, sorry." She struck herself, open-handed on the black tea-cosy, "I'm such a numpty, haven't even said what I'm after, have I?"

"A room?" I enquired hopefully, leaning against the desk and feeling, as I often did with Sal, that if I was with her long enough, I'd never regain a normal speech pattern.

"No. I mean yes. Actually, more than one?" She said. I tried not to look over-excited. "And, oh sugar! I haven't even asked, are you the proprietor? I'm only supposed to speak to the person in charge."

"Trust me." I said firmly, "If there's anybody in charge, it's me."

"Phew, jolly good, relief all round! Look this is my card." She was, it appeared, Charlotte Leavington-Rubicon, researcher for *All Seeing Eye*. "But call me Charley," she instructed, "Everyone does. Thing is, we're doing a series called *Lift Off* – following through on people setting out in different enterprises, that's why we picked on Oliver, he was the manager, but he just bought out the previous owners. Anyway, what we're after is the ups and downs, highs and lows, you know, personalities and problems behind the projects, fly on the wall – it's pre-sold to Channel Four, scheduled for Spring, we've already got a bakery, a nursery – tots not plants – and wedding dress hire under our belts, now we want a country house hotel, d'you see?" She paused and we both took a deep breath. I was indeed starting to see, and who'd have thought manna from heaven might turn up in a black woolly hat.

"You want to film a documentary here?" I clarified. "About us?"

"Well, in principle yes, although I do have to find out a bit about you and make sure you're interesting enough – although," she added hastily, "I'm sure you are. But like, at Westerly – there was the prize-winning dog – makes for interesting stuff, gets the viewers involved you know, we want the Ooh Factor, quirky or cute, either will do just as well."

I nodded enthusiastically, my mind racing. We'd have no problem with quirky, although I didn't think we were in with a chance when it came to cute. We'd also have to make sure Bella wasn't recognized by any less-than-satisfied clients from the London scandal, and I wasn't entirely sure whether Ophelia's light might best be hidden under a bushel or whether a celebrity relative, come down to help out, would be an additional attraction. I dragged attention back to Charley with an effort.

"...so you see." She was saying, "I've simply got to, got to, got to, get it all set up today." The pale blue eyes were swimming a little now and the right one had developed a small tic, this was one seriously stressed researcher. "We're all geared to go and Max – our director, terribly good, short-listed for a Bafta last year, but bit of a diva – will tear his hair out, and mine, if we're not all ready and raring. Please tell me..." she put one desperate, nails bitten to the quick, hand on my arm, "...that you're interesting?"

"Well," I said reflectively, patting the hand. "We don't have any prize-winning dogs, but we do have a tame wolf." I wondered briefly whether we could train him to stop purring and start howling. "And, it's really funny you should turn up now, because we do seem to be having a few curious goings-on."

"A wolf? *OMG* how wonderful is that?" Her grip tightened on my arm. "And goings-on?" Her nostrils flared, "What *sort* of goings-on?" I did my own bit of looking over the shoulder to check for listeners and she automatically mirrored me, before we both leaned in towards each other again.

"You'll probably laugh," I said hesitantly, "But we think we might be... haunted." I dropped my voice and cast my eyes downward, to indicate what a disaster that would be.

"*Oh*!" She said, face flushing, "*Oh, oh, oh, my giddy sainted Aunt*. That's just too, too wonderfully brilliant for words. A ghost, you've got a *ghost*?" I nodded modestly and tried to look rueful at the same time. She'd whipped off the woolly hat in the excitement and was fanning her hot face.

"And would you... would you be happy to have us film here?" She asked breathlessly. I pursed my lips and did the sucking air through the teeth thing again, I didn't want to come across as too easy – never a good start to a relationship,

"I will have to talk to my Great Grandmother, she's..."

"There's a *Great Grandmother*?" Charley's flush was becoming positively hectic and she was hopping from one foot to another. Much more excitement and I'd have to throw a bucket of water over her. "My *God* – viewers just *love* a Great Grandmother." I smiled grimly – I wasn't sure they'd love mine.

"Right, well she's the actual owner, although," I added hastily, "I'm running the show now, but I would have to have a word. And I'd need to know a bit more about what's entailed. And," I added tentatively, "Whether there's any financial inducement?" In truth, I thought the PR would be worth its weight in gold on its own, but no harm in asking – you don't ask, you don't get. "Perhaps we can sit down for a chat and you can fill me in on all the details. Coffee?"

"Yes, yes please." She said. "That would be wonderful, you're an absolute star. I'm dying for a wee first though, all that driving, you know." I directed her to the downstairs toilet I'd discovered earlier, then sprinted for the kitchen, where I was beyond frustrated to find no evidence of cleaners and still less of Ophelia on their case.

Time being of the essence, I boiled up just enough water for one coffee, threw two cups and saucers together spooned in granules, filled mine up with cold water, hers with the now boiled and legged it back, so I could usher her, in leisurely fashion into the library. I had to take a deep breath to avoid panting in an unseemly fashion – a little more time here and I'd either be fit as a fiddle or dead. Indicating a chair, I handed her the hot cup.

"Mmmm lovely, thanks a million," she murmured, unwinding her woolly scarf. "I needed this more than you can possibly know, you've saved my life in more ways than one." I smiled, warmly at her, the feeling was mutual.

CHAPTER THIRTY

Charley Leavington-Rubicon and I spent a highly productive period in the library while she recorded on her phone my potted history of the house, its conversion to a hotel and (judiciously edited), some of the family members and staff involved. And if, because just over twenty-four hours ago I'd known less about the set up than she did, there was a fair bit of imaginative gap-filling, she didn't know and I wasn't bothered. Mind you, it did belatedly occur to me, it might not have been a bad idea to record a few bits myself, so I could remember exactly what I'd said.

"Wow, what a background." She said, throwing herself back in her chair then bouncing forward again, "Now, tell me, tell me, tell me about what's been going bump in the night. Actually, you won't believe this but... " and she wriggled and shivered a little

"...I'm actually getting some odd sensations right now." I was pretty certain any odd sensations she was getting were due to the clapped-out springs of the armchair in which she sitting, because I was sitting on its companion and was getting some uncomfortable feelings in the nether regions myself. This, combined with the diabolical draught whistling under the library door, wasn't doing anything for anybody's comfort zone but still – all grist to the chill mill.

"Goodness." I said, wide-eyed, hand to chest. "You must be very sensitive Charley, most people don't sense her immediately."

"Her?"

"Well yes, it was in here you see that she..." I paused and took a slow sip of my icy coffee to give myself time to decide what exactly it was she'd done.

"My God, she killed herself, didn't she?" Charley gasped obligingly.

"But that's just incredible," I gasped back, "How could you *possibly* know that?"

"I just felt it." She said breathlessly, she now had her hand on her chest too. "Who was she?"

"One of the housemaids, a young girl from the village. Just sixteen years old, came here to work, and..."

"Wronged, she was wronged, wasn't she? A man? It's always a man." I nodded silently, maybe if I didn't say anything else at all, Charley would sort out the whole story for me. She leaned even further forward, so I did too.

"How did she... ?" she asked.

"Hanged herself." I said glumly.

"How?"

"With a rope?" I knew it – I was starting to talk like her.

"No, I mean, where from?" Charley was looking round the room expectantly, I could have kicked myself, maybe I should have stuck with the self-contained simplicity of poison.

"No, sorry," I amended hastily, "She actually hanged herself in the attic, but it was in here that she and he..." I paused delicately.

"The bastard!" The venom with which Charley spat that, led me to believe she'd had her own poor experience with the opposite sex in the not too distant past – I'd have to introduce her to my Mother they'd have things in common. "So, what does she do?"

"Do?"

"I mean, do you actually see her, or is it just noises, sobbing and that?"

"Ah, well, some people have certainly seen her, you know," I said vaguely, "Others just seem to hear her, calling out for him and yes there is a fair bit of sobbing now you mention and sadness, a terrible feeling of sadness. Good grief," I shivered dramatically in admiration, "It's just like you're tuned in to her already Charley, it's uncanny." She sighed with satisfaction,

"People do say," she conceded modestly, "That I am on the sensitive side. But Sandra, this is all just brill. First class. A1. Bloody brill, times ten over!"

Naturally, once I'd embarked on the tragic tale of the brief life and times of poor wronged little Polly Malone – I know, I know, not dead original – but you try being more imaginative, when you're thinking on your feet although I must admit, every time I paused for breath, Charley was in like Flynn. Honestly, the girl was wasted as a researcher, she should have been a member of the Screenwriter's Guild. We covered the whole sad tale in no time, both of us totally bowled over by how much she seemed to be sensing. Indeed, we agreed, it was almost as if she knew what I was going to say before I said it.

It transpired, the filming schedule was over the next six weeks and wouldn't be every day. She explained, this enabled them to work concurrently on other projects, but would also give a longer overview of what was going on with the hotel. They'd need three rooms for a couple of nights every week and on some weeks, four rooms. There would be herself, Maxwell Fearnstill the Director, Karl their camera guy and intermittently, Ffion Sykes who was doing intros, summaries and connecting pieces, but didn't need to be there all the time. Charley announced Ffion with some pride, and thereafter talked about her as the Talent, so although I'd never heard of the woman, I did a small 'ooh' with my mouth to show how impressed I was. Apparently, much of the narration would be added after editing, back at the studios, and the majority of the programme would be shot with Maxwell himself questioning us from off camera as we went about our daily business.

In view of the length and regularity of the booking, I was able to offer Charley a special rate for the rooms, although as I had no idea what the normal rate might be, this was truly a shot in the dark. However, I can't have been far off as she was most appreciative, and in the general bonhomie, I threw in breakfast for good measure, although made it clear we'd charge additionally for evening meals. By this time, I was starting to get a tad twitchy, we'd been uninterrupted so far, but the last thing I needed was one of the family walking in before I'd primed them. I glanced at my watch which showed we were coming up for 12.00.

"Look, I hate to be rude but…" I said, getting up from the chair and reflecting my bottom was probably permanently spring-scarred. Charley seized the hint with alacrity, as indeed she had everything else, she really was a most obliging sort of a girl.

"No, you've been beyond brilliant Sandra, I absolutely can't thank you enough, I've a heap and a half of stuff to go off and get on with now, and I can always call you for any more info I need, can't I? I simply can't believe how lucky I've been, this is soooo much better than an award-winning dog. See you first thing Monday then?" I hesitated, I could already see my avowed tenure stretching further than I wanted, but this was too good a chance to pass up.

"Super." I said. "Can't wait."

CHAPTER THIRTY-ONE

The documentary idea was greeted at the 5.00 o'clock family confab I'd called, with all the enthusiasm I'd expected.

"A *documentary!*" said Etty in Lady Bracknell tones. "Over my dead body." We were an uneasy gathering, and I for one was exhausted and not prepared to put up with any nonsense. I glared at her,

"That could probably be arranged" I said.

"Hang on a second Gram, hear her out." Roland, whose loose-limbed relaxation contrived to make even the rigid little sofa on which he was lolling look comfortable, was mushroom-colour co-ordinated today, cords and a jumper with leathered elbow patches. Etty, on the opposite side of the bow-legged coffee table was black and white in contrast and sitting bolt upright, both hands resting on the bird-head of her cane, which was as eagle-eyed as she was.

"I don't believe I have to hear any more, Roland." She said. "To know it is a totally absurd idea, and must you call me that, makes me sound like a new-fangled measurement?" My Mother, sharing the sofa with her brother, snorted softly,

"Nothing's changed then." She murmured.

"Meaning?" Etty's fiercely hooded, green granite gaze locked with Ophelia's.

"Your word." Said my Mother, "Still law."

"My house."

"And their home." Ophelia's impatient gesture took in Roland, Mimi perched tautly on a footstool near them, Bella and Devorah seated on a couple of upright chairs they'd drawn up and Henry, planted on the piano stool, bored and obviously present under duress. He was wire-less now, though the Elastoplast remained in place. He was picking desultorily at the piano keys in a tuneless way that made me want to brain him with the nearby harp.

"Pretty pickle they'd be in without my help." Etty's mouth was a thin grim line. "And," she continued, "I notice you came running back quick enough when you needed to." Ophelia barked a sharp laugh,

"Hardly quickly, perhaps I thought, after all this time there'd be more of a welcome, obviously I was mistaken."

"Wouldn't be the first mistake you've made." Etty said.

"And what's that supposed to mean?"

"You should know Ophelia – how many years is it now you've wasted, swanning round the country shoring up a third-rate vaudeville act?"

"I've done well out of it, thank you very much and been happy, happier than if I'd have stayed here."

"Well, you're not happy now, are you?" Etty came back. "Shown himself up in his true colours I understand." Mimi who'd been anxiously swiveling her head between the two stood abruptly, flapping her hands in agitation,

"Stop it, both of you, I won't have it. I don't know what gets into you when you're together... too much... it was always like this... too much then... certainly too much now... I won't have it, do you hear me, I won't have it." For all the notice Ophelia and Etty took, she might as well have remained silent. Roland chuckled, breaking the tension.

"Well, this takes me right back." He said, "Just like the good old days. Gram, Ophie, back off both of you."

"Answer me just one question." I said. I'd chosen to remain standing and from my position in front of the fireplace, I surveyed them all crossly. They all turned to look at me, with the exception of Etty who gazed steadfastly ahead.

"Are you." I said, and if my tone was that of a teacher with an unruly class it was because that was what it felt like. "In a financial position to turn down *anything* that might bring in a bit of income to prop up this place?" Roland shook his head, but it wasn't his agreement I needed.

"Etty?" I asked. Calling her Mrs Goodkind seemed ridiculous, but I certainly wasn't up for calling her Great Granny any time soon. She shook her head briefly, I wasn't sure whether in dismissal of me or in answer to the question. "Etty?" I persisted.

"No. We are not." She said coldly.

"Right. Well, as this documentary thing seems to have fallen into our laps, it would be crazy not to take advantage. It could give you just the sort of publicity you need to get everything moving. Now, because time's short and there's a lot to take on board, I've produced a fact-sheet." Devorah giggled and I glowered at her.

"Devorah, do you have something you want to contribute?" She shook her head, "Well shut it then." I said, handing out what I'd quickly put together on my laptop. I'd been confident that Henry would be able to print it out for me and he hadn't let me down, although bending over the printer, I hadn't been thrilled to find a hand that wasn't mine, resting on my bottom. I'd given it a good hard slap and its owner a sharp rebuke and a brief lecture on harassment he wouldn't forget in a hurry.

I'd bullet-pointed and numbered the steps already taken:

1 Ophelia's phone call to Jonathan Harper, together with the equally agitated email I'd sent to my office to forward on, so he'd received two similar complaints from completely different sources.
2 The phone call I'd made on the spur of the moment to the Pyschic Society, where an enthusiastic young lady had taken down details of our manifestation and promised she'd get a regional investigator to make contact.
3 Details on the documentary requirements gleaned from Charlie, including her weekly room bookings which were now nicely filling up some pages in the hitherto sadly blank register.

And finally, to ensure we were all singing from the same song sheet, I'd put down a few brief notes on the rise, demise and re-appearance of the unfortunate Polly, together with a few ideas – asterisked to indicate they were still in the planning stages – on proposed sightings. You might want to label me a little OCD, but years of helping Murray organise my parents, the crew and the dancers had taught me that nothing beats the clarity of a bullet point. Etty was singularly unimpressed,

"You cannot seriously believe, for one single second," she said, holding the fact sheet, of which I was really rather proud, in a fastidious finger and thumb, before letting it flutter down onto the table, "That this complete poppycock of a scheme will work?"

"Actually," mused Roland, "I think it's rather clever and just might."

"God Almighty you're certainly organised, are you sure you're really

Ophelia's?" Bella was still reading through her notes, a pair of reading glassed perched halfway down her nose.

"Never mind that," protested Mimi, "It's simply not true is it, not any of it."

"Mother," said Ophelia, "It's marketing."

"If she was hanged, would she have like a purple face and her tongue all swollen?" Enquired Henry with interest.

"Henry," snapped Devorah, "If you don't stop banging on that bloody piano, she won't be the only one with a purple face and swollen tongue." She turned to me, "I think it makes sense, anyway what've we got to lose?"

"Well?" I said, looking around.

"Well what?" Said Etty.

"Do we go ahead with this, or do I cancel everything and walk out of here right now?" There was a short silence, during which I honestly wasn't sure which way I wanted her to go. She cracked her stick sharply on the ground, once,

"Go ahead if you must girl. Just don't come crying to me if you make a complete fool of yourself, not to mention the rest of us. One condition though."

"Are you in any position to lay down conditions?" I asked mildly. She'd risen to her feet, waving away Mimi's helping hand impatiently, and now she looked across the intervening space between us.

"You're very young. There's a lot you don't know, for all you think you do and sometimes, when you open the lid of a box, it's very difficult to close it again." It was an unflinching stare from those strangely coloured eyes, and I felt the power of her at a deeply atavistic level, barely understood. I wasn't prepared to show that though, she may hold sway over the rest of the family – not over me. I raised my head and stared directly back and for just a few seconds, all extraneous sound dropped away and it was as if she and I were alone in the room. She lowered her gaze first, but only because she chose to.

"Your condition?" I asked.

"Be careful. Be very careful. You," she inclined her head at me, "Don't know anything about us. The rest of you," she slowly turned her head, looking briefly at everyone in the room, "Do." Mimi giggled nervously, but nodded as each of the others in turn, had done. "Mind my words then."

Said Etty and she stalked, stern-backed out of the room, trailing a wake of silence.

"She's not wrong, you know." I deliberately brought things down a notch or two. "There's going to be a lot of comings and goings and you'll all have to watch your p's and q's – you know exactly what I mean, no funny business, otherwise we'll have all sorts of publicity we *don't* want."

"Thought you said," pointed out Ophelia, "That you might want the odd 'performance' or two."

"Only if strictly pre-planned." I said repressively. "We can't have Mimi falling out of cupboards at unexpected moments or," and I turned a stern eye on Devorah "Simona floating all over the joint. And where's that ruddy wolf kept?"

"Enclosure, behind the annexe." Said Roland,

"But," Mimi piped up, "He likes to spend time with me, we walk a lot – he helps me."

"Helps you? With what?" Mimi adopted her daft little old lady look,

"This, that… and the other… you know, we potter around." I tsked impatiently,

"Potter? Mimi he's a bloody great wolf, not a craft project."

"Tame as a kitten." She protested.

"And twenty times the size. Now, I'm making it your responsibility to ensure he's kept well away from any guests and only brought out for the documentary people if, and when, I tell you. Is that absolutely clear?"

"As you say, Serenissima dear." I glanced at her sharply to see if she was being sarcastic, but she was busily re-reading her fact sheet, a small frown of concentration furrowing her forehead.

"Are we done?" Bella had risen, straightening her white coat, "I've another colonic irrigation coming in."

"Thanks for sharing." Murmured my Mother.

"I'd have thought," responded Bella amiably, "That a person who's spent her life, lying in a box while somebody sticks swords in her, is in no real position to be critical of what anyone else does for a living."

"Bella?" I interjected. Another of those worrying thoughts I seemed to be having a lot of lately had cropped up, "Are you actually qualified to carry out these procedures and treatments you're doing?"

"Naturally."

"Letters after your name and all the proper insurances?"

"No, I mean I'm naturally qualified – that's my gift." And she sailed magisterially out of the room, followed closely by Devorah and Henry. I turned to Roland,

"Does that mean what I think it means?" I asked with apprehension. He grinned amiably at me,

"You know sweetheart, if you're not ready to hear an answer, it's probably better not to ask the question in the first place." He uncoiled himself gracefully from the sofa, chucked Ophie playfully on the cheek, patted his Mother on the shoulder and followed the others out, closing the door softly behind him. Turning back to Mimi, I opened my mouth to reinforce the wolf warning, but she'd disappeared. Ophie met my furious gaze and shrugged,

"Mothers!" She said.

CHAPTER THIRTY-TWO

It's always gratifying to see a chain of events you've set in motion, progress satisfactorily. Like knocking over the first domino and watching the ongoing effect. Unfortunately, unlike domino displays, events don't always keel over in the right order.

Prior to our family meeting I'd checked and whilst there wasn't a miracle makeover in the kitchen, the four cleaners who'd finally pitched up, were even now wringing out cloths and contemplating their handiwork in the dim lighting. They'd done a good job. If it wasn't actually reaching state-of-the-art, at least it wasn't screaming botulism quite so loudly. It seemed a shame though, whilst I had four willing bodies and several blank cheques, signed by Ophie, not to take advantage. I dispatched them, under the able supervision of Elizabeth, to expend some more of their energy on further much-needed cleaning efforts elsewhere in the house. Double time, I said, because it was after regular hours.

The phone rang as I was on my way out of the kitchen. I waited a while to see if someone else was going to answer. As expected, nobody did. Why would they indeed now muggins was here? I grabbed it in an exasperated hand,

"Home Hill Hotel, Good evening."

"Look, this is purely on the off chance and really last minute but I don't suppose you have a room for a couple of nights do you?"

"Checking in tonight sir? Would that be single or double occupancy?"

"Just me, but happy to take a double, prefer a bigger bed." Do you indeed I thought, and with that voice I'm not surprised. He'd probably turn out to be a four foot eleven gargoyle, because life's like that, but right now, over the phone, he sounded charming.

"Bear with me just one moment." I cooed in suitably professional sing-song, holding the phone away for a couple of minutes and making tapping noises on the dresser with my fingernails to indicate some computer action, then "Thank you so much for holding. We can indeed offer you accommodation for tonight and tomorrow night, because I see we've just had a last minute cancellation." I paused, was this guy going to notice the distinct absence of any other guests when he arrived? I'd just have to ensure the family milled around a lot, but perhaps also best to box clever. "In fact," I added cunningly, "I see the cancellation was for a family group, so we do have more than one room available," My tone of slight surprise, indicated this occurrence was rarer than hen's teeth. "May I take your name and credit card details, to guarantee the reservation?"

"Harper," he said, "J, and can I book a table for dinner, I have dined with you before." I grinned to myself, well, well, well, the roving reporter returns, what a gratifyingly quick response.

"Certainly Mr Harper. Would 8.00 suit?" I'd have to make some of the family eat in the dining room too, to avoid him sitting in oddly solitary splendour.

"8.00. Perfect, and I presume your extraordinary chef's still with you?" He said. I looked across the kitchen. The door to the walk-in larder had just opened and Gladys had wandered out. She was wearing her flowered pinny, a pencil behind her ear and an absent expression. She had a leg of lamb swinging from one hand and some celery and carrots in the other. She stood there, head cocked to one side, swaying gently back and forward as if in a mild breeze. I turned back to the phone,

"Indeed yes," I said, "She's still with us."

"I'll look forward to it then." He said. Gladys had stopped swaying and started looking worried – I hoped it wasn't Sitting Bull on the way back in.

"As will we, sir." I put the phone down thoughtfully. I'd need to organise a little something over and above a meal and a room for Mr Harper, just enough to give him a really good story.

"Gladys?" I moved in front of her to gain her attention and she started and looked up enquiringly, "Gladys, that was Jonathan Harper on the phone, remember – restaurant critic, rave review?" She nodded silently, "Well, he's coming to stay again tonight, what's on the menu?" She looked blank, "Lamb, is it?" I prompted, looking at what she was holding.

"Possibly," she said. "Possibly not."

"Right." I said brightly, "Well, we haven't really got a lot of time to think about it, I'll pop back shortly, to see how you're getting on, shall I?" The phone rang again, I picked it up.

"I'm calling," it said, "About your issue. Now, I know you'll be worrying about my equipment." My mind skittered a little, trying to get its bearings. "Nothing too obtrusive my dear." The voice on the phone assured me. "And there's just three things I'm after, let's call them the three esses, shall we?"

"I'm sorry?" I said.

"Sight, sound and shiver factor. From what I understand, you've got all three going on."

"Look," I said sharply, gripped by a concern we might be fast forwarding into a heavy-breathing situation, and that the next question might well be what underwear was I wearing. "I've no idea who you are," I said, "Nor what you want but… "

"Well, I'm a complete idiot, that's what I am. Forgive me. Profound apologies. Completely carried away there. Harold, Harold Hugheson. You rang the Society? The Psychic Society?"

"Right, yes, of course I did, I'm so sorry. Couldn't think for a moment…"

"Well of course you couldn't, I know you've a great deal on your mind, unsettles people no end does this sort of thing. Now, Monday too soon? I understand you're a hotel so we won't trouble you over the weekend. Not to worry though, we won't worry the guests, we'll just blend."

"Monday?" Well why not, I thought, it would certainly give Charley and Co. something to document. "Monday's fine – you said we?"

"Two of us, Harold and Morwenna, my wife. Always best to work in pairs, double checks you know, science versus spooks and sceptics, proof's the thing isn't it, nothing beats an irrefutable bit of proof. Now, we're not that far away from you, so won't need to avail ourselves of your kind hospitality. Once set up, we'll just nip in now and then. But I'll run through all the instruments with you, make sure you're happy with them staying in place during the day. Whole thing'll probably turn out to be nothing more than a draught and an odd trick of the light. Fifteen years I've been doing this, not come across a real recordable yet. Still," he added wistfully, "Hope springs and all that."

"Indeed." I said warmly and then because I felt deeply guilty, added, "I look forward very much to meeting you both, thank you for coming back to me so quickly."

We said goodbye and I replaced the phone thoughtfully. Things were certainly acquiring their own momentum. All I had to do now, was make sure we staged just enough to fan the flames. Then the hotel could rest on its spooky laurels, reap the publicity rewards and Ophie and I could wend our way back to normal, or as normal as we'd ever been. I just hoped it wasn't going to be too late to bring Adam back to his senses.

"I think I should tell you, they're changing shifts now." Announced Gladys suddenly from behind me.

CHAPTER THIRTY-THREE

I jumped and swung round to face her. Changing shifts? Was that, I wondered, a good thing. Did it mean unhelpful influences were on the way out and Delia was on her capable way in and, more importantly that Jonathan Harper wouldn't be disappointed?

"Who Gladys?"

"Out there, in the garden." She was facing the window, I looked out too. The efforts of my eager cleaning students had made visibility a hundred times better than yesterday and although it was only about 4 o'clock, darkness had fallen, but there must have been a security light triggered, because a whole section of the outside area was brightly lit.

"See, behind that bush." She said. I followed her pointing finger.

"I don't see anything." I said.

"Because they're hiding."

"Why Gladys?" I enquired in kindly tones. "Why would you think they'd be hiding?"

"To watch Bella."

"Bella?"

"They take photographs all the time you know."

"Wait a minute," I said, "Are these *real* people we're talking about or um... others?" Gladys took a step back, meeting my eye for longer than usual in her indignation,

"I'm not mad you know, of course they're real people, they work for Simaxo."

"Who the hell's Simaxo?"

"Not who, what – it's the company Bella nearly did that deal with. Everything fell through when there was all that London kerfuffle, but they still want to find out how she gets her results. I'll tell you what it is, straight out, it's industrial sabotage."

"Espionage," I corrected absently.

"I know what I mean." She said.

***

Bella, when questioned was sanguine,

"My dear, they're always there, nothing at all for you to worry about."

"But we can't have men behind bushes," I pointed out. "It'll frighten the guests."

"Well, there's usually only one at a time, anyway I thought that was what you wanted?"

"I want spooks not spies."

"Well couldn't they just be extras?" She suggested amiably, I sniffed,

"Ghosts – with cameras and notebooks? I hardly think that's going to work, do you?"

"Actually, I feel rather sorry for them, out there in all weathers." She said, avoiding my comment.

"Why?" I asked. "They're spying on you, trying to steal your treatments?" Bella laughed heartily, the buttons on the white coat straining desperately to maintain a hold across her expansive front. Winking, she adopted a remarkably accurate southern drawl, "Honey, what I got, ain't nobody gonna steal! Anyway," she added in normal tones, "They're not very good."

I'd run her to ground in the annexe where mercifully, the colonic irrigation hadn't yet started, although there was an anxious looking lady in the waiting room and some ominous looking equipment laid out next to a treatment table. Bella took my arm and pointed into the gardens.

"Look, see what I mean." Sure enough, right at the edge of the lawn, there was a polished brown shoe protruding from behind a laurel bush. Bella opened the window and leaned out, "Oy, Cyril." She yodelled, "Shoe!" the brown shoe jerked and then was slowly drawn out of sight, perhaps he thought we wouldn't notice it moving if he did it slowly. Bella chuckled and shut the window against the chilly night air. "Nice chap, retired policeman, I take him out a cup of tea from time to time, although he gets embarrassed when I do. "Problem is," she paused to concentrate on fitting together two sections of the rubber tubing, whose purpose I didn't even want to contemplate, "There's not a whole lot for them to find – not if they lurked for a hundred years. Sandra, my dear, don't give them another thought, they've been here weeks already, they won't hang around indefinitely. We could have dealt with them of course, but I honestly don't think it's worth it. They'll get fed up soon enough."

"Flipping well hope so," I grumbled as I left her to the tubes and the anxious looking lady. It was all going to be tricky enough as it was. We'd have the documentary people here, Jonathan Harper had left a message to say his paper's photographer might stop by to take a shot or two and we couldn't forget Harold and Morwenna. At this rate, we were going to be fielding more photographers than you could shake a fist at. I could only hope none of them were going to catch Bella practicing without whatever it was one should have, before sticking tubes up other people's rear ends.

I was hastening back into the main house, ticking off a mental check list of tasks done and intended, when my mobile buzzed in my pocket.

"Sandy?"

"Hi Murray, where are you, it's very noisy."

"Hospital. Can't talk long."

"Oh God, what's happened? You OK? Adam?"

"It's Sasha."

"Sasha? What's wrong?"

"Knife wound."

"*Knife wound*?"

"Don't shriek like that, goes right through me."

"What happened?"

"Rehearsal."

"Rehearsal?"

"Sandy – I'm going to cut you off right here and now, if you don't stop repeating every blinking word I say."

"Sorry. Just tell me, can't you."

"Rehearsing, weren't they? At the theatre. Determined to go on with him, she is."

"And?" I carefully avoided any repetition. I knew Murray in this sort of snappy, frustrated mood he would indeed cut me off.

"The wheel routine." He paused. I filled in my own gaps.

"*Murray*." I yelled. "Why didn't you stop him?"

"Stop him? *Stop* him?" Murray yelled back, "You know you can't stop the stupid old sod doing anything he wants to – bleeding lucky I persuaded him to leave the blindfold off." I flopped down on one of the green leather chairs near the reception desk.

"Sasha, she's not… ?"

"Nah. went into her upper arm, the fleshy bit. Her own silly fault, she egged him on, insisted they do it. They're bandaging her up now, looked a lot worse that it was, lot of blood, but it doesn't even need stitches, they say she can go back home right away." He snorted, "Except it's not her home she's going back to, is it?"

"And Adam, he all right?"

"No he's not, he's in a right old two and eight. She keeps saying it wasn't his fault, that she moved. He keeps saying he's losing his touch. Losing his touch, my arse!" He snorted more noisily this time. "Sandy, you've got to get Ophelia back home, before something goes seriously wrong and someone really gets hurt."

"I'm doing my best, but she won't budge till I've sorted things out here."

"Well? Taking your time aren't you?"

"I've made a start." I snapped, "Rome wasn't built in a day."

"So how long d'you reckon – to get things straightened out I mean." Straightened out wasn't quite how I'd describe the interlocking series of events I was so busy choreographing, but I didn't think it would be a good idea to go into details and further fray Murray's nerves.

"Middle of next week, I should think."

"Blimey O'Reilly," he muttered, upbeat as ever. "There could be people pushing up daisies by then."

CHAPTER THIRTY-FOUR

By the time I'd finished the call with Murray I was standing in the reception area, so I thought I might just as well stay there for a bit, and plonked myself down on one of the unyielding green chairs. This might be a quiet moment to try and get my thoughts in order and maybe prioritise, but what was missing were my lists. Ophie and Adam always laughed at them, but I maintain, once you've got something on paper, you're halfway to getting it done. However, I'd put my notebook down and left it somewhere or other. In a little while I'd get to my feet again and hunt it out, but for now there was no-one around and I felt I'd earned the luxury of a few seconds without interruption, I rested my arm on the armrest, my head in my hand and shut my eyes.

"What exactly is it you think you're doing?" I kept my eyes shut, I thought I'd opted for no interruptions. "You really can't just swan in here and turn people's lives upside down, you know." This obviously was an interruption that wasn't going anywhere, anytime soon. I opened one eye and squinted upwards.

"Mr Heywood," I said, "You, here again, how nice."

"I've been seeing Mrs Goodkind. You and I need to talk." He said. I shut the eye again.

"I don't see why."

"She's told me what you've got in mind to put in motion and I must register my disapproval." I opened both eyes this time and stared at him, what a pompous ass. And what exactly had she told him?

"Your disapproval?" I queried.

"Indeed."

"And what business is it of yours to approve or otherwise?"

"Mrs Goodkind is my client, her welfare is therefore my concern. Now, I'm sure you mean well." He said, his tone indicating quite the opposite. "But you obviously haven't thought things through." I stood abruptly, so we were almost toe to toe. He didn't show any signs of backing up, so

I took a side-step. He had on an old-fashioned, dark gray waistcoat, to match his suit, complete with fob watch and chain – affected or what?

"Not," I said, "That I think it's anything to do with you, but I'm simply getting the hotel some much needed publicity, before it's too late."

"You're playing with fire."

"Isn't that a tad over-dramatic?"

"Can't you see, the last thing needed here is publicity, what d'you think's going to be made of the family, not to mention Gladys? Once some clever filmmaker gets her in his sights, she's going to come across at best, as completely batty and at worst as… as…"

"Are you saying she's not batty?"

"Eccentric, certainly. But what's that to do with anyone else? And what about Felicia – they'll love her, won't they?"

"Don't be silly, there's no need for them to even meet her." I said firmly. He grunted in exasperation and pushed his glasses back up on to his head, allowing him to better pinch the bridge of his aquiline nose with thumb and forefinger, a gesture I interpreted as a sign of extreme frustration.

"I can't make up my mind whether you're naïve or just plain daft." He said. "Don't you know the way they work – these documentaries? They flourish on sensationalism. What do you honestly think they're going to be more worried about – your well-being or their viewing figures?" I made to interrupt, but he didn't let me, "And Mimi," he said, "Exactly how are you going to keep her under wraps? Don't you see the risks?" He didn't add 'You stupid woman', but he might just as well have done.

I never respond well to criticism, and certainly not from someone with no business making it. I was close to losing my temper, despite the fact I'd had more than enough practice at keeping emotions well under control.

"I've made you angry." He said, then unexpectedly, "Good. What are you feeling now?" A few well-chosen, barbed responses that I was formulating, lodged in my throat as I stared at him. I felt honesty at this point was the best policy,

"That I'd like to pulverise you."

"And could you?"

"What?"

"Well, you're part of this family too – with all its 'foibles' – give that some thought." And he swung on his heel and headed out the front door.

It took me longer than I would have liked to calm down, following my encounter with the annoyingly meddlesome solicitor. There was no doubt he'd stirred up some unpleasant speculation – although nothing that hadn't already occurred to me during the last few days – it was just that hearing that voiced by someone else, was a little alarming. Even more alarming was exactly how much he did or didn't know about the family and their funny ways. I resolutely shoved all these clamouring questions to the back of my mind, where they could buddy up with a whole group of other things I didn't want to think about now (or indeed in the foreseeable future), I had more pressing matters on which to focus.

To reap maximum benefit from our journalistic visitor there were a few things I had to sort out before he arrived, and I felt Polly Malone's opening night was a matter best handled by the only person round here I could rely on – me. However, I needed some props so I thought before tackling the family meeting, I'd tackle Elizabeth.

"What d'you want with a cap then?" She said, eyeing me suspiciously. I'd run her to ground having a cuppa in the kitchen, where Gladys was bustling about like a thing possessed – which she might very well have been. Also present, sipping tea, humming quietly, dunking a chocolate digestive and intermittently jotting things down in a tattered open notebook, was a lugubrious looking individual who stood and formally shook my hand when I came in.

"Alfred." He said. I nodded,

"And I'm...

"Ophelia's girl." He supplied. "I know, been hearing quite a lot about you."

"What sort of a cap you talking about?" Interjected Elizabeth. Actually, she had me there. Although I'd put together quite a solid story on the misfortunes of poor Polly, Charley hadn't asked, and I'd neglected to decide, quite when this had all taken place. I thought I couldn't go wrong with around 1910, and then wondered if it ought to be a bit earlier, I didn't want any records being checked for authenticity.

"Old-fashioned housemaidy sort of a thing?" I asked hopefully.

"Mob cap, she means." Put in Gladys, as she whisked past at speed.

"You don't need a cap." Elizabeth looked me up and down, I'd changed from my jeans into the black skirt and white shirt she'd given me "It'd look proper daft, you'll do as you are."

"No, no, it's not for serving dinner. It's for… something else entirely." She pursed her lips. "Elizabeth," I said, in the voice I use to deal with Ophelia when she needs to be taken in hand. "It's a very simple question, have you or have you not, got something I can use?"

"Well there's a load of old tut in the cupboard next to Felicia's room," she said grudgingly, "You'll likely find something there. Mind you don't disturb her though." I nodded, reflecting as I trotted upstairs, that Felicia was disturbed enough already.

CHAPTER THIRTY-FIVE

In my experience, the average mind can accept only so many knocks in the course of a day, before it begins to recalibrate and take the entirely unexpected, manfully in its stride.

With Harper, J. booked in for dinner that night, I'd insisted on family back up. So when Roland came down to dinner, later that evening, in black fishnet tights, high heels and a not-too-far-above-the-knee-to-be-sluttish, black leather skirt, I simply blinked hard once or twice.

He'd topped the skirt with a baby-blue angora jumper, tastefully beaded around the neckline, a blond, chin-length, feather-cut wig and skilfully understated make-up. I had to admit he looked lovely although I did think, as they descended the stairs pausing, all three of them on the bottom step for a moment, like the Supremes taking a photo-call, that maybe they'd misinterpreted my instructions which I'd thought were quite clear – bring on the cavalry, I'd said, not the bloody cabaret.

Bella had swapped her white coat for a figure hugging little black dress, and there was a lot of figure to hug. She'd added a pair of hanging earrings, which would put any decent chandelier in the shade and the mass of black curls, piled high on her head was anchored with an extravagantly jewelled pin. Ophelia had opted for a mid-calf, full and floaty chiffon skirt in deep brown, her normal teeter-high heels, a long-sleeved, cowl-necked gold lurex top and enough Chanel No. 5 to rock you on your heels.

As all three sashayed past me into the candle-lit dining room, I made a firm grab at a gold lurex arm,

"I wanted," I muttered through smiling lips, "For you to make like normal guests, what the *hell* is Roland playing at?" Ophie grinned widely,

"It's just what we used to do, when we were kids, Bella and I would dress him up in our clothes – Etty hated it."

"So, what? He's a cross-dresser?" I asked. She pealed with laughter,

"Goodness me no my darling, nothing half so exciting I'm afraid – just an inveterate practical joker, did I not mention that about him?"

"That and a few dozen other things." I hissed. I let go her arm and she followed her two dining companions, as an unflustered Elizabeth ushered them graciously to a table in the middle of the room.

Devorah and Henry were already in situ at a table in the far corner, although both a little sulky. They'd been sitting there from 7.45 but were only being allowed a bread roll and dessert, on account of the fact that Gladys, and whoever she was working with tonight, had under-estimated on the lamb. I'd decreed therefore, that they had to appear to be at the end of their meal, when Jonathan Harper was just starting his and once he'd seen them, they could leave. Whilst I appreciated we didn't exactly present a bustling restaurant on a peak night, it was the best we could do, and I hoped the explanation re the cancellation would cover. I also prayed he wouldn't want to eat in again tomorrow night, I was running low on extras.

CHAPTER THIRTY-SIX

I had made it my business to introduce myself as the hotel manager (more or less accurate I felt), and I let myself be casually engaged in conversation by Jonathan Harper when I cleared his soup plate. I was relieved to see he'd finished, so it must have been reasonably OK, although I couldn't tell what it had been and Elizabeth had taken his order.

"Not that busy tonight?" He asked, I cast an eye round the dining room, averting it swiftly from Devorah who was making, when-can-we-go faces at me and trying not to let it linger on the Three Degrees in the middle of the room, who'd taken their role properly to heart and were chatting and laughing loudly, to show what a wonderful time they were having. Roland looked across at me, grinned, winked and gave me a little wave. I ignored him.

"Bit of a relief, to have an easy evening for once, to be honest." I said, "We've been rushed off our feet, but we had a group coming in tonight who cancelled at the last minute."

"So I understand. Have you been here long?

"Long enough." I said, with feeling.

"I hear that you've had... ," He paused, casually buttering what remained of his roll, "...one or two unusual things going on here recently."

"I don't think so," I said repressively. "Who on earth told you that?" He smiled smugly,

"I have my sources." I was relieved he didn't tap the side of his nose, which would have been naff in the extreme. Contrary to expectations, his voice wasn't too let down by his appearance. He was early forties with straight dark hair flopping over his eyes, in a way he probably imagined to be boyishly attractive, although it immediately made me want to utilise a hair-slide.

"Of course." I said, "This is a very old building, you know, lots of creaks and groans and things and sometimes, I expect, people's nerves get the better of them." I was busily doing that thing waiters do with the napkin to rid the table of crumbs, although I don't think I was doing it well, because most of the mess was ending up in his lap. However, I thought it politic to let him deal with that on his own.

"Oh, go on," he said, lowering his voice, "You know you can't keep this sort of thing quiet for long, word gets out, people talk."

"Well," I said reluctantly and in an undertone, "You might mean Polly."

"Polly?"

"Never seen her myself," I admitted, "Others say they have, although as I said, that's probably more down to over-active imaginations and bad lighting than anything else."

"You mean there have been actual sightings?" He leaned forward.

"Suppose you could call them that." I agreed grudgingly. He smiled up at me and I could see him setting up headlines in his head.

"You said Polly?" He asked, "How do you know that's who she is – was?" I took a breath to launch into Polly's CV, but was saved by Elizabeth bustling in with his main course. Over his head, I raised an eyebrow and she nodded reassuringly, Gladys was obviously holding her end up in the kitchen. Elizabeth placed an impressively professionally displayed plate in front of our guest and re-filled his wine glass. I seized the opportunity to move away sharpish, bearing the soup bowl and at the same time deciding how indeed we knew Polly was Polly. It was the unexpectedness of the question that had thrown me, but then I decided it wasn't that complicated at all, there can't have been hordes of housemaids doing away with themselves over the years, so if a ghost pitched up, it was odds on to be the one that had. Stood to reason.

As I left the dining room and made my way back to the kitchen, I was overwhelmed with a wave of tiredness, it had been a long and busy day and the thought of bed, even with my Mother and Ink, was suddenly very tempting. I made a swift resolution that the wisest course of action might be to let sleeping dogs or in this case housemaids, lie for a few hours, get a bit of much-needed sleep, set my phone alarm and then put on a show in the wee small hours.

I think, as I made my way upstairs a little later, I might have felt the teeniest bit smug. The sooner I got things sorted here, and there was no doubt, substantial strides had been made in that direction, the sooner

I could haul Ophelia back to base and start getting things sorted there. Under the circumstances, I felt I'd achieved rather a significant amount in an amazingly short time.

***

I woke up in the early hours, far earlier than planned because someone was suffocating me, although after a moment's panic-stricken flailing, it turned out to be Ink who, looking for somewhere warm to settle, had opted for my face. I'd set my phone for just after 3.00 and it was now 2.45, but it seemed silly to wait. Shoving aside one petulant cat, I got up quietly. Ophelia was snoring softly on the other side of the room, but enough moonlight was coming through the well-worn curtains to let me locate the shapeless, long black dress I'd extracted from the cupboard upstairs. It smelt decidedly musty, as did the white cap into which I stuffed my hair. Still, I reckoned Polly couldn't have been expected to be that fragrant after all this time, and anyway, she was only going to be putting in a fleeting appearance.

Ophelia didn't stir as I slipped out of the room and down the corridor, walking near the wall to minimise floorboard creaks. We'd put Jonathan Harper in the first room to the left of the staircase. I straightened my little white cap and knocked, three judiciously spaced but gentle raps on his door. The plan was he'd wake, stumble slowly and sleep-befuddled to the door and open it, just in time to see the back of Polly, turning into the darkness of one of the alcoves further along the corridor that housed a linen cupboard. I calculated, by the time he'd gathered his wits, I could be back in my room, sleeping the sleep of the just for the remainder of the night, job well done.

It was disconcerting therefore that I'd hardly finished my three sepulchral knocks, before he opened the door with a book in his hand and stepped into the corridor.

"Hello." He said, "Is there some kind of a problem?" It's not often I'm lost for words, but I was a bit stumped.

"I, um, thought I heard something." I said. I know, feeble in the extreme, but give me a break.

"What?" He asked with interest. Well, he had me there.

"Erm, someone moving around, I was worried one of the guests might have been taken ill or, or… needed something."

"I didn't hear anything." He said.

"Everything's OK in here then?" I said weakly.

"Thank you. Yes." He gestured with his book, "Dreadful sleeper, can't get my head down till the very early hours."

"Ah." I said, "Me too, but the other way around, a few hours from midnight then that's me done." There was an awkward pause, which I urgently felt the need to fill. "I like to use the time to catch up on stuff that doesn't get done during the day." I said. He nodded politely,

"Diligent." He said. "Always work to be done behind the scenes, isn't there?"

"Oh absolutely," I agreed. "And," I indicated my cap which was feeling more ridiculous with every second. "I hate dust getting in my hair."

"Understandable." He nodded. Straight-faced but only just, I didn't know what he was thinking but suspected I'd been well and truly sussed.

"Right," I said, "I'll just get on then, I'll…" I stopped, his expression had changed. He wasn't looking at me now, but over my shoulder and along the corridor.

"Holy shit." He said, and colour drained from his face. A shiver ran right up my spine, because genuine fear is instantly contagious. For a few seconds I was as frozen as he was then slowly and with an enormous effort, because I really didn't want to, I turned my head and looked behind me.

So swiftly had I been infected by his shock, I honestly didn't know what I expected to find leering at me. The fact that it was only Ophelia in a long, floaty white gown, now turning away from us and drifting slowly away back down the hall, was both a relief and a further complication. I swivelled back to Jonathan Harper.

"Please don't worry," I said, seizing the moment, "It's only Polly, nothing to be scared about. She'll vanish in a second or two, that's what she does." Flickering in and out like a bad television picture, clever of her to add that touch I thought, the figure in flowing white had slowed and stopped.

"Yes, indeed," I repeated, louder, "She'll just *disappear*." But she didn't disappear. No such luck. In fact, she slowly and gracefully collapsed to the floor and lay there, an unmoving, white heap, a few feet away.

"What the hell… ?" Murmured Jonathan Harper as much to himself as to me. I was silently grinding my teeth and making my jaw ache. I had no idea what she was doing. My bloody Mother, trust her to stick her oar in and muck things up so thoroughly that I hadn't the faintest notion what to do next. The one thing I was certain of was we couldn't stand there gawping all night. Honestly, the one time, the one and only time I'd actually wanted her to do some of her funny stuff and vanish and she wasn't obliging.

I started down the corridor towards her, I was just going to have to play it by ear. Maybe she really wasn't playing silly buggers, but had collapsed or something equally awkward. I could hear Jonathan Harper from the doorway, breathing unevenly behind me. I bent towards the motionless heap of silky cloth, topped with long blonde hair, and put a hand on her shoulder.

"Come on Ophelia, don't give me grief." I muttered under my breath, "Do something for God's sake." And she did.

CHAPTER THIRTY-SEVEN

As she began to uncoil and slowly rise, I automatically straightened up too. She still had her back to me, but she started to turn. Her heavy, long blonde curls were curving, fetchingly as usual, either side of her face, except it wasn't there – her face I mean. I was looking at a completely blank, dead white, featureless mask. Behind me, I heard a thump as Jonathan Harper slumped heavily against the wall. I didn't blame him I felt like a bit of slumping myself.

"For pity's sake Ophelia," I hissed. "Tone it down a bit can't you? I just want to give him something to write about, not a bloody heart attack." I didn't dare turn to see if he was OK, but she was certainly scaring the pants off me. I'd never seen her do anything quite as dramatic as this. She'd even managed to lower the temperature somehow, and as well as goose-bumps rising up and down my arms, my teeth were starting to chatter, it was freezing and I was fast losing patience.

"Now just stop it, this minute." I said, giving her a sharp, back-handed slap on the shoulder, which oddly enough, was higher up than it should have been. Yup, the wretched woman was doing some kind of stretching trick, rising taller and taller above me, so I was now looking up instead of across at her. I was dimly aware of a couple of doors opening farther down the corridor, but didn't have time to deal with any other troublesome family members right now. What did catch and hold my attention though was Ophelia, emerging from our room near the end of the hall, rubbing sleep from her eyes and tying the sash of her silk dressing gown.

"Serenissima?" She said,

"Oh shit!" I muttered, echoing Harper and pulling my attention back to what was now looming over me. I didn't think even Ophelia's many and varied talents extended to being in two places at once and the face with no features was even now, morphing in front of my eyes. A vivid red gash of a mouth was suddenly slashed across the white. It was yawning wide, rimmed impossibly with viciously sharp, tiny teeth and then, swift as a snake, she bent and struck.

I had no chance to move back out of range, and felt the agony of every single one of those teeth as they sank deep into the flesh of my shoulder and then withdrew – every bit as painfully – and she reared up and back again. Eyeless she may have been, but I knew, without a shadow of doubt, she'd find my throat next.

I was dimly aware of Ophelia, running down the hall towards me, followed by others, but things had suddenly acquired that unnatural black outline which means you're well on the way to losing consciousness. I could feel myself sliding slowly down the wall, I hoped to goodness I wasn't going to leave a blood-stain, they're so difficult to get out. As I hit the floor, I realised someone had interposed herself between me and the thing that definitely wasn't Ophelia. I looked up to see who'd come to my rescue. It was Mimi. Great!

Against the looming threat, she looked more insubstantial than ever, I struggled to get to my feet again, but without looking, she pushed me back to the floor with surprising strength. The thing in white, that no longer really looked like a woman at all, hissed harshly and swayed from its impossible height, mouth agape, teeth scarlet with my blood. Mimi, still holding me with one hand, extended the other, fingers spread wide and muttered something, very low, very fast. It reared back from her and in one sinuous move, whirled round to face Etty, who'd pushed her way past Ophelia. Goodness me, I thought vaguely, what a crowded corridor this was turning into, lucky we didn't have any more guests in residence right now.

Etty, night clad, didn't look that different from during the day. Buttoned to the neck in starched white, green gaze glinting she had her stick with her, but was standing fiercely upright. She looked at what swayed above her and spat out a phrase, extending her right hand as Mimi was doing. In an instant, the shape beneath the material was shrinking, shrivelling in on itself to become once again and unbelievably, a heap of unmoving white cloth on the floor. Etty poked it once with her stick, wrapping the material around the end and shifting it disdainfully to one side. She looked at Mimi and briefly nodded, in some kind of acknowledgment, then she looked down at me,

"I hope you're satisfied." She said icily. And she swung on her heel and made her way briskly back along the hall to her room. Halfway there, she stopped.

"Tomorrow morning," she said without looking round. "8.00. In the library. I want you all there."

Still on the floor, I was holding the agony that was my shoulder and didn't have the faintest idea of what to do next. Luckily I was surrounded by busy-bodies who did. Ophelia swept past me towards our journalist and I heard her murmuring to him as she shepherded him back into his room and closed the door behind them. Then there was a sudden heavy breathing in my ear, and an oddly comforting if massive weight against my uninjured shoulder as Rostropovich made his presence briefly felt, before being kneed firmly aside by Bella.

"You've been keeping that animal in your room again, haven't you Mimi?" She chided absently, as she leaned down, put both arms around me and lifted me swiftly and efficiently to my feet. Mimi humphed guiltily at her niece and winding her fingers into the thick fur at his neck, pulled the wolf away with her, holding up her pink flannelette nightdress with the other hand, to avoid tripping. I spotted the label on the outside, maybe this inside out thing was no accident, more a fashion decision. I chuckled, heard myself, and stopped abruptly, because it had in it more than a hint of hysteria. Roland moved up on my other side and together he and Bella got me along to her room.

"Devorah and the baby?" I asked.

"Fine, I checked in on them, both sound asleep," Bella said, "Devorah could sleep through the Second Coming."

"And the others, upstairs?" I asked. She shook her head,

"Probably didn't hear anything, nobody's come down." My teeth were chattering again and I was still freezing. Roland grabbed a blanket from the bed as they sat me down, and put it over my knees. I looked up at both of them, one on either side of me,

"What the hell just happened?" I said.

CHAPTER THIRTY-EIGHT

They exchanged a look over my head. Roland, elegant as ever in paisley silk pajamas and Bella, bursting out of a low-cut black lace nightie, beneath a matching negligee. For the first time, I realised they looked as shaken as I felt. Bella shrugged weakly,

"Blowed if I know." She said, "Roland?" He shook his head slowly, ruffling his hair from back to front with one hand.

"Beats me. Look, we need to deal with that shoulder."

"Must have been... some kind of illusion." I said. Goodness knows, I'd seen enough unlikely and seemingly inexplicable stuff pulled off on stage, this must have been just more of the same. Bella had unbuttoned the back of my black dress and pulled it gently down.

"Looks real enough to me." She said grimly. I twisted my head to where, just on the edge of my shoulder, raw, red, deep and perfectly defined, was a complete set of tooth marks. The pain of the bite had subsided for a brief while with so much adrenaline shooting through my system, but now it was hurting badly again and still-welling, blood-filled bites weren't part of any illusion I'd come across before. Bella brought a dampened towel from the bathroom and cleaned the wound carefully, while I did a lot of swearing and moaning, no stoic, me. Roland meanwhile followed her directions and dug out a first aid kit she kept in her bedside drawer,

"Kids were always doing something or other to themselves." She said, "Always good to have it handy. Nothing ever quite as dramatic as this though." She patted a hefty amount of stinging, antiseptic cream onto the wound and then carefully placed a gauze dressing over it, held in place by a couple of strips of sticking plaster. I think we all felt better once it was out of sight.

"Does she need stitches, Bel?" Said Roland, looking dubiously at the results of her handiwork. She shook her head,

"Don't think so, there are so many punctures it'd be nigh on impossible to stitch and anyway, think of the questions if we took her to hospital. We'll get Etty to look at it tomorrow." I flinched,

"I don't think so," I said, I didn't fancy submitting myself to what I couldn't imagine would be Etty's tender care. "It'll be fine."

"Here," Bella was holding out a couple of white pills and a glass of water.

"And these are?" I was apprehensive. She laughed at my expression.

"Nothing I've made, I promise, just paracetamol. Go on, get them down, they'll help, and then we need to get you back to bed. And drink this too." I raised another eyebrow at the glass with amber liquid, "For God's sake girl, talk about paranoid, it's whisky, good for shock." I obediently drank, choked and got my breath back.

"What...?" I started, my eyes still watering. Roland interrupted,

"Sweetie, I don't know quite what happened just now, neither of us do, but whatever it was, it wasn't anything good. Lucky Mimi and Etty were there, but this is way beyond anything I've ever come across." He glanced at Bella and she nodded her confirmation. "Point is, we're not going to find out anything more tonight. We might as well all try and get a bit of sleep. Etty's called this get-together, first thing – which I'm not looking forward to, don't think it'll be a load of laughs."

"But what if She... It comes back?"

"It won't," he said with confidence. "Etty knows what she's doing and she'll have set something up, around the house."

"Set something up?" I asked, then held up my good hand briefly, "No, skip that, I don't want to know."

CHAPTER THIRTY-NINE

"Do you have *any* idea at all, what you've done, girl?" Etty hadn't raised her voice above a normal speaking tone, but the words were razor edged and slashed the air.

We'd all turned up early in the library, but she was there first, sitting stiffly, her back not touching the carved wood of the chair she'd chosen. Black polished shoes below a grey flannel skirt, were clamped together as tightly as her lips and one hand rested atop another on the bird-headed stick. The fire was made up, although as yet unlit and the tall, maroon velvet draped windows weren't letting in any more light than they had to.

Devorah and Henry didn't seem to have been included in this family confab, but Mimi was perched on the piano seat, looking as if she wasn't quite sure what she was doing there, a complete contrast to last night. I wondered which was the real Mimi and which the act. Ophie and Bella sat at opposite ends of the small sofa to the right of the fireplace and Roland had drawn up another heavy chair alongside them, which left me only the chair nearest to Etty's.

I was bleary eyed and irate. I didn't think I'd had a wink of sleep and my shoulder was throbbing painfully, setting up a counter-rhythm to the dull ache at the base of my neck. I suspected I'd wrenched something, recoiling from whatever it was that had gone for me. I both wanted and didn't want to hear whatever Etty had to say. This whole set-up was giving me a familiar feeling of sickly unease in my stomach, recognisable from those times in the past when I'd tried to tackle my Mother about odd happenings. I didn't like that feeling one little bit.

I'd slept through the alarm and when I did open my eyes, there was no sign of Ophelia, she hadn't bothered to wake me and I had to move quickly to get myself sorted for Etty's 8.00 o'clock – I wasn't going to give her the satisfaction of pitching up late. I paused to grab a swift coffee from the kitchen, where Gladys was bustling and muttering – I didn't stop to find out who to – and on my way out, I bumped into Elizabeth who told me Jonathan Harper had checked out first thing, not even stopping for breakfast. I wasn't sure whether this was a sign he couldn't wait to start writing or couldn't wait to start running.

***

Last night Roland had walked me from Bella's room to mine, opened the door and pushed me firmly inside.

"Get some sleep."

"Ma's not here." I said, looking across the room to where the sheets were still flung back and Ink was perched at the foot of the bed, eyeing us suspiciously.

"I'm here," said Ophelia arriving behind us and making us both jump.

"Christ's sake Ophie, don't do that." Roland snapped.

"What did he say, Jonathan Harper?" I asked. Ophelia, wrapped in a black with vivid fuchsia roses, silk dressing gown, at first glance, looked her usual glamorous self. She moved past Roland and into the room,

"Not to worry, I've got him sorted."

"How?" I asked, with apprehension.

"Well, he was convinced at first that you were trying to put one over on him – that dress and cap – a little obvious my darling."

"He was supposed to be asleep." I pointed out resentfully.

"Yes, well he wasn't, was he? Anyway," she went on, "As he said, no-one pulls the wool over his eyes and he jolly well knows the real thing when he sees it." She paused and I saw she was, in reality, as disconcerted as the rest of us, just better at hiding it. "Luckily he didn't see too much, I think at the height of things he backed right into his room, by the time he screwed his courage up enough to stick his head out again, he'd missed most of it. Didn't even realise you were hurt, which is a good thing. I'd say you'll certainly get all the publicity you wanted, my sweet, he was gagging to get going."

"Yes, but what exactly is he going to say?"

"Probably more or less what you wanted him to in the first place. As far as he's concerned, he saw poor old Polly, clear as day and he probably won't want to mention he didn't see her for longer because he was hiding in his room, not too macho for a hard-boiled journalist."

"Come on you," said Roland, shoving me gently towards the bed again. "You're dead on your feet, get some sleep, you too Ophie. No point in chewing over all this tonight. Bed. Now. 'Night!" And he closed the door softly behind him.

Ophelia dropped her dressing gown, climbed into bed and unbelievably, despite everything, within two or three minutes was sound asleep. I couldn't settle. I still felt cold and shivery, and even lowered myself so far as to pick Ink up, on my way back from a trip to the bathroom. I thought at least she'd provide some warmth. Predictably contrary though, she wasn't having any of it and promptly jumped off my bed and back on to Ophie's. Honestly, in this life, you can rely on no-one can you?

***

Etty now was glaring green daggers at me and I glared back.

"Well?" She said.

"Well what?" However angry she was, I could match her step for step, I hadn't been dragged down here and into their mess, to be bullied.

"I asked you a question," she said. "Do you have any idea what you've done?" I stood abruptly, moving over to the fireplace, putting a distance between us.

"I have no idea whatsoever, although I've no doubt you're about to tell me. But before you do that, let's get a bit of warmth in here, it's like the Arctic." I bent and put a match to the kindling under the logs. The first one didn't take, nor the second; with the third I struck lucky and it caught. I straightened, taking my time because I knew it would annoy her.

Roland appeared, this morning, to be back to his usual lazily amused, urbane self. Bella and my Mother were quieter than I'd have expected, but both had applied make up and therefore looked a lot better than last night. Mimi was humming softly under her breath as I returned to my seat.

"May I be allowed to continue?" asked Etty, heavy on the sarcasm.

"Please do." I said politely.

"Exactly how much has your Mother told you?" She asked. I laughed, I couldn't help it. I glanced at Ophelia, who gazed disingenuously back.

"You have to be kidding?" I said.

"Do I look like a woman in the habit of 'kidding'?" Etty bit off each word and spat it at me. Roland tutted reprovingly,

"For Pete's sake you two, just cut the sparring can't you? Gram get on with it and Sandra, stop with the stroppy."

"Well, pardon me," I said, "But considering I only found out I had any flipping relatives, a couple of days ago, and that you lot make the Addams Family look average, I believe I'm handling everything quite well."

"She must have told you something about us?" Bella said reasonably.

"Not so you'd notice."

"Didn't you ever ask?" Queried Roland.

"Well of course I did," I snapped, "She had a whole detailed story about her background and supposed family, but it was so bloody harrowing, she could hardly bear to talk about it."

"She was always excellent at stories, top marks for her essays." Mimi piped up with somewhat misplaced, not to mention mistimed, maternal pride. Everyone ignored her.

"So, Ophelia, let me get this straight in my mind. The girl," Etty inclined her head toward me, "Has no idea about anything, anything at all?" Ophelia was defiant,

"She knows a bit. Enough."

"No I don't." I said.

"Yes, you do."

"No." I said, and then I stopped. Whose fault was that exactly? Disregarding Ophelia's deceit about her family – although now I'd met them, I could see why she'd preferred to keep them under wraps – it was true, I'd never ever wanted to delve too deeply into the 'funny stuff'. Always wanted to distance myself as far and fast as I could. I'd opted for ostrich but was now, belatedly perhaps, wondering whether hiding your head in the sand isn't simply inviting a kick up the bottom.

"Well?" Said Etty and if the room had warmed up a little with the fire, she hadn't.

"OK," I said. "I suppose I have seen things. So yes, I probably do know a bit." Ophelia abruptly rose from the sofa,

"If you don't mind, I'm really not feeling all that good. Think I'll just pop back upstairs and lie down for a bit, until… "

"Sit down." Said Etty.

"But... "

"Ophelia," Etty lifted the cane slightly and rapped it back sharply on the ground for emphasis. "All your life, you've turned tail and run from anything that didn't suit you. She's your responsibility as much as mine – more so. You chose to bring her here, and now, see what you've set in motion. You'll stay and be a part of this until I say otherwise." Ophelia sat. I'd never seen her headed off so neatly at the pass, nevertheless I didn't think she should be spoken to in that way, not in front of everyone. I was starting to think Etty had as much of an overdeveloped sense of histrionics as her granddaughter. I was also starting to think that this whole thing was turning far too serious for its own good and my liking. There was a part of me convinced Etty might prove to be the craziest of the whole crazy lot, but there was another part, equally worried she might not.

"Spit it out then." I said, partly because I wanted this session over and also because I didn't doubt that particular phrase would get right up her patrician nose.

CHAPTER FORTY

"So, you do know something of what your Mother can do?" Etty asked. I nodded slowly, "And you've seen things since you've been here?" I nodded again.

"*Filia matrem*," She said.

"And that is?"

"It's what we do; the passing of knowledge from Mother to daughter."

"Isn't that what everyone does?" I said dryly, "Isn't that just called bringing up children?"

"Don't be more obtuse than you need. What we pass down, has evolved through centuries. Generations of women, using what they are and what they've been taught, refining, re-shaping and re-defining."

"Right, and... ?"

"Such women, were known originally as the *Illustratum*. It means," she said, "The Enlightened."

"Well that's not what I'm feeling right now." I said. She ignored me.

"Over the years, we've been called many things: witches; magicians; sorcerers; seers and other names, far less flattering – because those who don't have something, fear those who do..." I interrupted again,

"Hang on one minute here – are we talking spells, incantations, that sort of thing?" I grinned broadly and bit back an additional barb on broomsticks, I didn't figure Etty's sense of humour was her strongest asset. Roland stretched impatiently in his chair,

"Sandra, can't you just shut up for one bloody minute and listen?" He said. Etty re-adjusted her hands carefully on the head of the stick before continuing evenly, as if neither of us had spoken.

"People put labels on things they don't understand, and therefore can't comprehend." She said. "Things that scare them. Ignorance calls it magic, but what I'm talking about is energy, resonance and focus; infinitely powerful when used correctly."

I humphed, I thought I did it quietly to myself but it came out louder than I intended. She carried on ignoring me.

"You're aware of what happens if you concentrate the sun's rays through a magnifying glass, aren't you? You're utilising the sun's energy and the focus of the glass to achieve a flame. Knowing where and how to harness all manner of things is instinctive, it's a part of us – part of you too. You could choose to learn all your Mother has chosen not to teach you."

"Why?" I stamped my foot hard on the carpet, and then wished I hadn't, too childish. "Why the hell would I want to? What on earth gives you the idea I want anything to do with any of this loony woo woo stuff?" She didn't answer me directly, simply carried on reflectively.

"Through the years, people like us have used what they have, sometimes to their own advantage, sometimes to the advantage of others, sometimes simply to take advantage. There have been doctors, scientists, midwives and healers as well as politicians, criminals, fraudsters – novelty theatre acts." She curled a lip and glanced at Ophelia. "There have been those who want no part of their inheritance and turned their back and others who have made it their obsession; those who've used it powerfully, to advance themselves and those who have used their power to stay hidden. Today, there are far fewer unbroken family lines. Many families, like ours, have chosen to take a step back; mind our own business, keep a low profile. After all, history has taught us some terrible lessons, hasn't it? Persecution, prosecution, torture, terrible deaths." Her words, so incongruously dramatic in that setting, dropped like stones into the silence of the room. I looked round at the others. I suppose I hoped one of them would give me a bit of an eye roll, show me we were all humouring a loopy old lady, but nothing like that was forthcoming. I was on my own. Nevertheless, I hadn't spent a lifetime defusing drama, for nothing,

"Well, this is all extremely fascinating," I said, "And thanks for the history lesson, much appreciated. But I've already made it plain, I'm not really interested in what you're telling me. To be blunt, I don't want to have anything to do with it, not interested, not bothered, not getting involved – not sure how I can make that any clearer." She turned the flint, green gaze my way,

"And last night?" She said.

"Yes, well that was a bit of a surprise." I admitted reluctantly,

"Not a surprise, Serenissima, merely a direct result of you sticking your nose in where you shouldn't have been sticking it."

"For goodness' sake, I was trying," I protested, "To improve the useless set-up you have here, and get some money coming in for you. *She...*" I turned an irate eye on Ophelia, who wouldn't meet it, "Flatly refused to leave and come home until things were looking up a bit, I had to do something didn't I?"

"The Enlightened," Etty, gazing ahead at the fireplace continued, seemingly at a complete tangent, "Was always a misnomer, some aren't in the least little bit enlightened and there have always been factions, alliances, rivalries and jealousy. As I said, we choose to keep a low profile. But now, you've brought us to the attention of those who think you're here for a reason." She paused, gesturing at the jug of water and some glasses on the table. Bella poured and handed her a drink. I found, in my frustration, I was gripping the carved wooden arms of my chair, far more firmly than was comfortable. I deliberately relaxed my hands as I spoke,

"A reason?"

"Look around, what do you see?" She asked. This was a tricky question, I wasn't sure whether she wanted comment on the general air of disrepair, the dodgy décor or the assembled family members. Apparently, I didn't answer swiftly enough and she sighed, actually it was more of a hiss.

"Mimi is my daughter, Ophelia is Mimi's daughter, you are Ophelia's daughter. But that's not all is it? Felicia is also my daughter and Bella has brought with her, her daughter and her daughter's daughter. There are eight of us here. Have you any idea what that means?"

"Surprise me."

"They think we're gathering." She said. I couldn't help myself, I laughed, this was sounding more and more like the script – and a crappy one at that – from a low budget film.

"Gathering?"

"You find that amusing?" She said. "You think I have an overactive imagination? Come here." I hesitated for only a second, before moving over to her. She reached up and with surprising strength, yanked down the arm of the loose t-shirt I was wearing. The cotton scraped painfully over my shoulder and I yelped. "Look." She said. I twisted my head; the circular wound, each tooth mark clearly visible, was red raw and certainly more swollen than the night before. It had been throbbing uncomfortably in the background all morning but now, material-scraped, it was truly sore.

"Looks infected to me." She said. "Painful, right?" I pulled my t-shirt back carefully over my shoulder and glared at her,

"Don't we have a spell for that?"

"Probably better off with Savlon." She said sourly, "Although," she added, "I hope your tetanus injections are up to date." Someone, probably Roland, cleared their throat behind us and at the same time I realised two things; firstly how childish and spiteful I sounded and secondly, however senseless this seemed, it was a situation in which I was embedded right up to my neck and to deal with it and get the hell out, I needed to get it sorted as much as I could.

"You should probably," she said, "Consider last night a warning." I nodded slowly,

"OK, consider me warned." She twisted a lip in a brief smile without warmth, as I continued,

"But, forgive me pointing out an obvious fact, nothing you've told me changes the current dire financial situation. Unless you start getting paying guests in and out, presumably you can't afford to keep this place on. Unless, of course, there's any way all your hokery-pokery can be used more constructively?"

"Not sure hokery-pokery's actually on the business course curriculum" muttered Bella. Etty glared at her and then, without breaking stride, back at me.

"What we know and what we do." She said, "Is of little immediate practical use in supporting a family, although it is of course fine for cheap stage tricks or making magic youth elixirs which don't last." I was impressed. With one swipe, on her way to squashing me, she'd comprehensively knocked Bella and Ophie over too.

"OK then," I said, "So, we're at a bit of a crossroads, aren't we. Either you throw in the towel, cut your losses, put this place on the market, see what you can get for it and move on. Or we give what I've got in mind a go, see if you can turn it into a going concern – at the same time," I added, "As convincing anyone it may concern, that the last thing you've got in mind is some kind of a – what did you call it – a 'gathering'? They have to be convinced there's no need for any action. I presume that thing that pitched up last night..."

"A *Malignum*. It was a *Malignum*" I turned in surprise to look at Mimi, she'd been so quiet I'd almost forgotten she was there.

"Which is?"

"Not good." She pursed her lips and shook her head firmly.

"Right, well I think I got that," I said, and my shoulder throbbed in agreement. "But whatever it was, wherever it came from, it didn't do too much damage, and probably did us a favour in the long run. "So," I looked around at each of them in turn, although I knew where the decision had to come from. "What's it to be. Do we throw in the towel or continue with plan A?"

"This is our home, and family stay together." Said Etty. In any other group, this pronouncement might have brought a tear to the eye and a group hug. As it was, there were merely a couple of nods. Etty stood, shaking off Roland's hand as he rose to help her and turning to me.

"Do what you think you need to do, I trust you," she said, although before I could get a lump in the throat, she continued, "Not to make too much of a pig's ear of it all." She moved briskly towards the door, just as it opened and a black knitted hat popped cheerfully round it.

"Oh goodie, goodie." Said Charley, "I know I'm not due until Monday, but I've just popped in on the off-chance, no rest for the wicked eh? Would now be a good time for a bit of a pow-wowy sort of a thingy with you Sandra, on how all this documentary thing is going to work?"

CHAPTER FORTY-ONE

"Hi Murray, look things have got a bit more complicated here." I said.

"Things have got bloody complicated here an' all. I'm telling you Sandy, my girl, Adam's right out of control and that Sasha, she's a conniving little so and so, for all she's so young. Let me tell you, she's been round the block more than a time or two, that one. She's got her eye on the main chance, no mistake. He's talking divorce." I swallowed, this wasn't good, this wasn't good at all, but I had more on my mind than just the domestic crisis and as always in a difficult situation, I needed to talk to Murray.

"That's terrible," I said. "I don't know what to tell you, other than I'm working on getting things sorted as fast as I can, so I can haul Ophie back where she needs to be, but listen Murray…"

"Well, you'd best get your skates on sharpish and pull a rabbit out the hat." Murray never met a metaphor he couldn't mix. "I'm telling you…" he said. I interrupted him sharply,

"Murray, for God's sake, can you just shut up a minute and listen to me." I was leaning on a wall in the corridor between the kitchen and reception, it was the one place nobody else seemed to be, but as I jerked in agitation, I knocked my sore shoulder – it hurt, far more than I thought it should, maybe it really was infected. I didn't really want to think about that, nor about what had bitten me. Murray heard the wobble in my voice and immediately switched into Mother hen mode,

"Sandy, what's the matter, you not well? What's been happening down there? Anything wrong?" I bit back a giggle, which had more of it's share of shrill than was healthy, where indeed to start?

"Murray," I said. "Do you believe in witches?"

A master of melodrama on his own account, Murray was nevertheless a paradigm of practicality and pragmatism when it came to problems I presented. Once I'd finally grabbed his attention, he listened carefully and without interruption to my probably rather garbled summary, and I could picture him, rubbing the toe of one shoe up and down the back of the opposite trouser leg as he concentrated. There was an uncharacteristic pause while he digested what I'd said, before he conceded there'd always been a touch of the odd about Ophelia, no denying it, he'd seen too many things he couldn't explain. And if that was the case, he pointed out, it stood to reason, now that this family had come to light, they were likely to be a bit blooming odd as well.

"But," he said thoughtfully, and I could hear him choosing his words carefully, "Whatever they want to call it, does it really matter? People always want explanations, to be able to stick things in one drawer or another, sometimes those are the right drawers with the right labels, other times they're not." I had to laugh at his unknowing echoing of Etty, "I hope," he said, "I've brought you up to not always believe the evidence of your eyes – we've both seen far too much stuff on stage to do that – but when there's no logical explanation, sometimes you just got to swallow that too. I reckon some of the things you've seen down there and that thing that hurt you last night, all come under that heading."

"But what about me, Murray?"

"What about you?" He said. I hesitated, then plunged.

"Do you think I'm one too?" He didn't bother pretending he didn't know what I was talking about, which was his usual way of dealing with unpleasant stuff. He was taking this dead seriously – I wasn't sure whether I was pleased or peeved by that.

"Listen to me." He said. "And listen good. Whatever this bunch want to call 'emselves, you said yourself it's all about knowledge passed down, right? Well, think about it Sandy, for Gawd's sake, your Ma wouldn't even *talk* to you about it – let alone pass anything down, so don't you go imagining all sorts."

"But, Murray," I protested, "I have to find out more don't I, especially if things look as if they're turning nasty," He humphed irritably.

"Listen, my thinking's you should get on with doing what you do best, bossing everyone around and getting things sorted with this blooming hotel thing they're trying to run. Don't go sticking that busy little nose of yours where it doesn't rightly belong, you hear me?" He was again unconsciously echoing Etty. I nodded, as if he could see me.

"OK." I said slowly, "Point taken." And I had taken his point, I just didn't altogether agree with it. As we said goodbye and I promised I'd call him back later, it seemed I'd been up for hours, but in fact it was only now coming up for 10.00 a.m. He was right in many ways though, however much I'd turned my back, all my life on what I didn't want to see, it had always been there, giving it a name shouldn't really make any difference one way or another. And nothing had really changed, well apart from something trying to take a chunk out of my shoulder, which was I felt the sort of happening probably best avoided, going forward. The practical problems however were still the same – Ophelia's late-developed conscience and her intractable determination to act on it, clearly wasn't going to let us go anywhere until things were running more smoothly, and nothing was going to run more smoothly unless I oiled the wheels. I felt a new list coming on, took my notebook and pen out of my pocket and began to jot.

"*Pssssssst.*" I jumped and whirled round, clapping my hand to my chest in the universal shock position. Gladys was right behind me in the corridor, looking if anything even more anxious and disarrayed than usual.

"*What*?" I snapped, she'd nearly finished me off and honestly who actually said Pssssst any more? She grabbed my arm, pulling me towards the kitchen.

"Gladys, what is it, for Pete's sake, use your words." I said in exasperation, automatically pulling back from her frantic grasp, but it appeared words had, for the moment, temporarily deserted our Glad. When I got into the kitchen I could see why.

Alfred and Elizabeth were close together in one corner, while on the other side of the room, near the back door was a chap standing in an unnaturally rigid position, his head bent forward at what must have been a most uncomfortable angle. Alfred and Elizabeth looked up as Gladys and I barreled in, the man didn't move.

"It's Cyril." Said Elizabeth grimly, with an inclination of her head.

"Cyril?" My mind was a blank.

"One of the men watching Bella," supplied Alfred "You know, from the pharmaceutical company."

"Well, what does he want?" I asked impatiently, then realised how silly that was and addressed him directly, "Uh, Cyril, hello there. What can we do for you?" There was another pause, as if my words were taking their time getting through to him. Then he suddenly moved a couple of faltering paces forward and looked up. I automatically took a step back at what I saw. Unfortunately, Gladys was standing a lot closer to me than I thought. I trod hard on her toe and she yelped.

He began to speak, his words oddly dragged out as he continued to move slowly forward. For a few seconds, I didn't listen to what he was saying, taken aback as I was by what had happened to his eyes. They had rolled upwards in his head, so what was staring at me were two sockets of ghastly blank whiteness. Then I began to make out the words he was intoning over and over, which didn't make me feel any better.

"Earth to earth, ashes to ashes, dust to dust." He was muttering. I'd backed as far into the corner as the wall and Gladys would allow, and was debating what might be a sensible next move when the back door opened, letting in the chill wind from outside and Bella. She paused in mid-bustle and took in the situation at a glance. She tutted, moved forward, grabbed Cyril by an arm, swung him briskly round to face her and clapped her hands once in front of his face.

"Stop it now," she said sharply. "Cyril, snap out of it." I could only see his back now, so had no idea what was happening eye-wise, although he was straightening up into a far more natural stance, looking around slowly as if he didn't know where he was.

"Where am I?" He said, proving how observant I was.

"Well, where do you think you are, you daft so and so?" Said Bella, shoving a kitchen chair behind his knees, so he had no choice but to sit.

"What happened to him?" I asked. "Some kind of a seizure?" Bella shook her head decisively.

"Befazed." She said. I looked at her, probably as blankly as Cyril and she shrugged. "You know – entranced, hypnotised. They used to call it bewitched, but we don't like that for obvious reasons. Haven't you ever?"

"Ever what?"

"Done it to anyone?" She said. I shook my head,

"Why would I?" I asked. Bella shrugged again,

"Well, it's just something we can do isn't it?" I moved over to another kitchen chair, the opposite side of the table from Cyril who was now looking more normal, if somewhat vague. On reflection, I suppose there might have been times, in intense conversation with someone that they had come over rather glazed, but I'd just assumed it was because I was being boring. I said as much and Bella laughed, puncturing the tension in the room.

"You probably were, but didn't Ophelia ever show you...?" I shook my head at the unfinished question and she tsked again,

"No I suppose she wouldn't have done." Alfred and Elizabeth had recovered their equilibrium remarkably swiftly. Elizabeth was getting on with some washing up, which I presumed was what she'd been doing when Cyril had made his unscheduled appearance and Alfred was making himself busy, I was glad to see, with the kettle and coffee. I felt I needed a little something round about now and even under this set of circumstances, it seemed a bit early to be hitting the wine. I looked around to make sure Gladys and her toe were all right, but she was just disappearing inside the walk-in larder.

"Look." Said Bella, "They're only out to frighten you."

"Well they're flipping well succeeding." I said. "And who are 'they' anyway? And did you hear what he was saying?" She nodded, frowning. I realised we were talking over Cyril as if he wasn't there, but he didn't appear to be paying much attention, so maybe it didn't matter.

"I presume they're the 'they' responsible for that thing last night." I said. I rubbed my shoulder and it throbbed back at me.

"Mmm," she said, "Have to admit, that's the first time I've ever seen anything like that – not nice was it? But sweetheart," she added slowly, "I honestly don't think it's anything to worry about, it's all bangs, flashes and trickery – bit like the stuff your parents do all the time, you should be used to it. It's just to put the wind up us." She nodded thanks to Alfred as he handed us mugs of coffee. He put another one in front of Cyril, who looked at it as if he had no idea what it was.

I was watching Bella closely. I didn't know her that well, but well enough to know that I didn't entirely believe what she was saying, and she didn't either. Underneath all the brisk and businesslike, she was acutely uneasy. Uneasy and baffled. She looked up, met my eye, took a couple of long gulps of coffee, an avoidance tactic if ever I saw one and got up to leave.

"Oh no, you don't." I said, reaching across and grabbing her wrist.

"Couple of questions." She sat again reluctantly, reaching with her left hand into the right side of her white tunic to find and restore a bra strap which had slipped.

"I don't know what you want to know." She said.

"Oddly enough, I don't really know either. But there's no doubt, things over the last couple of days have turned more than a bit unpleasant." We both looked at Cyril who was still gazing vacantly into the middle distance. "Will he be all right?" I asked.

"Yes," she waved her hand dismissively. "He'll be fine, he won't remember a thing about it."

"OK. First things first." I said, "I'm assuming Alfred and Elizabeth are um, like the family?" Bella chuckled and Elizabeth turned to glare at me, I was starting to realise that what she heard and what she didn't hear, depended more on inclination than anything else.

"Not bloody likely." She said. "Don't you go tarring me with that brush. I don't hold with any of this stuff, I'm a God-fearing woman me, and none of this has got anything to do with us. I just work here and turn a blind eye."

"And Gladys?" I said, "Is she…?" Bella laughed, "No, of course not, she's just common or garden bats, nothing beyond that." At that point, Gladys emerged from the larder, carrying a load of ingredients for goodness knows what. She saw me watching and smiled happily,

"Breakfast went really well, earlier." She said, "Jamie and I whipped up a smashing healthy buffet, just like that – bish, bash, bosh. Lovely it was."

"Right," said Bella taking advantage of the interruption. "Appointments; sorry, must dash." I put out my hand again,

"And Roland?" I asked. "Can he… ?" She looked at me as if it was a really stupid question.

"No, not really, he's a man isn't he, they've never really been any good at picking it up. Occasionally, you get one that does, but no, not Roland – think that's why he became such a practical joker, felt he was never getting his share of attention unless he made his own spotlight. Look I've really got to go." She'd been sitting the same side of the table as Cyril, and my attention had been on her rather than him, which was why I hadn't noticed that he'd picked up some viciously sharp scissors which had been lying on the table, next to a bunch of roses from the garden.

As Bella stood, so did he. Her hair, piled as usual atop her head, provided an instant hand-hold and wrapping his fingers into the dark mass, he pulled her swiftly backwards and in towards him, forcing her head sideways into an awkwardly cricked angle. The point of the scissors was digging into her neck, around about where I thought her carotid artery might be. The lethally sharp tip of the blades had already broken the skin and there was a thin trickle of blood running down. It found a home in the collar revere of her white tunic, where it spread in that alarming way blood does and I saw, with apprehension that Cyril's eyes had headed due north again. For a moment, I think we all froze, as if we were auditioning for Madame Tussauds, then Bella shifted slightly and started to try and say something, but the scissors dug a little deeper and she shut up.

CHAPTER FORTY-TWO

"Well, this is a little awkward, isn't it?" Said Ophelia, and I don't think I've ever been so glad to see anyone in my life.

She'd pushed through the swing doors of the kitchen and, as Bella had done earlier, I saw her take in every aspect and implication of what was happening, with instant understanding. She narrowed her eyes and raised an index finger. The scissors flew out of Cyril's hands, landing noisily on the tiled floor. She used her index finger again, sharply lowering it this time and he slumped down bonelessly, right next to them. Bella moved away swiftly, her hand over the bleeding nick in her neck.

"Glad to see you can still make yourself useful." She said, a little breathlessly to Ophelia who'd stepped daintily over the body on the floor and was now putting the kettle back on to boil. Ophie looked back over her shoulder at her cousin,

"You could have done it yourself?" She said.

"Scissors. Neck!" Exclaimed Bella.

"Hmmm. So," said Ophie, again stepping carefully over the unconscious body, but this time with a coffee in hand. She pulled out a chair, "What's going on then?" I rapidly emerged from temporary, fear-induced paralysis.

"You tell *me* Ma, you bloody tell me what's going on. You're the one who hauled me down to this madhouse. And now," I continued, gesturing fiercely at the still unmoving Cyril, "He's tried to murder Bella and I'm going to have to call the police and what's that going to look like, with the tv crew arriving?" Ophelia added sugar generously to her coffee, stirred and shook her head firmly.

"You can't phone the police."

"Of course I'm phoning the police, we've got an unconscious, homicidal maniac on the floor who could wake up at any time and do God knows what – how else would you suggest we handle it?" Ophelia sighed,

"He's just befazed." She said.

"I *know that*," I snapped back. "Bella's already said, but I've actually no idea exactly what that means, who's done it to him, why they've done it, nor what he's going to do next – he might just fetch an axe and chop us all up into little pieces."

"Look, it's probably my fault." Bella was holding a damp cloth that Elizabeth had given her, against her neck, and when she took it away the cut looked a lot less frightening. "I thought he'd played out, didn't realise there was more to come – careless of me." I looked from one to the other of them in frustration.

"Aren't you rather missing the point here Bella? He nearly slit your throat, and if what you say is right, someone or something primed him to do it. I don't think," I added sourly, "Careless really covers it. Anyway, what are we going to do with him? He can't stay there and we don't know what he might do when he comes round, and," I paused again because another, even more awkward thought had just occurred. "He will come round won't he? What exactly is it you've done to him, Ma, he's not dead is he?" Ophelia sighed again, she had a range of sighs she could call upon, and this was the one that reduced me to the status of a tiresome offspring.

"Well of course he's not dead, my sweet. What do you think I am?" I really couldn't think of anything polite to say to that, so kept quiet. "I simply wiped away whatever was done to him." She continued, "I assure you he won't remember a thing about it. "He's one of those chappies keeping an eye on you, isn't he?" She turned to Bella, who nodded.

"Then," said Ophelia, "Best just put him back outside where he came from?" Bella nodded again. They both briefly closed their eyes and Cyril suddenly wasn't there any more.

"Where is he?" I asked wearily. Bella inclined her head towards the window and I got up to look. Sure enough, our Cyril was in the process of scrambling back behind the bush where I'd first seen him. I turned away from the window and took out my notebook again. It felt like the lunatics had taken over the asylum and a well-constructed 'To Do Next' list might be the only thing, at this juncture, to keep me together.

The unpleasant Cyril incident, threw into sharp relief the fact that our current situation divided itself into two halves of a whole. One half was the purely practical issue of getting the hotel kick-started with a hefty dose of ghostly notoriety. I was confident that if we could get that particular ball rolling, it would run and run and once the initial publicity died down, we'd get a follow-up boost from the tv programme when it was shown. The other half was more problematic, not to mention increasingly hazardous.

It seemed though to be based on a simple misunderstanding, by person or persons unknown who apparently believed there was a sinister motive for the family convening. We needed to establish who it was who thought we were up to goodness-knows-what, make contact and explain they were laboring under a misapprehension. We needed to establish that far from this being a gathering of the clan for nefarious purposes (as if), our intentions were purely for commercial gain. Therefore none of the unpleasant and scarily violent stuff was the least bit relevant or necessary. Once we did this I felt, we'd have things back on track and certainly, breaking it down that way, made me feel it was a lot more manageable and in reality not too much of a problem at all.

CHAPTER FORTY-THREE

Not unnaturally, one of the things Charley was most keen on, was talking to all the family and staff – she was after candid trains of thought and reflections, off the cuff, as they were going about their business. Not unnaturally, one of the things I was keenest on was that this shouldn't happen unsupervised. I was aware that preventing it could prove a little tricky, but thought I had a solution. I caught up with her on Monday morning on the pretext of making sure they were happy with their rooms, that the late breakfast we'd laid on, had been to their satisfaction, and that Charley herself was as relaxed as it's possible for a stressed-out researcher to be.

"Look," I said, "Don't know if it will help at all, but I've made up a list for you of who's who, and where and when you're most likely to find them – thought it might save you some time." We were at the door of her room and I could see, glancing over her shoulder, that she was of the Ophelia school of unpacking, as all available surfaces were now obscured by clothes and toiletries.

"Wow!" She said, as I handed her the list, "You are a truly wonderful woman, I think I love you?" With enthusiasm, the rising tone at the end of each sentence was even more exaggerated than before. She leapt forward and hugged me enthusiastically. Released from the woolly hat, her hair was a mass of exuberant chestnut-red curls and until she let me out of the hug, I was swamped. Released and able to draw breath again, I smiled modestly, I did in fact feel the list was rather helpful.

I'd divided it into staff and family, given room locations where necessary and had added short explanatory notes, detailing who was related to who and how, and where there were minor eccentricities to watch out for – that had taken a little time and thought. I'd wanted to put down enough to keep Charley and Co. enthralled, but not so much as to alarm them unduly. I'd left Felicia off the list completely on the assumption that if she hadn't been downstairs in twenty years, she probably wasn't going to start now.

Charley had flopped down on the bed, shoving aside a pile of clothes to peruse the details, suddenly she jumped up again and shrieked. I jumped too, my nerves were a bit on edge I think.

"Ophelia?" She said. "Ophelia Adamovitch – *the* Ophelia Adamovitch?" I nodded.

"Oh. My. God! I think I'm going to pass out, here and now." She said, "I sometimes do that when I get over-excited you know." I took a cautious step forward and she put out a hand, "No, I promise I won't this time, I'm doing deep breathing, but I can't believe it, this is the most wonderful thing that's happened all year. Max will just adore me, she looked at me in awe, "She's actually your Mother, your *Mother*?" I conceded that indeed she was my Mother, but by this time Charley had continued down the list and found Bella, which produced several more shrieks, an excited little dance on the spot and some more deep breathing, after which she grabbed me and pulled me in for another hairy hug.

"Bella Belinfante? *Shut Up!* I don't believe it. It is, isn't it? Bella – Bella Donna?" I nodded again, extracting myself.

"Well, yes. Yes, it is, but you know there were a few small problems..." I paused delicately, "Nothing Bella was to blame for, you understand, but she's just taking some time out to work on more research, before releasing anything else on to the market, so maybe..." I stopped again, there were so many questions I'd rather weren't asked, I didn't know where to start.

"Okey dokelah," said Charley, "Gotcha, I can see what you're concerned about, but discretion's my middle name, not to worry." I smiled at her, completely un-reassured, I knew full well, when it came to impressing an audience of any kind, discretion was usually the first thing that flew out the window.

***

I'd made a duplicate of my list, and had tried to establish with Charley the sort of order in which she might like to meet people, and what kind of schedule they might have in mind when it came to the filming, but she'd done an emphatic curl-shake.

"Sorry, sorry, sorry. No can do. Max is, you know, a bit of a law unto himself. He's so, so, innovative he just kind of marches to his own drum –

it's like, he sometimes doesn't even know what he's going to be doing next, until he's doing it."

I personally felt that for a director, that was really no way to run the show but there you are, some people are anally organised, others not so much. I'd been introduced earlier to Maxwell Fearnstill, who looked far less arty, farty than I'd expected. He had wavy sandy hair, a rounded face with a softly receding chin and an oddly long, pointed nose – like a Mr Potato Man on which someone had stuck the wrong feature, but hadn't yet got around to remedying it. The nose seemed to bother him too, even during the brief time we were speaking, he kept pulling at it absentmindedly, as if astonished it went on for so long.

"Thing is," Charley continued, "Max, well, he absolutely *loathes,* I mean hates, hates, hates to be tied down in any way, won't have it – has to go as the mood takes him – makes for some amazing footage and lets him dig really, really deep. Although," she allowed a small frown, "That doesn't make life any easier for moi! Still, that's what it's all about, isn't it? But not to worry, I'm sure your family hasn't got too many dark secrets?" We both laughed heartily, although I was perhaps a little less hearty than her, realising I'd definitely have to do a continuous mad dash around, making sure everyone was as fully briefed as they could be, before they got in front of anybody's lens.

I had also (belts and braces) taken the precaution of running off a short crib sheet for everyone, with some underlined warnings as to what they were supposed to be saying and what was verboten, although my thoughtfully executed instructions had received a typically mixed reception.

I caught Henry in the kitchen, along with Elizabeth and Gladys. Turned out it was half-term so he wasn't in school, which I felt was an added and un-needed complication. I briefly explained to the three of them, the importance of everything going right when it came to the documentary, emphasising if this didn't come off as planned, they might have to be thinking of finding somewhere else to lay their heads in the not too distant future. Henry, passing me on his way to the fridge to grab a sandwich, made the mistake of grabbing a quick pinch of my bottom too. I rounded on him and gave his hand a good hard slap.

"That's exactly what I mean, keep your hands to yourself you little shit." I was livid. "Do that to anyone else and you'll find yourself with a sexual harassment charge slapped on you. I made an educated stab in the dark. "I bet Etty doesn't know about some of your revolting little habits, does she?" Henry paled. "Right," I said, "You just mind yourself and we won't say any more about it. But one more single step out of line and I'm going to take you by the ear and drag you to see Etty, and you can discuss it all with her. Do I make myself absolutely clear?"

Elizabeth meanwhile had been digesting the crib sheet I'd produced for her and Alfred,

"Nothing here that's not plain good common sense," she grumbled. "Not stupid are we, know which side our bread's buttered. Been with the Goodkinds more years than you've been on this earth young lady, never put a foot wrong in all that time, no cause to be doing that now." And she grabbed a pile of just-ironed table-cloths and stalked out. Gladys was shaking her head, mournfully.

"I'll try my best dear, you know I will, but I can't always be responsible for my actions, not if there's someone coming through."

"I know," I said soothingly, but you'll see I've made a suggestion or two, should that happen. She read on and nodded doubtfully,

"You think that would be all right?" She asked. My thought had been, should she feel any of her regular visitors about to put in an unscheduled appearance, she should immediately claim a crippling migraine, and go and lie down on the nearest flat surface with her eyes tight shut, totally incommunicado. This may have been a bit extreme, but was the best I could come up with at short notice. I also felt I'd covered a lot of bases by putting in brackets next to her name on Charley's list (excellent cook, but please note, highly eccentric!).

Leaving the kitchen, I went in search of Bella and Devorah, tracked both down in the annexe and was surprised to find Ophelia with them. I went through the same speech and handed out the crib sheets which were received in much the spirit I'd expected. Ophelia laughed, Devorah shifted baby Simona to an alternative hip, grinned and called me OCD, while Bella tutted did I think they were all complete morons.

Roland I wasn't so worried about, I wasn't sure whether he'd actually be around much while filming was going on, and I trusted him enough to think he'd know exactly what to say and not say. As he'd already proved, when it came to amateur dramatics, he could out-perform anybody and

I suspected he could carry off what I wanted, better than the rest put together. But it did occur to me that perhaps I should have tackled Mimi first, next to Gladys, she was probably the loosest cannon we had. And then of course there was Etty, I wasn't looking forward to that. I was on my way upstairs to find both, when the screaming started.

CHAPTER FORTY-FOUR

Funny isn't it, and I'm sure I've said this before, how we try to rationalise things, struggle to make them fit known parameters?

I must have remained frozen for a good minute or so on the stairs, trying to make sense of what I was hearing. Perhaps Gladys was having a bad recipe experience. Perhaps Elizabeth had found the agency hadn't done the cleaning as well as she wanted. Perhaps a treatment of Bella's – colonic irrigation sprang to mind – had gone terribly wrong; but somehow none of those eventualities, any one of which could have brought on a noisy reaction, seemed to fit the bill or the decibel level. I turned and belted back down. I had my list of dos and don'ts and screaming wasn't on it.

At the bottom of the stairs, I ran slap bang into my Mother, Bella and Devorah. For once it seemed we were all singing from the same song sheet, we paused only to exchange baffled looks then, in a body, made for the living room, which was where all the noise was coming from.

There were several people standing around, but only one of them was doing the screaming, which I suppose was something to be thankful for. Mimi (damn, they'd got to her before I did) was standing by one of the dark brown leather sofas, wringing her hands anxiously. Charley had her arms around Ffion Sykes, who was the screamer, Maxwell Fearnstill was looking horrified and massaging his nose anxiously, while Karl, the camera guy was busy filming what I could instantly see would make great tv. At first I couldn't spot what the problem could be and when I did, I could make no sense of it.

On the other side of the large room, opposite the door through which we'd just burst, were the two, beautifully proportioned, high arched windows, with sills deep enough to feature seating cushions. The windows were either side of double doors, leading into the gardens. On the outside of one of the closed doors, a black cat was swinging slowly back and forward. For the first few seconds, I thought it was Ink and could hear Ophelia's gasp behind me, but it wasn't, it was far too thin.

The unfortunate animal was upside down and there didn't seem to be much doubt that it was very dead indeed. As if to underline that, the body, moving with the wind – its tail was attached to a piece of rope – rotated slowly and hit the window again with a dull thwump. I was tempted to join Ffion and do a bit of screaming on my own account, but I had my hand clamped tight over my mouth and enough sense left to realise, doubling the noise would do no-one any good.

I looked across swiftly at Mimi, she caught the glance and its implicit question and shook her head in bafflement. Ophie, chalk white from the initial impression it was Ink, also shrugged imperceptibly as did both Bella and Devorah. Great, nobody knew what the hell was going on. By now Ffion, shrieking more softly had collapsed on to the nearest sofa, Charley still holding on to her. I remembered her saying her prime role, a lot of the time was taking care of the Talent. She was doing her best now, under trying circumstances.

"Right." I said briskly, relieved to find my voice was still working. "Well, I'm really very sorry about this," I forced a laugh. "Honestly," I said. "What is he like?" Everybody turned to look at me with varying degrees of bemusement. "Roland." I said, chuckling some more. "That man, he's never grown up has he, the only teenager I know who's hit his forties. Except sometimes, a joke can go just that bit too far, can't it and doesn't that ghastly thing look real?" Everyone turned their gaze back to the window. I hoped to God, no-one was planning to go out and check. Ophelia, bless her for once, caught on and pitched in,

"My brother," she said, adding her own light laugh, "I'm afraid it's a long-running thing, we've done it since we were kids, we'd all try to scare the pants off each other." She looked at Bella who nodded enthusiastically, "This time though," Ophelia went on, "The silly sod's gone a bit far, hasn't he?" Bella continued nodding agreement,

"It is blooming life-like." She said. "I nearly had a heart attack."

"You mean it's not real?" Maxwell had taken up a place, the other side of Ffion who although obviously distraught, still bore the slightly startled look of the recently botoxed as he patted her shoulder. I chuckled again,

"Well, of course it's not *real*, what kind of a joint do you think this is?" I looked at Bella and Ophie and they obligingly chuckled too.

"But," Max unobligingly put his finger firmly on the flaw in the argument, "It can't do your business any good, can it, if this sort of thing is going on, when you're just starting up – with guests and all." Karl had swung the lens around to me for my response and I resisted the urge to smack it and him away.

"Oh, trust me," I said firmly, "This is the last you'll see of Roland's sense of humour. I expect it slipped his mind we had you coming today. Look, why don't you take yourselves into the library, you can chat to Mimi in there and we'll get Elizabeth to bring some coffee, Devorah, would you mind organising that?" As they trooped out, Charley gave me a reproachful glare over the shoulder of the still sobbing Ffion and the sad little body hit the window hard again – as if it was knocking to come in.

The cat had no obvious injuries and apparently didn't belong to anyone at the house, goodness knows where it had come from, but one thing was for sure, its appearance wasn't designed to spread happiness and good cheer. The Talent certainly hadn't taken it well – I suppose we were lucky she hadn't departed forthwith and scuppered the whole ruddy deal. A tight-lipped Alfred, summoned from the garden where he was doing something useful with secateurs, had used a ladder to detach the cat from the rope and had then wrapped it gently in an old cloth. I had no idea how he was going to dispose of it and didn't ask, sometimes delegation seems the best bet.

CHAPTER FORTY-FIVE

"And they believed you?" Etty had been in her bedroom when I tracked her down, and apparently hadn't heard the screaming. I hadn't been in that room before, and dearly wanted to look around, but she'd fixed the green glint on me, as I recounted the sorry tale of the dead cat, so I couldn't take in my surroundings half as much as I'd have liked.

It was a much larger room than some of the others and surprisingly uncluttered, don't know what I'd been expecting, maybe a cauldron on the go and a selection of unidentified sinister objects hanging from the ceiling, I subdued a grin. She'd been sitting writing at an old-fashioned, roll-top desk when I knocked. There was a chair at the side of the desk and I flopped into it without being asked. The surge of adrenaline that had flooded my body with the cat fright, seemed to have beaten a retreat and I felt knocked out.

"Yes, they believed me." I said. "It was a truly daft story, but no crazier than somebody actually stringing up a dead cat, anyway it was the best I could do at short notice."

"Are you all right?" She asked, looking at me slumped in the chair. This was possibly the first time she'd spoken to me as if I was a person rather than a problem, and it took me aback.

"Bit shaken up. It was just..." I paused, my Mother's histrionics had pushed me to pragmatism all my life, "...a bit unpleasant." The solid, dull, thwump of the limp, black-furred body hitting the window came back to me and I swallowed hard before continuing. "And I don't suppose anyone's had time to tell you about our other little set-to, with one of those chaps who are watching Bella?"

Etty slowly screwed the cap onto the fountain pen she'd been using, but didn't put it down, holding it absently between her fingers and rolling it gently as I summarised the Cyril incident. The skin on the back of her hands was tissue-paper creped, roped with veins standing clear, but her fingers were still elegantly slim and as familiar to me as my own, because they echoed Ophelia's – I'd always admired my Mother's hands, especially as I'd inherited my Father's far stubbier digits.

"What do you plan to do?" She said, she'd reverted to her usual clipped tone.

"Do?"

"Well, action's got to be taken, things are escalating and you've brought this to our door, you must have a view." I sat up indignantly,

"Hang on one minute. Not me – Ophelia, she's the one who hauled me down here." Etty dismissed my Mother with a wave of her hand – something I'd often wished I could do so easily.

"Ophelia made her own decisions many years ago." Etty said. "She always wanted to pick and choose. She wanted none of the family obligations, only to use whatever suited her. She made her choices and she's lived with them very happily and successfully all this time. She's one of those people who are somewhat self-centred, and thus live life in a far more relaxed manner than the rest of us." I laughed, couldn't help myself,

"Tell me something I don't know." I muttered, before remembering this was no laughing matter.

"Look," I said. "I don't know how I can make myself much clearer on this. Until a few days ago, I didn't even know this family existed. When I did find out, I didn't want anything to do with you all, and now I know a whole lot more, I can see how right I was."

"But there *are* issues you can't avoid." She pointed out.

"My only issue." I retorted, "Is getting Ophelia back home to sort things out with my Father."

"But that's not strictly true, is it?"

"You think?"

"Indeed. You have a conscience, which is precisely why you couldn't leave well alone and leave right away, as you thought you wanted to. Because of that, you've muddied the waters and drawn us to the attention of quite the wrong people.

"Yes, I know that." I said impatiently. "You've already said, and they're behind all the dodgy stuff, right?" She inclined her head in silent assent. "But don't you think you might be making a bit of a mountain out of molehill?" I said, then I thought of the scissors at Bella's throat and the dead cat and regretted the molehill, I continued anyway, "Surely the solution couldn't be simpler. All we need do is let them know we're not up to any funny business, none of this ridiculous gathering or whatever it was you called it. All I want to do is get the hotel bringing in some money, and then get the hell out." She barked a laugh, but it wasn't of amusement.

"My dear," she said, and that wasn't an endearment either. "You have no idea what you're dealing with do you? What do you have in mind? A cosy chat over a cup of tea? Posting a letter? Sending an email? Making a phone call? Where and how exactly do you imagine you're going to get such a message across?" I stood abruptly, so I was looking down at her – it felt better.

"Well," I said briskly, "We'll just have to come up with something, won't we? But if you think that's going to involve getting me into the woods to dance starkers round a fire with the rest of the coven – you can bloody well, think again! I turned to leave the room and she laughed, this time with genuine amusement, a surprisingly warm sound.

"Honestly Sandra, I really don't know where you get your ideas – they're a tad antiquated, apart from which, they're really rather insulting." She leaned back in her chair, hands on its carved arms, her eyes briefly hooded. She raised a hand and gestured me back to the chair. I paused before I came back reluctantly.

She was silent for a moment, then,

"Through the years, there are those of us who have owned the knowledge and many more who, for one reason or another wanted to think they did. That's where your 'covens' came from, women who wanted, needed to believe they were something they weren't. And it was those women who sadly, but most usually, ran into the deepest and nastiest trouble. We, who know what we are, have always hidden in plain sight, Ophelia mastered that perfectly didn't she?" I nodded despite myself, because it was so patently true. She acknowledged my agreement,

"Think about it girl, hearsay and heresy, two words with only a couple of letters difference between them, yet what a dreadful and dangerous difference." She paused again, but I didn't move or say anything. I both did and didn't want to hear what she was saying – talk about a dilemma. She looked up at me then with full green intensity.

"Understand this. We're not a coven. We're a family, that's how it's always been, how it will always be. It's never about strangers coming together, how could it be? It's about blood, shared DNA, complete connection. And you can't run away from that. It's who you are, wherever you are. You may choose not to use it in any way, that's entirely your decision, but you can't deny where you came from."

"OK," I said slowly. "Supposing I accept what you say – and I'm not necessarily saying I do – what is it exactly these others, the ones who are giving us grief, are afraid of?" She tutted impatiently,

"Power, how can you not see that? We all have varying degrees of power on our own, but together we are stronger." I sighed, this was turning silly again.

"So what're we going to do? Take over the world, turn lots of people into toads?" She didn't move, but suddenly the chair on which I was sitting did. I completely lost my sense of balance as it heaved, bucked and surged beneath me.

"Toads?" She said, "Toads? This isn't Hans Christian Andersen, you stupid child. This is about the ability to control and manipulate both reality and perception. I told you before, there is a strong but delicate power balance that exists. Always has done, always will. Various families run a lot of things in this country, indeed worldwide, some of them manage things with good intent and succeed much of the time, others with not such good intent and they succeed much of the time too. I, we, have chosen not to be involved in any of that. Don't like it, don't want it. But that's not necessarily how it appears now." As she spoke, my chair was gradually regaining stability, I wished I could say the same of my stomach. I pulled my arms in, I'd flung them out to catch hold of the desk next to me, to try and prevent myself falling, now I folded them defensively over my chest. She raised an eyebrow at my discomfiture, then continued in an even tone, as if nothing in the least bit untoward had happened,

"We're manipulators, highly skilled manipulators, playing with people's minds, other times altering a small part of reality. You know this to be true, don't pretend you don't." And she was right. I was hearing all this ridiculous, unbelievable, impossible stuff yet somewhere, deep in my gut, I knew it to be irrefutably true. I was being dragged, kicking and screaming away from my ostrich philosophy. I felt very sick.

"Get your head down, between your knees." She leaned forward, put her hand on the back of my neck and forced it down. I knew my neck and the back of my head were drenched with sweat, but she didn't pull away. "Better?" She released her grip on me, although I stayed where I was for a minute, resting my forearms along my thighs and noting the shaking of both. I hoped the nausea would pass, I really didn't want to compound embarrassment by throwing up, over what looked like a very expensive rug. "Here." She handed me a glass of water. "You might want to think of what we can do," she said, "As being in possession of a knife. A sharpened blade can do miraculous things in the hands of a good surgeon, dreadful damage in the hands of the ill-intentioned." I reluctantly raised my head, it hadn't stopped spinning but I couldn't stay down there indefinitely.

"So," I said. "All these things going on now, how do we put a stop to them?"

"Any way we have to." She said.

"And if I want no involvement?" I asked, Etty shrugged.

"I really don't think, at this point you have a choice."

"Well, I don't agree. I'll do what I think best to do, and I'll do things my own way. Quite apart from which," I added, with some satisfaction, "I don't know anything, don't have anything to use – all my Mother's ever passed on down to me is a ton of aggravation." Etty was already turning back to her desk and her interrupted writing, but over her shoulder, as I rose to leave, she said quietly,

"Most of us are taught, but there are also those who act purely instinctively, without that instruction."

"And?"

"And you probably won't ever know which you are, unless or until you're in a situation where it's a straight choice, between your principles or your life."

As I left the room, I closed the door unnecessarily sharply, not exactly a slam but not far off – if there's one thing I can't bear it's someone who has to have the last word.

CHAPTER FORTY-SIX

"You feeling all right? You look dreadful." I'd huffed out of Etty's room and stomped downstairs with a lot going on in my head. Consequently, I'd descended into a reception area milling with people before I'd had a chance to rearrange my face into managerial mode, and the less than flattering assessment on my appearance had come from the tall, skinny solicitor. I couldn't for the moment recall his name, although I did remember he took milk and sugar in his tea and that I hadn't taken to him either the first or the second time we'd met, the third didn't seem to be going too well either. He was waiting at the foot of the stairs, with a briefcase anchored between his feet.

"What the hell's going on?" I muttered, more to myself than to him, but he obviously thought we were having a conversation, because he started to explain.

Apparently, he was here for an appointment with Etty, and Elizabeth was going to pop up and let her know he was here, as soon as she'd finished dealing with this lot. He inclined his head to where Elizabeth was manfully, and probably for the first time in the hotel's history, dealing with a queue at the reception desk.

A second glance helped resolve things a little more and I could separate the crowd into various groupings. Near the front doors, Bella was ushering what I presumed to be her latest victim/client, on their way to the annexe. In the middle of the reception area was the media contingent, with Charley apparently doubling as the make-up department and powder-dabbing Ffion's nose, which presumably hadn't fully recovered from being blown a lot in the aftermath of the feline fatality.

While this was going on, the attention of Max and Karl was on a third man and I could see he was being filmed, although with all the hub-bub, I couldn't imagine how they'd hear a word he was saying. His back was to me until Karl moved him into a slightly better angle for the light and I was disconcerted to see it was our local friendly hack – Jonathan Harper.

He caught my eye and raised his hand in a wave, before brushing back that unnecessary lock of floppy hair, I hoped he had the sense to keep well away from anyone with a pair of scissors and a proactive attitude. I had no idea why he'd turned up now nor, more uncomfortably, could I guess what his recall of the other night's little adventure might be.

The couple talking to Elizabeth at the desk, had a formidable pile of luggage by their side although I didn't think we had anyone else booking in, and they looked like they might be arriving for the long haul. Then Elizabeth looked up and from the acidity of her glare, I deduced it must be the people from The Psychic Society, come to set up, and that wasn't luggage it was equipment. I gulped and wondered, as had been happening more and more frequently recently, whether I'd thought this through sufficiently. It was one thing pulling the wool over the eyes of J. Harper, especially when he'd retreated as far from the action as he could when things got dicey, it was another matter altogether to subject anything I might put in place, to scientific scrutiny.

"Look, I don't want to be a nuisance," said Whatshisface, the solicitor from behind me, although he obviously wasn't much bothered whether he was or wasn't. "But as Elizabeth is tied up, perhaps you'd be kind enough to let Mrs Goodkind know I'm here, she's rather hot on timeliness." I sighed ungraciously, and had just turned and started up the stairs again, when there was a shrill cooee from the doorway. Another new arrival – God help us – who for some reason was waving enthusiastically at me.

"Therenithima, hellooo!" She yodelled. I shut my eyes for a second and shook my head slightly. Surely not. I was imagining things, must be the stress. There was a touch on my arm, that ruddy solicitor again,

"I think," he said, helpfully indicating with his head, "There's someone over there trying to catch your attention." Two familiar figures had now appeared behind Sasha. Murray, looking as disgruntled as I'd ever seen him and my Father, pausing as he always did for a few seconds, framed in the doorway, allowing himself to be seen recognised and acknowledged. Sure enough, Karl's camera swung that way as if magnetised.

"Serenissima," my Father had spotted me standing on the stairs, and the mellifluous tone which hit the back of any auditorium with ease, had no problem reaching across the reception area. He swept towards me, people automatically parting to let him through as he advanced, like Moses tackling the Red Sea.

"My darling, darling girl." He boomed, enfolding me in his arms, as if we hadn't seen each other for years, rather than just last week. "You've no possible idea how much I've missed you." And he swung me round slightly so he could get a better view of the audience reaction – they were rapt. They were even more rapt when Sasha joined the fray, putting her arms round both me and my Father in a kind of awkward group hug and beginning to cry.

"If you only knew," she declared, "How much I've always wanted a daughter of my own to love and now, deareth t Therenithima, I have you." I debated whether I should point out I was, in fact, several years older than her, and then I wondered if perhaps this wasn't really happening, maybe I was befuddled or befazed or whatever it was they called it, or maybe Etty was simply getting her own back because of my overt scepticism. And then, over the top of Sasha's blonde curls, currently buried in my bosom, I caught the jaundiced eye of Murray. He shook his head morosely. It was a small gesture that yet conveyed so much, and I knew this was no hallucination and the only thing that could possibly make it worse was if Ophelia were to pitch up.

"Adam." Said Ophelia from the top of the stairs. "What an unpleasant surprise!"

CHAPTER FORTY-SEVEN

I don't like to blow my own trumpet, but then again, if I don't, who will? And I must say, considering the rather complicated set of circumstances, some of which were directly my doing, others which weren't, I think I pulled myself together as well and as quickly as could have been expected.

Ophelia, after commanding the stage briefly from the upstairs landing and freezing everyone in their tracks, had swung decisively on her heel and headed off to her room, slamming the door behind her in a way that seemed to shake the whole building. The reverberation had the effect of setting the temporarily immobilised masses back in motion.

Karl, swift as you like, swooped the camera back down to focus on my Father. I could see Pa was more than a bit fraught, because he was forgetting to present his left side, which he always maintained was his best, to the lens. Director Max had begun striding back and forth busily in the background, muttering frenzied notes into his phone, while Charley, powder puff in one hand and Ffion in the other, was wide-eyed and hopping from left leg to right, with palpable excitement. I could quite see how this whole thing was turning out to be beyond her wildest expectations and, like her could see the Brownie points accumulating towards her future career. Sasha had now unhanded me and was clinging tightly, two handed, to my Father's arm. I took a step back, right onto the feet of Jonathan Harper who was far closer than he should have been, and who was also making use of his phone, taking shots of Pa and Sasha over my shoulder. That wasn't good.

Out of the corner of my eye, I saw the double swing doors from the kitchen corridor open and Gladys pop her head round. I had no idea what she wanted or indeed who she might be, but felt she was more than I could deal with right now. I shook my head fiercely, jerked it back in the direction of the kitchen and mouthed "Not now". Thankfully she withdrew, as Elizabeth looked across at me with a silent query. The couple in front of her were gathering their cases and I mouthed 'Library.' She nodded and started ushering them briskly down the hall.

I turned sharply, plucked the phone from the astonished grasp of J. Harper and whilst he was still protesting, moved forward and put my other hand firmly over Karl's lens, which had turned in my direction and was now so close, it felt he was filming up my nose.

"No." I said, far more authoritatively than I felt. "I expressly do *not* give my permission for this to be filmed or shown. Nor," I flung over my shoulder at Jonathan Harper, "Will I allow you to publish those pictures you've just taken. You're taking advantage of a private and personal situation."

"Actually," he pointed out. "That's what I do – journalist, remember? Anyway you can't just take my phone like that."

"I believe I just did, and unless you agree to co-operate," I gave them all the hard-eyed stare I'd picked up from Etty, not only will you be allowed no further access, but we will be suing for, for… ," I paused at a temporary loss.

"Invasion of privacy." Suggested the solicitor, who I'd quite forgotten was still there.

"Precisely," I said. "As our lawyer has just stated. Now, I suggest," I said to Charley and Max, "That we have a brief session, so we can definitively establish what I will and will not authorise for broadcast. I strode to the door of the main lounge and flung it open, casting an apprehensive glance at the window where thankfully, no more dead cats were hanging around. I chivvied the tv team briskly in, pointedly ignoring a fraught Ffion who was muttering she wouldn't, couldn't possibly go back in there. Hysteria, I've often found is best dealt with by being ignored.

"I'll join you shortly." I said firmly, shutting the door on them. "And you," I turned to Jonathan Harper, If I hand your phone back, I want to watch you delete those photos right now"

"I'm sorry but I absolutely refuse to do that." He said, tossing the hair back defiantly, then he noticeably flinched and clapped a hand to his jaw. "Ouch," he said and then, "Owww!" He'd turned a bit pale. "Bloody, tooth abscess." He muttered. "All sorted last week, but ow, it's started right up again." He really did look in pain and was hopping about a bit, the way you do when you want to take your mind off something giving you grief. "Give me that phone now." He demanded. "I've got to call the dentist, I'll have to have more antibiotics."

"Photos first." I said. "Or you're going nowhere." He stared at me appalled, as did everyone else, indeed I was a little shocked at myself. But if those pictures got out, Ophie would be so beyond livid, there'd be no chance of peace being declared any time soon.

"Sod it all." He swore, rocking back and forward a bit more and clasping his jaw, which appeared to be getting redder and visibly more swollen by the minute. He grimaced, grabbed the phone and standing next to me, so I could see, deleted the photos. "See, all gone. Satisfied?" He said sourly. I nodded and smiled graciously.

"Thank you so much. I appreciate that and I'm sure you understand. Family first." He seemed to belatedly remember that there was still a great story to be had here, and nodded reluctantly.

"OK," he conceded, "You got me, for the moment, but I still get first dibs on the ghost, right? He started backing away, then stumbled over Mimi, nearly knocking her off her feet, she'd appeared right behind him, although he hadn't noticed,

"Oops, God, I'm so sorry." He grabbed her arms to steady her,

"Entirely my fault." She straightened her cardigan which was, oddly enough, the right way round today. "You get along now young man, and I do hope that tooth gets sorted. So very painful these things aren't they?" I looked at her suspiciously, she didn't meet my eye.

"*Mark*?" Next to me, the solicitor heaved a small sigh and looked up.

"Mrs Goodkind." He said. Etty was descending the stairs, one hand on the bannister, the other grasping the cane.

"I was," she said, "Expecting you a little earlier."

"Not his fault," I interrupted, "He was actually here, bang on time but things got a bit… out of hand." She sniffed, as if this was no less than she'd expect from me and turned a hooded, eagle eye on my Father from her superior position on the stairs.

"You, I assume," she said, "Must be the magician." She imbued the word with a wonderful wealth of disdain. He stepped forward with an outstretched hand which she ignored, looking instead at me. "He can't stay here, you know. We haven't got rooms ready and Gladys is up to her eyes."

"No, no, of course, we wouldn't dream of imposing, made our own arrangements, all very last minute you know." Adam had switched on the charm which never failed to work, although it was obvious that here he was battling on stonier ground. "We're at The Westerly Manor. Just down the road." He couldn't resist adding, "2 Star Michelin chef I believe." I bit my tongue. Not, I thought, unless said Chef had returned the wife and the Dalmatian, still, that was of minor interest right now.

"Mark," said Etty, ignoring my Father. "We'll go into the library."

"No." I said.

"No?" She raised an eyebrow.

"There are people in there already." I thought it best not to elaborate.

"Very well," she turned towards the living room.

"Um, sorry people in there too." I said. She glared at me. "Dining room?"

"Cleaners." I said.

"In that case, perhaps we could find a small space for our meeting in one of the studies?" She looked at me and I nodded – I hadn't even realised there were studies. Etty led the way to one of two closed doors further down the hallway which I hadn't yet explored. The solicitor grabbed his case and followed smartly, throwing me a polite if distracted smile over his shoulder. I didn't bother returning it. It also belatedly occurred to me that I should really have introduced my Father to his Mother-in-law. I looked around for Mimi, but she'd gone again. Perhaps that was for the best.

"Blimey," said Murray, speaking up for the first time and rubbing his ear reflectively. "Weren't kidding were you, when you said it was a bit of a madhouse?"

CHAPTER FORTY-EIGHT

As always, Murray had summed up succinctly. In truth, by the time I'd hurriedly ushered the three of them out of the entrance hall and into the room next to the one Etty had just appropriated, I was rather losing the will to live. I was also aware the tv lot were waiting for me to draw the parameters I'd threatened, and was trying to mentally list exactly what those were.

The room we'd entered, was one of the two at the end of the hall, next to the swing doors and kitchen corridor. Wallpapered in dark flock, it obviously hadn't been used for some considerable time. The armchair my Father flopped into, released a cough-inducing cloud of dust and made Sasha and Murray a lot more cautious as they too, seated themselves on a nearby small sofa. I moved across to open a window to see if I could dissipate the smell of foxed paper from the piles of books stacked every which way on shelves, across the surface of a leather-topped desk and on assorted occasional tables. This was obviously also a dumping ground for items of furniture that didn't have a home elsewhere, and the place where mismatched and damaged table lamps came to die.

"Nice!" Commented my Father dryly, looking around.

"Don't give me nice." I said crossly. "What are you doing here Pa? Why didn't you at least let me know you were coming. And anyway how did you find out exactly where we were?"

"Murray called your office, we thought Sally would know." I glared at Murray and he ostentatiously looked the other way.

"We've come." Said Sasha, smiling brightly at my Father, "To make arrangemenths."

"Arrangements?" I said.

"And to talk about the divorth."

"Don't you think that's a matter to be discussed privately between my parents?" I said coldly. I was on a short fuse, but also aware it wasn't going to get anyone anywhere, if I lost my temper.

"Sandy's right, course she is." Said Murray, getting to his feet again. "Said you should've phoned ahead Adam, didn't I? Can't just arrive out the bleedin' blue. C'mon, drive you back to the hotel, then you can fix to meet up with Ophelia later, or tomorrow. On your own." He added pointedly. My Father nodded slowly and stood too. I heaved a small sigh of relief that just for once, he was seeing sense and not seeing red. Sasha pouted prettily, but could see she was outnumbered. I sent Murray a grateful grin.

"Right then," I said, opening the door, "I'll tell Ophelia, you'll call her, shall I?" And I led the way back down the hall and out through the double front doors. The attack, when it came was swift, violent and shocking in its unexpectedness.

***

They came from nowhere. One moment the circular gravel drive surrounding the miserable mermaid on the green was empty, except for Mimi who was trotting away from the house, muttering softly to herself. And then a solitary crow swooped down from a tree.

Slick and oily black, the afternoon sun on its feathers made it look wet. It circled slowly, catching our attention and then its wings folded backwards and it dropped like a stone, straight towards the slight figure making slightly uneven progress away from us. We heard the sound its beak made as it cracked into her head. I was already running towards her, Murray cursing, close behind me, when the other birds came. First just one or two from the trees and then suddenly, the air was full of them.

Mimi, astonishingly hadn't gone down with the first blow, she was still standing, but if she was screaming, I couldn't hear it over the grating caw and rattle of the birds. They'd completely surrounded her and impossible though it seemed, looked to be taking turns in drawing back in order to dive down again, rising higher and higher to increase the impact when they did.

I knew I was running fast, but didn't feel it was fast enough and then from somewhere at the side of us, I felt the rush of air as he passed. A huge, loping, silver gray shape, moving more swiftly than I ever could. He left the ground in a massive leap, soaring up and then down, knocking Mimi flat and standing over her, teeth bared, snapping, snarling using jaws and claws to lash out and tear viciously at the attackers. Yet still they came.

Straddling Mimi, and I couldn't even tell if she was conscious or not, Rostropovich was shaking his massive head back and forth, barking and growling, snapping and grabbing. But no sooner had he disposed of one bird than others were there, zooming in, razor-sharp beaks breaking through fur to skin. The silver of his back and sides was becoming increasingly bloody, his or theirs I couldn't tell, but he couldn't keep this up. Somebody had to do something. I looked around, but other than Murray, next to me and as horrified as I'd ever seen him, there was no-one else. Goodness only knows what I thought I could do and the last thing I needed was a lead role in a Hitchcock production, but I couldn't just stand there. I strode into the fray.

Woman and wolf were surrounded by a growing carpet of torn and bloody little corpses, but there seemed to be no decrease in the blackness swirling and darting above. As I moved forward, I'd automatically folded my arms over to protect my head, but oddly enough, the birds didn't seem to go for me, so I stopped being terrified and started being angry instead. I rarely really lose my cool, but now I could feel rage bubbling and building inside me. The single-minded savagery of what was happening wasn't any kind of natural event, and whilst I didn't know what I was doing, I knew fire had to be fought with fire.

I took my arms from my head, looked up into myriad black shiny, pitiless eyes and raised my right hand high, fingers spread wide and rigid as I'd seen Mimi and Etty do the other night. Of course, they'd known what they were doing, known what to say. I didn't. So, standing alongside Rostropovich and the fallen Mimi, I simply let the fury I was feeling, soar and speak for me. And it did.

The effect was amazingly immediate. The numerous birds lying on the ground around us were going nowhere, but the others, the flying mass, reacted instantly. They circled once, twice, three times more, packed so tight together I could clearly hear the dry, clicker-clatter of wing against wing. And then, as one, they wheeled away and disappeared up and away over the trees.

CHAPTER FORTY-NINE

For a few beats, there was complete silence, then Rostropovich raised his bloodied muzzle high and howled, a sound not of triumph but of grief I thought, and I was suddenly convinced that below him, lay a lifeless body.

I put both my arms around his massive neck – no I probably wasn't thinking straight – and tried to haul him off her. He resisted, I'm not sure he was convinced the danger was fully past and in fact neither was I, but I threw all my weight into pulling and he started to shift over reluctantly. Then suddenly there was help, another pair of arms, longer and stronger than mine.

"I see it's just another quiet day at the old homestead." Roland muttered grimly. I didn't answer, I think we were both scared stiff of what we were going to find. Together we managed to persuade the reluctant animal to one side to reveal the ridiculously small figure he'd been shielding. She was bleeding heavily from her head and for a few tense seconds didn't move, but then she hauled in a gasping breath and stretched out an arm to touch the huge head which had lowered to lick the side of her face.

"Goodness, but you weigh a ton." She said to him and then, "Roland, you're home early dear. Good day at the office?" Roland shook his head, let out the breath he'd been holding and briefly stroked the cheek that Rostropovich wasn't licking,

"Come on Ma, you daft old bat, let's get you up and in, see what the damage is."

Murray had moved forward and between them, he and Roland were half carrying Mimi back to the house, although she was noisily protesting that she was fine, really she was. Murray, still a whiter shade of pale, turned his head to look at me as I followed them and widened his eyes briefly in an expression asking far too many questions – most of which I didn't have answers for. I shrugged helplessly and absentmindedly patted Rostropovich who was trotting along next to me, Murray's eyed widened even further.

My Father, Sasha still clinging tightly, had retired to the haven of the hall and seemed undecided as to whether it was safe enough to venture out again. However, not surprisingly, Charley and Max were hastening towards us in a state of high excitement, and flipping Karl was making with the camera again. We really would have to have that little chat about what could and couldn't go into the documentary.

"O.M.G! O.M.G! O.M.G!" Charley had her hand to her chest which she was patting wildly, to indicate the double-time her heart was doing. "That was incredible, incroyable! You were so, so brave." I wasn't sure whether she was talking to me or the wolf so didn't say anything, just in case.

"What *was* that?" Said Max, walking backwards as we advanced, so he could talk to us. I saw he had his phone, recording in his hand. "Never seen anything like it. Was she feeding them? Was that it, was that why they swooped like that?"

"Seen seagulls do that." Supplied the normally taciturn Karl, also skillfully walking backwards so he could continue filming and I swallowed an impulse to knock the camera right out of his hand and give him a good slap. "Mind you," he added reflectively, "Not so many at the same time. Got some great shots of them going for her." He said, turning with satisfaction to Max, who cast a cautious look at my glowering frown and shook his head slightly at Karl.

"Later, eh?" He said, then to Mimi, "Could we just have a quick, heat-of-the-moment quote?"

"I think not." Said Roland firmly then, turning to Murray, "I'm sorry, who are you exactly?" And I realised, in all the excitement, I'd forgotten my manners.

"Murray." I said. "This is Roland, he's my Uncle and Mimi here is my Grandmother." Murray nodded as if it all made perfect sense, although I could see he was as stunned as I'd originally been at this sudden influx of near and dear.

"And Roland; Murray is..." I paused, how to describe him – the nearest thing I'd had to family before you lot turned up. My Father swept forward just then, interrupting me, he'd been out of the limelight too long.

"You were beyond magnificent, my darling." He said to me, "I have no idea how you managed to scare them off like that, you were amazingly brave and then to Roland, "Adam Adamovitch." The two nodded at each other and I was glad I couldn't see what either was thinking.

Etty had also come to the front doors, accompanied by the solicitor. She stopped Roland and Murray as they reached the steps, and gently angled Mimi's face up to look at the head wound.

"A & E d'you think?" She asked.

"No," said Murray, with years of experience of slipped saws, hammered thumbs and people falling off high things. "Don't think so, looks pretty surface to me, don't think it needs stitches, heads always bleed a lot don't they? Probably a nip of brandy couldn't hurt mind, for shock." Etty and Roland both nodded agreement.

"Ophelia." Etty turned to my Mother who'd appeared behind her, "Take her into the kitchen, it's warmer in there and Elizabeth's got a first aid kit." My Mother looked horrified.

"I really don't think... , " she murmured, Etty interrupted,

"I didn't ask you to think," she snapped, I asked you to see to your Mother." Having dealt with that, she looked at me as I followed them up the uneven stone steps and pursed her lips.

"Do you want to talk?"

"No. Thank you," I said primly. I wasn't, at that point in time, sure of a great deal, but on a couple of things I was rock solid, not only did I not want to talk – I didn't even want to think!

***

"What in the name of sweet frigging Fanny Adams, have you gone and got yourself into Sandy?" As the rest of them trailed inside, Murray grabbed me by the elbow and held me firmly back. He'd regained a little of his normal ruddy colour but he was pretty shaken, he'd been a lot nearer than anyone else and had therefore had a front row seat for Mimi and the Birds.

As often happens, an adrenaline-fueled incident, led to a bit of an anti-climax. Roland and Ophelia had taken Mimi, Rostropovich close at their heels, to the kitchen and the ministrations of Elizabeth although I hoped, not Gladys. The tv team had beaten tracks upstairs to look at 'what they had' and to get Ffion to 'put some things down'. I wasn't sure precisely what all that added up to, but decided I'd tackle censorship issues tomorrow.

Etty said acerbically that if I could manage to keep an eye on things for just a short while, without further chaos ensuing, she was resuming her meeting and stalked off, followed by the Heywood chap, both pointedly ignoring odd noises coming from the library, which I could only assume was the Psychic Society 'setting up'.

My Father, Sasha remaining attached limpet-like, said they'd probably better revert to plan and push off now and he'd come over to talk to Ophelia tomorrow. They took off for the car at a faster pace than normal, and not without a lot of apprehensive upward glances at the surrounding trees and sky.

"Well? I'm waiting." Hissed Murray, still holding my arm and shaking it hard in his agitation. "What in hell's name is going on here and what were you playing at back there, who do you think you are, flaming Harry Potter?" I removed myself gently, pushing my hair back and away from my eyes with my hands. I saw they were liberally blood spattered, whether it was Mimi's or the wolf's I had no idea. Murray followed my glance and grimaced. "You need to go and get cleaned up, are you hurt anywhere, did the little buggers get you?"

"Don't think so, don't think they touched me."

"No," he said slowly, "They didn't, did they? So, what was all that... that business with the hand?"

"You know what Murray," I said, "You wouldn't believe me if I told you. In fact, I don't believe it either. So no, I don't know what I've got myself into, other than a right royal mess."

"Can see that much. Blimey O'Reilly, what a cockamamie set up!" He said. I sighed, he didn't know the half of it.

"Murray, hey *Murray*, what are you faffing about up there for?" My Father was leaning out impatiently from the passenger seat of the Jag. "Get your arse over here and get us back, I need a drink." Murray looked at me,

"Look, I'll be driving him and," he added with ire, "Her too I expect, over again tomorrow, we'll grab a bit of time then, you and me, and talk properly. Right? Or," he paused, "Do you want to come back with us now?" I shook my head,

"Can't leave now, you know me, job half done and all that." He nodded reluctantly,

"I do know you," he grumbled. "And didn't expect anything different.

But listen, I was worried sick about you before we got down here and now," he turned his mouth down. "I'm worried sicker!" I gave him a long hug, thinking not for the first time, what would I do without him. He held me for a minute then humphed himself free.

"Come *on* Murray." Bellowed my Father, who I noted without surprise, didn't appear to be worried about me in the slightest. "Or I'll bloody well drive myself."

"Right, and then we'll really be up shit creek." Murray grunted and with a last squeeze of my arm, he turned and hurried over to the car. My Father's driving was notable – and not in a good way.

CHAPTER FIFTY

"Of course, we mustn't forget about poor Polly, must we?" Stated Charley firmly, the following morning. I looked at her blankly. "Polly Malone, the girl who, you know…" she held her fist above her cocked-to-one-side head, crossed her eyes and stuck her tongue out, too graphic by half, especially so soon after my hurried breakfast. Gladys had insisted on making me eggs again and they were still uneasily lurking, somewhere just south of my ribs.

"Goodness, no, not for one moment." I agreed, although poor old Polly had rather slipped my mind, what with everything else going on. I guiltily recalled the ghost recording equipment in the library – 'very unobtrusive', I'd been earnestly assured by Harold Hugheson. Morwenna had nodded enthusiastically – she didn't seem to be one for talking, but was an enthusiastic nodder. They hadn't finished the setting up until about 10.00 yesterday evening and said they'd give it a couple of days before a return visit, to see if anything had been set off. I definitely needed to organise a little something, to justify their time and trouble and make sure our haunted reputation was enhanced. I really mustn't allow myself to be distracted from the main aims for the hotel's forward progress.

Last night had, after the varied ups and downs of the day, been a quieter affair, and as far as I knew, everyone had slept, other than me. I'd been so exasperated after a brief conversation with Ophelia, that even after both she and Ink were snoring in harmony, I'd tossed and turned for hours, having an animated if silent discussion with myself on the complete perverseness of my Mother; a level of unreasonableness rivalled only, as I knew from past experience, by my Father's.

"Ma," I'd said, broaching the subject cautiously. "You're going to have to talk to him you know, now he's come down here."

"Only if I choose to." She said, creaming off her make-up and surveying her face critically in the dubious light of a table lamp she'd moved on to the dressing table. "And then only if he doesn't have that little cow hanging off his arm." I could see her point.

"Well, of course not." I said, "That's fair enough, but maybe you should hear his side of the story." She snorted,

"His side? *His* side? He hasn't got a side."

"But think of all the years you're throwing away, so much time, all those shared experiences. Not to mention your career." I said. She gave a half snort half laugh,

"My darling, he's throwing away far, far more than I am. And, if he's deluded enough to think the act can go on without me, he's more of a fool than I thought." She suddenly changed the subject,

"Has Etty spoken to you?"

"About?"

"You know damn well, don't be obtuse."

"She has."

"And... ?"

"And what?" I said. Ophelia shrugged.

"You probably think I should have told you more, over the years." She said. "But to be honest, sweetie, you never really seemed to want to know anything very much, so what would have been the point?" She wasn't wrong, I'd known what I'd known and hadn't wanted to know any more. "Anyway," she went on, "I left here so as not to have anything to do with it all."

"But you didn't," I said. "Not have anything to do with it – you used it, as and when you wanted." She looked at me as if I was crazy,

"Well of course I did, why wouldn't I?" I gave up and brought the conversation back to where it had been originally,

"Look, you and Pa have to be reasonable, there's too much at stake to make decisions in a temper." She tightened her lips and turned away and I could see, to my intense frustration, I probably wasn't going to get anything else out of her, nobody tightened their lips quite as finally as my Mother.

***

Charley snapped me back to the present by unexpectedly grabbing my wrist, I yelped and nearly jumped out of my skin, I was obviously more on edge than I thought. We were sitting on one of the uncomfortably slippery, leather sofas while we waited for Max to finish a 'terribly, terribly important' phone call which he'd taken out into the hall. He and I had already had a frank and at times, slightly heated exchange about what I would and wouldn't agree to going in the documentary. I just needed to make sure he and Charley had that completely straight and there was no room for misunderstanding, misunderstandings being in my experience, the root of most problems.

"I've just thought," she said breathlessly, "Those dreadful birds, yesterday, they couldn't have had anything to do with her – Polly, I mean – could they?" I shook my head,

"Course not, just one of those freaks of nature things that happen – you know, like it raining fish. Or Sahara sand." I added vaguely. I was keen on giving the hotel a high profile, but felt random wild-life attacks weren't quite what we were aiming for.

"Still," she said. "Dead scary and really, really weird, wasn't it?"

"Weird indeed." I agreed. I realised I was having a bit of a problem keeping track of things I thought I'd arranged and differentiating them from those I hadn't. I definitely needed more than ever, to get my house in order.

"And the *wolf.*" Charley wasn't to be deterred, her voice rising more than ever at the end of every sentence. "Just how cool was that – wow, I mean seriously wow, we got some wonderful shots of the whole thing, start to finish, didn't we Max?" Max who'd just come back in, nodded reluctantly, I could clearly see he wished Charley would put a sock in it. He met my querying eyebrow with an exaggerated sigh and shrug,

"No, Sandra, please don't look at me like that, we've already agreed you can see an edit." But he couldn't resist a snide addendum as he sat down to go through some stuff with Charley. "Although this is a documentary you know, and that's what we're doing – documenting."

CHAPTER FIFTY-ONE

"We're worried, Mimi's acting oddly." Said Bella, cornering me as I came out into the hall. I was planning who or what I was going to tackle next, but couldn't help commenting,

"How can you tell?"

"That head wound's still looking pretty nasty," Bella hadn't smiled back. "She must have been rammed pretty hard. We're worried she might have a concussion or worse. I think she should get checked out, but Roland's in court today and left early. Could you take her? Nearest A&E's about twenty minutes away." I sighed, contemplating a day spent hanging around in a noisy, blue-curtained cubicle, while my task list burnt a hole in my pocket. Additionally, I didn't know what time my Father was planning on putting in an appearance, and I did feel I needed to be around for whatever fireworks might ensue; my parents in full flow were not for the faint hearted.

"Well?" Bella had been rushing and was breathing heavily, I hoped the buttons on the tight white tunic weren't going to give up the ghost. I could see though that she was indeed worried.

"OK." I said ungraciously, "If there's no-one else who can do it."

"Thank you sweetie, honestly I'd come with you if I could, but I've two clients booked in, one after the other, and it's too late to phone and cancel. Maybe Ophelia?" We both thought about that for a second then dismissed it. Ophelia would be less use than a sick headache in a thunderstorm.

"Where is Mimi now?" I asked, extracting my car keys from the reception desk drawer where I'd left them.

"Upstairs, if you just bring your car up to the door, I'll get Devorah to bring her down."

"Will do," I said, "Oh, and ask Devorah to pop into my room and grab my handbag, so I've got some cash on me – it's on the bed." Bella was already on her way up, raising a hand in acknowledgment as she went.

It was par for the course, that my car wouldn't start. I cursed and kept re-turning the key, the way you do even when the thing's so obviously deader than a dodo. I cursed some more, it had been fine when we drove down. I gave it a hard slap on the roof as I slammed the door. I knew that wouldn't do any good either, but I was fed up.

I could see Devorah had brought Mimi down and they were waiting at the top of the steps – she didn't look so hot even from that distance, pale faced and I could see how heavily she was leaning on Devorah's arm. Mind you, had I known what she was going to look like, a little while into our journey I'd have been a darn sight more unsettled. I was trotting back to the house to meet them, thinking we'd have to get a cab there and back, when another car crunched the gravel behind me.

"Problem?" It was everybody's favourite solicitor, in a black SUV, honestly the man was always under foot, didn't he have a Practice to be running? However, the SUV had the advantage over my car, in that it had an engine that was working. I summarised the situation for him, I guessed Etty might not be his biggest client, but she was probably the scariest and I suspected he therefore might want to stay on her good side. I wasn't wrong.

"I'll take you." He said obligingly.

"Might be a long wait, once we're there." I belatedly felt a bit guilty.

"Have laptop, can travel." He patted the computer bag next to him on the seat, Smug or what? But I thought, beggars and choosers etc and thanked him nicely. We got Mimi, wearing a warm, red knitted cape, into the back of the car and Devorah hopped in after her with a nod at Mark.

"Brrr." She shivered, "Brass monkeys, isn't it? Cold enough for snow."

"Didn't realise you were coming. What about the baby?" I asked.

"With Elizabeth," she replied. "She was so like, worried about Mimi, she didn't even grumble when I asked her." Mimi's forehead had blossomed sickly blue and green around the original cut and every now and then she put a hand to her head, as if surprised by all the discomfort, but she wasn't keen on going to the hospital.

"This is ridiculous girls, big fuss about nothing at all, I'm quite all right." But she so patently wasn't that I found I was beginning to catch some of Bella's panic. I took a calming breath or two – everything would be fine, we'd get her to the hospital, get her checked out and given the all clear. Then I'd get back; umpire the parents; get the hotel plans back on track and sort out the journalist, the tv people and the Psychic Society respectively – it was all perfectly doable.

"You do know where you're going?" I turned to Mark as I got in.

"Lived here all my life." He said. He'd circled the mournful mermaid, in a business-like fashion, headed out the main gates and we were now on the sort of narrow winding road that makes you clench your buttocks in a vain attempt to make the vehicle thinner, but he was a steady driver and obviously knew what he was doing. "By going this way," he said, "We cut out most of the traffic. Slightly longer mileage, but shorter timewise."

Through canopied trees above us, the low, late November sun was strong and strobed and was making my eyes ache. I shut them briefly. When I opened them again, there was a child, six or seven, a dark-haired small boy, running right across the road in front of us. As we bore down on him, he turned towards us and stumbled. Mark didn't slow down one iota, he was deliberately steering straight at him.

I screamed, long and loud, jerking over at the waist to grab the wheel and wrench it with all my strength to one side. The vehicle swerved violently, smashed all the way through a thick hedge, lurched into a deep ditch beyond, mounted the ditch's far side and then shot rollingly back down again. It came to a teeth-jarring stop at a forty-five degree angle. My head whacked viciously back against the head rest and I saw flashing lights.

"What the *hell* do you think you're doing?" Mark had shoved me away hard and still had a hand on my shoulder, holding me as far from him and the wheel as possible. "You nearly got us all killed, are you bloody crazy?"

"A child, boy, he was there – right in front of us." I pointed, my hand shaking alarmingly. I used my other hand to steady it at the wrist then whipped round to the others for confirmation, "You saw him too? You did, didn't you?"

Neither Devorah nor Mimi answered, they were looking at me, but they weren't seeing or saying anything. Devorah still had her arm around Mimi and they were still seat-belted into place, but where their faces should have been were two pale ivory, rotting skulls. I screamed again – and honestly that wasn't like me, Ophie usually did the screaming, I did the calming. But these were unusual times.

CHAPTER FIFTY-TWO

Events seemed to have slipped into slow motion, so I was hyper-aware of every detail; Mark's baffled, furious face close to mine, mouthing words I couldn't hear; the ghastliness in the back seat; my whiplashed neck which now felt barely able to hold my head. It seemed that screaming and keeping on screaming, might well be a reasonable option under the circumstances, but I could see it wouldn't be helpful, so I was almost glad when he grabbed me with both hands on my shoulders, and shook me hard. My teeth clamped together and I didn't move my tongue out of the way fast enough, so tasted blood.

"Stop that." He said, "Shut up, shut up!" he was trembling with shock or anger, probably both. He was as white as a sheet or indeed as white as what was in the back of the car.

"Look." I hissed urgently. "*Look* at them." He turned and said something, then turned back to me frowning. "They're OK, they were strapped in, they're not hurt, but they bloody well could have been. What are you playing at?"

"The boy," I said, "We nearly hit him, you were heading straight for him, he wouldn't have had a chance, I had to make you stop. We have to get out and make sure he's all right." He shook his head,

"There wasn't anyone there," he said wearily, "You imagined it." He didn't add, 'You daft cow.' But I could clearly see him thinking it. He sat back in his seat, ran his hands through what he had left of his hair and loosened his tie. "I have to see if we can get ourselves out of this, otherwise we'll have to call for help." He re-started the engine then paused. "Look, you'd better get in the back and hold on to Mimi, this could be bumpy."

"In the back?" I licked dry lips, "No, I'll stay here, or I'll get out and push, that would help wouldn't it?"

"Yeah, sure, tell you what, why don't we put a tow rope round you and you can just pull us out. Don't be so damn stupid." He snapped, "For Christ's sake, can't you just do what you're told for once." I got out, didn't have any choice, opened the back door and climbed in on the other side of Mimi and – oh thank God – the two faces that turned to me were pale and shocked, but they were faces. I let go a breath I didn't know I'd been holding and Mimi reached for my hand.

"Not your fault, dear." She said. "Whatever you saw, you saw." I gaped at her and shook my head, big mistake because my neck hurt so much. She glanced at Mark, but he was fully occupied trying to reverse along our tracks, and she continued more softly. "They're doing this because they want to frighten you."

"Right. Job well done then," I snorted. "I'm flipping terrified."

"They want you gone," she continued. "You'll be fine, so long as you're not here, with us."

"Well they're thinking along exactly the same lines as me then." I said. And then I stopped. Her warm, thin hand was holding mine, surprisingly firmly. I looked at her and at Devorah. What is it they say – you can choose your friends, but you're stuck with family? Well, this was my family, like it or not, crazy as they were, and whatever was happening, was hitting and hurting them as much as me. After all, we'd just ended up in a ditch and, as my no-longer so friendly legal friend had pointed out, could easily have been killed. I certainly did want out of there, but I don't take kindly to bullying. I'd set myself a task to do and I intended to see it through and I'd make my own decisions as to when and how I left.

I grasped the hand in mine harder, not sure whether for her comfort or mine and we all ignored the range of surprisingly colourful curses drifting back from the front seat. After a couple of false starts and with some stomach-churning rocking, dipping and sliding as the wheels caught then slipped, he managed to reverse us up the slope and through the great ragged hole torn in the hedge, although not without incurring some viciously deep-sounding scratches on previously immaculate paintwork.

"The problem is, you see," said Mimi breathlessly, hanging on grimly to Devorah's arm with the hand not occupied by mine. "They think you're something you're not. They think you've been brought up in the traditions, they have no idea you've no idea! They think you're a greater threat than you are and yet," she paused thoughtfully, "They don't know how great a threat you could be – and quite frankly my dear, neither do you." I huffed in exasperation.

"For crying out loud Mimi, do we really have time for riddles, I mean *really*? Can't you say something that's just a little more constructive?" My patience was running out, my neck-ache running riot. Mimi shut her eyes and Devorah and I exchanged looks. Had she dropped off? Had she passed out? Was this the concussion, or was she just thinking? We waited anxiously and after a minute she opened them again.

"There is no time to teach you all you should have been brought up knowing, it's far too late and there's far too much, but it would seem you're an Instinctive, Etty knew of course, soon as she saw you."

"An Instinctive?" Maybe this was the concussion talking after all. I glanced at Devorah again, she shrugged and started to say something, Mimi shushed her with a look at our thoroughly cheesed off driver, who was currently tramping round the outside, blowing exasperated breaths into the frigid air and picking bits of hedge out of windscreen wipers, back and front so he could see where he was going, not to mention where he'd been.

"I don't know how much more plainly I can put it?" Mimi's voice was low but urgent. "For whatever reason, you're one of those oddities who has the ability without the knowledge. You're a risk, to yourself and others, you have to be careful."

"Look," I said. "I've no idea…"

"Rubbish." She said sharply, "You have; you just won't admit it because you're pig-headed, like your Mother, she's always shut her eyes to anything she didn't want to see too. You dealt with those birds because you felt you had to, there was no-one else to do it. You may not know how you did, but you did." I sighed and slipped my hand out of hers. I didn't want to hear any more. In my mind, I'd ring-fenced the birds, I didn't want to think about them. I'd scared them off, it was as simple as that, no mumbo-jumbo involved, goodness knows, a scarecrow could have done as good a job.

"I've already told you." I said, "I'll do what I can to help sort things out with the hotel, and if I have to get some of you to contribute some crazy daisy stuff, well so be it. But I don't choose to be any more involved than that. How hard is it to get you to understand?

"Hmm." Mimi suddenly had a touch of Etty's iciness and for the first time I saw the likeness. "I'm afraid it's you who doesn't understand, dear girl. You talk about choice. What makes you think you have any?"

CHAPTER FIFTY-THREE

Nobody expects their trip to A&E to be a bundle of laughs, and having a near fatal incident on the way, hadn't enhanced ours a whole lot. At the hospital entrance, I'd tried to insist to Mark Heywood that we'd be fine on our own and could easily get a taxi back, but he obviously felt having taken on a task, however onerous, it should be seen through to its conclusion. I wasn't particularly appreciative, muttering something along the lines of him not blaming me if we had to sit there all day. He ignored me, and in retrospect I hoped he hadn't heard, because they weren't very busy and Mimi was called in after only twenty minutes waiting. Devorah went in with her, leaving us to cool our heels in purse-lipped silence.

Mimi was duly checked over thoroughly and other than the nasty head cut, to which they applied a special type of glue and a small dressing, they pronounced her in full working order. The nurse who came out with her, said we could take her home, but she had to take it easy for the next few days and we should keep an eye on her, she wasn't a young woman and such nasty experiences, didn't go into your boots!

***

When we got back to Home Hill, things hadn't stood still, in fact it was rather a dysfunctional hive of activity, with raised voices coming from any number of directions. It took me a while to establish what was going on and who was doing what to whom. My first stop was the kitchen where, as I opened the door I narrowly avoided being hit in the chest with a large onion, hurled at speed by an irate Gladys. I bent to retrieve it from the floor and Elizabeth nipped past me, with an armful of linen.

"Off to turn out the rooms," she said, "Not risking all sorts down here."

"*Shallots*, I told them, *shallots*." Yelled Gladys, "What sort of effing greengrocer can't tell a shallot from a pigging onion?"

"Gordon Ramsay, unless I'm very much mistaken," muttered Elizabeth, making an identification and a hasty exit, seconds in advance of another hurled onion. I sighed and put both onions on the table.

"Everything OK Gladys?" I enquired cautiously. She glared at me,

"That's an effing stupid question, isn't it?" She snarled. "Does it look as if everything's OK? Well does it? Why don't you get on out of here and leave me to get something done? You'll be expecting dinner tonight and who d'you think is going to cook for the whole bloody lot of you? And how much help have I got? Sod all, that's what." I sighed and followed Elizabeth's example, heading out of the kitchen to see if I could track down the next set of shouty people.

These turned out to be Adam and Ophie who were going at it, hammer and tongs in the study we'd occupied before. I opened the door cautiously, wary of any other flying objects. They were facing off across the desk and exchanging recriminations briskly. My Father, it appeared had raised the issue of the bronze horse she'd hit him over the head with, whilst she was querying the state of his mental health when it came to believing that a girl, younger than his own daughter, was after his body and not his wallet.

"Hey." I said. Neither took any notice but I could clearly see, what my Father apparently couldn't. Whilst he was fully involved in the argument, bellowing and doing a fair bit of desk thumping because he was on the defensive, her pain was palpable. She was putting on a show, giving as good as she got and normally she enjoyed a good row as much, if not more than he did, but this time her heart wasn't in it – or maybe that was the problem, it was.

She looked tired and her under-shadowed eyes – she must have forgotten the Touche Éclat – were bright with unshed tears. This was worrying, because tears were invariably the sure way to bring him to his knees and as far as Ophelia was concerned, a useful ploy was never to be sneezed at. But I realised, that was when she knew exactly where she was with him, when there was never any doubt as to the outcome of the argument, nor the passion of the resolution. I felt slightly sick, maybe this really was the end of the road, a new reality I might have to accept. I didn't know what to say, so I backed out and shut the door quietly behind me.

I assumed that where Adam was, Murray wouldn't be far away and I found him and Sasha sitting opposite each other in the main living room, which for once had a reasonably cheerful fire going and lamps on, to combat the outside gloom. Murray, who'd had years of watching Adam and Ophelia knock chunks off each other, was taking the ructions next door in his stride, Sasha not so much. She was sobbing quietly to herself. I wasn't sure whether this was guilt due to her own role, or concern that things might not be going the way she wanted. She obviously wasn't getting any sympathy from Murray and when I came in, she leapt up and launched herself at me with such force, I staggered back and we both nearly lost our footing. I felt this was a bit rich, we'd never really been that friendly and I didn't think it fell to me to be offering a listening ear and comforting arm to my Father's extra-curricular activity. Perhaps she felt my recoil, because she didn't stay attached for long, but flopped back down on to the sofa.

"How long d'you think they'll be in there?" She asked. Murray frowned at her,

"That's for them to know and us to find out, because it's none of our damn business." He said. She sniffed and started to say something, but I jerked my head towards the door,

"Murray, a word? Sasha, would you excuse us one moment?" Murray followed me out into the reception area, from where we could clearly hear Gladys cursing comprehensively in the kitchen – Murray looked at me and I gave him a 'don't even ask' look – and my parents yelling at each other from the small study. I had no idea where the tv people were right now. I could only devoutly hope it was somewhere well out of earshot.

Finally facing Murray, with the chance to talk, I opened my mouth, only to find nothing much came out other than a cross between a sigh and a sob. Murray humphed and held out his arms. He didn't do long cuddles, never had, wasn't his style, but a brief hug was enough to inhale the familiar aroma of his favourite Famous Grouse, overlaid by the far stronger one of TCP antiseptic, with which he gargled religiously every morning.

"So?" He said, dropping his arms and moving over to the two green chairs. Seated, I started to tell him what had gone on this morning, but he stopped me before I'd even got properly started, shaking his head decisively.

"No, I don't need to know the whole of it. I've seen enough to know whatever's going on here makes no sense at all, and by my reckoning it's not going to, whichever way up you put it. If you want my opinion, there's no point in delving into things any deeper. In this world there's more things we don't know about than we do. And the deeper you dig, the less you might like what you dig up. We need to get you out of here and the quicker the better.

"But..." and I nodded towards the door, behind which neither Ophelia or Adam had run out of steam. He shook his head again,

"Look, don't know what's going to happen there, anybody's guess. It's not good, I'll tell you that much, she's..." And he jerked his head towards the living room where we'd left Sasha, "...proper got her claws into him," He down-turned his mouth, "This is different from all those other times, when he was only too pleased to be hauled out of the mess he'd made. This time he thinks it's 'for real'. Point is, Sandy my girl, whatever's going to happen between your Ma and Pa is going to happen. I know it's tough, but it's not as big a bloody risk to you as what's going on here." He shivered, a completely un-Murray like gesture, "Don't know what it is about this place, but it's giving me the willies, I've got a bad feeling about it and I don't usually do feelings." I nodded slowly, he was the most pragmatic person I knew.

"But..." I started again. He interrupted sharply,

"None of your 'buts'. If you can't see what's under your nose, then you're a fool, and I've never thought that about you."

"What if Ophelia won't come with me?" I asked. He shrugged,

"My guess is she will, whatever she says. You know she'll opt for what's going to be least trouble for her. Truth is, as much as you blame her for you not being able to get away, you and I both know it's more likely your own pig-headedness, never could resist a challenge, could you? All your life, never met a muddle you didn't think you could mend. And God knows," he sighed, "This is one bugger of a muddle. But trust me, this isn't the time for proving how clever you are."

"He's right." The voice from the top of the stairs wasn't raised, but it carried. We both looked up, I don't know how long she'd been standing there listening, but as she moved down the stairs towards us, hitting each step with the bird-headed cane, I saw she was taking the measure of Murray, as he was of her. There was silence as they weighed each other up, then Etty nodded briefly at him and turned to me.

"You," she said, "Need for once, to listen to the voice of common sense."

"But..." I started again. She rapped the cane sharply on the parquet floor and gave me the green glare. I was getting a bit sick of not being allowed by anyone, to finish a sentence.

"No." She snapped. "No more buts, you mean well and you think you're helping and maybe I thought you were too, at the beginning, but now it's clear. Not only are you not helping, you're placing yourself and all of us in the path of something that's not going to stop, until it's inflicted terrible damage. You're exposing us, the family, to the sort of risk I've worked a lifetime to keep us away from.

"What about the hotel?" I asked.

"We managed before you got here, we'll manage well enough after you've gone."

"I don't understand what..." I said. She cut in again,

"You don't have to understand. But you do have to leave and while you're at it, you need to get rid of those ridiculous documentary people, not to mention the lunatics in my library, looking for ghosts." She turned on her heel and put her foot on the first stair. I hadn't finished though, and to stop her moving away I put my hand over hers where it lay on the carved wooden post of the bannister. It wasn't an affectionate gesture, far from it, more a custodial one born of frustration, but as our flesh touched, a jolt went through me, jerking my body from head to toe, it was like nothing I'd felt before and certainly nothing I ever wanted to feel again. I gasped and pulled my hand back as if I'd been burnt.

"Sandy?" Murray had stepped forward too, but my gaze was on her.

"Now." She said, "Now do you see, girl? It's you and me. Together, we're the risk that can't be taken." She turned from me to Murray. "You," she said. "Need to get her away from here and from us. Is that clear?" Murray nodded slowly.

"Do my best." He said. She didn't look at me again, but continued up the stairs and over her shoulder she said,

"I expect you to do better than that."

"Depends," he said. "Look." We turned. For once the big, black double front doors were closed, but we could see through the arched windows to either side. In the time since we'd arrived back from the hospital, the light outside had turned an ominous iron-grey, and it had started to snow.

CHAPTER FIFTY-FOUR

Outside, the falling snow was spreading its false blanket of calm and charm. Inside, all wasn't quite as serene, and the mass exodus that Etty had in mind, didn't look as if it was going to be taking place any time soon.

Roland arrived back, bursting through the front doors, vigorously shaking flakes from the cashmere camel coat and cursing the state of the drive. He'd nearly, he informed us, upended several times in those potholes, we really had to get them seen to.

Adam and Ophelia erupted from the study and Sasha, who must have had an ear to the door of the living room, emerged at the same time and re-attached herself proprietorially to my Father. Then the front doors opened again on a gust of wind, to admit Max and Karl, thrilled with the great shots they'd got of the house, looking moody in the failing light. They were followed by Charley, shepherding a grumbling Ffion, who clearly wasn't the outdoor type at all.

Etty, whose stately progress up the stairs had been derailed by the snow news, watched all this coming rather than going, with a weary eye, tutted and turned to Murray again.

"Don't forget what you must do." She insisted, before continuing upwards without another backward glance.

"It won't lay." Said my Father categorically, "Come along Murray, we need to get back to our hotel while we still can."

"Not sure you'll make it." Roland shook his head doubtfully, "It's coming down thick and fast at the moment. The roads might be OK where they're gritted, but our drive's a nightmare and the drive at Westerly is well over a mile long and, I suspect, in a worse state than ours. Don't suppose you've got snow chains, have you?

"Snow chains?" Pa couldn't have been more incredulous if Roland had mentioned a sledge and team of huskies.

"Well, you're not in London now." Roland pointed out. "But I shouldn't think it'll last."

"But Adam, what will we do in the meantime?" Wailed Sasha, "Are we going to be trapped here?" Murray grunted,

"Better off here, than stuck in a snowdrift, trying to get back." He pointed out. Sasha looked aghast, as did my Mother. Charley who'd been unabashedly listening in, clapped her hands in glee, encouraging the snow, gathered on her knitted hat, to drip damply down on to her Parka.

"Oh, my days!" She exclaimed, bouncing up and down like the ruddy Duracell bunny. "Could things get any better, honestly, could they, could they? Trapped in a snowstorm in a haunted hotel. Max, this is too wonderful, isn't it?" Max didn't appear quite so excited, and Sasha gave a small shriek, her lisp exaggerated by alarm,

"Haunted? Adam, what'th she talking about, haunted? She'th joking ithn't she, she ith joking, Adam?"

I surveyed the assembled gathering and heaved a sigh. Any kooky conspiracy theories circulating in Etty's head, would just have to go on the back burner for now, as would my departure. It didn't look as if anyone was going anywhere at the moment. One of the downsides of that, of course, was they were going to have to stay right here, which meant they'd have to be fed and accommodated somehow. It was a logistical challenge, but practicality's my middle name and far better to be dealing with problems I could get my head around than those I couldn't.

I did a swift mental calculation of available bedrooms and then, mounting the first couple of steps to give myself authority, put two fingers in my mouth and whistled the piercing whistle Murray had taught me, perfected over the years to drag the attention of unruly dancers and crew, back to where it should have been in the first place. The response was, as always, satisfactory and all heads whipped round towards me. Time to muster the troops, although I realised the troops were a bit thin on the ground, just my Mother and Roland right now.

"Roland," I said, "Would you go into the kitchen and explain the situation to Gladys?" He looked alarmed, which I ignored. "Tell her it's going to be dinner for 14 tonight." Roland blanched a little but nodded, sketched a salute and strode off to do battle. I knew we'd had deliveries scheduled from both the butcher and the greengrocer that morning, so assumed we'd have enough food in stock, although depending on whether or not Gordon was still with us, I didn't give too much for

Roland's chances of getting in and out without a profanity laden, ear-bashing.

"Ma." I said. "I need you to find Elizabeth and help her sort out the rooms."

"Certainly, I will find Elizabeth," she said and added. "Although I'm sure she can manage very nicely on her own and Alfred will lend a hand." I nodded, didn't have time to argue, I hadn't imagined for one moment that 'all hands to the deck' would work with my Mother.

"Pa, you and Murray won't mind sharing, will you? I said. Sasha opened her mouth, but I just looked at her and she shut it again. I re-did the initial head and room count, to make sure I hadn't missed anybody out, and was relieved to find it was all doable – just – and mercifully without having to involve the top floor, and risk Felicia scaring the pants off anyone.

I was heading off to the kitchen to reinforce Roland, and thinking we could organise an early meal for the family, to be eaten in the kitchen. That would then allow us to provide dinner for the paying guests ie: the documentary crew, as well as the unexpected influx of Murray, Pa and Sasha. After all it was still important, I felt, to preserve the illusion of a well-run, smooth and professional hotel operation. I was halfway down the kitchen corridor, when I met myself coming the other way.

CHAPTER FIFTY-FIVE

I have heard it said, that when you can't believe your eyes, you don't. And I didn't. My mirror image and I came to a stop, a few paces from each other, while my brain struggled to rationalise. The best case scenario I could come up with was that the accumulated strain of the last few days had finished me off and I needed sedation, and possibly putting away in a locked room.

How long we would have stood there, staring at each other I really couldn't say, but Roland emerged from the kitchen, not looking his usually laid-back self, as one might expect if Gordon Ramsay was still holding sway in there. He was brushing what looked like flour from his jacket – I wondered what had been thrown at him – when he saw the two of us. The light in the corridor was dim and I watched as he also struggled to make sense of what he was seeing. The other me, turned slowly on her heel to face him and tilted her head slightly to one side.

"Sandra?" He said. I took a breath and opened my mouth, I wasn't sure I could get anything out, but thought I should make the effort. A fine shaking had started in my legs and was slowly moving up my body.

"It's me." I said urgently, "I mean, *this* is me." It didn't make much sense, so I tried again, "Roland, I don't know what that is, but this is me." My voice sounded high and shrill and I didn't feel as if I'd clarified the situation much, but it's not really the sort of situation you expect to have to clarify is it? She/me was wearing exactly what I was wearing, and as she started to move towards the now backing-away Roland, I saw she moved the way I moved. I thought with horror, if she spoke, if she said anything at all, I'd be lost.

I did the only thing that made any kind of sense in that moment, I leapt forward and threw both my arms tight round her body. It felt indescribably repulsive, because she/I was completely solid in my grasp and she was wriggling and bucking violently to get away. In that instant, I knew exactly what I had to do, the only thing to do. I reached up to her/

my face, clamping my thumb and forefinger bruisingly on her/my lower jaw, turning her face to mine, forcing her mouth wide with the pressure of my fingers. I hauled in a breath, feeling my lungs expand and then I hissed it out, hard, into her.

It was a long, sibilant, snake of a hiss, full of the complete revulsion I was feeling and the face, her/my face, so close to mine began to melt, falling away like wax in a flame. And if you've never watched your own face melt before your eyes, it's not something I'd recommend.

The progression from drooping misshapen flesh, to bare bone, to bone dripping down a melting neck, was swift and appalling, and then the still-wriggling body in my arms, disintegrated and fell away completely. On the uncarpeted floor was a pile of ash, shifting slightly back and forward in the draught and with a shining, unmoving, solid object in the middle – the gold chain and initial necklace I often wore, I put my hand to my throat – was wearing now.

Roland moved forward and caught me as my legs gave way, mercifully pulling me away from what was on the floor and towards him. Wordlessly, he put one arm round my waist and half dragged, half carried me down the corridor, the short distance to the kitchen. I found I was still holding firm to my notebook with my pen hooked into the wire binding, that was good, you never know when you might need to make a note or two.

Elizabeth and Alfred were taking small bottles of shampoo and tablets of soap from the cupboard below the dresser and putting them in a plastic basket on top of towels, and Gladys was washing vegetables in the sink and heaping them unevenly on the draining board. As we came through the door, they turned and took in our faces. Alfred was quickest to react, pulling forward a chair for Roland to dump me on. I slumped on the seat and Roland leaned shakily against the table.

"Shit." He muttered. "Shit, shit, shit!" I didn't say anything, there wasn't really anything I could add, he'd summed it up.

"What is it, what on earth's happened now? Gladys, there's some brandy in the larder." Elizabeth was bending over me, brushing the hair away from my face in an unexpectedly maternal gesture. She tutted as she felt how clammy I was. "Alf," she said, "Damp one of those towels there, quick as you like." She handed me a glass provided by Gladys, who I was relieved to see, now seemed to be Gordonless, "Here," said Elizabeth, a firm arm round my shoulder, "Get this down you." I choked violently on the sharpness of the liquid, welcoming the reality of the sensation, as she patted me hard on the back to stop me coughing.

"That's the ticket." She said. "Good for shock. Have a drop more, finish the glass. Roland, you have some too, you look terrible. What in God's name happened?" The lights were on in the kitchen, but weren't doing much to illuminate anything, and thickly falling snow was already accumulating on the panes of the window, making everything even darker. Roland and I looked at each other.

"What… ?" I asked. He ran his finger and thumb absently down either side of his face, so they met at his chin, and shook his head,

"Never seen anything like that. We'll have to go to Etty."

"No." I said.

"Well, out with it, what was it then?" Elizabeth said sharply. Roland said nothing, so I answered her, hearing the stupidity of what I was saying, even as I was saying it.

"It was me. It was something that looked like me." I said. Elizabeth and Alfred exchanged a glance that said nothing good, and Alfred shook his head, grunting "Situ omnia naturali et turbaverant."

"What's that mean?" I asked.

"Situation normal, all fouled up!" Said Roland grimly. "He's not wrong. Come on you."

"Where?"

"Talk to Etty."

"No, later. I've got to help get things sorted here. Look I'm fine." I made a huge effort and stood up. I was still shaky, but didn't need him to see that. Neither did I want to discuss what had just occurred. It had happened and I'd dealt with it, which was part of the problem. From fear and panic had been born my sure knowledge of exactly what to do and how to do it – I really didn't want to go into that right now." Roland shrugged,

"Have it your own way, you usually do, but when I see her, I'm not going to keep quiet – that'd be plain daft." And nodding briefly to the others, he took himself off. I turned to them decisively,

"Right," I said, "Let's get ourselves organised." Elizabeth snorted, reverting to type.

"What makes you think we're not?"

"Well," I said, "It's rather a turn up for the book isn't it, suddenly lots of extra people?" She sniffed and went back to sorting towels.

"Young lady," she said, turning her back on me, "Years ago, this house used to be full of any number of guests at any one time, parties and the like. We coped then, we'll cope now."

"I know that," I said placatingly, "Of course I do." The last thing we needed was Elizabeth throwing a strop. And then, another worry, "What do we do about Cyril, we can't leave him out there?" She didn't answer me, not sure whether she couldn't hear because I wasn't facing her, or whether she was just choosing to ignore me. Alfred gave me a wink.

"Not to worry," he said, "Cyril took himself off ages ago and we've got everything well in hand here. Rather agreeable to be rushed off our feet for a change. Take yourself upstairs now for a few minutes peace and quiet, strikes me, you're not going to get any down here." I turned to Gladys,

"You OK too then?" She nodded, the most animated I'd seen her. "Don't you give it another thought lovey, get your feet up for a bit. As it happens, I think I feel Nigella coming through."

CHAPTER FIFTY-SIX

The hotel reception was mercifully empty when I passed through on my way upstairs. Everyone must have dispersed to various rooms. Actually, I didn't really care where they were, as long as I wasn't having to deal with them. My sense of responsibility had taken temporary leave of absence, and lying mindlessly on my bed for a while, seemed like the most desirable thing in the world. It wasn't to be.

Devorah met me at the top of the stairs, Simona on one hip and a worried expression on her face.

"Mimi's disappeared." She said.

"Well, she's always doing that, isn't she?" I said reasonably, moving past her, pillows on my mind.

"Not like this."

"Try looking in the broom cupboard, maybe she's got stuck." I knew that sounded sour, but honestly, I was all out of oomph. Devorah grabbed my arm, with the hand that wasn't anchoring Simona.

"Listen, you don't understand. When she's here, when any of us are here, we can feel it." I stopped and stared at her.

"Feel?" I said. She shrugged,

"Don't know, can't explain it, but like, we all know who's near and who isn't and roughly where they are – and right now she isn't. You know what I mean?" I shook my head.

"Devorah, I've no idea what you're talking about, give me a break. She'll turn up, she always does, doesn't she?" I didn't add 'like a bad penny', although I was tempted. She shook her head,

"Look," she said. "There are some funny things going on right now."

"You don't say!" I muttered, still making for my lie down. Unfortunately, Roland and Bella had now appeared from their rooms, both kitted for the outdoors.

"We can't find Mimi." Said Bella as she passed.

"I know, Devorah said."

"Go get Alfred," Said Roland. "Ask if he could check out by the annexe, we'll head out the front."

"Well, actually I was…" I started, then gave in and peevishly turned to stomp back downstairs after Roland and Bella. We were stopped in our tracks by an unearthly, not unfamiliar howling from outside, which rose and fell and rose again.

Rostropovich was highly agitated, outside the front doors, pacing rapidly up and down in the still heavily falling snow and stopping every few steps to throw back his head and give vent, his breath clouding and hanging. As we came out he watched and waited impatiently until we'd negotiated the icy stone steps, then turned and loped off, across the circular gravelled area and down the drive. I'd grabbed the first jacket I saw from the coat rack on the way out and luckily hadn't changed my shoes from my earlier outing, although they were immediately soaked through and not a lot of help on the thin but treacherously slippery surface.

Roland and Bella, were both equipped with torches, even if they weren't making much of an impact because it wasn't quite dark enough. We were trailing Rostropovich as best we could, although there was no way we could keep up with him but, clever animal, he was well aware and kept pausing, turning to face us and pawing the ground in impatience, whining at our unevenly clumsy progress. Every time we reached him, he set off again at a brisk pace, and by the time we'd followed him into the thicket of trees, I was embarrassingly short of breath, and sweating like a pig in the jacket, which turned out to have a fur lining.

The wolf didn't hesitate, leading us deeper and deeper into the trees, so Roland who was in front, had to force his way through low-hanging, ice-encrusted branches, holding them from swinging back and hitting us in the face as we followed. He was muttering something about bleeding Indiana Jones and the forest of doom, Bella laughed breathlessly, but neither of them were concealing their anxiety. In the short while we'd been going, full dark had fallen, but any moonlight was deadened and diluted by pregnant clouds, whilst the snow was becoming ever more wind-driven and stinging sharply into our faces and mouths.

We'd never have found her in a million years on our own, but Rostropovich led us unerringly to where she lay, a small unmoving bundle of material in the darkness of a clearing. Face down in the snow, all we could see was her red knitted poncho, topped by what at first glance, in the dancing light of the two torches, looked like a black fur hood. But it wasn't a black fur hood. It was Ink. A stiffly dead, Ink.

Roland gently lifted the cat's rigid body, seemingly so much less plump now.

"Did he do that?" I asked, looking at the huge animal who had settled back on his haunches. Roland shook his head briefly as he laid the small corpse gently to one side on the snow.

"Shouldn't think so, there's not a mark on her." He turned swiftly to help Bella move Mimi carefully over on to her back. Bella had already stripped off her thick glove and was feeling for a pulse, eyes closed in concentration. None of us said anything, comment seemed pointless. The front of the red garment was completely snow encrusted and there was no movement of her chest and no discernible colour in her face, other than the black gash of the bird-inflicted wound. It seemed an inevitability that Bella would shake her head as she slowly did, then she paused,

"Wait, I'm not sure, Sandra, quick you feel." She'd reached up behind her, dragging me forward and I dropped to my knees next to her. I didn't have gloves, so my hands were numb, apart from which I hadn't had a lot of experience of checking for life, so had no idea what I was feeling for.

"There," Bella was pressing my two fingers firmly into Mimi's neck. "Can you feel…?" She said. I shut my eyes as she had, and thought there was a fractional, butterfly fluttering beneath my fingers. Bella's anxious breath was on my cheek, her fear and uncertainty mirroring mine.

"Think so… very faint. Honestly, not sure." I whispered. I don't know why, it seemed important not to disturb the silence. Roland moved rapidly then, pulling open his thick jacket, bending and scooping her thin frame up in his arms, so she was pressed against the warmth of his body, while Bella wordlessly pulled the jacket closed as best she could, shielding Mimi from the still-falling, spitefully slanting snow.

"Come on, quickly." He said, already moving off, following our footsteps back out of the thicket. Rostropovich stayed as close as possible to him, at the same time, careful not to impede him in any way. I hesitated and Roland threw over his shoulder,

"Leave the cat, we'll come back for it tomorrow." But I couldn't do that.

Ink and I were never that close and God knows, I'm the least sentimental person on this earth, but I couldn't just abandon her, lonely and frozen. I bent and picked her up, death-diminished in my arms, and set off after the other two, hurrying to catch them up because without the uncertain light of their torches, the blackness was complete. We were all breathing heavily by the time we broke out of the trees back onto the drive and once we weren't battling branches, we were able to put on some cautious speed.

We'd almost reached the base of the stone steps, when the music started blaring. Shockingly loud, totally incongruous, it hit us physically, reverberating through our chests as it assaulted our ears. It was Bing Crosby, and to our astonishment, he was dreaming of a White Christmas, which was really a bit previous, being as it was only November.

"For pity's sake who's put that on?" I shouted at Bella, as wincing from the noise-blast and gripping each other's arm for balance, we staggered up the steps after Roland. "I didn't even know we had a PA system." I said.

"We don't." She said grimly.

CHAPTER FIFTY-SEVEN

As we made it through the front doors, the music was head-splittingly invasive from all around us, with Bing begging for sleigh bells in the snow. The three of us stopped short for a few seconds, dazzled by warmth, light and noise before Roland moved towards the living room door which was standing open.

"Someone find where that's coming from and shut it off." He yelled, as Alfred and Elizabeth burst through from the kitchen corridor. Devorah was running down the stairs towards us and above, on the landing stood Etty with Ophelia slightly behind her.

"Mimi?" Etty asked.

"We think she might be OK." Bella looked at me for confirmation, but I couldn't help thinking of the uncertainty of that flutter under my fingers, would it still be there after our desperate dash through the cold? Unconsciously I shook my head slightly and Devorah gasped. I turned to her quickly.

"Call an ambulance."

"They'll never be able to get here." She protested, we were all yelling, to be heard over the music.

"I'm sure they will, we have to try anyway." I said, nodding towards the phone. "Do it." And then to Etty,

"Come on, quickly, there may be something you can do and where's that bloody music coming from, can't we stop it?" She made her way down, pausing halfway to close her eyes. For a moment, she was still and then, mercifully the noise was wiped out, leaving a vacuum into which the silence fell. She tutted, perhaps to herself. "Childish." She said disdainfully, as she hurried past me.

"Serenissima?" Ophelia had moved too, to halfway down the stairs. She was looking at what I carried in my arms.

"Ma. I'm so sorry." I said. She nodded once, pressing her lips together tightly, before turning and moving slowly up again and back along the corridor. I watched her go. I had no idea how to cope with that. Hysteria, tears, shrieks, wailing, beatings of breast were all on the cards and could be handled. I wasn't sure what to do with genuine grief.

"Here," said Alfred, stepping forward, "Let me." For one stupid instant, I felt protective towards what I cradled, then I held out my arms and he took her from me.

"Don't know what happened." I said. "Maybe..." I trailed off, I didn't really know what I was going to say, and going through my mind was the sheer implausibility of sedentary Ink voluntarily going for a snow stroll with Mimi and meeting a frozen end.

"I'll take care of her." He said gently, "Don't you worry yourself." As he turned away, it occurred to me that it had been easier to think about Ink than about Mimi, perhaps misplaced priorities.

I knew I should go and see how Mimi was or indeed wasn't, although I hadn't heard any overt sounds of distress from in there, so maybe the worst hadn't happened. But still jacket-clad, I sat for a moment on one of the green leather chairs. The chairs had clearly been designed by someone to whom comfort was not a prime consideration; hard and slippery in a bottom-repelling way, they had straight up and down backs that actively discouraged any form of leaning. I knew a review of the chairs was simply a way to avoid thinking about everything else, because right now I didn't, to use one of Murray's favourite phrases, know which way was up and couldn't have told my arse from my elbow. But if for a brief while, thinking about the shortcomings of a pair of chairs took my attention, that was no bad thing. I shut my eyes briefly. Maybe anybody passing would just ignore me. No such luck. I was forced to re-open them by a hard rap on the parquet floor. It was the bird-headed cane.

"A word, if you don't mind." Said Etty.

"I'd really rather not."

"I'd really rather not, too." She said. "But there you are, we can't always have what we want can we?"

"Mimi? Is she OK?"

"She will be."

"We have to thank Rostropovich," I said. "He saved her life, we'd never ever have found her in time. What about the ambulance?"

"There's a wait of over two hours, unless it's a life or death emergency. There are apparently road traffic accidents all over the place, so we cancelled the call."

"This isn't an emergency?"

"Not the sort they can deal with." Said Etty grimly. "She just needs to get warmed up, Elizabeth's seeing to her. She's tougher than she looks."

"Who, Elizabeth?"

"Don't be stupid; Mimi."

"Right, of course. Sorry, feeling a bit..." I swayed suddenly on the chair and Etty moved forward, although what she could do to help me if I slipped off, I had no idea, I'd knock her right over. I giggled weakly at the thought of Etty and I going down like a pair of skittles.

"We need to get her upstairs." I blinked up at her, not sure whether she was talking to or about me, but with the familiar scent of whisky and antiseptic, I realised Murray had turned up. So pleased to see him. I put out my hand, but couldn't seem to focus properly.

"Murray." I said. And then because I really couldn't think of anything else to say, tried it again "Murray?"

"Come on, quickly now, before those wretched people turn up again with the camera." Said Etty.

"What's wrong with her?" Murray had an arm round my waist and was helping me up from the chair. I chuckled again, swaying as I stood, because I was taller than him and we made an odd couple. I didn't give much for our chances of getting up the stairs in one piece.

"She been drinking?" He said accusingly to Etty.

"Brandy." I said. "Elizabeth gave it to me. After the double."

"Double what?" Said Murray anxiously, as we followed Etty who had already turned to go upstairs.

"No. Not double what." I elucidated carefully. My tongue seemed suddenly to have become rather larger in my mouth than it usually was, it certainly didn't seem to be working in its normal fashion. "It was a double of me. A whatdoyoucallit?" I shut my eyes, the word was on the tip of my tongue, but closing my eyes to try and find it was suddenly making me very dizzy, so I opened them again hastily. "Doppelgänger," I said triumphantly. "Yup, that's the chappie, a doppelgänger!" Etty turned. We were now about halfway up the stairs.

"Ah." She said. "I see." I waggled my head at her,

"Well, jolly glad somebody does." I said, "Because I'm blowed if I do. Roland," I added, "Wanted me to tell you, but I… I…" I paused, I really couldn't think what it was I'd wanted or not wanted to do. I giggled again. It was really all rather funny, one way and another and added to that, was the fact that both legs felt like cooked spaghetti, no use whatsoever for walking on.

"I told you." Said Etty to Murray, as we reached the landing and she indicated her room at the end of the corridor. "I said you had to get her out of here." Murray, panting now but still doggedly hanging on to me as I swayed at his side, managed to swear quietly under what breath he had left.

"I *know* you ruddy-well told me, but who knew we were heading into a blizzard? We're all bleeding stuck here aren't we, until it clears up a bit. Nothing you nor anyone else can do about it, is there?" Etty opened the door to her room.

"Better put her on the bed." She said. "Then you can go."

"Oh, I don't think so." Murray drew himself up and gave her a look I knew well. He hadn't had years of dealing with Adam and Ophelia without developing a highly effective stroppiness of his own.

"Excuse me?" Etty wasn't used to being gainsaid. "I would like to speak with my Great-Granddaughter, privately."

"Well that's tough isn't it, because I'm going nowhere, and she may well be your Great-Granddaughter, but she's been my responsibility a bloody sight longer than she's been yours."

"Awwww." I muttered. I was swaying between the two of them, like a rag doll who's a bit short of stuffing and Murray, giving in to my increasingly dead weight, shuffled over to the bed, onto which I collapsed gracelessly while they faced off over me. Etty broke first,

"Very well." She said icily. "Have it your own way, but please don't hold me to blame if you don't like what you hear."

CHAPTER FIFTY-EIGHT

"Here, drink this." Etty was holding a glass to my lips. I turned my head away, I was getting bit sick of people giving me things to drink, after all the brandy hadn't done me any favours.

"What is it?" Murray, leaned forward suspiciously from a chair he'd pulled up next to the bed. Etty, perched neatly on the other side, tsked briskly.

"For goodness sake, it's a glass of water, what do you think it is, eye of newt and toe of frog?" I squinted up at her, surely not a joke? She frowned and I decided, more like habitual sarcasm. But my throat was dry and raspy, so I reached for the glass. I didn't feel right but thankfully, a lot less 'not right' than earlier. Murray stood up, reached behind me and propped the pillows up behind my back, so I could sit more comfortably.

"Come on then." He said to Etty. "Let's be having it. Whatever you've got to say, better out than in. Seems to me there's a ton of iffy stuff been swept under the carpet up till now and I reckon Sandy's got a right to know what's what." Etty might have been the only person who could sit with ramrod dignity on the side of a bed, and now she turned the green glint gaze first on him dismissively, then on me.

"When was it?" She said, "When did you see this doppelgänger?" I rubbed my forehead in the hopes that might stimulate sensible thought.

"This morning," I said. "Least I think it was this morning. To be honest I can't seem to think straight, just so much going on." She shook her head,

"It's not that, you feel the way you do because of what it's taken out of you. You know what they say about a doppelgänger – when you see yours, you die." I shook my head,

"No, actually I didn't know that." I said. "Thanks for sharing though, made me feel a whole lot better." She ignored me and continued.

"It's about the energy. To create a perfect double, whoever is doing the creating needs to draw off your energy, your essence. It leaves you depleted, you literally take leave of your senses. If the doppelgänger continues to exist, it continues to draw from you." She looked at me, "But it didn't continue to exist, did it? You knew exactly what to do."

I reached out again for the glass of water and drained it, deciding that depleted or not, someone had to take charge and even feeling as I did, the person I had most faith in was still me. Whatever she thought she wanted to talk about, I needed answers to questions. There was no doubt things were escalating way too fast, and not in a healthy direction. It would seem that saving the hotel had moved into slightly second place on the list. Our first priority had to be making sure no-one else got hurt or worse. Etty opened her mouth to continue, but I held up a hand.

"Let me get my thoughts in order." I said. She raised an eyebrow but I ignored that, she wasn't the only one who could do bossy. I saw Murray settle back in his chair with a relieved look, he obviously preferred me imperious to insensible.

"Right," I said. "Before we can work out how to handle this, we need to know the who, what, where, why and how. So first of all, who's orchestrating everything that's been going on?" Etty frowned.

"I can't tell you specifically, but they're doing it because they think I've brought you here deliberately." My turn to frown,

"But you had absolutely no idea Ophelia and I were going to turn up." I said.

"Well of course I didn't." She said impatiently, "If I had, don't you think I'd have stopped you?"

"What do they want?"

"They want you gone. Away from the rest of us."

"Why?"

"I've already told you this, did you not listen? There are those who use what they are to achieve exactly what they want. If you're hungry for money, influence, power, there's nothing to stop you using what you have, to get it. Some people have overreaching ambition, yearn for the spotlight, others not so much or not at all. Everyone's choices are their own."

"OK, OK, I get all that and all the stuff about energy, focus, yada, yada, yada. But what I need to know is what's real and dangerous to us, and what are just scary Mary smoke and mirrors tactics, and how to tell the difference." She laughed with no amusement.

"Who's to define reality? We can only go by the evidence of our own eyes and ears. We all saw the Malignum, the other day, that was reality, so were the birds. On the other hand, none of us saw what you saw on your car trip – yes Mimi told me about that. That was something successfully messing with your head, but it didn't make it any less real to you, did it?" I shuddered, the memory was still strong and she was right, anything was as real as I thought it was – and thus dangerous. I realised I'd been tensed, leaning forward as I questioned her and my back was beginning to ache, I sat back against the pillows.

"I still honestly don't see what it has to do with me, why I seem to have set the cat amongst the pigeons." I thought of Ink and regretted that particular turn of phrase.

"I've told you, the balance of power is just that – a balance." She said impatiently. "But it can easily be tipped one way or another and any change at all to the status quo is a threat to those who want it left as it is." I snorted crossly,

"But this is all so stupid. I don't know anything, don't want to know anything, in fact want to run as far and as fast from your hokery pokery as I can. How can I possibly be any kind of a threat?" Another thought struck me, "Anyway, if it's me they've got a gripe with, why is it Mimi who seems to be getting the brunt of it?"

"They see a family chain, with her as the weakest link." Said Etty. Murray who'd been listening to all this, his face expressionless, leaned forward.

"Hang on in there a minute. Just want to make sure I've got this absolutely straight. Make sure you're saying what I think you're saying, get it all out on the table and call a spade a spade. All this, all the rum stuff Ophelia's pulled off through the years, it's because you're what? Witches?" Etty scanned his face.

"And if I say yes?" She asked. He shrugged and grunted.

"No skin off my nose. Been around the block enough times to know, there's a bloody sight more things in this life that don't have any kind of sensible explanation, than those that do. What I'm more interested in right now, is how dangerous all this is. And most importantly, how the hell do we put a stop to it?"

"I've already told you." Etty didn't raise her voice but thumped her stick once on the floor in exasperation. "You need to get her away from here."

"And you know, bloody well." He snapped back. "We don't have a hope of doing that until this weather clears up a bit. So, what's to do in the meantime, eh?" They glared at each other.

"Oh, for goodness sake," I said. "Don't you two come to blows, we've got enough on our plates as it is." I looked at Etty. "Isn't there something you can do, I don't know, some sort of protective something or other? Aren't you supposed to be able to do that sort of thing. Or isn't there some clever way of getting me out of here with a bit of… you know?" She looked at me witheringly,

"Well of course." She said, "Why didn't I think of that? Tell you what,why don't I just pop you on a broomstick and send you up the M40? Don't be any more stupid than you have to, girl. This is real life, not a fairy tale." Murray and I exchanged looks, this was the kind of conversation you don't quite believe you're having.

"Aren't we still missing the main point here?" Said Murray. "What is it precisely they're afraid of? What is it they think she can do." Etty didn't have a chance to respond, because the screaming started again.

CHAPTER FIFTY-NINE

It was Devorah doing it this time. As Etty, Murray and I tripped over each other, hurrying out of Etty's room, Devorah was standing at the other end of the corridor clutching Bella's arms and Ophelia was hurrying out of Devorah's room, shaking her head.

"She was there, she was there, I put her down, she was there." Devorah shook Bella's arms frantically. "Someone's taken her, Oh God, where is she?"

"The baby," Ophelia said to us as we came towards them. "Devorah thinks she's gone."

"I don't *think*." Shrieked Devorah, "This isn't something I'm not *sure* of, you stupid woman!"

"How long?" Said Etty. Devorah turned a wild-eyed look on her.

"What?"

"How long is it since you put her down?" Etty said, Devorah dragged both hands through her hair,

"Don't know, don't know, not that long, like maybe half an hour. I was tired too, so I popped on the bed for a bit, must have dropped off, not for long though. When I woke up she wasn't there. God, don't just stand there everyone, we've got to find her, please, *please*."

"Look, I'm sure it's just a misunderstanding," I said, although I was sure of no such thing. "Maybe she was crying and someone heard and popped their head round the door, saw you were asleep and… " I met Devorah's anguished glare, "Of course we'll start looking, she can't have been taken far can she?" I looked at my Mother, Great Grandmother and Aunt, "Can't you lot 'do' something?" I said.

"Such as?" Said Ophelia. I hissed in exasperation,

"Well what use is all the crazy-maisie stuff, you all do without a moment's thought." I said. "If when push comes to shove and we really need the stops pulled out, you're all stood here like a collection of chocolate tea-pots?"

"You really shouldn't... " began Ophelia, but we didn't have time for discussion or debate.

"Bella," I said urgently, "You and Devorah check all the rooms upstairs, Etty and Ophelia, you do all the rooms on this floor, they're probably not locked but if any of them are, get hold of Elizabeth's keys. Check the cupboards too." Devorah moaned quietly and slumped against the wall. "Just a precaution." I said, patting her arm. Look I'm sure she's fine. Murray," I continued, "You and I – downstairs." I turned to go, then swung back as something occurred to me.

"The baby," I said, "Could she have um gone anywhere... I mean, on her own? No? OK, just checking. Come on Murray." Then I stopped for a second time, looking at Devorah. "Hang on, what you told me before, can you 'feel' her?"

"No." Devorah said quietly, and that was more unnerving than any scream. "I can't feel anything."

We checked the kitchen first because Elizabeth was the most likely to have heard Simona and brought her down, but she shook her head,

"No, course not." And I was up there not that long ago, making-up the two new rooms for your Dad and him." She nodded her head at Murray, "And one for that girl." She added, a sniff indicating Sasha hadn't made the best of impressions. "When I went past, baby was in her room, heard her burbling to herself, happy little soul she is. Didn't know whether Devorah was in there or not, but the baby was fine enough, didn't need seeing to, so no, didn't go in."

Alfred, cleaning some silver cutlery, looked up and shook his head too. Gladys, wiping her hands on a dishcloth, seemed to be herself, although I didn't know whether that was a good or bad thing, she looked blank as well, said she hadn't been out of the kitchen and hadn't seen Devorah and the baby since there was all that fuss earlier with Mimi. I recalled guiltily that I hadn't given Mimi much thought over the last hour or so. Once we'd sorted out where Simona was, I'd check on her.

Roland came in through the back door, grumbling and stamping snow off his boots. He was accompanied by an icy draught and Rostropovich. At Elizabeth's protest, he shrugged as he peeled off gloves and coat.

"Lizzie, my love, I've been trying for flipping ages. Took him down to the kennel, but he wouldn't stay, howled like a banshee with depression. Honestly, what was I supposed to do? Look he can settle down in a corner, he'll be no trouble." Then catching sight of my face, "Sandra? Christ Almighty, what's wrong now?"

Adam and Sasha were seated, like ill-matching bookends at either end of one of the sofas in the living room. He was reading what must have been yesterday's newspaper, while she was talking at him, presumably not appreciating he was a past master at tuning out anything he didn't care to listen to. I recognised the technique and briefly wondered what that said about where their relationship was right now.

I was relieved though to see, that whilst Mimi was still tucked up on another sofa, facing the fire, she was sitting up and looking perky, though a little twitchy. On closer inspection, it turned out she was listening to an iPod with earphones – I detected Henry's touch – and wasn't twitching, just moving with the music.

None of them had anything helpful to say, and I had to persuade Mimi to stay where she was for the time being, the last thing we needed was her getting mislaid again. I met up with Roland in the hall.

"The tv lot are in there," he indicated the library with his head. "Except for that girl, you know," he sketched the knitted tea-cosy, pom-pom, hat in the air. "She took herself off to her room to make some calls apparently. They've had to re-arrange their schedule or something, with the weather, anyway they haven't seen or heard anything." A particularly vicious gust of wind hit the front doors making us all jump, and we looked at each other. Murray shook his head,

"Don't be daft, the kiddie can't possibly be out there."

"Mimi was," I said.

"Yes but," said Murray. "She's a bit away with the fairies anyway, isn't she?" He looked at Roland, "No offence."

"None taken."

"She must have wandered off for some reason and got herself lost."

"And Ink?" I asked. Murray frowned,

"Well known fact." He said. "Cats often take themselves off somewhere when it's their time, and face it, the poor old girl was getting on a bit." I thought about the other cat, the one hanging outside the window, but didn't say anything. There was a feeling of panic in the pit of my stomach, and it was increasing with every passing minute.

"Sandra, anything?" I looked up, Bella was at the top of the stairs. I shook my head and she put her hand to her mouth.

"I'll call the police." I said.

"Goodness, no need to do that." A cheerful voice sang out behind us. It was Charley and – oh thank God – she had Simona comfortably against her shoulder. The baby was cooing happily, turning and holding out her arms to Devorah as she rushed down the stairs towards us, Bella on her heels.

"Why don't we all go into the library?" Said Charley, "They've got the fire going there, and it's almost cosy. She made a wry face to show she knew, as well as we did, that one of the things the library wasn't ever going to really aspire to was cosy. She turned, the baby still in her arms and moved ahead of us. Devorah, her tear-stained face regaining a little colour, stepped in front of her,

"I'll take her now."

"No." Said Charley, "Not yet. Come into the library." She turned. "All of you."

"Hang on just a minute." Said Roland, moving forward next to Devorah, so they were blocking her path. Charley tilted her head to one side and smiled. She had her right arm firmly under Simona's plump nappied bottom and now she moved her left hand flat against one side of the baby's face.

"If you don't do as I ask," said Charley reasonably, "I'll break her neck."

CHAPTER SIXTY

Odd, isn't it, how your reaction to a given situation, isn't ever what you think it might be? Maybe because the primitive part of your brain kicks into gear, way ahead of any kind of reasoning process, making sure you do what seems safest, without stopping to ponder overmuch.

Devorah made a small sound, deep in her throat and then turned and led the way. Roland and Bella followed her. I looked at Murray, his face was as expressionless as mine. Charley glanced up. Etty was coming down the stairs slowly, Ophelia behind her.

"That's the ticket." Said Charley approvingly, shifting the baby more comfortably against her. "Ah, wait," she turned to me. "We're missing someone, where's your Grandmother?" I inclined my head towards the closed door on the opposite side of the hall. "Be an angel would you," said Charley, "Nip in and get her. Just her."

Adam and Sasha both looked up when I came in, I could see he wasn't in the best of moods and she was doing some extreme pouting.

"Thank goodness." She said, getting up as I came in. "Where is everybody, I'm bored, there's no-one to talk to. And I want to watch some television, where is it?" I looked at her blankly. I had no idea, I didn't think I'd seen a television anywhere, but I had more pressing matters on my mind.

"Don't think they've got one." I said shortly and was about to suggest a book, when it occurred to me the place to find one of those might be in the library, so I buttoned my lip. "Mimi," I turned to her. "We've found the baby, but I need your help with something. Would you mind?" She nodded, throwing off the blanket and swinging her legs obligingly off the sofa.

"I think I might just have a wander around the place, stretch my legs, maybe see if the weather's let up at all." Said Adam, also rising. "And where's that damn Murray? Haven't seen hide nor hair of the lazy little sod for ages. Probably sloped off for one of his naps, I've got some calls I want him to make for me."

"No." I said.

"No?" Boomed my Father. Mimi jumped, unaccustomed to the volume.

"Pa, there's a bit of a thing going on."

"A thing?"

"Yes, sort of a family thing." I said. Mimi looked at me anxiously,

"Dear me," she said, heading for the door, "Always bickering, what are they like? I need to go and sort it out. I knew there'd be clashes now Ophelia's back.

"That's all very well," said my Father, "But you can't expect me to stay penned up here till everything's died down. Anyway, Ophelia and I still have things to discuss."

"Not now." I said. Pa humphed in frustration,

"Will you ruddy well stop saying that." He snapped. I clenched my teeth. Mimi was already halfway out the door, I couldn't let her head into whatever was going on, without a word of warning. I also didn't know how long Charley would consider it took, to transfer a grandma from one room to another, she might be getting impatient and something told me, in this odd new incarnation, impatient wasn't the way to go.

"Adam," I said tersely. "For once in your life, just shut up and do what you're told, will you. I've asked you to stay in here, and in here is where you're staying." Hurrying out after Mimi, and as I pulled the door closed behind me, I saw there was a key in the lock. I used it with no compunction.

***

For someone who liked to play the batty article, Mimi cottoned on pretty smartly as I hissed a quick situation summary, she closed her eyes briefly, before nodding and saying calmly,

"Turn up for the book eh? Best get in there then, see what she wants."

The library was looking the best I'd ever seen it. There was a healthy fire flaming in the grate and reflecting in the shining black veneer of the piano, the maroon curtains had been drawn against the snow, and the standard lamps were on, soft against the muted colours of leathered book bindings on the shelves. Even the cherubs surrounding the mirror above the fireplace, seemed in a plumply better mood. But if the room was looking comfortable, the assembled company wasn't.

As Mimi and I walked in together, Charley turned towards us with a welcoming smile. Etty was sitting, upright and expressionless on the sofa at right angles to the fireplace, hands immobile on the bird's head cane. Ophelia and Roland were unrelaxed on either side of her. Murray had taken an upright chair and pulled it up on the other side of the sofa, so he was within protective, touching distance of Ophelia. Devorah, red-eyed, white-faced was sitting close to Bella on the piano bench that had been drawn up next to Murray's chair. Max, Karl and Ffion, looking as blank as the rest of us, were seated in the shadows in the far corner of the room and didn't seem to be taking an active part in proceedings. I couldn't blame them.

Charley was leaning back on the sofa opposite Etty, a cushion comfortably in the small of her back and Simona on her lap, starting now to get a little fretful. There were a couple of empty chairs, between Murray and Bella, towards which Charley graciously waved us. Mimi sat, I didn't. I was calculating what chance I had of moving forward and snatching the baby. Charley looked up at me, eyes bright with excitement.

"No." She said, "I wouldn't do that, if I were you." I moved to stand behind the seat she'd indicated, and rested my hands on the top of its carved high back. Charley looked exactly the same as usual, pale freckled face, unruly red curls and she still had her chunky jumper tucked into her trousers – a decision that never, in the history of womankind, did a waist any favours. My mind was doing that drifting-away thing that often happens when you don't want to deal with a current situation and I yanked it back sternly. I had no idea what had got into her but in reality, how dangerous could she be? She certainly did a nice line in threats, but then she'd always seemed a bit hysterical, maybe the stress of the job had got to her and she simply needed to be talked down firmly. I thought I'd start as I meant to go on.

"If you don't mind Charley," I said. "I won't sit down. This shouldn't take long. Obviously, there's something on your mind, so what's it all about? Before we start though, why don't you let Devorah take the baby to feed and change, then we won't be interrupted. Charley jiggled the baby merrily on her knee and shook her head firmly.

"Don't waste my time by pretending you don't know what's going on." She said, then looking across at Etty. "Is she really that stupid?" Etty glanced over at me briefly.

"Not stupid," she said, "Just not in the least bit interested. Although I don't expect you to believe that."

"Too right." Charley said, looking back at me again. It was becoming clear that this might possibly not be a work-induced nervous breakdown after all.

"So, Sandra, what do you think it is that people fear most?" Asked Charley, seemingly at a tangent.

"Finding dead cats all over the place?" I suggested, "Or no, wait," I added. "Perhaps it's having someone kidnap and threaten their baby?" Charley tutted,

"It's change." She said, "Change that's feared the most and therefore must be prevented from happening. You must have guessed we'd know you'd turned up here, and that we'd know exactly why." I'd been leaning against the back of the chair, now I straightened up, so I was looking down on her even more.

"Hate to disappoint you, but you obviously don't *know* very much at all." I snapped. "Coming down here certainly wasn't my choice." I glared at Ophelia who looked the other way. "And I've only stayed this long out of a stupid sense of obligation to this lot," I waved a hand at the assorted assembled.

"And yet," she said, "Nothing we've done up till now has scared you off."

"Trust me, as soon as I can, I'm out of here."

"Well, we've been sent to make sure you do go and to inform you of what will happen if you don't. We will not allow you to stay." I stared at her, distracted.

"We?" I said. She nodded at Max and Karl, who looked back impassively. Ffion seemed not to be listening and was looking down at her feet expressionlessly, although that might just have been the botox. I turned back to Charley,

"Are you telling me, this whole ruddy documentary thing, isn't genuine? I was getting angrier by the minute; after all, the documentary was one of my main business plan props. "And who exactly is it you think has 'sent' you?" She didn't answer either question,

"Go away." She said, "Get lost. Go back where you came from. Do not even think of returning here and we'll leave you alone, leave all of you alone." I gripped the chair-back and opened my mouth to start detailing some of my thoughts, but Etty turned her head and stopped me,

"You need to listen to what she's saying."

"I'm sorry," I snapped. But I really don't respond too well to bullying." Murray, leaned forward,

"For Gawd's sake girl, will you for once stop digging yourself in even deeper. Whatever crazy stuff is going on here, this isn't the way to handle it." I ignored them both.

"Neither." I said to Charley, "Am I very good at taking orders. You want me to do something? You ask me, don't tell me. You want me to leave? Then explain nicely why, don't try nasty little scare tactics, all smoke and mirrors. And now, before you say another word, hand that baby back, or deal with the consequences." No, I don't know what I had in mind to do either. There was a concerted intake of breath and someone, not sure who, muttered something, not sure what, and then things went a bit pear-shaped.

CHAPTER SIXTY-ONE

Charley didn't move, she carried on smiling and jogging the baby on her knee, but suddenly, something infinitely older looked out from her eyes and I felt a stinging pain in mine.

The agony and the shock of it was such that both hands immediately flew to my face, a belated and useless protection. Temporarily and terrifyingly blinded, I was aware of all sorts going on round me, then Murray on one side and Bella on the other, moved me into the chair behind which I'd been standing. I couldn't immediately see, but knew they'd then stationed themselves either side of me, because I could hear Murray cursing to himself and Bella had a hand on my shoulder. She was holding me down.

Through tears still streaming, I saw that a shocked Roland and Ophelia were also on their feet. Etty remained seated, unmoving and seemingly unmoved. Turning my head to the left, forcing open what felt like vastly swollen eyelids, I saw Mimi, also still seated, looking straight at me. She shook her head briefly whether in admonition or warning, I had no idea.

I don't usually lose my temper, I get cross, become irritated but it's always been important to me to never lose control. After all, I'd grown up watching my parents do it and knew what foolish, oft regretted things could be said and done under the influence. I also knew that going red in the face and screaming until your throat was raw, wasn't productive. But what was rising in me now, was something rather different. Not hot but cold. Cold and knowing.

I shook Bella's hand off my shoulder, Murray's off my arm and stood up. Charley immediately stood too and as she did, Devorah seized the moment, darted forward and snatched the baby.

"I don't know exactly who or what you are," I said slowly, "Although I understand what you want from me, because you've made that very clear. However, I have also made it clear that I will not be intimidated by whatever it is you think you have up your sleeve. I will leave here, as and when I choose. My timing, not yours. I don't appreciate scare tactics and I will not have you threatening my family. Take your camera; your microphone; your team and your inflated idea of your own importance in the scheme of things and get the hell out of here."

Charley looked across the room to Karl and Max, they were standing too now, and between them they held Ffion, who appeared to have passed out, maybe all the excitement was just too much for her. Whatever it was, she was being held by the arms, dangling between them like a piece of washing on the line. Charley looked back again, but not at me this time – at Mimi, and suddenly Mimi was on the floor. Very still. There was a concerted movement from the others towards her, but Charley held up a hand and stopped them.

"Not yet." She said, looking at me. And without knowing what I was doing, yet knowing completely what I was doing, I lashed out at her. I didn't touch her, but she doubled over and pitched violently forward. I heard her head hit the rug with a surprisingly loud crack – of course, the rug was worn and not very thick and the parquet flooring beneath was unforgiving. She lay, face-down in front of the cheerfully burning fire and like Mimi, she wasn't moving. Neither was anyone else for a beat or two, then as if someone had murmured 'Action, take one,' everyone got going.

Bella and Murray reached Mimi first, but she was already regaining consciousness. Typically Mimi, she seemed no more or less dazed than usual, although she was already looking apprehensively to where Roland was bending over Charley. He looked up sharply, in shock and disbelief.

"I think she's dead." He said. I sat down abruptly in the chair I'd only recently vacated.

"Can't be, don't be so daft." Murray moved from the body that was now sitting up rubbing its eyes, to the body that wasn't doing anything of the sort. He turned her over so she was on her back, then bending lower, put his cheek almost over her mouth. After what seemed like an age, he straightened, his normal ruddy complexion paled to a sicklier shade.

"She's not dead, but I think she's in a pretty bad way. What the hell did you do to her, Sandy?" From the other side of the room, where Devorah had retreated, Simona started to whimper. I felt like joining her. I looked up and met Etty's eye. She and I were the only ones still sitting so were on a level. I opened my mouth, but she shook her head imperceptibly, as Mimi had done earlier. I had no idea what that meant but obviously, whatever Etty was thinking, there were steps that had to be taken.

"I'll call an ambulance." I said.

"I don't think so." Said Ffion.

CHAPTER SIXTY-TWO

I suspect, engrossed in the Charley situation, most of us had almost forgotten Karl, Max and Ffion. But something was happening to the woman who'd been slung limply between the two men. Impeccably coiffed, and dressed in business-like black skirt and short, double-breasted jacket, with something colourfully Butler and Wilson on the lapel, her face, as she raised it to look at us, still bore the slightly shocked imperturbability that botox brings. Then it began to change. For a moment, I was reminded of the melting features of the doppelgänger and thought irreverently, she'd probably want words with her aesthetic facial specialist and a refund, then I realised – not melting, re-forming.

Now, beneath the blonde, sharply defined and deftly highlighted bob was incongruously, a far older face, dominated by fleshily broad lips, a heavy jowl and hooded wrinkled lids over a green glint gaze that wasn't unfamiliar. The new face was disproportionate to its body, it really wasn't a combination that worked, and the discrepancy was unpleasantly disconcerting. She looked around, chuckled briefly and phlegmily at our expressions, then frowned as the baby started crying again.

"You," she said to Devorah, "Get that out of here, now." Devorah looked across at Bella, then me as if to say what did we want her to do. Bella made a shooing motion with her hand and I nodded quickly. Devorah backed to the door, opened it and slipped out, the fear on her face the last thing we saw, as she closed it quietly behind her.

Ffion – well not Ffion, but in the absence of introductions, Ffion would have to do for now – nodded in satisfaction. "That's better. Can't stand the noise, grates on my nerves." Her voice now wasn't Ffion's modulated presenter's tone, but something far rustier. She turned the new head stiffly on its neck and looked directly at Etty, who looked impassively back.

"Etty Goodkind," said re-formed Ffion, "I'm sorry it's these circumstances we meet under, especially after such a long time." Etty, inclined her head.

"Indeed." She said.

"You do understand," said Ffion, "There is no personal animosity involved. This is pure contingency." Etty, hands folded and still on the bird-headed cane, was equally polite but similarly firm.

"And you don't seem able to understand what has already been extremely clearly stated." She said. "My Great-Granddaughter has neither intention nor inclination to stay here. She wants nothing to do with anything we are. Is a word from one of my family, no longer worth anything?" Ffion threw her head back – I hoped it was firmly attached to its new neck – and laughed.

"You always were the idealist, Etty Goodkind. You've seen, we've all just seen." And she indicated with a perfectly manicured index finger, Charley prone in front of the fireplace, "What she is. What she can do. We can't, are not prepared to take any risks. In fact," she paused thoughtfully, "I'm starting to wonder whether her leaving here, might not now be enough."

"Enough?" Repeated Etty, and she rapped the cane sharply once on the floor. Ffion's face appeared to want to grimace, but force of circumstance and the botox were against her, so she settled for an odd little head wiggle which should have been comical, but somehow wasn't at all.

"Don't pretend ignorance Etty Goodkind." She hissed, "You and I have both been around long enough to know what's what. We, the remaining families, all have a place in the hierarchy. In the past, you've chosen to slink away, lie low, not practice the art, and that's entirely your choice – as long as it stayed that way. But did you honestly believe we wouldn't notice what you are doing now? The status quo is set, but this," she waved her arm to take in all of us, "This gathering says something else altogether."

"Oh, for goodness sake," I said, hauling myself to my feet again. The stinging in my eyes was dying down, although not the anger at this ridiculous, crazily melodramatic stand-off. "Here we go again with the gathering." In my frustration, I moved towards Ffion, then thought better of it and stopped where I was. "I... we've told you the truth. You're putting two and two together to make five. Who the hell do you think you are to come here and put on this absurd performance?" Out of the corner of my eye I saw Ophelia start forward, her hand out in a 'stop it now' gesture, but my gaze was riveted by the cold green one before me.

"I'll show you who I am." Said Ffion softly and as I watched, the face changed again, and again, and again, slip sliding from one set of features to another, each completely individual. Different eyes observed or glared, individual mouths twisted in bitterness or sneers, morphing swiftly if not always smoothly, from one to another, to another – too many to count, it really was most unpleasant to watch. And then the thing that had been Ffion was back, spitting triumph.

"Did you honestly think I would risk coming alone? I stand here with the strength of the many, the mind of the majority." And interrupting as Etty, standing now, started to speak. "No, Etty Goodkind, save your breath, you were always mistaken, it was never a sisterhood, only alliances of convenience." As she turned back to look in my direction, I felt the full force of whatever she was – it went through me like an electric shock and the hairs on the nape of my neck rose in atavistic response. I was moving slowly forward, not sure what I had in mind to do, when the door of the library was flung open with some force – he always knew the value of an impressive entrance – and there stood an irate Adam with Sasha still attached to an arm.

CHAPTER SIXTY-THREE

He may have been a past master at a showy entrance but he was, as ever, impervious to atmosphere.

"Serenissima," He boomed in best baritone. "What do you think you're playing at? I had to bloody-well pick the lock to get us out of that room you left us in. What on God's good earth is going on here?" Then belatedly, looking around, even he picked up on the fact that this wasn't your normal social situation.

Ffion's head swung, slow and snakelike in his direction and in that instant, most of us in the room knew what she was going to do. I moved quickly but Ophelia was quicker, she flashed out of one spot and re-appeared in front of him, lips drawn back in a snarl of defiance, arms spread wide as if creating a defensive screen. I was taking the more prosaic route across the floor, so was too slow to stop what happened next.

Ffion spat out a phrase, jerked her head and Ophelia was flung backwards against Adam with such force that we heard the breath knocked out of them as they collided. Arms and legs tangled, they fell heavily. Sasha screamed once, loudly. I don't think she'd been hurt, but she dropped as fast as they had, I think she'd fainted dead away, which was probably for the best.

I was bending down, with dreadful trepidation towards my immobile parents, when a dismembered arm flew heavily over my head, so close I felt the weight and wind of its passage. Ducking reflexively, I turned to look behind me, then wished I hadn't. Heading into the library was what looked like an army of the dead, and they weren't all in one piece. I guessed this might qualify, in Alfred's phraseology, as situation normal even more fouled up!

Hurtling at speed, and unerringly hitting their now cringing, flinching targets were arms and hands, so many hands, not to mention truncated torsos and disembodied heads – bone-white, petrified clay, yet full of vicious intention and attrition and seemingly moving of their own volition.

Ffion, Karl and Max were being herded into a corner of the room by the swirling, heaving mass around them; limbs and bodies hitting limbs and bodies, crashing, batting, lethally swiping.

Felicia, pink-quilted to the neck, was standing in the doorway, her own hands folded primly before her.

"I waited," she said acidly, "For someone to bring up my afternoon tea. But everyone was obviously too busy to bother." She surveyed her family reprovingly, letting her eye run over Charley, still comatose in front of the fire, Adam, Ophie and Sasha piled up by the doorway and then the three, besieged in the corner and shook her head.

"Honestly!" She said and moved back towards the stairs. As she turned, the swirling, twisting hands, arms, faces and figures began to smash to the floor, the air was filled with noise and clay dust.

"Wait," I called out, as nobody else seemed inclined to stop her. She turned to look at me. "Thank you." I said. She sniffed,

"Down to you now, Ophelia's girl. I've done my bit, given you a breathing space, but you know it's not finished. Now get your act together, or pack and go, you've brought nothing trouble to this house. I'll be in my room, should anybody want me."

Murray, Roland and Bella were busy with my parents and Sasha.

"Spark out," reported Murray. "Like her." He jerked his head at Charley. He looked terrible, his mouth drawn down by worry and fear and he shook his head slowly at me. "Can't be doing with all this business Sandy, heart won't take it." He put a pained hand to the offended organ as I stepped in front of him and the others, facing the three in the corner. Enough was enough, it was time to defuse the situation before things became even more lethally horrifying.

Etty had remained seated and impassive throughout – did the woman have no nerves? I looked over briefly at her and she met my eye and raised an eyebrow, but that wasn't a road I had any intention of going down. I turned away, I'd do it my way, not hers, on my own.

Ffion straightened up slowly, as did Max and Karl, either side of her. Neither of the men had been particularly remarkable before, in fact Max's receding chin and overlong, pointed nose had previously lent him a slightly silly, rodent-like air, but now neither he nor Karl looked harmless at all. Their expressions were a combination of fury and deep, deep affront. Ffion's impeccable bob was no longer quite so impeccable, and she impatiently blew an irritating strand of hair away from her nose. She should have looked slightly ridiculous, she didn't at all, rather she was all green glinting malevolence. This seemed to have turned into something of a power struggle and I sensed it came with the heft and accumulation of years of similar struggles. But for God's sake, this was the twenty-first century and wasn't it about time that sheer common sense and self-preservation prevailed.

I held up my hand, the dignified effect of which was immediately spoilt as I was nearly knocked off my feet by a weight hitting the side of my legs. There was a bit of heavy breathing, both his and mine as I regained my balance and Rostropovich, still leaning protectively against me, growled low in his throat. I raised my right hand again and let the left one rest on the wolf's head, it was a convenient height, and to be honest at this point, support wasn't to be sneezed at and I was kind of getting used to having him around.

"This stops here." I said. Ffion sneered which I didn't take as a good sign that negotiation might be on the cards. She circled her head on her neck as if it was stiff and needed kinks removing. Then she made an odd little moue with her mouth and a wasp slowly crawled out.

For a moment, it hung there on her lower lip, then took flight, lazily circling above her head. I tried to keep my face immobile but don't think I successfully hid my instinctive revulsion. Ffion smiled and opened her mouth again, expelling several more large wasps. The circle grew bigger and more crowded and in the silent room, the ominous buzzing of busy wings was audible. Next to me, Rostropovich growled again, I could feel the deep reverberation run through his body under my hand. He made to move forward, but I said softly,

"No." And he instantly stopped, you've got to love a well-trained wolf. Out of the corner of my eye I could see Charley, beginning to stir in front of the fire. Great, just what we needed, someone else to join the party. I wanted to step back and away from the widening wasp circle, but knew instinctively, that would be seen as weakness. I was holding Ffion's gaze and she was drinking in and relishing my reaction. As wasps continued to crawl lazily, one by one out of her mouth, I could feel a sapping of my strength alongside growing dizziness and nausea. I staggered a little, and the animal beside me adjusted his weight so he was supporting me better, I now had my hand twisted in the thick fur at his neck and hung on gratefully. But I could feel something odd happening to my mind, it was that sensation you often get as you fall asleep, a slipping away of reality to be replaced with another equally strong reality that makes no sense whatsoever, before you drift away from that too.

"Sing!" Someone commanded, as if from a great distance. I ripped my gaze from Ffion's, blinking and trying to re-focus. Mimi was moving towards me urgently, arms outstretched. "Sing, she can't get to you if you sing."

Over the head of the wolf, I stretched out my hand to Mimi, except I seemed to be doing it in slow motion. She was walking towards me, but so unsteadily I was frightened she'd fall, she too was being affected by whatever Ffion was doing and, poor old soul, it had obviously tipped her over the edge. I'd no doubt a family sing-song might be the sort of fun, bonding thing people did and that was all well and good, but this was neither the time nor the place. I shook my head gently at her and as our hands met and gripped, I felt a faint echo of the shock that had reverberated through me when I touched Etty earlier. But there was no time to think about that, because Mimi has already hurled herself headlong, her voice warbling a little at first and then getting into stride, surprisingly strongly.

"*Ten green bottles, hanging on the wall, ten green bottles, hanging on the wall, and if one green bottle should accidentally fall, there'll be nine green bottles, hanging on the wall.* Come on," She said breathlessly urgent, "Sing, now." So I did – "*Nine green bottles…*"

In front of me Ffion's bemusement must have comically echoed my own, before her gaze hardened as she realised what was happening – she was way ahead of me, I still had no idea why or how this was working, but did know I was feeling measurably less dizzy and disorientated, which could only be an improvement.

Behind me, I was aware of Etty rising to her feet and to my astonishment, pitching in firmly with her daughter, and then Bella's lower tones, joined a beat later by Murray's tuneless bellow, harmonising unsteadily with

Roland who, needless to say, sang as smoothly as he dressed. I didn't think we'd reach competition standard any time soon, but however completely ludicrous this all was, it was working. We were robustly surging into seven, when Ffion let loose her wasps.

CHAPTER SIXTY-FOUR

Up till then, in the heat and confines of the room, the sound of the insects circling lazily overhead had been acutely alien and uncomfortable, but now the buzzing changed tone, and there was no mistaking, it wasn't a change for the better. It was menacing enough to be heard even over our discordant chorus. And then they attacked, so we never made it to six.

They went first for Mimi. Poor Mimi, of all of us she'd certainly had a basin-full, one way or another. As the surge of yellow and black viciousness launched itself, our voices fell away one by one. She let go of my hand and did something swiftly with her arms, and only a couple of the insects seemed to be able to reach her, but we could see from her face the pain those instantly inflicted. I wasn't sure why she simply hadn't disappeared, then I guessed if she did, she'd probably take some of the wasps with her, so it would do her no good. Beside me, Rostropovich was twisting and snapping as some of the insects dived for him. In front of me, Ffion tilted her head to one side, stretched her neck, smiled, opened her mouth and breathed out more insects. Cold knowledge rose in me and I made my decision.

My parents had come round, although appeared still dazed, and were clinging tightly to each other on the floor, Murray was crouched, with an arm firmly round each of them. Bella and Ronald had moved close to Etty. I could feel the power radiating from the family, multiplied because we were together, I also knew, with certainty that however strong they were and they were indeed strong – they probably weren't strong enough to combat what was being unleashed against us. Things had gone too far and, like it or lump it, I had a responsibility. Without looking around, I reached my right arm behind me and knew, without seeing that Etty was instantly moving forward, fingers outstretched to meet mine.

As our hands touched, slid together and grasped, I felt and knew she did too, the thrust of the power which swept through both of us; an unimagined, almost painful intensity. It rocked me back on my heels and rocketed through my body, so for a few seconds it felt quite possible it couldn't be contained within me and the top of my head might simply blow right off. I can't say I was thrilled, I don't know what I'd thought would happen, but definitely nothing as physically overwhelming as this, and if it was having that effect on me, I hoped it wasn't going to finish Etty off completely. But her hand, bony and cool in mine, didn't flinch, maybe she was made of sterner stuff or perhaps she'd had an inkling of what was coming.

The three facing us, knew in that instant, they'd failed. The precise thing they'd been sent here to prevent had gone ahead and happened. I wanted to point out that it really was their own stupid fault. If they'd only listened to what I'd been telling them and cut out the threats and unpleasantness, everything could have been brought to a far more amicable conclusion. But I wasn't given time to tell them anything.

Ffion drew her head back sharply and hissed in frustration and fury as Karl and Max moved in close behind her. I felt them mustering their own power, at the same time as harvesting that of all those others we'd had the pleasure of briefly glimpsing earlier. The force created was unseen, yet none the less malignantly fierce. I gently loosened my hand from Etty's, the connection was there now, it couldn't be broken, and I did the only thing I could, under the circumstances. I turned that force around, and with what I now had, magnified and sent it right back to them.

All three went down without a sound, other than the dull thumps they made as they hit the ground which would have hurt I supposed, had they been more compos mentis. Thankfully the wasps, at the same time, seemed to lose all motivation and began flying around in far less menacing, aimless and ever decreasing, circles. Within a minute, they'd given up the ghost and dropped to the floor, forming several desiccated little yellow and black piles. Then from my left, jarring my already sorely beleaguered nerves, came an impossibly high-pitched, eldritch shriek. Charley, it seemed was ready for a come-back.

CHAPTER SIXTY-FIVE

I have to say, she had proved herself a bit of a disappointment all round. I'd thought she was sweet – annoying speech pattern admittedly, but basically a good, reliable sort, which just goes to show, first impressions can't always be relied upon, because now she was heading for me at speed, hands outstretched, fingers clawed, lips hauled back over clenched teeth and eyes so wide and white rimmed, they looked at risk of popping out altogether.

Sandwiched and now restrained between Mimi and I, Rostropovich was a wolf who had just about reached the end of his tether. We felt him bunch powerful muscles, growl low in his throat and then with a snarl to match Charley's he sprang, and the two hit each other full-on, in a crashing coming-together that should have knocked both of them out. I really didn't know what had got into Charley at that point, but she certainly wasn't the slightly harried young researcher we'd all come to know and like. She looked much the same, but this version was rolling and growling on the floor with a fully-grown wolf who wasn't in the best of tempers, and she was fighting back with a strength and feral ferocity that took us even further into not-believing-what-I'm seeing-territory.

I'm not sure how long we'd have stood there immobilised and gawping, had there not been a brief pause in the fray, into which came a polite knock on the closed library door. Adam, Ophelia and Murray, who were on the floor blocking the entrance, shuffled clumsily out of the way and it opened to reveal not Elizabeth or Alfred as we'd thought, but Mark Heywood, the solicitor.

"Thought I'd just walk over." He said, "And make sure everything was OK over here – see whether there was anything at all you needed." He was wearing a business-like, fur-trimmed parka and pulled down the hood, as he cast an eye around the room. He took in my parents and Murray, helping each other up from the floor; Sasha still spark out in a corner; Charley pinned flat by the wolf, and the bodies of Ffion, Karl and Max and it belatedly occurred to me, we didn't know whether or not I'd killed them.

The latter three were surrounded by dead wasps and assorted sculptured clay body-parts from when Felica had lent us a hand, in fact, several hands. I bit back a small giggle, but it came out anyway and sounded slightly more hysterical than I'd have preferred.

"Well, I see you've been keeping yourselves busy then." The Heywood chap observed. It was, I felt, a tricky situation. Etty stepped into the breach, as upright and restrained as ever.

"Mark," she said levelly, in what might have been the understatement of the century, "You've caught us at a slightly awkward moment. As you can see we've had a few… issues." She was interrupted by a sharp yowl of pain from Rostropovich. We all spun round. Charley, still on the ground, goodness knows what the wolf on top of her weighed, now had her eyes tightly closed and with what little breath she had left, was chanting something. Whatever she was doing, was obviously hurting him. Neither Mimi nor Etty hesitated, but did the rigid hand thing and Charley once again opted out of the action. It added to the body count, but by this time I was kind of past caring. Mimi called the wolf back to her side and he moved to lean against her, casting a low warning growl every now and then in the direction of the recumbent Charley.

"Mr Heywood lives just across the field." Etty said in explanation, continuing as if nothing had happened. I nodded politely and moved to sit down, my knees suddenly weren't working as well as they should. Still, I felt I had to keep my conversational end up, as nobody else in the room seemed ready to say anything yet.

"Is he, you know,… one of you?" I asked.

"Of course not." Etty tutted as if I'd said something ridiculous. "However, his family have been handling our legal affairs for several generations now and have always been in our confidence."

"Well, that's a relief." I said "Otherwise, all this," And I waved an encompassing arm. "Might have given him a bit of a turn." And then, to my utter mortification, I fainted dead away.

CHAPTER SIXTY-SIX

"So," said Murray, "What now?" The sun was shining fiercely and, despite the biting wind, it was seeing off the snow in no uncertain terms. It seemed ridiculous that only the previous day, weather-wise, it had looked and felt like the end of the world.

Murray had come into the kitchen about 9.00 that morning, whilst I was knocking back a much-needed cup of coffee under the watchful eyes of Gladys, who seemed to have appointed herself guardian of my general health and well-being, and Rostropovich who had been granted kitchen privileges because of the bitter weather and his heroism.

Murray said he thought a bit of a walk was called for, to blow away the cobwebs. If by cobwebs he meant yesterday's events, I thought it might take more than a bit of a walk. But I grabbed a jacket and scarf and cautiously negotiating the front stone steps, which still held some treacherous ice patches and arm in companionable arm, we paced around the mermaid, who was looking no perkier, and slowly down the drive.

"No. Absolutely nothing's changed." I said, in answer to his earlier question. He didn't say anything, so I carried on, "Not as far as what I'm going to do. I want to get back to normal as quickly as I can because normal, right now, is looking more attractive than it ever has. All this," I waved my hand at the house behind us and included in the gesture all that had gone on, "Isn't for me, it's not who I am, is it? I know I got hung up on getting everything sorted business-wise, but I've got the family started on what needs to be done, they'll have to stand or fall on their own now. After all, they were managing before I pitched up, they'll manage after I go. I'm out of here, leaving this afternoon if nothing else happens to stop me." He was silent for a beat or two. Then,

"And can you?"

"Can I what?"

"You know, just go back to your everyday stuff, you've had a taste of something." He shook his head, "Don't know quite what, but whatever you want to call it, can you just forget about it, isn't it part of you?"

I thought about what he'd asked, thought about the painful intensity of the connection with Etty, the overwhelming and frankly terrifying strength of what had been generated between the two of us. I thought about how, although it was completely new, there was a knowingness in me that recognised and welcomed it back. And I knew I had to reject it and why. I tried to put it in words for him.

"Growing up," I said slowly, "I deliberately turned my back on what Ophelia is, pretended I didn't see, didn't know, although of course I did, deep down. But what I felt then and what I feel now hasn't changed one iota. It's not me, I don't want it, don't want to use it, don't want it to use me. My decision, my choice." My breath was coming faster, vapourising in the frigid air, He squeezed my arm, held in his,

"OK, Sandy, don't get your knickers in a twist, up to you. You know I'm right behind you whatever you want to do." I nodded, there wasn't much I was sure of after recent events, but Murray's backing was and always had been, solid as a rock. We walked on in comfortable silence.

***

Due to my humiliating opting out yesterday – I never faint, that's Ophie's territory, Sasha's too, certainly not mine – I found myself a bit hazy on the way things had panned out. I hadn't properly come round until I was being dumped unceremoniously on my bed upstairs, by Roland and Mark Heywood. They were both panting a little, having apparently made a chair-lift of their hands to get me upstairs. Roland was pulling the bedspread over me,

"Blimey," he said, "You're heavier than you look."

"Thanks." I said. Mark Heywood, putting a glass of water on the bedside table next to me, frowned,

"Well, it would have been easier if she hadn't struggled all the way up. Don't you," he said to me, "Ever do what you're told?" I wanted to say something crushing, but was feeling too much on the woozy side to think of anything worthwhile. However as my senses returned, I struggled up to a sitting position, grasping Roland's arm in panic.

"I shouldn't be up here, what's happening downstairs – did I, did I…" I couldn't quite bring myself to say it.

"Kill them?" Supplied Mark, obviously not the sensitive type. Roland and he exchanged looks above my head. "We don't know." He said.

"What do you mean you *don't know*?" I squeaked, then lowering my tone to something that not only dogs could hear. "How can you not know?" They exchanged another look, if they didn't stop doing that I was going to thump one or both.

"They went." Said Roland.

"Went? What do you mean went?" He shrugged,

"Well, you dropped down with such a thump, everyone's attention was on you and by the time we'd got you back on the chair, they'd gone.

"Gone?"

"For Christ's sake Sandra," snapped Roland, "Will you stop repeating everything I say? I can't be any more specific than that, they'd gone, disappeared, vanished, pouf – there should have been a puff of smoke but there wasn't – one minute they were there, all over the floor and then they weren't. Ffion, the two blokes and Charley, all gone."

"But that's impossible." I said. Mark Heywood sat down on Ophie's bed opposite and laughed. I glared at him and then Roland started to chuckle too.

"I really don't think," said Roland, "Impossible's a word that can apply in any way, to what's been going on, do you?" I shook my head slowly, he wasn't wrong.

"Is everyone else all right?" I asked, "Devorah and the baby?" He nodded.

"Bit shaken, but fine. Bella's with them now."

"Ophie and Adam?" I said. "They were completely knocked out."

"I think Ophie took more of a hit than your Father." He said. "But they're both all right and she's playing wounded martyr to the hilt." I grinned, her brother knew her as well as I did. "She says," he elaborated, "That she's never going to forgive him, but they're canoodled up on the sofa downstairs, so I suspect all might be well."

"And Sasha?" I asked apprehensively. Mark Heywood answered with a brief slashing gesture across his throat, I gasped and he chuckled,"

"Don't be daft, I just meant she was history. Whatever plans she had for your Father seem to have gone down the tubes and she's sulking somewhere. Murray said he'd stay with her until she calmed down. She was hardly a match for Ophelia anyway." He added.

"But what does she say about what happened, everything she saw?" I couldn't begin to imagine how we could explain things. Mark shook his head,

"From what I understand, she actually didn't see too much, I gather it all happened so fast and she passed out at an early stage."

"But didn't she have a whole load of questions?" I asked.

"I don't think," he said reflectively, "That she's the sharpest knife in the drawer, and anyway she was far more preoccupied with the way things were going between her and Adam."

"Mimi's fine too." Roland supplied, before I could reach her in the roll call.

"And Etty?" I asked with trepidation, remembering what the impact of our touch had done to me. He smiled,

"She's a game old bird, my sweet, you should know that by now. Turned her nose up in disgust when you fainted, said she thought you were made of sterner stuff and stalked off upstairs, mind you she did hang around long enough to make sure you were all right." I grimaced,

"And here was me worrying about her." I said, sitting back against the pillows then hauling myself back up again.

"I need to…" I started but Roland gave me a gentle shove back.

"You don't *need* to do anything. Elizabeth's bringing you up a cup of tea, just stop being a busy-body for a bit, if you can manage that.

"But what if… ?" I started again.

"Don't you get it?" He said, "Our so-called tv friends – shame about that documentary, it might have been the making of us – were here to frighten you away. Not only didn't they succeed, but they failed at stopping the very thing they'd come to prevent." He paused. "But you've seen them off for now."

"For now?"

"Well, there's no doubt, the stakes just got higher." He said. I shook my head firmly,

"No, they haven't," I said, "Because I won't be here."

CHAPTER SIXTY-SEVEN

My morning stroll with Murray had cleared my head and confirmed my thinking, and I saw no reason not to immediately put everything into action. Of course, I wasn't going to just disappear without a word, so I packed the few things I had with me – not a lot, it had only been intended to be a couple of nights stay – and set off to do the rounds.

In a route reminiscent of my tour of the house a few days ago, although it seemed a lot longer, I started at the top. Henry was as expected, wired up to the computer, but not half as cocky. Other than greeting me with,

"What's up babe?" He was so busy not meeting my eye, that it was difficult to know whether he was even listening to my goodbye.

"For goodness sake," I said in exasperation, "Stop working that keyboard and just pay attention to me, what's the matter?" He muttered something I didn't catch, so I put out a foot and swung his swivel chair round to face me.

"Very sorry." He muttered, chin down to chest. "Didn't pitch in."

"What d'you mean?"

"Yesterday... all that stuff going on. Heard it all start up and..." he paused.

"And what?" I said,

"Put the headphones on and turned up the volume. Sorry." I laughed wryly at his guilty expression,

"Don't be silly," I said. "Strikes me as the most sensible thing to do under the circumstances. Don't give it another thought," He muttered something else which I didn't catch.

"Look, I've just popped in to say goodbye," I said, "I'm off later."

"OK." He said. "Bye." And swiveled back into position with rather more relief than regret.

I knocked on Felicia's door with some apprehension and entered in answer to her imperious, 'Come'. The huge room was darker than I remembered because of the residue of snow on the skylights, but still dazzling after the dimness of the hallway. It was also startlingly empty. I turned slowly on my heel. There were one or two odd pieces lurking in a corner, but other than that, nothing. She was standing by the table, looking at me expectantly and still pink-quilted. I wondered if she ever got dressed. As if she'd heard the thought she replied,

"Never waste time dressing and undressing, pretty pointless, unless it's for a special occasion, so you'll have to forgive my informality." I smiled,

"I've come to thank you."

"Oh?" She said.

"For yesterday, you were brilliant." She nodded briskly,

"Well, somebody had to do something, the rest of the family aren't much use, are they? And it was, as you might say, a call to arms." I looked at her sharply, was that a joke? She gave a brief twitch which could have been the beginnings of a smile, or maybe just a twitch. I thought of all the smashed years of clay piled in the library,

"All your work though, what will you do now? I asked. She looked at me as if I was mad,

"Start all over again, of course. Now, if you don't mind, I am rather busy."

"I came to say goodbye as well as thank you. I'm leaving." I said.

"Good." She said, "Nothing but problems since you arrived."

"Right." I said, backing out the door, a hug didn't seem to be on offer.

Devorah and Bella, when I tracked them down in Bella's room, more than made up for Felicia in the embrace stakes. As soon as I stuck my head round the door, I was pulled into firm hugs against first one capacious bosom, Bella's and then a second, Devorah's, with the ever-amenable Simona, slightly squashed but cheerful, between us.

"You were like just awesome." Devorah said when she'd let me go and,

"I won't say I didn't think you had it in you," said Bella, "Because I did. But you're not going to hang around are you?" I shook my head. "Didn't think so." She said and I was surprised at the regret in her voice, she might be the only person not pleased to see the back of me. We were interrupted by a resounding thump against the bedroom door which turned out to be Mimi, looking unusually disheveled – and that was saying something – Bella helped her up and she smiled at us all.

"Goodness me," she said. "I didn't mean to be here at all. I was on the way to ask Elizabeth something, although," she ran a hand distractedly through her halo of fine white hair, "I can't for the life of me think now what it might have been." She looked at us enquiringly, as if we might have an idea.

"Mimi," I said, "I'll say my goodbyes now, because I might not see you before I leave." She looked at me sharply, confirming yet again there was more behind the daffiness than she chose to show.

"Yes, I see." She said, "Well, it's been really lovely having you to stay, given us a chance to find out a bit more about each other, hasn't it?" Devorah smothered a snigger behind me, but I ignored her. Mimi reached up a little and placed two forefingers briefly on my forehead, an odd gesture yet like so much else, disconcertingly not unfamiliar. "I expect we'll see you again, sooner or later." She said and headed out of the room and down the corridor. She'd got a little way before she obviously remembered what it was she wanted to impart to Elizabeth, she exclaimed and disappeared. I sighed and turned back to the other two women.

"She's right you know." Said Bella. "We'll probably see you again."

"Not if I can help it." I said, squeezing her arm to show no hard feelings as I leant over and kissed Simona's plump cheek.

The visit I was looking forward to least was next and, coward that I am, I rather hoped she might not be there, but in response to the knock on the door Etty asked me to come in. She was as before, writing at her desk, and didn't glance up for a moment or two. I felt we were past the standing around awkwardly phase, so sat myself firmly on the chair and waited. She finished what she was listing in a lined notebook, she was near the end of the book and I could see slips of differently coloured paper sticking out as markers from between lots of the pages. Was this I wondered, the Etty Goodkind Book of Spells. She snapped the cover closed, slipped an elastic band round it and looked over at me.

"Well?" She said.

"I'm afraid I'm leaving." I said "And..."

"Don't be afraid. By far the best thing, don't you think?" I nodded, of course it was. I had no doubts about what I was going to do, but perhaps a polite remonstration on her part wouldn't have hurt. There was a short pause then,

"Is there anything else?" She enquired. I'd thought I'd used up a month's store of emotional stuff yesterday and didn't have any feelings left, turns out though I did. I sat up straighter.

"Are you not going to say anything at all about what happened?"

"What would you like said?" She asked with interest. I clenched my nails in my palms. Bloody woman had the power to get up my nose as much as Ophelia, must run in the family. She sighed,

"Look, I warned you what would happen if you stayed," she said. "The assumptions that would be made and the danger those would bring. You didn't believe me. You stayed. You attracted that attention. It was a... difficult situation, but it was dealt with adequately."

"And?" I asked. She raised a brow over the green glint,

"And nothing. You've made your own decisions all along. You made a clear choice when you reacted yesterday, it had to be free-willed, would only work if you came to it voluntarily."

"It was hardly a choice." I said, "It was them or us."

"It always is."

"But now it's my choice to forget about it, get the hell out of here and get on with my life."

"Good luck." She said.

"Meaning?"

"Exactly what I say. But you're misguided if you imagine you're leaving it behind. It's who you are, always has been. What happened yesterday merely confirmed what we all knew."

"Which was?" I asked.

"Don't play games." She snapped. I turned away from her. She was right, no question. I'd tasted my strength, felt the power of Etty and knew I was her equal if not more. But that made no difference, I was only what I was, if I chose to be, and I chose not to be.

I rose to my feet, looking down on her where she sat upright, back not making any contact with the chair. It wasn't that my feelings for her weren't strong – they were, they just weren't particularly fond – nevertheless she was old and she was indisputably family. I softened my voice,

"I'm sorry," I said, "If I've been a disappointment, but I hope you'll respect my decision and know that I'm saying goodbye with no hard feeling between us." She nodded in acknowledgement and, still seated, held out her hand. I hesitated before I took it and her mouth twitched in amusement, although I needn't have worried, it was just a handshake, an oddly formal gesture.

Ophelia and Adam were indeed snug on a sofa in the living room downstairs. Murray was seated opposite them and they had a tray of coffee and biscuits into which they were tucking with enthusiasm. It all looked very comfortably domesticated. Both my parents got up when I came in, and Ophelia flung out her arms dramatically.

"Darling, darling girl," she said. "I feel so terribly guilty for pulling you into all this." She paused, presumably for me to reassure her. I didn't say anything. I was wondering whether, what and how things had been explained to Adam, but decided I wasn't going to worry too much about it, I'd leave it in the capable hands of Murray and my Mother, who always seemed to have managed things satisfactorily until now. Murray glanced at my overnight bag, packed at my feet,

"You're off then?" He said. "The roads should be all right. They're saying so on the radio, everything's running more or less normal today, but still, be careful. I nodded, and seeing my parents were murmuring sweet nothings to each other, mouthed at Murray,

"Sasha?"

"Taxi, to the station, 'bout an hour ago." I nodded in relief.

"Ma?" I said, reclaiming her attention. "Are you driving back with me? Because I want to leave before it gets dark."

"Darling," she said, "I think I'm going to be totally selfish for once." I glanced at her sideways but no, there was no irony involved, "And go back," she continued, "With Murray and your Father, you don't mind honeybun, do you? I am," she murmured, leaning further into Adam, "Totally exhausted, with all that's been thrown at us over these last few days." Murray followed me out into the hallway,

"We'll be leaving soon and all." He said. "And don't worry, I've settled up with that Elizabeth for the rooms and food and such. She didn't want to take anything under the circumstances, but I insisted, said to her, you're not running a blooming charity here." I smiled, trust Murray to do the right thing.

"You OK?" He said.

"I will be."

"And all sorted," he jerked his head, "With the family, I mean?" I nodded.

"I'm just going to find Roland," I said. "Then I'm off." He patted me gently on the back,

"Drive safely hear me? You've had a lot on your mind, I don't want you not concentrating." I laughed,

"Trust me Murray, concentrating on the motorway is going to be the most relaxing activity I've done for days."

Roland was in the kitchen with a half-finished cup of coffee in front of him and was watching Gladys with mild apprehension. She was back on the silver tray and rocking, so I guessed the Chief was with us. Still, there were no dinner or room bookings for the next few days, so perhaps he'd head for the hills before we needed her to be constructive again.

"I'm heading off." I said to Roland. He nodded and smiled amenably. "Bet you can't wait to see the back of us. Hasn't exactly been an uneventful visit. Still, very appreciative of what you've tried to do." I pulled out a couple of sheets of paper from my shoulder bag.

"Look," I said, "I know you'll think I'm bossy."

"As if!"

"I've put together a bit of a forward plan of action and some lists. This gives you several things to follow up on."

"Well, we've already had Hugh Whateverhisnameis and Morwenna, in from the Psychic Society this morning." He said. "They were in a high old state of excitement, practically hysterical," he grinned. "That equipment they'd set up in the library apparently recorded all sorts of power bursts and a cartload of inexplicably odd sounds. They were quite beside themselves." I frowned at him, worried.

"What would they have picked up?"

"Not to worry." He said, "Nothing dodgy, everything's calibrated to pick up things outside the normal range of speech or vision – apparently that's the wavelength ghosts prefer to work on. Don't ask! Anyway, suitably leaked, it should generate some good publicity for us."

"So you will follow through then?" I asked, pleased.

"Much as I can. You talk up a good plan, niece of mine. Now come here and give me a hug." I complied and was just pulling away, when Elizabeth and Alfred came through the back door. She was pulling a small trolley on wheels, with logs for the fire and he was bent double, steering it from behind.

"You off then?" She said. "Thought you wouldn't hang around longer than you had to – blimey there was a mess and a half to clear up in the library, what the devil did you get up to in there."

"Elizabeth," I said, "Trust me, you really don't want to know."

"That's as maybe," she said, "All I'm saying is things were a darn sight more normal before you happened along." I glanced at Gladys, chanting and rocking, and wasn't sure whether I went along with that, normal hadn't ever seemed an integral element of Home Hill. She sniffed, "S'pose, you'll be wanting a sandwich to take with you, long drive, you might get peckish." I smiled and reassured her I was fine, but I was touched, I suspected that was the nearest Elizabeth might get to gushing.

I realised, as I went through the front doors that I hadn't commiserated properly with Ophelia about poor old Ink, and was feeling dreadfully guilty about that as I dumped my bag in the passenger seat. I was frightened the car would play up again and not start, although Alfred had looked at it for me, muttering what he didn't know about engines, wasn't worth writing home about and bless him, it started first time and actually sounded a lot smoother than it ever had done before.

As I let off the handbrake, there was a rapping on the window, I jumped. It was the solicitor again, I spotted his flashy SUV parked the other side of the mermaid. I wound down the window.

"You're going?" He said. I shook my head,

"Nope, just thought I'd sit in the car with the engine running – it passes the time." He ignored the sarcasm.

"I need your phone number." He said. I looked at him in surprise, I didn't feel we'd hit it off that well – in fact I couldn't think of a polite word we'd said to each other.

"I don't think so." I said. He caught my meaning and laughed,

"No, I can assure you, I wasn't thinking of a date, but I will need to make contact at some point in the future."

"What on earth for?" I asked. He waved a vague hand,

"Legal stuff." He said and I frowned at him,

"I really don't see... " I started. He lost patience, although from what I'd seen, he didn't have a whole load to start with,

"For goodness sake," he thrust his phone into my hand, "Just put it in there will you and then you can go." I couldn't be bothered to argue, so did as he asked and then, for some reason, felt the need to justify my leaving, but like everyone else he really didn't want me to stay.

"Sooner you go the better, nothing short of all hell's broken loose since you came on the scene." I thought that was a bit on the harsh side, but who cared what he thought anyway. "And," he added helpfully, just as I was taking off the handbrake, "You've got a great big smudge on your forehead."

I pulled the mirror sharply down in annoyance, but he wasn't wrong, must have come from touching the car door which was smutty from the snow, or maybe Mimi had something on her fingers when she touched me.

I thanked him politely, I knew my manners even if he didn't, spat on a tissue with perhaps a little more force than necessary and cleaned up. But as I turned away, something was odd and I looked back quickly. For a moment, I'd thought my eyes, always unobtrusively hazel, had glinted green. But it must have just been a trick of the light.

~ the end ~

BY THE SAME AUTHOR

REVIEWS FOR *RELATIVELY STRANGE* & *EVEN STRANGER*

"OHMIDAYS! OHMIDAYS! What a book!" – *Melanie Lewis*

***

"With the author's deadpan humour and observational wit, I read this book with a huge smile on my face, eagerly following Stella through her various exploits. A truly fabulous series which I hope has at least one more book to come, I need to know what happens next! 5 stars." – *Tracy Fenton. TBC Founder*

***

"Suddenly it was no longer a gentle humorous saunter, but a chilling, violent, situation which develops into a gripping plot. A good and thought provoking read." - *Zandra Johnson*

***

"I have not been so enthralled with a story for a long time. I really don't want to give too much away but the story had me page turning like a woman possessed. I really hope other people enjoy this book as much as I did, and I hope that there will be another one to follow because I'm already missing Stella." - *Angie T.D*

***

"One part of this book spooked me so much, I think it knocked a good few years off my life!" - *J. Mortimer*